Praise for the novels of *New York Times* bestselling author HEATHER GRAHAM

"Captivating...a sinister tale sure to appeal to fans across multiple genre lines."
—*Publishers Weekly* on *The Death Dealer*

"Mystery, sex, paranormal events. What's not to love?"
—*Kirkus Reviews* on *The Death Dealer*

"An incredible storyteller."
—*Los Angeles Daily News*

"Graham's latest is nerve-racking in the extreme, solidly plotted and peppered with welcome hints of black humor. And the ending is all readers could hope for."
—*Romantic Times BOOKreviews* on *The Last Noel*

"Graham peoples her novel with genuine, endearing characters."
—*Publishers Weekly* on *The Séance*

"A writer of incredible talent."
—*Affaire de Coeur*

"Graham's rich, balanced thriller sizzles with equal parts suspense, romance and the paranormal—all of it nail-biting."
—*Publishers Weekly* on *The Vision*

"There are good reasons for Graham's steady standing as a best-selling author. Here her perfect pacing keeps readers riveted as they learn fascinating tidbits of New Orleans history."
—*Booklist* on *Ghost Walk*

HEATHER GRAHAM

DEADLY HARVEST

MIRA®

MIRA®

ISBN-13: 978-0-7783-2560-4
ISBN-10: 0-7783-2560-1

DEADLY HARVEST

www.MIRABooks.com

Printed in U.S.A.

For Sharon Dale, with so many thanks, the wonderful folks at the Peabody Essex Museum, the House of the Seven Gables and the beautiful city of Salem, Massachusetts.

Prologue

It began when Mary and Brad Johnstone went to the psychic fair and happened upon the tent offering readings. Neither of them believed in such things. Still, as Brad said, with a wry grin, "When in Rome… And this looks like the place that guy at the museum was talking about."

Of course, it was possible to get a reading just about anywhere in Salem, Massachusetts—especially now, on Halloween. They'd already been through several haunted houses, visited costume shops and met locals ranging from wiccans to historians. A guy they'd talked to at a museum dedicated to local history days had told them to get a few readings, because they would all be different, and given them a rundown of some of his favorite places to go.

Not long after that, Mary had gotten her first reading in a shop called the Magick Mercantile, run by a couple of real wiccans, Adam and Eve Llewellyn. She looked like a hippie, and he dressed all in black. He chewed gum nonstop, though, which made him look a little more normal. Brad doubted that Adam and Eve were their real names—everyone here seemed a little theatrical—but they had been nice. Eve had looked at

Mary's palm and assured her that her ability to dance would take her far. Talking about it afterward, they were both sure they hadn't mentioned her profession. "Maybe they saw you on that local access show you did," Brad suggested. In any case, it had been a nice look into the future.

This guy, though… He was pure Halloween creepy. He was wearing a cape and a turban. Tall, dark and lean, he had piercing eyes darkened by liner and shadow.

Inside his tent, he had a small table covered in dark fabric lightened only by a design of moons and stars, with a crystal ball on a stand in the middle of it. Everything was so carefully arranged that his tent could have passed for a permanent place of business. There were sculptures everywhere: Egyptian gods and goddesses, dragons, demons and more.

Mary immediately asked, "Are you a wiccan? A witch or a warlock?"

The reader offered her a wry smile. "There are no warlocks in the wiccan religion. Wiccans are just wiccans. And, no, I'm not a wiccan. Just a simple reader of signs, of the moon and the stars, and all that has come before."

"I'm Mary Johnstone, and this is my husband, Brad," Mary said. She almost tripped over the word *husband.* She remembered just how recently they had been headed for divorce.

"And I am Damien," the reader told them.

"Can we stay together?" Mary asked him. "A double reading, I guess."

She was actually feeling a little chilled, she realized, then told herself not to be silly. This was Halloween.

Things were supposed to be scary. Like a horror movie. What good was a horror movie if you didn't jump a little?

She still felt oddly uncomfortable. But she would be fine if Brad stayed in here with her.

"Of course," Damien said with a smile. "What I see…will be what I see. Sit down. There are two chairs."

They sat at the table. Brad squeezed Mary's hand. She reminded herself that they were on vacation, far away from the Florida beaches of home and doing something entirely different. They were trying to heal old wounds and start over again. They were going to have fun.

"Now, look into the ball," Damien told them with a flourish.

Mary looked, and decided the man was certainly a master of effects. The clear crystal ball began to swim with mist. As she continued to stare into it, she thought she saw fire. A fire leaping toward an unseen sky. Then the fire faded away, and she found herself looking at a desolate hillside. There were a few scrawny trees, with gnarled branches. And there were people. She couldn't hear them properly, but they seemed to be chanting. Suddenly a scream broke through the chanting. She almost jumped, but she realized Brad was at her side, grinning, having fun. She had too much imagination, he always told her that. And she was too timid.

She reminded herself they were repairing their relationship. That they both needed to work at it, even if he was the one who had strayed. He never would have wanted a lifetime with Brenda, she told herself. She had only appealed to him because she was brash, willing to take chances, and because she was…slutty. Mary couldn't help a moment's rancor.

Brad loved her, and she knew it. But she had been hurt. Still, she didn't want to ruin their future by dwelling on the past. She was going to make some changes, starting with becoming more adventurous.

Brad's hand was tight on hers. He was with her now. She believed that he loved her, and that they could make it.

"In the dark and in the mist, there lie the places of danger. Let not the hand that holds you slip, for when the wind blows and the trees dip, there you find death," Damien said. "Look to the ball, keep your eyes on the crystal."

She was *compelled* to look back. She heard screaming again, and sobbing full of deep agony. The branches of the trees were like skeletal hands. Snow began to fall, and then…

Suddenly she was staring at the corpse of a woman, dangling from a hangman's noose tied to one of the skeletal branches. A scream caught in her own throat as the body rotted right in front of her eyes.

"Indians," Brad said. He sounded almost bewitched. "Sorry, Native Americans."

She managed to tear her eyes from the deathly scene to stare at Brad. He was smiling, clearly seeing something entirely different.

"The first Thanksgiving dinner," he said, marveling.

She had to get out of there.

"You're really good," Brad told Damien.

Damien smiled at him, then turned to Mary, and she thought there was something nasty in his stare, something licentious and…evil.

"Touch the crystal," Damien commanded them.

No. She wasn't going to do it.

But she was compelled. It was a projector of some kind, she told herself. It was a holograph. Had to be.

Whatever it was, whatever the compulsion, Brad felt it, too. Their hands still joined, they touched the crystal ball.

Now, when she stared into its depths, she saw corn. Rows and rows of corn.

Cornfields filled with scarecrows and an overwhelming sense of evil.

Was Brad seeing the same thing now? Whatever he saw, he was staring at the ball as if hypnotized.

"You are in danger," Damien told Brad. "You loved, but you betrayed, and now you're weak. And because you're weak—" he turned to Mary "—*you* are easy prey." Damien spoke as if the words gave him pleasure. "He lacks the faith in himself necessary to fight for you, so you will be lost in the mists of evil."

Brad stood abruptly and looked down at Damien, furious. "What the hell is this? You should be arrested. We didn't come here for this kind of crap."

Damien rose, too. "I'm sorry you didn't like the reading, but the crystal tells the truth. It speaks, not I."

Brad threw a twenty on the table, then grabbed Mary's hand firmly and pulled her out of the tent with him.

Back on the pedestrian mall, they were surrounded by people laughing, having fun. A group of kids burst out of one of the haunted houses, laughing. An old man, trying to avoid all the rush, slipped into a coffee shop. A woman walked by with two little girls dressed up as fairies. Even the dogs walking by were in costume.

"Leave it to me to pick the jerk," Brad said apologetically.

"Hey, don't worry. He felt he had to put on a show, that's all." She was careful to speak lightly. Brad had been really angry, maybe even shaken. It was strange, the way Damien had been able to sense the tension they were escaping and home right in on it.

But now, out here, surrounded by shrieks of delight, quiet conversations, silliness and games and laughter, the visions in the crystal ball seemed like fading images, nothing more.

"I'll tell you, though, that turkey dinner looked fabulous. I'm starving," Brad said. "I swear, I could almost smell turkey. Though now that I think about it, I'm not sure those In—Native Americans were sitting down to dinner. They had hatchets, and they looked angry."

Mary smiled. A breeze was blowing. It felt fresh and clean. She already felt like laughing, though it did trouble her that she hadn't seen any turkey dinner. A holograph should have been a holograph, right? Or maybe there were different projectors. The guy might be an asshole, but his act was a good one.

And she was *not* going to let herself be unnerved by it.

Still, over a late lunch she couldn't help asking him, "Brad, was that turkey dinner all you saw?"

"Well…"

He sounded reluctant, she thought, and wondered why.

Finally he went on. "At the end…I know this sounds crazy, but there was this cornfield, and this body that…" He looked at her and said, "Forget it. It was just some stupid illusion."

"Why were you so angry?" she asked.

"Because he pegged me for a jerk," he said, looking at her apologetically. "If Jeremy were here, he'd know how the guy pulled it off. In fact…" He laughed. "I can just see Jeremy staring at that stupid crystal ball, then getting up and figuring out where Damien—or whatever the jerk's real name is—keeps all his special-effects equipment."

Mary smiled. "He's in New Orleans almost all the time now, huh?"

Jeremy Flynn had been Brad's partner when they had both been forensic divers for the police department. He'd been Brad's best man at their wedding, and through everything, he had never lied to her, remaining her friend as well as Brad's. And Brad was right. Jeremy would have revealed Damien as the fraud he was.

After lunch, Mary announced that she was ready for some actual history, so they headed toward one of the town's famous cemeteries. It struck her as a poignant place, and she couldn't help the tears that filled her eyes.

"What's the matter?" Brad asked.

"Nothing. I was just thinking," she said.

"Well, let's get out of here," he told her. "It's this place that's making you sad."

No, it's not really the cemetery, she thought. It's that man, Damien, and the things he said.

"I love you, you know," he told her.

She looked into his eyes. "I know. And I love you."

She was shaking slightly; she knew he thought she was too easily frightened.

"I'm going to look at a few more of the graves, read

some of the stones," she told him. She squared her shoulders and walked away from him with quick steps, pulling a small guidebook out of her purse and calling out to him, "I've been reading about this. The garland symbolizes victory in death, and the winged hourglass is for the swiftness of passing time. Skeletons and skulls are for mortality. These angels are for heaven, and these ones here are for little children."

Brad seemed to be getting into the spirit. He was standing by a stone several feet from her. "There's a hooped snake on this one. What's that for?" he asked.

"Eternity," she informed him.

He walked down the path, putting more distance between them, and found an aboveground tomb. He sat down on it, watching her. "Hey, my feet are starting to hurt. How about we find a nice happy hour?" he asked.

"I don't think you're supposed to sit on someone's grave," she warned him. A broken stone seemed to beckon her from its spot by one of the huge trees that punctuated the cemetery. The tree's expanding roots had broken through several of the nearby stones.

"Hey, don't go too far," Brad called to her, lying back on the stone tomb and staring up at the sky. "People are leaving. We don't want to wind up locked in here."

"We'll be fine," she assured him.

As she walked toward the stones, she felt the breeze pick up. And, she realized, darkness was coming. Fast. And with it, though she hadn't felt or seen any sign of fog before, a silvery dew thickening the air.

She walked more quickly, stepping past the tree to get a better look at the stone that had caught her attention, and stopped dead.

Someone had cleaned and re-etched the stone, which dated from the late sixteen hundreds. It looked almost exactly like dozens of others. There was a death's head at the top, and scythes and hourglasses along the borders.

And then she noticed the name.

Mary Clare Johnstone.

Her name.

Her name *exactly*.

She felt something clutch at her throat, and weakness swept through her. She went down on her knees and placed a hand on the stone, as her dizziness grew worse.

From somewhere, she could hear laughter. Children having fun. Mothers calling out to them. Husbands speaking to their wives.

She closed her eyes against the sight in front of her and saw the hill and the tree. The tree with the skeletal branches and the hangman's noose.

And the woman, dangling at the end of it.

The mist swirled around her in a fury, and she heard laughter again.

Damien's laughter…

His face rose before her.

He was there. He had her hand, and they were standing on a hill, with the wind sweeping around them.

His laughter was…evil.

He couldn't be real; the hill couldn't be real. But she could feel the wind against her legs, the earth beneath her feet and the chill of descending night.

"And now you're mine. Playtime, my love," Damien said.

His laughter came again, blending with the wind.

1

Rowenna saw scarecrows.

They stood above the cornfields, propped on their wooden crosses, and from a distance their faces were blank and terrifying.

The cornstalks grew high, marching toward the horizon in their neat rows seeming to stretch on forever.

And then, like sentinels, rising in a line and towering over the tall stalks that bent and waved in the cool breeze, stood the scarecrows.

She felt as if she were drifting through the corn, borne on the breeze, as the mist settled down over the cornfield, a dark blanket against the burst of beauty and light. She was looking down from above, almost as if she were a camera, coming into focus.

She dreamed, but she fought it and came so near to waking, struggling against the nightmare, against the threatening whisper in her mind.

Light… She needed light. Needed the spectacular beauty of the autumn colors to drive away the creeping darkness.

She was going home, so maybe it was natural to dream of the place where she had grown up, where the colors of fall were so beautiful that they belonged not in the real world of the unreal, but in a land of dreams.

Golds, oranges, crimsons, deeper reds, softer yellows, all dazzled from the trees stretching from the great granite rises to the windswept seas and calmer harbors, where the whitecaps of the waves warned that winter was on its way.

But before the ice and cold of a New England winter arrived, there was the fall. The glorious fall with its brilliant display. The gentle sweep of the breeze came first, a touch of sweet cool breath on the cheeks. And before that touch became the chilling grip of icicle fingers, there was the reaping, the bonfires of fall, the harvest brought home.

And so, in her dream, they stretched before her, rows and rows of cornfields, the stalks undulating mesmerizingly in the sweeping breeze. She had always loved the cornfields; she could remember racing through them as a child, her grandfather chasing her, her laughter filling the sky.

The crows were always there, too, their black wings shimmering, their wicked cawing carrying high in the air, but the farmers, with a wisdom carried down from generation to generation, knew how to manage the voracious thieves.

They fashioned scarecrows and set them above the fields, and those scarecrows had personalities of their own. Mrs. Abel's scarecrow wore a wild garden hat sporting stick pins to stab the feet of any unwary crow that tried to land. Ethan Morrison's wore a billowing cape and a hideous, toothed grin. Her grandfather's scarecrow was dressed in denim overalls and a plaid shirt, and carried a shotgun; its hat was straw, and it had a mop of white hair.

Eric Rolfe's creation was the most frightening—and the most remarkable. The most likely to come to life and speak, for he had created his scarecrow's face from a plastic skull and Halloween makeup. Huge eyes stared out from the bony face, eyes that moved on battery power, and it wore a black frock coat, arms outstretched, barbed wire protruding from its head like a razor-sharp fright wig.

Some of the older residents had a problem with Eric's creation—Puritanism was long gone from the area but never really dead. Regardless, Eric loved it, and so did the kids.

Sometimes, though, when she was running in the cornfields, her grandfather close behind, her laughter would die when she came to that scarecrow. The eyes would be looking at her from their sockets, and the wind would seem to rise, not howling, but breathing out a high-pitched whisper of mingled fear and seduction. She would stop and stare, the cornstalks rustling around her, and uneasiness would steal into her heart, a fear that if she opened her mind, she would see something ancient and terrible that had occurred here, would share the evil impulse of its creator and the horror of those it had touched.

She had grown up with the stories of the local witch trials, when men, in the service of their God, tortured and condemned their fellow men, when children wept and accused, and evil was done in the name of righteousness.

In such a blood-drenched land, how could an impressionable child not feel something of the anguish of those times?

Despite that, the cornfields had always entranced her, along with the spectacular color palette of fall.

And now she was going home to see those fields in truth, so it was only natural, in that strange twilight stage between sleep and wakefulness, to see them in her mind's eye, to dream of running through them like the child she had once been. She heard her own laughter as she ran and knew she would soon come upon Eric's gothic monster of a scarecrow, but she didn't hesitate, for she was no longer a child but a woman grown, and the fears of the past could not haunt her now.

But she was wrong. The fear *was* there.

She saw it now, in the distance, and fingers of dread reached for her heart as she waited for it to see her, because she knew it would.

She didn't want to go closer.

But she had to.

Then the scarecrow raised its head, and a scream froze in her throat. The eye sockets were empty, the head a skull covered in rotting, blackened flesh, and somehow she knew it could see her, though nothing remained of what had once been its eyes.

What was left of the mouth was open, as if in a final scream. A ragged coat hung from the rotting body, the white gleam of bone showing through, dried blood staining fabric and bone alike. And as she stood there, her scream still trapped inside, the skull began to turn toward her, as if whatever evil consciousness still lived within it was drawn to her.

A crow landed on the gruesome figure's shoulder and plucked at the putrid flesh hanging from one cheek.

The skull began to laugh, as the wind rose and the sky was suddenly filled with the fluttering of brilliant fall leaves. And all the while, those eye sockets stared at her, and then red tears suddenly spilled from them, down the ravaged cheeks, as if the rotting corpse was locked in the field for all time, weeping blood.

Then the fingers of bone and rot began to twitch, reaching out for her, as a chant from her childhood echoed on the air.

"Don't fear the Reaper,
Just the Harvest Man.
When he steals a soul
It's a keeper, so
Don't fear the Reaper,
Fear the Harvest Man,
For when he steals a woman's soul
She'll go to hell or deeper…."

Rowenna Cavanaugh jerked up to a sitting position in bed, gasping, startled…and scared.

She took a deep breath and reached for calm. What a nightmare. She was surprisingly shaken by it, and she couldn't allow herself to be. She told herself that she had simply drifted off to sleep while thinking about home, even though she wasn't going back for a few days and Halloween would come and go with her here in New Orleans.

She missed home. Massachusetts was always so beautiful this time of year. And Salem… Salem was still just a small town in so many ways. She'd been elected harvest queen in her absence. At least that gave her something enjoyable to look forward to after the upcoming debate with Jeremy Flynn, scheduled to raise funds for Children's House, the charity he ran here. Besides, her appearance would help her to sell books. And she had been adrift since Jonathan, the man she'd planned to marry, had died—had it really been three years ago?—so she'd welcomed the chance to get away. Not that she really needed an excuse for coming to New Orleans, because she loved the city. But she was ready to go back home now, nightmare or not.

When she'd been a kid, they'd played games like harvest man. The Puritans had believed that the devil lived in the dark forests surrounding their settlements, just waiting to steal unwary souls. Superstition and fear had reigned supreme then, but she knew better, no matter what nonsense her subconscious had decided to dredge up.

Still, she had to wake up, had to get out of bed before she fell into another dream that was as bad or even worse.

She was living in the real world, the world of today. She had to pull herself together—and somehow manage another day in the company of Mr. Jeremy Flynn.

Ah, yes, Jeremy Flynn. Ex–police diver, now a partner in a private investigations firm with his two brothers, intelligent, articulate, charming, gorgeous…and not in any way shape or form attracted to her. In fact, he seemed to actively dislike her, but maybe it was just her opinions he didn't like. To be fair, he was never rude or actively hostile. Of course, he probably didn't dare, since his sister-in-law, Kendall Flynn, was one of her best friends and had been for years. Tonight there was going to be a Halloween party at the Flynn mansion, which Kendall and her husband had moved into a year ago, and where they now managed a community theater and hosted various charity events. It would be a great party, and Jeremy would politely greet her, then find a way to be on the other side of the room all night.

She got along just fine with Aidan, Kendall's husband, and the youngest brother, Zach, was unfailingly friendly.

Unfortunately, she was attracted to Jeremy and had been since they first met. She had been stunned, because she hadn't dated at all since Jonathan's death. Not that she believed in some archaic mourning period, she simply hadn't met anyone who attracted her enough to want to go out with him, or even to wonder what it would be like to have sex again, to touch another person intimately. But with Jeremy, she all too often found herself watching his mouth when he spoke, or his strong hands, with long fingers, the tips calloused because he played guitar. And he was a phenomenal musician. She knew, because she had seen him play.

But he clearly wasn't interested, so she kept her dreams of wild, rampant, in-the-dark-at-first sex with Jeremy Flynn a complete secret. She wondered if her hidden fantasy meant she was being disloyal to Jonathan's memory or merely human.

She wondered how he could ignore all the heat and electricity whenever they met. It was as if sparks filled the space between them, as if all they needed to do was touch and the very air would burst into a beautiful sizzle of mutual desire.

Or did that feeling exist only in her own mind?

She knew she needed to get up and take a shower, but

she couldn't stop thinking about him. It wasn't just the vision of sex, either. It was like a yearning in her heart.

I admire you. I love listening to the tone of your voice. I love the passion in your eyes when you talk about a cause. I would love to spend just an hour in real conversation with you, without being on a show, when your attention was all for me, when I could honestly know what was going on in your mind, what makes you tick....

But it wasn't to be. It was ironic that she'd finally met someone she was interested in and he wasn't interested in her, but that was that. He'd made his opinion of her clear, and she wasn't about to make a complete fool of herself by throwing herself at him. She would keep on being polite, and she would never give up her friendship with his sister-in-law—or his brothers, for that matter.

She stretched, sighed and took hold of the sheets, ready to throw them back and get up to face the day.

She touched something in her bed and frowned then gasped, incredulous at what she found.

A corn husk. A single brown corn husk caught in her sheets.

2

"Jeremy?"

He looked up, and was quick to feel a surge of annoyance. Rowenna Cavanaugh. Author, speaker and historian—and advocate of the powers of the mind. Her books were popular, he knew. She wrote about places to go where strange events had been documented, abandoned prisons and mental hospitals, historic battlefield sites and the like. She never came right out and said that ghosts or anything else otherworldly existed, only that no one had proved they didn't. She had come to town to debate paranormal possibilities with him as a way to publicize last night's Halloween benefit for Children's House. Their regular radio debates had been popular, and ticket sales and donations had soared.

This would be their last on-air appearance, though.

He was proud of everything he'd done to establish the local branch of Children's House, a special home for displaced children, something he had given himself to wholeheartedly when he had left the Jacksonville police and his position as a forensic diver to work as a private investigator in partnership with his brothers. Their inheritance of the Flynn plantation, outside the city, had kept him around, along with his charity, but now the trust fund had reached a substantial amount and was being run by local agencies, and the plantation was thriving, with his older brother, Aidan, and his sister-in-law, Kendall, in residence. Zach, their youngest brother, had already headed home to man their Florida office, and as for himself…he was ready to take some time off. Head to the islands for diving that had nothing to do with work or death. Drink sweet concoctions filled with fruit while he sat on a beach.

He wanted to reply curtly to Rowenna, but he refrained. He didn't know why she'd instantly gotten his back up.

She was a stunning woman. Her hair was nearly pitch-black, her eyes strikingly amber. Not hazel. Not brown. Amber, like gold, and shaded by ridiculously thick lashes. She was both tall and slim, but curved in every place where a woman should have curves. Her voice had a husky quality that reeked of sensuality, perfect for public speaking.

Too bad they weren't on television. No, thank God they weren't on TV. No one would even notice *he* was there, nor would they give a damn what *she* was saying. They would nod at anything, drooling on the floor all the while.

So what's your *problem?* he mocked himself.

Their debates had been sponsored by various businesses; the sponsorship money went straight to the charity. They'd been going on for two weeks, and he felt that he knew her fairly well from a distance, if that made any sense. The distance was something he had imposed.

Maybe it all had to do with everything that had gone on out at the plantation a year ago.

Rumor said the property was haunted. At first, it had been part of the charm of the place. Now he was sick of it. He adored his sister-in-law, and no way was he going to get into a fight with her over her belief in ghosts or what she had been through out in the family burial ground. But as far as he was concerned, the bad things in this world were brought to light not because of voodoo, mysticism, ESP or any other hocus-pocus.

He believed in hard work, science, logic and intelligent investigative techniques. The work of forensic scientists combined with detectives going door to door, wretched hours in stakeouts and a mind trained to slip into the psyches of others. Those things solved crimes. A crime scene was simple. A killer always took something away with him and always left something behind. Not every case was solved, but the ones that *were* all got solved in the same way. The lost were found by retracing footsteps, by detecting liars, peeling away layers of subterfuge until the truth was at last laid bare.

Any psychic was simply damned lucky—and probably smart enough to detect and follow clues—to solve a murder or pick up the trail of a kidnapper.

If only logical arguments could drive away the dreams that plagued him. The scenes that came to him when he was sleeping, of the bodies he had found floating. Of the children.

He'd been a police diver, and that meant you found bad things in the water. And he had found plenty. But nothing like the children. The van had been seen going into the water, and the dive team had been assembled fast. But the St. Mary's River was brown, mucky and deep, and the van had plunged into the deepest part. He'd been the first to reach the van and had gotten the cargo door open, only to find the cargo was children, foster children in the care of a couple whose only interest was in the payments they received each month, and each child was strapped into the car. Not seat-belted, *strapped*. Six of them, ranging from two years to ten, five of them staring sightlessly into the void that had stolen their lives. And then there had been Billy.

Billy had been alive. Jeremy had used his knife to cut the cord that bound the boy to his seat, and Billy had seen him, had tried to smile. Had reached for him. When he'd gotten Billy to dry land, he'd performed CPR until the paramedics arrived. He'd driven with Billy to the hospital. And then, despite the desperate efforts put in by truly caring medical personnel, Billy had died.

Jeremy could still see Billy's eyes. In his sleep, he could feel the boy's hand, grasping for his, as he drew him from the van.

That was the worst of the nightmares that plagued him. It was the nightmare that had made him decide to leave the force and join his brothers in an investigation agency. He was sane; he'd seen the police shrink. He knew that nightmares were nightmares. They were repeats of what was unbearable by day, of what the mind couldn't endure, not the visitations of restless spirits.

He lived with them.

He didn't attempt to put them into any cosmic per-spective.

He dreamed of Billy alive, looking at him with his huge brown eyes, and sometimes he dreamed of standing on a hilltop with Billy holding his hand. Maybe Billy represented the child he'd never had—

and perhaps never would. Maybe he represented what infuriated Jeremy about of the failure of the overburdened social welfare system. He didn't know and he didn't care. He only cared about making things better for the children who were left.

Anyway, even the shrink said he was doing the right thing, using his time to create facilities to help other needy children. It seemed to be working. And maybe, someday, the nightmares would stop, not just for days at a time, but for weeks. Months. Years. Maybe even forever.

But that future was unknown and would remain so until he got there. He didn't look for signs in tea leaves. He didn't believe that a line on his hand indicated the direction his life would take.

He reminded himself that it wasn't as if Rowenna ever said flat-out that there were ghosts in the world, much less claimed that she sat down to chat with them. She simply pointed out strange things that happened, phenomena for which there was no clear explanation.

He and Rowenna were professional combatants, nothing more. They could have been friends, if he'd been willing, because it was clear that she was open to the idea. They had been the guests of honor at several fund-raising lunches, even headlined a few cocktail parties and dinners. She had been a big draw at all those events. She was charming, articulate and approachable. They had a shared indignation at injustice, and a passion for the rights of others. But something in him wouldn't let her get close.

"Jeremy?" She repeated his name, a frown forming between her delicate, perfectly arched brows. "Sorry. Are we on?"

She nodded, as the producer spoke to them from the booth and started his countdown.

They introduced themselves, falling easily into the give-and-take they were there to provide, given how many shows they'd already done. She had an easy manner on the air, making her point but never breaking in or turning rude or abrasive. He had a feeling it was her calm approach that made her so believable. She didn't have to be fanatical. She spoke just as she wrote—she didn't tell ghost stories, she reported on events and let the listener decide. She presented things well, too. He found himself nearly hypnotized, almost believing her at times.

He was making a pitch for the real, the definable, the touchable, the things that could be seen. She stared at him, those gold eyes of hers sparkling teasingly. "Explain a remote control."

"Like a radio, there are frequencies."

"I can't see a frequency, but I believe it exists," Rowenna said.

"So you're telling me ghosts absolutely exist, even if we can't see them?"

"I'm not saying anything is absolute, but take the case of the MacDonald twins…." She went on to describe a brother, injured in the Middle East, who somehow not only told his identical twin he'd been injured but also raised a welt on his brother's stomach in the same place where he'd been hit by shrapnel.

"It's documented," she said, looking at Jeremy.

He decided not to respond directly. "What's frightening is when people believe in magic and in spells. Even when what look like miracles occur—an unexpected recovery from disease, for example—there are underlying principles at work, even if, like frequencies, we can't see them."

"Now, wait a minute. Even doctors acknowledge that a positive attitude can help in a person's recovery. The will to live can be very strong," she argued.

They went on in that vein until it was time for a commercial, and when they went back on air, the phones began to ring off the wall.

Most of the callers were for Rowenna.

Many of them admitted looking at her picture on the Internet; most of them were keen on the idea of the supernatural, as well.

That was okay. There were calls for him, too, applauding the work the police did in solving crimes and bringing killers to justice. Frustratingly, Rowenna was just as happy when those calls came in, and she agreed with every caller.

What the hell was his problem with her?

Fear?

Fear of *what?*

He was single, self-supporting and over the age of twenty-one. He liked women. He'd never felt women were "easy come, easy go," but at the same time, he'd just never found anyone with whom he wanted to share his life.

Someone with whom he would really want to share his soul and his mind. So much of what he had seen, as a cop and even now, as a private investigator, was horrific. How the hell did you share that with someone?

He almost laughed aloud at himself for the way he was thinking. He and Rowenna hadn't even been on anything close to a date. He hadn't been rude, though he'd certainly been cold and distant on every possible occasion. Something about her was too compelling. It was almost as if there were something, well, *magical* about her. As if—as crazy as it sounded—she owned his soul.

She had never tried to seduce him. She had been friendly, nothing more. She never seemed to feel the sparks that always hit him like an electric current.

Their segment at last came to an end, and they both laughed about their disagreements. Jeremy even quoted Voltaire. "I may not agree with what you say, but I will defend to the death your right to say it."

The producer waved an all-clear and the newscaster came on. Together, they headed out to the anteroom, where Jeremy stopped dead still, his attention caught by a newspaper lying open on a coffee table.

"What is it?" Rowenna asked, sounding genuinely concerned.

He glanced up at her. "Nothing," he lied. "Something just caught my eye, that's all."

"Oh, okay." She sounded doubtful, but clearly she wasn't going to push it. "Well, this was it, last show. Let me buy you a drink?" Her smile deepened. "You never have to see me again after today, you know."

He never flushed, but he did then. *He would like to have that drink. He would like to have a hell of a lot more.* It was her last day, and it would be churlish to refuse.

Except today he really did have other—and much more pressing—concerns.

He inclined his head slightly. "I would love to take you up on that, actually. But the truth is…a friend of mine is missing, and I'm kind of anxious to find out more about it." He indicated the paper.

"I have a laptop in the car," she offered. "And there's bound to be a wireless signal we can pick up."

He hesitated. He had an odd feeling he was standing at a crossroads, and that if he accepted her offer, he would be making a life-altering decision.

Bull.

To prove the ridiculousness of the thought, he decided to take her up on the offer. He told himself it was just because it would be faster than heading back to his hotel, where his own computer was. "All right. Thanks."

They said goodbye to the people at the station, then headed out to her car.

He was able to bring up the Internet easily and quickly found what he was looking for. His old partner, Brad Johnstone, and his wife, Mary, had been on vacation in Salem, Massachusetts, when Mary had disappeared at dusk from a local historic cemetery. The police had found Brad alone behind the locked gates, screaming for his wife. A search had begun quickly, but nothing had turned up other than her cell phone and purse, which were found lying on top of an old grave. The article mentioned that the couple had been estranged and were trying to repair their marriage.

Brad was made to look bad, with mention of an affair.

The worst was that Mary's parents were convinced Brad had done away with his wife, and someone had suggested that Brad's law enforcement background would have given him the skills to kill Mary and dispose of her body, before putting on a desperate-husband act.

Rowenna, reading over his shoulder, said, "I'm sorry. It looks like terrible news."

"I worked with the guy for years, and I know his wife pretty well, too. Hell, I was in their wedding. This guy was my partner for several years. They went through a really bad spell—she's a professional ballroom dancer and travels to competitions. Her partner's gay, and there isn't a soul who'll tell you she does anything but dance when she goes out of town. I think Brad just got a little lonely.… Anyway, they worked through it and got back together." He stopped talking, realizing that he had given her a lot of information, and she hadn't really asked. "I know Brad, and I don't believe for a minute that he would hurt her, but when something like this happens, it seldom ends well. I hate to say it, but the odds are she's dead, and the cops are likely to waste time focusing on Brad instead of going after the real killer."

She shook her head sadly.

"It's very strange," she said, and briefly looked his way. "Sorry," she added in response to his quizzical frown. "I mean it's strange the way she disappeared. Into thin air. Without anyone seeing anything. Salem at Halloween is insane. There are people everywhere. It's hard to believe no one saw anything."

"Oh? How do you know so much about it?"

She offered him a dry smile. "Salem is my hometown. I was born there. Well, not in the city proper— my area is still unincorporated—but I grew up on stories of the witch trials. It would have been a plain old fishing village like a hundred others if not for that."

"I knew you were from New England," he told her. "I guess I just figured Boston, from the PR bio they sent me before you got here."

"I went to college in Boston," she said. "Actually,"

she added with a laugh, "I went to college in a number
of cities in a number of states." She smiled self-deprecatingly. "What can I say? I like school. And one
interest led to another."

Jeremy idly ran his fingers through his hair, staring
at her. "Just how many degrees to you have, Miss
Cavanaugh?"

"Two. Philosophy and communications," she
assured him. "I like electives. I have tons of those.
Ancient Greek legends, Roman beliefs and superstitions, and a lot of history." She looked away for a
moment, then went on. "Naturally I looked into the
history of my own area. Back in the time of the witch
trials, people were convinced that Satan actually
walked the earth. Thousands were executed in Europe.
Despite the madness, it never got as bad over here."
She grimaced. "My family was already in the area
when it all happened. My great-great-great—well, a lot
of greats, anyway—grandfather was arrested. His
family had the money to get him out of jail, so he
survived. The thing is, what went on then has nothing
to do with Salem now. Today's witches are completely
different."

"Today's witches?" Jeremy echoed skeptically.
"Great. Mary disappeared in a town where everyone
thinks there are still witches."

She was silent for a minute. "You're missing the
point. Today's so-called witches are really wiccans.
Wicca is a pagan nature-based religion. There's no
relation between what wiccans practice today and what
the witches of the past were supposedly doing."

"Oh, please, you don't buy into all that, do you?"
he asked her.

"I'm not a wiccan, if that's what you're asking, but I have friends who are," she said, keeping as much indignation as she could from her voice. "Wicca is a recognized religion, you know. If a soldier comes home to be buried, he can have the sign of the pentagram on his marker, just the same as he could have a Star of David or a cross."

"I'm sorry," Jeremy said. "It's just that…well, bringing that kind of woo-woo superstition into things always complicates matters."

"It shouldn't. Wiccans don't believe in doing evil. Whatever one person does to another is returned threefold. So a wiccan wouldn't hurt anyone, because they would be hurt three times as badly in return."

"Yeah, and if you're Christian, you go to hell if you kill someone. That doesn't stop a lot of Christians from turning into cold-blooded murderers."

"I agree with you there," she said.

He'd had enough of the discussion suddenly. "Look, we're not going to solve anything here, so why don't we head over to the Quarter?"

"You're taking me up on that drink?" she asked.

He was. He wasn't sure why, but he was. He liked the sound of her voice. He was interested in the things she had to say. He was drawn to her—well, hell, any heterosexual male was going to be drawn to her—even though he still felt as if he needed some kind of barrier between them.

Not that it really mattered now. Today was it. She was leaving after tonight's party. No more debates. Their paths would not cross again.

"Yeah, let's do it," he said. "In fact, how about we grab some lunch?"

They headed toward Royal Street and a quiet restaurant, where Rowenna ordered tea and crawfish and he decided on jambalaya.

"So go on," he told her, once they had been served. "I want to know more about what witches are today."

"Really?" she asked.

"Yes, really."

She arched a brow, doubtful, then plunged on. "The Salem witch community started in the early 1970s, when a woman named Laurie Cabot, who's now considered the official witch of Salem, moved to town. There are now several thousand practicing wiccans in the area. They would have been in real trouble back when the Puritans were in charge. Ironically, they left England looking for religious freedom, then went on to persecute anyone who didn't worship as they mandated. But wiccans—if there had been wiccans back then—would never have practiced Satanism the way the Salem witches supposedly did. The devil is a Christian concept, a fallen angel. So wiccans *can't* worship the devil or sign a pact with Satan, because in their religion, he doesn't exist. That's not to say there aren't Satanists out there, because there are, but that's a different philosophy entirely."

He stared at her and nodded gravely. Was it a lecture on the ironies of man that he really needed? Maybe, in a way.

Brad and Mary had gone to Salem. Mary had disappeared. He needed to know anything he could about the place, and Rowenna knew a lot about it. She was also beautiful and, frankly, enchanting, and the scent of her cologne was arresting. Mesmerizing. He felt his pulse stutter.

She had never claimed to read minds, but he felt that she knew what he was thinking. That he didn't really think witches or Satanists, real or imagined, past or present, had anything to do with Mary's disappearance and the probability that something terrible had happened to her.

Unless someone out there believed he was following the dictates of Satan.

She smiled. "You think anyone who decides to practice an ancient and long-dead religion is an idiot."

"I don't care if you want to worship palm trees—as long as you don't use your belief as an excuse to hurt or kill anyone else," he told her.

She laughed. When she did, her eyes were like liquid gold, he realized. "You'd like the wiccans just fine, then. Like I said, they do no evil, because evil comes back threefold." She shrugged. "I don't think anyone has the answers to the questions that plague the universe. We all want to think people who hurt others will be punished—in this world or the next. Or, better, now *and* in the afterlife, assuming you believe in an afterlife."

"Are you saying you don't?" he asked her.

"I definitely do." She gave a little shiver as she said it.

"You're thinking about something else, aren't you?" he asked.

She looked startled, then offered him a rueful grin. "We have a legend up where I live about a sort of bogeyman. We call him the Harvest Man. He's a creature of evil—drawn from old pagan practices, even Native American beliefs, and the concept of Satan, as well. When someone disappears, when something awful that can't be accounted for occurs, we chalk it up to the Harvest Man. He doesn't have horns and a tail. In fact, he doesn't really look all that scary. He wears a crown of autumn leaves and a cape the color of the earth. He's taller than most men, too. Huge."

"So he goes after young women?" he asked.

"I don't know how the legend got started, to tell you the truth, but the oldest story I know is from a few hundred years ago, sometime after the witch trials, when a series of young and beautiful women disappeared. They never caught the killer, so colonists, probably influenced by the local tribes, said the Harvest Man was out there, stealing their souls."

"Don't tell me you're saying Mary was taken by the Harvest Man."

"Of course not. I'm just saying it's New England, there's a story to go with anything that can happen. But if you're wondering if I think there's a real-life killer out there, someone just as evil as the Harvest Man, then I'm afraid it's a real possibility."

Just then his phone rang, and he had the strangest feeling, even before he glanced at the number, that it was going to be Brad.

It was.

He excused himself, and stepped outside.

Rowenna played idly with the straw in her iced tea, wishing she'd made a hasty goodbye when Jeremy had taken the call.

Maybe it was just having too much time to think while their conversation was still fresh in her mind, but she had an awful feeling she knew what was going to happen. Brad was going to call Jeremy for help—in fact, for all she knew it was Brad who had called just now—and Jeremy would come to Salem.

She felt her heart pounding a bit too hard, and she tried to still it. She wouldn't see him, even if he did. He didn't like her, so he would hardly give her a call or ask for her help.

But she *would* wind up seeing him.

Detective Joe Brentwood would call her, and Jeremy's eyes would widen when he saw her, and she could only imagine his anger—and his opinion, whether kept inside or voiced out loud. "My friend is in trouble, and you're going to bring a psychic quack in on it?"

"Will there be anything else?"

The waitress startled Rowenna, who barely managed not to jump. "No. Thank you. May I just get the check, please?"

As soon as she had paid the bill, she slipped out and hurried to her car. He wouldn't be heartbroken to discover her gone, and she knew that even though he owned one-third of the Flynn plantation, he wasn't living out there and instead was staying at a small, privately owned hotel just the other side of Jackson Square.

Her own hotel was just down Royal, and as she drove those few blocks, she couldn't help wondering whether she would be stuck dreaming about him for days to come, and paradoxically hoping both that he wouldn't show up in Salem…and that he would.

Upstairs in her room, there was little to do. She had organized almost everything over the last few days, knowing she would be heading out in the morning.

Feeling absurdly disconsolate, she sat on the bed, then nearly jumped sky-high when her cell phone rang. She expected it to be Jeremy, wondering why she had walked out on him without even saying goodbye.

So much for psychic connections. It was Kendall.

"Hey," Kendall said.

"Hey, yourself."

"You're leaving tomorrow—you weren't even going to call?" Kendall asked.

Guilt washed over her. She had known Kendall for years, having first met her at Tea and Tarot, the shop Kendall had owned until recently, when she'd sold out to an employee, so she could give her full attention to her marriage and the theater she had dreamed of founding since college.

"No, of course not," Rowenna said. It wasn't a lie. She would have remembered to call. Wouldn't she?

"Why don't you come out for dinner?" Kendall asked her. "We won't keep you late."

Rowenna looked around the room. She thought about lying, about telling Kendall that she was a mess, that she had a million little things to do to get ready to leave, after having lived in a hotel room for two weeks.

But she wasn't going to. Kendall had been her friend forever. Yes, she was married to Jeremy's brother, but that wasn't worth ruining a friendship.

"I just had a late lunch," Rowenna said.

"I won't make you eat a lot," Kendall told her.

Rowenna laughed. "Sure, I'll drive on out. Thanks. It will be good to say goodbye one last time."

"Hey, don't say that," Kendall protested.

"Sorry, I didn't mean it that way. I mean, before going home."

"Great."

"Hey, you know, you guys could come up my way for Thanksgiving," Rowenna told her.

"It's hard to leave here right now. I've got the little kids doing a First Thanksgiving play on the Wednesday right before. But Aidan and I will come up soon. I promise. Come on over now, why don't you? Or as soon as you're packed and ready. Is your flight early?"

"No, it doesn't leave until noon."

"Great," Kendall said. "Get your butt on over here, then. Or, even better, Jeremy's heading out to talk to Aidan about something, so he can pick you up. I'll have him call you to tell you what time. See you soon."

"No! No, no, I'd rather have my own car. In fact, maybe I should just stay here and get some things taken care of. Kendall?"

Rowenna realized she'd been talking to the ether. Kendall had hung up.

Great. Just great.

What to do now? Behave normally, that would help.

The phone rang again. She hoped against hope it was Kendall calling back, but of course it wasn't.

It was Jeremy.

"I hear I'm picking you up. Would an hour be all right?"

"It would be fine, but I'm not sure I should go."

"You have to go. You picked up the lunch check. I owe you a meal, but since my sister-in-law is taking care of that, I'll have to settle for playing chauffeur. By the way, I'm sorry my call took so long you decided to ditch me."

She winced. She would have loved for him to speak to her so pleasantly a few weeks ago.

"So…an hour?" he asked.

"Sure, fine, thanks."

When she hung up, Rowenna hesitated, then put through a call to Joe Brentwood.

"Hey," he said, picking up his cell phone. "You still coming home tomorrow? I'd like your take on something that happened here."

"Joe, you're supposed to say you've missed me and you're delighted I'm coming home soon."

"I miss you and I'm delighted you're coming home soon. And have I got an interesting case for you."

"It's about a man named Brad Johnstone and his missing wife, Mary, right?" she said with a sense of fatality.

"Damn. You *are* psychic."

She wasn't psychic. She couldn't meet people and hear the spirits of their loved ones talking to her, passing on messages. But there were times when she opened her mind, let herself think and feel and add in some good common sense, and could figure things out. Maybe there was something different in her subconscious, something her research had honed to a fine and useful edge. But though she wrote about other people's encounters with the supernatural, and though she admitted to a knack for sensing things when others didn't, she would never call herself a psychic, not when—no matter how much Jeremy Flynn apparently doubted the truth of this—she didn't believe in the reality of the paranormal, only the possibility. No matter what others sometimes called her, as far as she was concerned, all she did was use her senses, all of them, along with her brain, to see possibilities and draw conclusions based on the available evidence. And she made very, *very* certain that no hint of her involvement ever reached the media.

"No, Joe, nothing psychic. I read it in the paper. And I have a…friend who is involved in a strange way."

"What?"

"The guy I've been working with down here used to work with Brad Johnstone."

"That investigator?" Joe asked. Like most cops, he didn't like private investigators. He thought they were pains in the ass who messed up the official investigation into any case they got involved with.

"Yes."

Joe's silence clearly transmitted his opinion.

"He's a decent guy, Joe."

"Yeah, yeah. Great. Well, I'll see you tomorrow. Wait, you called me. What's up?"

"The Johnstone case," she said dryly.

"If you read the paper, you know what I know."

"But—"

"You're coming home. Give me a call as soon as you're back and we'll talk."

"Sure."

She hung up. Since her own parents were dead and she had no siblings, Joe was the closest thing she had left to family. He'd lost his wife to cancer a decade ago, and their only son, Rowenna's late fiancé, had been killed overseas, serving in the military.

Even though he was Jonathan's father, he was always the first one to tell her she needed to move on with her life. He'd told her once that he was grateful she hadn't forgotten him and started over again too soon, but his son was dead and buried, and there was even moss growing on the tombstone when he didn't keep up with it. Time for her to build a new life.

He was also a detective with the county. Her

"career" with him had begun over coffee one cold winter's night when he had been talking to her about a recent murder. She'd asked him to show her the scene, and on the way, he'd told her what he knew about the victim. Sunny Shoemaker, thirty-four, depressed because she'd been let go at the real estate agency where she'd worked, had gone out to a bar with a few sympathetic co-workers. After a few drinks she'd left to go home, telling her friends that she was fine. She'd been discovered with a knife in her back beside the high fence of the old prison. Her handbag was gone; the presumed motive was robbery. The M.E. had found a hair, but that wouldn't do them any good without a suspect with whom to compare it, and so far, they hadn't found one.

When Rowenna stood there and closed her eyes, she could imagine what it might have been like to be Sunny. She hadn't heard the footsteps of her attacker, so she hadn't turned around. And she hadn't fought to keep her purse. But wouldn't a random thief have tried to wrest the purse from her first? Purse snatchers didn't usually stab their victims in the back, then steal their purses.

Rowenna had noted the proximity of the bar, a place where the locals hung out after work, and, on a hunch, gone in the next evening.

She chose the same stool the bartender said Sunny had used, and sitting there, sipping a glass of wine, she watched the people around her, listening, trying to picture herself as Sunny once again. In her mind, she allowed a part of herself to become Sunny. An executive type, who'd been sitting with another man at a table, came up to the bar, taking the stool next to her.

As the bartender mixed his drink, they joked about the fact that he just couldn't stay away from his customary stool, and that he would have to reclaim it as soon as his client left. The man left an empty glass on the bar. When the bartender turned, Rowenna confiscated the glass. She gave the glass to Joe that evening, and one thing led to another, until Joe had a suspect.

It turned out that the man was a broker from Sunny's firm and had been skimming profits from his partners. Sunny hadn't known anything, but he was afraid she did and had been the one to fire her. Angry, she had threatened him at the bar, convincing him that she really did know what he was up to, and he had panicked, following her, picking up a knife on his way past the bar, where the bartender had left it after slicing lemons.

After that, Joe had decided that she had psychic abilities. It wasn't true, but she hadn't been able to convince him of that. It was a talent to get into the head of another person, she admitted, but there was nothing mysterious about it. After that, he often came to her for help on puzzling cases, but she made him swear that he wouldn't mention her name to the press. Some of the other guys at the station knew that he consulted her, but he kept any mention of psychic ability out of it, so no one really worried about it and they all liked her.

She hoped she would be able to help them find Jeremy's friend, even though she knew how he would react if she were brought into the investigation.

She felt pathetic, like a lapdog hoping for a sign of approval.

Rowenna stood up and brushed her hair, trying to imagine being Mary Johnstone. A woman with a husband who loved her but had cheated on her. A husband who was trying to rebuild their marriage. Someone she really loved.

She hadn't walked out on him. And this wasn't a practical joke; she wasn't pretending to disappear to get even with him for his transgressions.

She closed her eyes. She knew the cemetery, and she could see it plainly in her mind's eye. She felt the sea breeze that came in from the water, cool now, with the touch of fall. She could see the fallen leaves in their brilliant colors.

As she stood there, "becoming" Mary, soaking in the atmosphere of the cemetery and the beauty of the day, she was startled by a wall of sheer black settling over her vision.

And once again she saw the cornfields that had so terrified her in her dream.

Crows shrieked, as she ran through the corn. She wasn't a child, and she wasn't Mary. She was herself, an adult, running and running, seeing the scarecrows towering above the fields, running toward the one scarecrow that terrified her the most.

And there was something beyond. No, some*one*. A figure in the distance, clad in a dark cape, nothing more than darkness amid shadow…

The Harvest Man.

There was a sharp knock at her door. It was as startling as an alarm bell.

Her eyes flew open, and the cornfields vanished. She realized that she was shaking, that her hands were clenched at her sides, her palms damp.

"Rowenna?"

Jeremy Flynn was here to pick her up. And she was

glad, and not only because she was going to have one more chance to spend time with him.

She'd been afraid to reach the scarecrow in the cornfield.

No, not afraid. She had been terrified.

3

He could tell immediately that Rowenna was tense when she opened the door. He might not have a psychic bone in his body, but he could read the strain in her features and the tic that pulsed rapidly at her throat. And he noted the change in her expression, from something white and frightened to a false, tight smile when she greeted him.

"Hi. Hey, I'm sorry you had to come for me. I could have driven out myself," she said. "I just need, um…to get my purse. And a jacket."

She turned away from him and hurried to get her things. She had a nice room. His eye was drawn directly to the huge canopy bed, and he quickly reined in his wayward thoughts. He'd picked her up at the hotel once before, for a promotional appearance, but he hadn't gone up to her door; he wondered why he had done so tonight.

With her purse and jacket in hand, she paused, staring at him.

"What's the matter?" he asked her.

She didn't deny that something was wrong. "I know the detective on your friend's case," she told him bluntly.

Her words startled him. "Pardon?"

"I…I just didn't want it to be a surprise when you found out. The lead detective on the case is a man named Joe Brentwood. I know him. He's a…friend of mine."

It was the last thing he had expected. He felt a new wall of distrust going up between them. Not her fault. His.

"And you know he's on the case…how?" he asked.

"I called him."

"I see." He hesitated for a moment. "But how did you know to call him?" His tone sounded suspicious, even to himself.

She looked away from him. "I knew you were concerned for your friend. I thought I'd ask him if he knew what was going on, so I gave him a call. Shall we go?" She strode past him, hurrying toward the elevators.

Was she behaving in a guilty manner, or was it his imagination?

She didn't say anything more as they rode down in the elevator. The valet was waiting with his car, and he seated Rowenna and took the wheel before he spoke again. "And what did your friend say?"

"Honestly?" She looked at him.

He hiked up a brow. "Yeah?"

She looked forward again. "He isn't fond of private investigators."

He laughed. "The guy likes psychics and he looks down his nose at P.I.s?" He groaned. "This is going to be bad," he said grimly. "Small town, witches, hostile police department—just great."

She didn't look at him, but he saw her lips tighten. He could have bitten his tongue. He hadn't meant to be so offensive; he had just spoken without thinking,

filled with a sense of dread. Brad had sounded crazy
on the phone. He was coming undone, and he badly
needed help. The only person up there who seemed to
believe him was a beat cop named O'Reilly. The detectives—presumably including Rowenna's friend—
were all treating him with suspicion, even hostility.

But that was the way it was. When a woman was
dead or missing and there was no obvious suspect,
suspicion fell on the husband. It was natural, a matter
of statistics. Brad was a cop, and he knew that. He and
Jeremy had found the bodies of too many wives and
girlfriends who had been weighted and tossed overboard by the men who supposedly loved them. It was
simple mathematics that told the cops to suspect the
husband when his wife disappeared. Especially when
he was the last one to have seen her.

"Are you going up there?" she asked him.

"Yeah." He nodded. "Sorry," he added, his tone stiff.
He owed her that apology, but it was hard to give.

"Joe Brentwood is a good man," she told him.

"I'm sure he is."

"I'm serious. If you work with him, he'll work with
you."

He had a sense she was making a promise she
wasn't sure would be kept—not surprising, given the
way most cops responded to what they saw as civilian
intervention. But all he said was "I hope so."

She fell silent. The atmosphere was strained. He
fished in his mind for something to say, but nothing
came to him. Strange, they had talked nonstop earlier
today. He had discussed Brad's situation at length, and
she had been filled with information, which he had
been ready to listen to. But now…

Then, she had been leaving. Going home. He hadn't expected ever to see her again, to have to fight his response to her again.

Now, he was following her. Was that the difference, creating this distance that crouched between them?

The drive to the plantation seemed to be taking forever.

She turned to him. "Joe Brentwood was almost my father-in-law," she said suddenly, as if she'd made a decision and was going to follow through, no matter what. "I was engaged to his son, Jonathan, who was killed three years ago in a helicopter crash overseas. He was military. Joe and I are still very good friends, so don't go thinking he's some weirdo or isn't everything in the world a good cop should be. He isn't a wiccan, but he couldn't care less what religion others choose to practice, as long as they're law-abiding. He respects his fellow human beings, again, unless they break the law."

He was startled by her sudden attack, because though the words had been evenly spoken, it had clearly been an attack nonetheless.

"Sorry," he said again, feeling defensive.

"He respects his fellow human beings—so long as they're not private investigators?" he found himself asking.

She sighed in aggravation, and he decided maybe silence was better than conversation after all.

At last they reached the Flynn plantation. As he stared up at the big white house, he felt a surge of pleasure and pride. Life was ironic. Aidan had been the one who wanted to sell the place rather than get involved in the heavy responsibility of restoring it. But

it was Aidan who lived in it now, with Kendall. They had turned the derelict manor into a masterpiece of beauty.

The house stood proudly now, a fresh coat of paint gracing her fine lines. They had preserved history, and, in the community theater, they had created something new and wonderful, as well.

As they drew closer, he noticed a poster over by the barn, announcing a Thanksgiving show featuring area schoolchildren. He had seen Kendall at work; she managed to involve every child. His elder brother, Aidan, had been known as the skeptical hard-ass of their trio. He'd lost his first wife to a car accident, and it had been as if anything optimistic in him had died as well. Kendall had changed all that. She was energy and faith in motion, and he was grateful for her.

He just wished she'd told him more about Rowenna.

As he parked in the graceful, curving front drive and they got out of the car, Kendall came out the front door, smiling. "Hey!" She gave Rowenna a hug and a kiss on the cheek, then did the same with him. "Thanks for picking up Rowenna," she said. "Aidan is out in the barn office. He wants a couple of horses now, did he tell you that?" She smiled, shaking her head. "I guess it won't be hard to add a small stable, since we're using the old barn for the theater. Rowenna, come on in. We're just about ready for dinner. Jambalaya for your last New Orleans meal for a while."

"Sounds wonderful," Jeremy said, opting not to mention that he'd had jambalaya for lunch and hoping that Rowenna would also keep that quiet. "I'll go find Aidan and tell him it's time to eat."

He headed for the barn, wondering what the two

women would be talking about and marveling again at the changes Aidan and Kendall had wrought in little more than a year. The old stables were sparkling clean, with a stage in the back and fold-up chairs stacked to one side, and, like the house itself, it was sparkling with new paint. The office was in the old tack room, and it, too, was entirely refitted with a mahogany desk, chairs, a small sofa and a phone, computer, printer and fax.

"Hey," Aidan said, looking up at his arrival. "I did like you asked and pulled everything I can find on what else happened in Salem that day."

"And?"

Aidan shook his head. "Nothing out of the ordinary. A few lewd and lascivious charges, a couple of drunks dragged in and one woman who refused to leave a store at closing time. Nothing major. So when are you leaving?"

"Tomorrow. Brad's pretty much a basket case."

His brother was silent, staring at his computer screen.

"What?" Jeremy said, frowning.

"I suggest that you stay open to any possibility. And by any possibility I mean, no matter how strange, if it seems like a clue, follow it up."

"Hey, you know me. I'm good at what I do."

"I know you are. But you always want the visual, the bird in the hand, the rock-solid evidence. I'm just advising you to be willing to accept things that look…less than rock-solid. Follow every path, whether it seems absurd or not."

Aidan had definitely changed, Jeremy thought. Hell, he'd married a one-time tarot reader, though Kendall

had always told him that she'd only been a performer. But Kendall *did* believe that the plantation was haunted by benevolent ghosts. She had said as much many times after her experience last year with a real-life murderer in the hidden chamber under the family tomb. But Aidan...

Aidan had raised him after their parents' deaths. He'd put his own life on hold to keep all three of them, Aidan, Jeremy and their youngest brother, Zach, together. Jeremy had all the respect in the world for his elder brother. He loved him and would fight any battle in his defense.

But Aidan had been down in that crypt with Kendall, and it had put him a little bit over the edge, at least when it came to the whole ghost thing.

He didn't want to argue with his brother, though.

Something in Aidan had changed when he lost his first wife, and then, just when he had dared to fall in love again, he had nearly lost Kendall.

Every man had his own demons, and his own way of dealing with them. If Aidan wanted to think there was something more out there, a gentle hand guiding events from the grave, that was his own business.

"Sure, Aidan. I promise. I'll keep an open mind," he said.

Kendall looked over her shoulder, even though they were alone in the kitchen. "Jeremy told you about it, right? About his friends up in Salem?" When Rowenna nodded, Kendall shivered and went on. "I'm so afraid she's dead. Mary Johnstone, I mean. I know Jeremy's worried about the same thing. He called Aidan about it earlier and asked him to look some stuff up on the

computer. Jeremy is convinced Brad is telling the truth and that he had nothing to do with her disappearance. And why wouldn't he? The man is his friend. He was his partner for years. They were responsible for each other's lives. The thing is…" Once again Kendall hesitated, looking over her shoulder, as if afraid her husband or Jeremy had slipped in without her seeing them. "Rowenna, I know we haven't talked a lot about how I feel about this, but ghosts *do* exist. I know it. And they can help us. All we have to do is let them."

Rowenna just looked at her, waiting for her to go on.

Kendall nodded. "Rowenna, you write books about the fact that there are things out there that can't be explained by logic and science."

"I know, but…Kendall, I never suggested that a ghost could just come in, sit down, drink tea and discuss the weather."

Frustrated, Kendall said, "I'm not saying that, either, and you know it. But I know you've helped the police figure things out in the past, and I hope you'll help them now. I hope you'll help Jeremy."

Jeremy doesn't want my help. He doesn't want yours, either. He wants the cold hard facts, ma'am, and that's it, Rowenna thought.

"I can try," she offered.

"Sometimes ghosts come in dreams," Kendall said.

Dreams. Rows of cornstalks. Scarecrows looming above them. Crows cawing high in the air, then alighting to pick at rotting flesh clinging to skeletal remains.

"Have you had any strange dreams lately?" Kendall asked her.

A chill settled over Rowenna, and she jumped to her

feet. "I think something is boiling over on the stove," she said, knowing even as she spoke that the excuse was transparent.

Just as she rose, Aidan and Jeremy came in from the back. Aidan greeted her with a kiss and a hug, and assured her that they would all miss her in New Orleans.

Except for Jeremy, who would be following her home the next day.

After dinner, Kendall hugged her goodbye at Jeremy's car and whispered, "Listen to your dreams. Promise me you'll listen to your dreams."

Words. Just words, Rowenna told herself.

But she couldn't forget the images that had plagued her sleep.

Jeremy planned to drop Rowenna at the front door of her hotel, but he didn't make a move to leave, even after he opened her door and then stood on the sidewalk while she thanked him for the ride.

She hesitated, then asked, "Do you want to come up? I have coffee and tea, maybe even a bottle of beer or two in the minibar."

"No thanks. We're both leaving tomorrow. I'm going to head back to my hotel and pack. I'm sure I'll see you up there. Thanks again for your help, though."

She nodded. "Thank *you* again for the ride."

She still just stood there. So did he. He found himself thinking of all the time they had shared, all the occasions when they had sat close together in the studio and he had breathed in her perfume. He thought of the amber lights in her eyes, eyes a man could get lost in. Suddenly, after all the times when he had felt

the need to stay far away from her, he wanted to be close. Touch her flesh and see if it was as smooth as it looked, find out if the texture of her hair was really as silky as he dreamed. If the passionate fire of her speech translated into the way she made love.

"Yeah, sure, of course. My pleasure."

"See you, then." With that she turned and headed into the hotel.

It wasn't late, Rowenna thought. Over on Bourbon Street, the bands would still be playing for hours.

She thought about heading out for a drink and some music, then decided against it. She opted for a long shower, followed by a light beer from the minibar. She wanted to sleep—*needed* to sleep—and she was afraid to sleep.

Kendall had told her in all seriousness that ghosts came in dreams, and now she was afraid to go to sleep.

She tried to watch some television until she was too tired to stay awake, but even as she aimed the remote, there was a knock at her door. And she knew, even before she went to answer, that Jeremy Flynn would be standing on the other side. Her heart began to hammer. She felt a flush rising to her cheeks.

Speaking of dreams...

He was leaning against the door frame, and for a moment his expression was completely unguarded. She was wondering what he was doing there. Thinking that he was insane. That he should go straight back to his hotel.

"You're not supposed to open a door without asking who's there," he said.

"I knew it was you," she told him.

"Psychic?" he asked softly.

"I knew," she repeated.

She hoped he didn't want to talk.

He didn't.

She drew him into the room. Other than the pale glow streaming from the bathroom, she had already turned off the lights. And she was glad of that, because she didn't want to talk, either. Nor did she want to study his expression or let him study hers. Most of all, she didn't want him asking permission.

She had donned a silk kimono after her shower, and now she let it slip to the floor, then cupped his face in her hands, rose slightly on her toes, found his lips and kissed him. His arms came around her, strong and tight, and his mouth opened to hers with equal passion, lips molding against hers, tongue thrusting deeply, evoking a rise of hunger within her that was both intoxicating and frightening.

She was afraid. What if she had forgotten how to make love? Was it really like just hopping back on a bicycle? Could she fail? Be too awkward…?

He caressed the length of her back while his mouth remained locked with hers, wet and hot, his fingers skimming along her flesh like the brush of wildfire. He stepped back, his deep auburn hair tousled by her roving hands, his breath coming hard, his gray eyes an enigmatic storm. She was afraid she had gone too far, been too eager, made a fool of herself, but he had moved away only to ease the sweater he wore over his head and cast it aside, and when their mouths merged once again, she felt a fever of electricity fill her and instinctively moved her hands to the waistband of his jeans, working the button free.

The next few minutes were a blur. She remembered his hand on her face, his fingers tracing the bones of her jawline and cheek. And she remembered his eyes on hers, remembered the color of them, the tempest within them, their touch as real as the stroke of his fingers. His shoes and jeans were discarded in quick succession, and then they were lying together on the bed, and she realized that her dreams had been nothing but teasing foreplay compared to the reality of the man. She was fascinated by every aspect of him, the sun-bronzed sheen of his flesh, the strength of his fingers and their calloused touch, the length of his legs, the hard muscles of his chest... She felt as if they'd been touching forever, as if his kisses fell everywhere. He moved with unbridled passion, and she met him with the same. They made love feverishly, desperate for the moment of climax, yet holding back, unwilling for this wordless communication to end. They were bold lovers, shy lovers, anguished and eager. In the end, she lay still long enough to feel the teasing progress of his lips and tongue down the length of her, and then the weight of his body atop hers, those storm-gray eyes locked with hers once again, and the delicious slide of his erection inside her, and that, like his first touch, was like a hot wind that seemed to sweep through her entire being.

They moved in a symphony outside of time, slow and deep, then faster, feverishly, more urgently. She clung to him, nipped his shoulder, bathed his neck with kisses, and felt the fullness of his possession with an intensity that threatened her sanity. She was lost in the rampant thunder of their hearts, the gasping of their breath and the eternal rhythm that had taken root in her being.

His fingers threaded through hers, clutching, and she closed her eyes against the climax that exploded through her like a storm in a desert. And she felt him above her, tension constricting his every muscle, then releasing, and heard him cry her name as his own climax seized him. He was with her when the ricocheting thunder of her heart began a slower beat, when she began to breathe again as if there were suddenly more air in the world, and when the room itself came back into focus.

Then, suddenly, she began to wonder what to say as the ticking of the clock became audible and she felt a chill along her naked flesh.

But words were apparently not so hard for him. He rolled to his side, but his arm remained around her, pulling close, and he whispered softly, "Do you know how long I've fought this?"

"I thought you didn't find me attractive," she admitted.

She was grateful for the husky sound of his laughter, and the way he touched her again, his fingers moving over her cheek and jaw, as if marveling at the structure of them. And his eyes, gray mist now, slightly clouded, stared at her as if he couldn't believe how foolish she'd been. She wondered if she would ever really know him, know what lurked behind his strength and passion, his determination, his confidence. And then she was immediately afraid that she'd been out of the game for too long, and that she was reading too much into one night of sex, however wonderful, and if the secrets of his mind were something that weren't meant to matter to her.

But at least he wasn't rude; he didn't jump right up and start putting on his clothes, ready to leave.

She was stunned when he said, "You scare the hell out of me."

"Me?"

"You."

Because I'm...a fruitcake? she wondered.

"Why?" she whispered, looking away, suddenly afraid of what she might hear.

"Because you're...you," he said. When she turned to him, he was smiling a little ruefully, and she decided to leave it at that. "And I'm glad," he added, pulling her closer. "I felt like a fool coming here, you know."

"It's all right. I panicked after I opened the door."

"You panic really well," he said.

"Thanks."

He let out a deep sigh. "When's your flight?"

"Noon. When is yours?"

"Eleven-thirty. I go through Chicago. You?"

"Charlotte. When do you actually arrive?" she asked.

"Three-thirty. And you?"

"A quarter to four."

"Want a ride?"

"You don't have to wait for me. I can get a cab from the airport."

"I'm sure you can. But wouldn't you rather just ride with me?"

Sex? Yes, she thought. A ride?

"Sure. If you don't mind the wait. And you can... You don't have to take me all the way home. I have to stop and see a...a friend when I get there."

What a lousy liar she was, she thought. Not that she was lying, exactly. She just wasn't telling the whole truth. She knew she had stumbled over her words, and that her face was reddening. Maybe he wouldn't notice in the dim light.

"To see your friend the detective, right?" he asked, and there was an edge to his tone.

She was about to say that she could introduce them, but he spoke before she could. "That's all right. I need to call Brad as soon as I get in, anyway."

"I would appreciate the ride, though," she said, and she knew she sounded ridiculously prim, especially considering her current position.

"Fine. I'll be glad of the company—and the directions."

He started to rise. To her own surprise, Rowenna held him back. "You don't need to leave, you know," she whispered.

He looked down at her and smiled slowly, then shrugged. "Okay, I won't."

He lay back down and found her lips.

Making love was easy, she thought. So much easier than she had imagined.

Far easier than hopping back on a bike, she added with a silent giggle.

Later, with him still beside her, she drifted off to sleep. She was glad he was with her, and glad, though still just slightly embarrassed, that she had taken such direct steps to keep him there.

When she started to see the cornfields again in her mind's eye, she fought the vision.

No, no, please. Not now, not tonight.... Please, just let me have tonight, let me have *him*....

It was almost as if her prayer had been answered.

She wasn't alone in the cornfield.

Jeremy was with her.

"Show me," he said.

"You don't want to see," she told him, but she couldn't stop the motion of the dream. They were running together. Running through the rows and rows of corn.

She knew what was waiting ahead, could already see those malevolently empty eyes, and she tried to stop. But she couldn't, could only look pleadingly into his eyes, gray, now with a touch of something darker.

Gray, like the color of the sky, and with that hint of the darkness that would soon engulf the fields.

She heard the first crow scream, and knew that it, too, was soaring toward them like a cruel shadow, black against the roiling gray of the sky.

"Run," he told her. "Run!"

And so they ran.

"Rowenna!"

She woke with a start. He was leaning above her, eyes dark with concern, hair disheveled, his weight on his elbow as he shook her gently.

She stared back at him, the dream fading. Damn Kendall, she thought. Listen to her dreams? Oh, yeah, that was just what she needed.

"I'm sorry," she said aloud.

"Nightmare?" he asked.

He sounded solicitous, sympathetic.

He was probably thinking that his first impression of her had been right and he was sleeping with a basket case.

"I…guess," she told him. "I'm sorry I woke you."

"I have to get going anyway," he told her.

An inexplicable chill washed over her, and she clung to him, then laughed, forcing herself to let go. "Sorry. It's morning, isn't it?"

"Morning enough. It's about six-thirty. And I have to finish packing."

He rose easily, unselfconscious. But then, he probably didn't have any hang-ups about nights of wild sex based on impulse. She watched him as he dressed, relishing the breadth of his shoulders.

Light was seeping in around the edges of the drapes, and she felt a vast sense of relief. For some reason, she'd become far fonder of the day than of the night.

In his jeans, pulling his sweater back over his head, he came back and sat on the edge of the bed as he slipped into socks and shoes. "Can I help?" he asked.

"Help?"

"With your dream. Your nightmare."

"Oh. No. I don't even remember it," she lied.

"You're sure? You could tell me about it. Make it go away."

She forced a laugh. "No, I'm fine, I promise." Lying was becoming easier, and that was probably not a good thing, she thought.

For the moment, she was grateful for the ability, though.

He kissed her lips briefly, paused, and kissed her more deeply.

"I'll see you in Boston, then," he told her. "Call my cell when you have your luggage. I'll just pick up the rental car and come around for you."

"Sounds good, thanks," she said, smiling.

He didn't linger or say anything more about her nightmare, and she was glad.

"Lock up behind me," he said at the door, and he did hesitate then. "And though I'm exceedingly grateful that you opened the door for *me,* don't open it again—don't open *any* door—unless you know who's out there, okay?"

She smiled again. "I'll lock it. I promise."

When he was gone, she leaped out of bed and locked the door, then turned on every light in the room. *And* the television.

A little while later, as she was showering, she wondered if there was any way to shut and lock the door to her dreams.

Except that...

She was very afraid that the cornfields in her mind's eye weren't a dream at all but something very—and terrifyingly—real.

4

Logan had never been Jeremy's favorite airport, but for once his connection had not only run smoothly, but his flight had also actually arrived ten minutes early, and it was almost as if someone had unloaded the baggage and gotten it onto the belt ahead of them. His gold card accessed his reservation without a hitch at the rental agency, and he was waiting when Rowenna called to say she and her luggage were ready to go.

Her directions were perfect, and they arrived in Salem with enough time before the meeting he'd set up with Brad that he offered to take her all the way home, but she assured him that Joe would give her a ride later. Instead, she offered to give him a quick walking tour of the central tourist area.

He wanted to see the cemetery, and after pointing out a few of the more important weathered graves, she let him wander by himself.

The cemetery stood right in the middle of the tourist track. There were a few museums nearby, and just across the street was a pedestrian mall.

But despite the modern-day surroundings, he found that the cemetery itself felt intriguingly authentic.

There was something about the place, something

about the old stones, that was poignant and haunting. He tuned out the mothers chasing toddlers, the fathers reminding their children to respect the dead. He could vaguely hear a guide droning on in the background, clearly eager to finish his speech and move on. Jeremy didn't blame him. Darkness came early this time of year, and it was no doubt time to call it quits and get away from a place with such eerie associations.

Especially now.

Dusk was definitely coming.

To say that it was simply falling would be a misnomer. It seemed to be curling in from both ground and sky, a silvery mist sweeping in around the old tombstones.

When he had first landed, it had been a beautiful fall New England day. The colors had been spectacular. Trees seemed to drip with oranges and golds in a mystic beauty that was like a siren's call, fascinating and sensual. And yet they were also a promise of the winter to come, when everything would be blanketed in bone-chilling cold.

Jeremy stood by the stone where Mary's phone and purse had been found and pictured what Halloween must have been like here, the ancient mingling with the new as children decked out as fairies or monsters moved along the streets. Most of the adults would have been in full costume, as well. But Halloween was over now, and the tempo and mood had changed just as the seasons did. Every season was celebrated here, not just summer to fall, but the more subtle nuances of Halloween to Thanksgiving—although, like everywhere else, Christmas was already making its presence felt. However, at least the shops here seemed to acknowledge that there was still a Thanksgiving holiday between Halloween and Christmas.

Pumpkins and pilgrims decorated store windows, along with horns of plenty, and scenes of the Native Americans and the settlers, sitting down to the original Thanksgiving feast. On the farms nearby, it was a time of reaping.

How the hell could anyone just disappear from plain sight in a city so full of tourists?

How had Mary been whisked away, given the teeming crowd that must have been everywhere on Halloween? Admittedly, the day had been darkening, the lights of the commercial district unable to penetrate fully into the cemetery, where night created a realm of shadows.

"Isn't it wonderful?" Rowenna called to him.

"It's a graveyard," he said.

"I mean fall. The colors…"

He looked over to see her standing amid the stones. She bent down and scooped up an armful of fallen leaves, then straightened and let them scatter around her. She might have been a pagan goddess standing there, her face lifted in delight, the leaves falling all around her, the waves of her pitch-black hair cascading down over the velvet cloak she was wearing. He could imagine her as a statue, raised to celebrate the advent of autumn, although he wondered if any artist could catch the enthusiasm with which she embraced life.

He was surprised when he felt a sudden twinge of unease, as if he were afraid for her.

Afraid for her? Why?

He was just worried in general, he decided. A

woman—a friend—had disappeared from right where he stood, and she still hadn't been found. And yet, watching Rowenna now, he was startled by the depth of feeling that rose in him.

Then again, a lot of things had surprised him since he'd met Rowenna.

First he'd been surprised by his instant animosity to her. He couldn't figure it out. He'd never had anything against Kendall, and she had read tarot cards for a living. But Rowenna… Well, for some reason she was different. Then there had been that immediate inner warning, telling him that he needed to keep his distance from her, because of his fascination with her. And now…

Now, more than anything, he was surprised by the mere fact that he was here with her. Because now, everything had changed. Last night, when he had left his hotel and walked right to her door, he had known. Known that if he followed the path that was beckoning him, everything in his world was going to change. He would be on a course straight toward emotional danger, with no way back.

It hadn't mattered. He'd had to go to her, even knowing she might slam the door in his face.

But she hadn't.

He watched her. She was blessed with porcelain skin and perfect features, highlighted by those glimmering golden eyes, and her long, slim body teased him even from under the billowing cloak. There was just no figuring attraction. She drove him crazy, but he cared about her. Cared *for* her. Maybe it had just been man's natural instinct for survival and self-preservation that had made him so wary of her, knowing that what he felt for her could destroy him if he gave it free rein.

She was so good at an argument—yet he had found himself seeking her out to argue, because she was a challenge, and because she was so fully herself. She didn't possess an ounce of pretension, and her laughter was as charming as her pigheadedness.

Her forthrightness was his undoing. Last night, when she had opened the door, let him in, then dropped that silky nothing she'd been wearing and risen up on her toes to kiss his lips... In the darkness of the elegant old bedroom, the drapes whispering in the breeze behind her, every vestige of intelligence and thought had slipped from his mind.

And later, when they had slept, and she had started to toss and turn, crying out in the midst of her dream...

He knew that feeling. Being so deep in a dream, desperate to awaken, afraid that he wouldn't, that the dream would play out over and over again for eternity, an endless loop of hell.

The department had made him see a shrink, but in the end he had left the force, determined to beat the nightmares on his own by doing something to combat the problem that had caused them in the first place.

It had been almost two years since the accident that had killed the children, and the dream still came to him now and then. And he always remembered it when he awoke.

He had the feeling that Rowenna had remembered her dream, too.

So much for her being entirely forthright with him, he thought.

Time would tell.

Time... Dusk turned to darkness. An uniformed watchman was asking everyone to vacate the cemetery.

He would come back in daylight, he decided. He would walk every inch of the ground, check every gravestone, and he would find out if Mary had been taken away through some secret exit, like the one in the family plot back at the Flynn plantation, or if she had somehow been dragged away through the Halloween crowd. It would have been easy enough. A gag shoved in her mouth, a hooded costume thrown over her, hiding her face, and then she could have been carried off between two coconspirators, as if they were a trio, the two sober members supporting the third, who imbibed a few too many spirits throughout the day.

"Rowenna?"

He didn't see her at first, and panic flared through him. "Rowenna!"

"I'm over here." She stepped out from behind a tree that had hidden her from view. "I was trying to read this tombstone. It has my initials on it," she told him.

He was shaking when he reached her. "What the hell is the matter with you?" he demanded sharply.

She turned to him, startled. "What are you talking about?"

"You disappeared."

"I was standing right here."

"You didn't answer when I called," he said, still angry. He knew he was overreacting, but...

A woman had disappeared—and her phone and purse had been found by a tombstone that bore her initials.

"I answered you. You just didn't hear me."

She turned and started for the exit. He followed her. He could see by the set of her shoulders that she was angry.

So was he. For God's sake, after what had happened, she should be thinking about what she was doing. "I was worried," he said curtly.

"Well, this is my home turf. You don't need to be worried." She stopped so short that he almost plowed into her back.

"What?"

"There's Joe," she said.

"Your friend, the detective Joe?"

She nodded. The white-haired man in a plain leather jacket was strolling along the street as if he hadn't a care in the world. But he had seen Rowenna, and a smile lit his lips—until he saw Jeremy standing behind her. The smile remained, but it had tightened, as if he was trying not to let it turn into a scowl.

"Joe!" Rowenna called, hurrying out the gate.

"Ro!" The man came forward, capturing her in a giant bear hug. Rowenna was five-ten, but the man seemed to dwarf her. Jeremy found himself standing a little straighter as he waited for an introduction.

"Welcome home, Ro. No, wait, it's welcome home 'your majesty,' isn't it?" he teased. He looked at Jeremy then, not trying to hide the fact that he was assessing him carefully.

"You're the private detective, huh?" Joe Brentwood said, keeping Rowenna at his side and taking a step forward.

"I'm a private investigator, yes," Jeremy said, offering his hand. "Jeremy Flynn. You're Detective Joe Brentwood. Glad to meet you."

"So Johnstone is an old friend of yours," Brentwood said, automatically offering his hand in return.

"Friend, and former partner. I used to be a police diver," Jeremy said.

"He's a loose cannon right now," Brentwood told him.

"I'm meeting him tonight at seven. I'll see what I can do."

"Well, Ro and I have a little catching up to do," Brentwood said. "In fact—" he turned to look at her consideringly "—I thought I would have seen her earlier."

"My fault," Jeremy said, stretching the truth. "I asked her to show me the cemetery first, and time just got away from us."

Jeremy wondered what it was about the human race. He and Joe were just standing there talking politely, but both of them were tense and rigid. They were like a pair of roosters sparring for the attention of a hen. The older man was her friend. *He* was her lover. All right, so far he was a one-night stand, but he didn't intend for things to stay that way. His instincts had been right, though. If he'd just stayed away from her, he wouldn't be feeling now as if he had to fight for her in the midst of a modern world where she was free to make her own decisions—even decide against him, if she wanted to.

Rowenna seemed to sense both men's agitation. Who knew? Jeremy thought. Maybe they actually looked like a pair of puffed-up roosters.

"Why don't we all go have a drink together first?" she suggested.

"That would be great," Jeremy said casually, staring at Joe Brentwood.

First round to him for appearing to be friendly and cooperative.

"Red's is right across the street. It's a bar and grill, and I'm famished," Joe said. There was a note of reproach in his voice, as if to say he and Rowenna should have been having dinner alone.

"Sounds fine to me," Jeremy said.

They settled at Red's, where a waitress brought a round of drafts while Rowenna and Joe pored over the menu. Jeremy, who was waiting to eat until he met with Brad, leaned forward. "You say that Brad's a loose cannon?" he asked.

Joe let out a long sigh, shaking his head. "The kid's in bad shape." He looked at Jeremy and shrugged. "It's probably a good thing you're here. He needs someone. His wife's parents are threatening to come up here, but they've been suggesting he had something to do with it, so even if they show up, they're just going to make things worse for him."

Jeremy nodded. He knew Mary's parents, knew they'd wanted her to file for divorce, but she had decided to fight for her marriage.

"So, do you have any experience in this kind of work?" Joe asked him. "You were a police diver. There's a lot of difference in looking for objects underwater and finding facts above ground."

"Are you asking if I've worked missing persons and murder cases? Yes," Jeremy assured him.

"Well, cheers, then. We seem to have one hell of a mystery on our hands."

"Want to catch me up?" Jeremy asked.

"There's probably not much to tell you that you don't already know. Dave O'Reilly, a patrolman, found your friend Johnstone in the cemetery shouting for his wife, supposedly only moments after she disappeared. And I have to admit, I've asked around, and as near as I can tell, it seems he's telling the truth about how they spent the day and the timing of her disappearance. The only one I haven't found to corroborate the story was some guy who managed to pitch a fortune-teller's tent in the middle of the psychic fair without a permit. He's long gone. But other people remember seeing the tent, and some of them went in for one of his readings. Anyway, that doesn't really matter, since the Johnstones were seen together afterward. In fact, they had a late lunch right here."

"So it looks as if it's true, as if Brad and Mary were having a nice day together—and then she just disappeared," Jeremy said, thinking that he would have to come back and ask questions here at the restaurant when Joe Brentwood wasn't around.

"That's what it looks like," Joe agreed.

That's what it *looked* like. It was obvious that Brentwood was still suspicious of Brad.

Jeremy noted that a couple had entered the restaurant and were pointing at Rowenna, huge smiles on their faces. The woman came forward quickly, unwinding the black scarf she'd been wearing around her neck. "Rowenna, you're home!"

Rowenna stood, hugged the woman, and then embraced the man as he came up behind the woman. Joe Brentwood's eyes rolled. "The Llewellyns," he said, shaking his head slightly.

"Eve, Adam, it's great to see you." Rowenna turned with a smile on her face to introduce them to Jeremy. "Adam and Eve Llewellyn," she said.

Jeremy stood, shaking hands as he examined the newcomers. The man was tawny-haired, tall, and perhaps a few years older than Rowenna. The woman was petite, and he thought that her hair had been dyed to its jet-black color. Her eyes were a powdery blue. She was cute rather than pretty, with an engaging smile. "Jeremy Flynn," he said.

"Hi, wonderful to meet you," Eve said, pumping his hand.

"A pleasure," Jeremy said.

"How do you do?" Adam said.

The wife had a more sincere handshake, Jeremy thought.

"Adam and Eve Llewellyn, huh?" he asked.

"Oh, the name is for business," Adam said.

"Adam and Eve. Catchy," Jeremy said.

"My name is really Eve, and his really is Adam," Eve said, grinning. "But Llewellyn is kind of like a stage name. We were the Eidenwiesses."

"We had it changed legally," Adam said. "Hey, Joe, how are you?"

"Okay, all things considered," Joe said, greeting the couple with a nod.

"They're wiccans, and they run a store specializing in magical items," Rowenna explained.

The Llewellyns weren't looking, and Joe rolled his eyes at Jeremy again. So much for Rowenna's claim that Joe respected any and all religions equally. At least the guy seemed ready to side with him on something, he thought. Good. He would have to use it.

"Oh, Rowenna, we're so glad you're home." Eve was clasping Rowenna's hands as she glanced over at Jeremy. There was a question in her eyes, even though she spoke casually. "And you've come with a friend."

"Jeremy is a private investigator, and he's here because he's working for Brad Johnstone," Joe said curtly.

"Really?" Adam looked at Jeremy with new interest. "Terrible thing. They were in our shop that day. They seemed to be a really sweet couple. I can't believe he would have hurt her." Almost as if to emphasize his words, he cracked the gum he was chewing.

"I can't believe people are suggesting that he did." Even as Jeremy heard himself say the words defensively, he knew they were stupid. It was easy to believe; it was even procedure. In cases like this, it was imperative to clear the spouse first.

Joe was looking at him with a hint of dry amusement, apparently glad that he'd so quickly betrayed a weakness.

"So you'll be investigating her disappearance, too?" Adam asked.

Jeremy nodded.

"So you haven't found anything, Joe?" Eve asked sadly.

"I'm glad Brad has a friend in his corner," Adam said when Joe didn't answer, then looked over at the older man as if afraid he might have offended him.

Joe neatly eliminated that possibility. "I'm an old cop, so I don't mind any help I can get. If Mr. Flynn can find any information that will help solve this case, I'll be more than grateful."

Oddly enough, Jeremy thought that he meant it. He was finding it difficult to get a good reading on the man. He almost missed it when Joe added softly, almost to himself, "And Ro is home now."

Jeremy glanced at his watch. It was close to time to meet with Brad. "You'll have to excuse me, but I have an appointment over at the Hawthorne Hotel bar. Nice to meet you," he told the Llewellyns. "I'll be seeing you, I'm sure." He started to reach into his pocket for his wallet.

"Hey, put that away. I can afford to buy you a beer," Joe said.

"Well, thanks, then. Thanks so much."

"And I'll be seeing *you,*" Joe assured him.

"I'm sure you will," Jeremy said dryly. "Rowenna…"

"I have to get my things from your car," she reminded him.

He shook his head. "If it's all right with you, I'll come back and get you and drive you out to your place in an hour or so. I'd like to see where you live and get a feel for the area from someone who knows it well."

"I can take Rowenna home," Joe said.

"I'm sure you can, but if Rowenna doesn't mind…?"

She was studying him, he noted, with a slight frown. Had it just been a one-night stand? He didn't think so. Not with her. He was sure he'd read her right. No doubt she'd dated, had known men over the years, but she'd never let them in, never let them get close.

Rowenna flashed him a quick smile, then turned to Joe. "Actually, it will be easiest if Jeremy gives me a ride. That way we won't have to bother moving my luggage around."

"Where are you staying here in town?" Joe asked Jeremy bluntly.

"I'm renting an old house over on Essex," he told Joe, reminding himself that the old guy had been through a lot, so no wonder he was protective of Rowenna. God knew, he didn't even want to imagine what it would be like to lose a son. Parents weren't supposed to outlive their children. Sons should bury their fathers, not the other way around.

"I'll come join you after we eat," Rowenna said.

"I'll walk her over," Joe promised.

"Okay, see you then."

As Jeremy walked away, he was aware that they were all watching him until he had left the restaurant. He knew that he would be the topic of conversation for at least the next few minutes.

It was just a few blocks down the quiet streets to the hotel bar where he was planning to meet Brad Johnstone. The night was cool and crisp. Streetlights lit the way, but the businesses were closed for the day, and a forlorn feeling had settled over the street, along with the fallen leaves of autumn.

The hotel had been built in the early part of the twentieth century, but it was surrounded by buildings that dated back to the late 1700s. It was near the town green, where Pilgrims had once grazed their livestock. Now a concert was advertised for the following weekend.

The hotel offered a wave of warmth after the chill of the streets. He found the bar, and there, slumped in a stool at the bar, head resting in his hands, was Brad.

Jeremy walked over and set a hand on his shoulder. When Brad looked up, the hope in his eyes was so great it was almost alarming. He stood and threw his arms around Jeremy, hugging him tightly. Jeremy patted his back, feeling awkward, and extricated himself from his friend's grasp.

"What's your poison?" the bartender asked, coming right over.

"I'll take a draft, thanks," Jeremy said.

"We can move to a booth over there," Brad said, grabbing his glass, which was filled with what looked to be bourbon. "Hugh," he said to the bartender, "this is my friend Jeremy Flynn. He's here to help me find Mary."

"Sure hope so," Hugh said, handing Jeremy a beer. Apparently the bartender was on Brad's side, Jeremy thought.

But not everyone was. That was apparent immediately. Three women and two men were sitting nearby, and as he slid into the booth that Brad had pointed out, he saw one of the women nudge the other and whisper something as they stared at Jeremy. The second woman shuddered visibly.

"Thank God you're here," Brad told him.

"I'll do anything I can to help," Jeremy assured him. "You know that. Still nothing?"

"If I'd heard anything," Brad said glumly, "the world would know." He groaned. "To tell the truth, I'm just waiting for someone to come and slip the cuffs on me."

Jeremy shook his head. "Brad, no one can arrest you without evidence, and there isn't any evidence, because you would never hurt Mary. The thing is, no one disappears into thin air, so there *will* be evidence of something, somewhere. What we have to do is track down that evidence."

"Do you know how many times I've gone over our every footstep?" Brad asked him.

"Doesn't matter. We're going to do it again," Jeremy said.

Brad nodded glumly.

"I'm so afraid."

He was definitely telling the truth on that score. His fingers were trembling as he picked up his glass. "Last night…for just a second, I thought…"

"You thought…what? You saw her? Heard her? What?"

Brad shook his head ruefully. "I thought she called me on the phone. But it wasn't her, it was her mother. She was crying, begging me to give Mary back to them. I think she'd been drinking. Then Mary's dad got on the line and told me he was going to kill me."

"He isn't going to kill you."

Brad ignored that comment and went on. "He's given her up for dead. I can't do that." He hesitated and looked at Jeremy, his eyes unfocused, as if he'd had a few bourbons before this one. "She isn't dead, Jeremy. I think that I'd feel it. I know that sounds stupid, but I really think I'd feel it. But she's…she's in danger. If we don't find her soon, she *will* be dead. Oh, God." Bourbon nearly sloshed over the rim of his glass when he picked it up this time, draining half the contents of the glass in a swallow. "Jeremy, we walked into the cemetery and Mary disappeared. That was it."

"Brad, it was Halloween. There were dozens of people around. Someone must have seen something. We just haven't found that person yet."

Brad went on as if he hadn't even heard him. "Now the whole world knows we were having problems, that we'd just gotten back together. They write about me in the papers as if I'm a monster."

"What they write in the papers doesn't matter."

"Oh, yeah? People stare at me, Jeremy."

"Toughen up, Brad. Hell, you're a cop. You know what people think, and you know it doesn't matter. What matters is thinking of every single detail, of following every little clue."

Wincing, Brad nodded. "I know that, and I've tried.

We've thought of everything… Hell, the cops here have even looked at the idea that Mary was pulling a disappearing act to get even with me. But she didn't. Mary isn't like that. You know her, and you know she'd never do anything like that. Plus we found her cell phone and her purse, with her credit cards and ID still in it, lying on a grave."

"Have they investigated the grave?" Jeremy asked.

Brad shook his head, reaching for his drink again. "It wasn't disturbed. Jeremy, it really is like she disappeared into thin air."

"I told you, no one disappears into thin air. No matter how efficient the kidnapper was, he'll have left evidence. For now, tell me everything about that day."

Brad shook his head. "You must have heard everything already by now. I'm sure you were on the Internet two minutes after I called you."

"I want to hear it from you. The whole day, from start to finish."

Brad almost smiled. "With details? We started the morning off with a wild bout of sex. Honest. That's the best thing about making up, starting over. Man, the sex has been good again. Had been good," he added in a whisper.

"The rest of the day, Brad. Everything. You had sex. And then…?"

Brad nodded. Took a deep breath. Started talking. He had street names down pat, along with museum and shop names. But he hesitated when he got to the afternoon.

"It was that Damien guy. I know it. He was a real creep. He liked Mary right off. I saw the way he looked at her."

"That guy—you're talking about the fortune-teller the police haven't found yet, right? The one who didn't have a permit," Jeremy said.

"There was something wrong with him. He was... scary," Brad said. "And Mary... Mary was freaked out by him, too."

"But nothing actually happened in the tent, did it?" Jeremy asked.

"No. Yes. No." Brad was frowning, thinking back. He shook his head. "Not physically, but the guy...said things. He said I was weak. That Mary was in danger. And his special effects, the stuff in his crystal ball...it was freaky. I mean, you could see things in that ball as if they were real. It started with a turkey."

"A turkey?" Jeremy repeated. He looked at Brad's glass. The bourbon was all gone. He wondered just how many his friend had drunk before this one.

"A turkey dinner," Brad said impatiently. "I could see it as if it were real. It was like I could smell it, too. Almost taste it."

Jeremy sat silent for a minute. "What did the guy look like?" he asked.

Brad was thoughtful. "Showy—you know, like he was having fun being dramatic for Halloween. He was tall, or maybe it was the cape."

"Okay, he was wearing a cape. Ethnicity? The color of his eyes? Come on, Brad, you know how to give a description," Jeremy reminded him.

"He was wearing a cape *and* a turban. Tall, dark and lean. But it was hard to really read his features, because he was wearing makeup. You know, around the eyes— maybe he had darkened his skin, too, I'm not sure. But he was real—lots of people saw him and the tent. The thing is, it's been hard for the cops to track him down, because it was Halloween. The city was full of tourists, and most of them have gone home. Besides, the cops think I'm just grasping at straws, pointing the finger at that guy. Mary didn't even disappear right after we saw him. The thing is, they didn't see what I saw in his tent. They didn't hear the way the man talked. As if he knew us. As if he was threatening us."

"You have to remember exactly what this guy said," Jeremy told him.

Brad hung his head. He looked as if he was going to start crying at any minute.

"Look," Jeremy said firmly, "I'm going to walk you to your hotel, and I'll be back for you at nine tomorrow morning. We're going to retrace every step you took that day. All right?"

Brad nodded, then looked up at Jeremy. "Sure," he said listlessly.

"Brad, it's important."

"It won't help."

"Why not?"

"Because that Damien guy is gone, and no one knows where he is. But he took Mary. I know he did."

"Brad, did this guy claim to have any special powers? Did he say he was a wiccan or anything?"

Brad shook his head. "Oh, no. He wasn't a wiccan. He told us that right away, when Mary asked."

"Did he say anything about having a local business? Did he say where he was from? That he belonged to a magicians' union or something?"

Brad solemnly shook his head again. "No. He didn't

say anything at all. But I know what he is." He stopped, his expression grim.

"And what's that?" Jeremy prompted.

"The devil," Brad said seriously. "He's the devil."

5

Rowenna saw Jeremy sitting alone at the bar when she went in and joined him.

"Hey," she said, sliding onto the stool next to him. She flashed Hugh a smile, and he came over immediately.

"Hey, yourself. Welcome home. The usual?"

"Sure, thanks, Hugh," she said.

Jeremy was looking at her, a slight smile on his lips, one brow arched. "You know everyone in town?" he asked her.

She shrugged. "I grew up here, remember?" she said. "But no, I don't know everyone. Hugh graduated high school a few years before me. He was on the hockey team."

"And you were a cheerleader?"

"No," she told him with a laugh. "But half my friends were." She grew serious. "Where's Brad?"

"I just walked him home."

"Oh. How's he doing?"

"Not well." He turned to look at her. "He's sure that he has the answer, but proving it… Let's just say it won't be easy."

"Oh? He knows who took Mary?"

"He says the devil did it."

"You're joking."

"I'm dead serious. Well, the devil in human form, I guess. He's convinced that the fortune-teller they went to that afternoon did it. Did you learn anything else?" he asked her.

"Hey, I introduced you to Joe. You know what I know."

"I thought he might have said something else to you." Jeremy was still watching her, eyes intense. "And hey, if you're worried about being seen with me, I can behave like a casual acquaintance."

She was surprised by his words, then surprised again when she felt herself blushing. Joe had definitely been hostile when he'd met Jeremy. Why?

Because Jeremy was a private investigator? Or because Joe sensed the chemistry between them?

No. Joe thought she should move on, have a life. He had said so often enough.

But did he really mean it?

"Don't be ridiculous," she said. She stared at him openly. "I do what I choose to do," she said softly. "I never let others influence my choices."

He turned back to face the bar, so she couldn't read his reaction to her words. "Still, people around here will trust you before they trust me," he said.

"I'm not sure why any of that would matter. A woman is missing. Everyone around here is hoping she'll be found alive and well. Hoping—and praying."

"Not everyone," he said.

"Oh, come on! Wiccans are not—"

"I didn't mean wiccans," he said, staring at her again. "I was referring to the person who took her."

"Oh," she said. "Of course." She had to stop letting her feathers get so easily ruffled.

"Tell me about your friends," he said.

"Which friends?"

"Adam and Eve."

"They're very nice people."

"Wiccans?"

"Yes. So?"

"Just curious."

"They're nice. I went to school with *them*, too. I've known them both forever. They have a shop where they sell a lot of the usual tourist stuff—and a lot of not-so-usual items. They work with a lot of local artists and jewelers."

"What about powders and potions? Do they sell those, too?"

"Yes. And tea," Rowenna said, hearing the edge in her voice.

"Sorry," he said, and set his glass down. "I guess I should get you home."

"Sounds good." She slid off her stool and waited for him.

When Hugh walked over with the check, Rowenna smiled at him. He grinned back. "See you," he said.

"Yeah, you will. Thanks," Jeremy told him. He set a hand on Rowenna's waist, guiding her out.

The air outside was beautifully cool. The harsh cold of winter had yet to make an appearance.

The city seemed very quiet. They might have been the only ones out as they walked to Jeremy's rental car.

He pointed to one of the houses they passed on the way.

"My new residence," he told her.

"Oh? A whole house?" she asked.

"Hey, it's leaf season," he said. "It was better to rent the house than pay the ridiculous room rate at a hotel. I was just lucky to get the place when someone had to cancel. Did you know that even the locals like to travel to see the foliage?"

"Yes, but they'll be going farther north soon," she told him. "Vermont, Maine."

"It's pretty," he admitted.

"You don't really get the seasons down where you live, do you?"

"Sure. We have killer hot. Just plain hot. Almost cool. And sometimes, in the shade, there's almost a nip in the air."

She laughed.

"I'm exaggerating," he told her. "We've actually had snow in the north of the state, and there have even been days when it's been colder in north Florida than in Chicago."

She thought then, as they moved along the street, that she really loved his smile. She wished that they weren't together only because a woman was missing. And she wondered what would happen when they reached her house.

At the car, he opened the door for her. "Thanks for letting me drive you home," he said casually.

"It made sense, and since you didn't mind…" she said, hoping her tone was just as breezy.

As they left the town behind, she found herself noticing how much darker things got. The coastline of New England was well-populated, and had been since the Pilgrims came and others followed. But they were moving inland, into farm country, she thought as she pointed out the road signs to Jeremy, so he would know exactly where they were going and how to get back.

"Just how far out are you?" he asked her.

"Now? Twenty minutes. In what we call rush hour? Thirty. Well, on a day like Halloween, more like an hour."

She didn't live all that far from the city, but the streetlights grew fewer and then stopped altogether when they reached the cornfields. She stared at the stalks, tall, pale sentinels in the night. They stood high, this near the harvest. They swept by in a blur of shadow and darkness with the speed of the car.

She didn't realize how tense she had become until she almost jumped at the sound of Jeremy's voice.

"Do you own much land?"

She shook her head. "No. I just have a few acres. I love the house, though, and the country is pretty. I've always thought I'd like to get a horse one of these days, when I'm not traveling quite so much."

Shouldn't they have passed the cornfields by now? she wondered. Surely they should have reached her house by now. No, she was just misjudging distance, because the cornfields were spooking her.

She told herself not to be ridiculous. She lived out past the cornfields. She was used to them. This uneasiness was utterly neurotic. She had to stop it. She loved her home, and she couldn't allow herself to become afraid of it because of some stupid nightmare.

"Are you all right?" he asked, glancing her way.

"Fine. Why?" she asked him.

"You look pale."

"Don't be silly," she said, hoping her laugh wasn't as shaky as she felt. "It's the light. Or the lack of light."

They had passed the cornfields at last. Of course, they were still out there. Lurking in the darkness. But there was the old MacElroy place, and next road led to her own home.

"There, take a right," she told him.

She drew a sharp breath when her house came into view. It was dark. It shouldn't have been. Ginny MacElroy, spinster aunt of the current Dr. MacElroy, always looked after the place when she was gone and left a different light burning every night.

Only the glare from the car's headlights kept the house from being swamped by the night.

"Strange," she murmured.

"What?"

"Oh, I guess a bulb burned out, that's all," she said casually.

He looked at her speculatively but didn't say anything.

Rowenna stepped from the car and headed up the walk to the wooden steps to the porch. The house was a total mishmash of architecture, with one room from the 1600s, an addition built in the very late 1700s and a final addition from the 1850s. There was gingerbreading on the balcony across the front of the second floor, and on the wraparound porch at ground level. She kept the house in good repair, aware that even in a place where historic buildings were common, her house and its history were unique and deserved to be cared for.

The steps were old, just like the rest of the place, and creaked when she walked up them. She searched through her large, over-the-shoulder travel handbag, found her key and opened the door, then fumbled for the light switch. She was relieved when the simple iron chandelier in the mudroom came right on.

"Come on in," she said to Jeremy, who was standing right behind her, carrying her suitcases.

She walked through the mudroom, hitting the lights for the foyer. It wasn't a grand entry by any means, but rather a glorified hall that opened to the oldest section on the left and the newer wing—the section added on in the 1850s—to the right. The stairway ran along the right wall and led to a picture-perfect landing above, complete with cast-iron balustrade. On the second floor she had her bedroom, guest room, office and a room she mostly used for storage. The stairs to the attic were in the storage room, and the attic was filled with all kinds of wonders that she meant to go through at some point.

"Where would you like these?" Jeremy asked, hefting her suitcases. There were two of them, and they were heavy, just missing the cutoff, after which she would have been charged extra by the airline.

"Right there is fine," she told him quickly.

He set them down, and she watched him as he surveyed the house. He met her eyes and grinned at her. "This is one big place to be stuck out in the middle of nowhere, huh?"

"It's not that big, and I do have neighbors—we passed their place," she said.

"But you live here—alone—and have for years, right?"

"Yes. I've lived here all my life, really, except for college and a lot of traveling," she said. "It's good to have somewhere that's home."

"Do you have an alarm system?"

"No."

"And no big dog, either."

She laughed. "I'd love a big dog, but he'd starve to death, since I'm gone half the time."

"Want me to walk around, check things out?" he asked.

Yes!

She managed a casual shrug. "Sure. If you'd like."

She walked him through, telling him the architectural history of the place as she did so.

"You've never been afraid out here, huh?" he asked.

"What? Are you trying to scare me?" she asked him.

At least he had the grace to look apologetic. "No, sorry. I'm not trying to scare you. I guess…" He paused, frowning.

"You guess…what?"

"Oddly enough, when I didn't see you in the graveyard, I found that far more frightening than knowing you live out in the boondocks."

"This is hardly the boondocks," she protested. And it wasn't. On a quiet night, she could probably scream loud enough for her neighbors to hear her. She was twenty minutes from the city. She wanted to live out in the country, but she didn't want to be *alone*.

"Want some coffee or something before you drive back?" she asked, starting toward the kitchen, which had once been a large pantry, in the rear of the house. She assumed he would follow.

She *hoped* he would follow.

He did.

"Hmm, no milk for the coffee," she said, rummaging in the refrigerator.

"I don't want coffee," he told her, then walked over to her, drawing her into his arms and looking down into her eyes. "Do you want me to stay?"

Her heart quickened. She wanted to say yes, and she didn't want to say yes. She didn't want him staying because she was afraid. She wanted him staying because *he* wanted to stay, and she wasn't sure that he would believe her if she said so. But she had to ask.

"Do you want to stay?" she asked seriously.

There was a tenderness in his eyes that seemed to take away all the darkness of the night. Being held by him, feeling the warm, hard strength of his body and his arms around her, seemed so sweet and foreign that she felt a rush of dizziness.

"You know I do," he said huskily.

"Then I definitely want you to stay," she whispered in return.

The next hours passed in a glorious haze. In the morning, she would put the memories in order by where she found her clothing. Sweater in the kitchen, one shoe at the foot of the stairs, another halfway up. Shirt at the door to her bedroom, skirt halfway across the room.

Her underwear, at least, made it to the side of the bed.

It had been late. Time to slip naturally into bed, to enjoy the darkness, fumbling to touch one another in the shadows, even to laugh a bit at the urgency that brought them together. In his arms, she didn't mind the darkness.

She didn't even think of shadows.

There was just him, his body long and smoothly muscled, vibrant and hot against her own. There was touching him and marveling again at the feel of his skin beneath her palms, knowing that first night they had shared was not a fleeting moment to be cherished forever, relived in memory but never to be repeated. She loved the way he stroked her face, as if learning the structure of it, and she loved the way his lips felt on her skin, as if he were branding her with kisses of fire and ice. She loved the pressure of his body against hers, the intimacy, the electricity. The hunger and the longing, and the sense of climbing, escalating, being so desperate for something and yet savoring every tiny, anguished step to reach that goal. Then there was the exultation of climax, like a scorching blaze that lit up the sky within her own mind again, and then again….

The simple beauty of being held, the slick warmth of passion and even the chill of aftermath, the slowing beat of pulse and heart, and still being together.

Maybe, for a while, she could live the dream. He would leave eventually, of course, and then all the wonder would indeed be confined to memory.

But it was foolish to envision the future. It would come soon enough. Somehow, she had to teach herself to be glad for the moment. Guard her heart, but live fully in the moment.

Easy enough to say, but almost impossibly hard to do. She was so tired, though, so on that note, she slept.

She heard the cawing of a crow.

It was coming from the darkness, except that the darkness was easing. Morning was coming. An overcast, cold morning, a forerunner of the winter that would so quickly follow the fall. But she was home, standing on the balcony just outside her bedroom window, and she was watching as the light of day struggled to pierce the mist and the night. She could hear the crow screeching again and again.

From her vantage point, she could see the cornfields.

And she could watch the crows.

They were circling over the cornfield.

She knew that she had to go out, that the crows were calling to her, showing her where to go. She tried to turn, to go back into the house, but she couldn't. A crow had landed on the railing and looked at her, cocking its head as it let out another terrible scream.

It lifted off from the railing and joined the flock circling…something in the middle of the cornfield. She knew what it was.

And she didn't want to see.

"Rowenna!"

She woke with a jerk and instantly winced. The dream had been dispelled by the sound of his voice, but she was still afraid to open her eyes.

One nightmare was easy enough to explain.

But two?

He was at her side. And it *was* the crack of dawn, the light as misty as it had been in her dream. They hadn't bothered to draw the drapes before tumbling into bed, and now the thin light was creeping into the bedroom.

His face was beautiful, she decided, though a man wouldn't want to hear such a compliment. Jawline strong, nose straight and perfect, mouth generous and wide, shock of dark auburn hair a perfect complement to the gray, wide-set eyes and ruggedly arched brows. His forehead was furrowed now with concern. He had risen earlier, she thought, because he was already dressed.

But he was back on the bed now, seated at her side, holding her.

"Um…good morning," she whispered.

"You were dreaming again. Another nightmare."

"I'm sorry. I don't do it all the time—honest," she said.

"What was it about?"

"What?"

"Your dream. What were you dreaming about? I hope you're not having nightmares about me," he teased.

"No, of course not."

"Then what?"

"I don't remember."

"Then maybe you *are* having nightmares about me," he said. "Seriously, you really don't remember?"

He sounded concerned, she thought, but when she shook her head, he just rose, looking down at her.

"I made coffee," he told her. "I found some little packets of that powdered cream stuff."

She noticed that his hair was clean and damp. Apparently he'd also found the shower. He'd obviously been up for a while, and she wondered how long he'd watched her dream before he'd awakened her. She didn't understand why it bothered him that she didn't remember what the dream had been about.

Because she was a lousy liar, and he didn't like being lied to? Maybe.

But she had the strange feeling that it was more.

"Coffee," she said, "sounds divine."

He nodded briefly and headed downstairs. She found herself wondering if she had done something to disturb him. Didn't new lovers find it almost impossible to resist one another?

She headed for the shower herself, then found him getting ready to leave when she went downstairs a little while later. "I have to pick up Brad at nine. We're going to retrace his every step that day, see if there isn't something, somewhere, anywhere, that we've missed so far."

"Good idea," she said, wondering why she suddenly felt uneasy. The daylight was coming, and this was her home, for God's sake. She was going to be fine. She was going to unpack.

And then, as she had promised Joe when he had dropped her off at the Hawthorne last night, she was going to go into his office and talk with him. Alone.

"Want to meet us for lunch?" Jeremy asked, breaking into her thoughts.

"Sure, if you don't mind a late lunch. I have a few odds and ends to take care of here," she told him.

He kissed her on the lips, stared into her eyes and smiled. "See you then. Um, you have a car, right?" he asked.

She laughed. "I have a car. It's in the garage out back," she told him.

He hugged her, and as she held him, she felt the gun in his waistband. For some odd reason, it gave her a little jolt. He was licensed to carry a concealed weapon, she knew. It shouldn't have been a shock.

But it was.

"What time?" he asked.

"How about two?" she asked.

"Sounds good. Where?"

She chose a restaurant down by the water. If she was going to meet Brad, she didn't really want to be too close to the cemetery. Let the guy have lunch without staring at the place where he'd last seen his wife.

"I'll see you there," Jeremy told her, and left.

She listened to the sound of his car as he drove away. Then she looked at her suitcases and decided that she would unpack, then run over to the MacElroy place and let them know she was back and they might be seeing a strange car in her drive. Then she could head in to see Joe.

When they left Brad's B and B, Jeremy told Brad again that he wanted to retrace the day of Mary's disappearance step-by-step.

"We were all over town," Brad told him.

"So we'll go all over town," Jeremy said, and started walking.

They stopped at the Salem Witch Museum first. Brad nearly broke down as he told Jeremy that it had been Mary's favorite museum, in large part because she'd thought they'd done an excellent job accurately recreating history with few theatrics. They stayed for the twenty-minute presentation, and Jeremy decided that he agreed with Mary. Since none of the people working in the shop or welcoming visitors had been there the day Mary went missing, they left as soon as the presentation ended.

Brad explained that they had skipped the Peabody Essex Museum, planning to spend the next day there, and had instead gone on to visit a number of the mall's haunted houses, which were gone now, having been set up specifically for Halloween. Jeremy and Brad boarded the tram and went to the pirate museum, a wax museum and a monster museum. Then they went to one that advertised History! Just History, and Nothing More!

No sooner had they entered than a man came over to greet them. He looked to be in his late twenties or early thirties. He had brown hair, brown eyes, glasses, and was tall and slim. He walked right up to Brad, who clearly recognized him. From the conversation, Jeremy realized the man, a museum employee who introduced himself as Daniel Mie, had struck up a conversation with Brad and Mary that day, and that he'd been hoping to get a chance to tell Brad how sorry he felt about what had happened.

"Jeremy and I used to be partners," Brad explained, after Jeremy introduced himself. "He's a private investigator now, and he's here to see what he can find out."

Daniel smiled at Jeremy. "Glad to hear it."

"So what about you?" Jeremy asked. "Did you notice anyone suspicious, maybe someone paying more attention to Mary than he should have been?"

The man looked thoughtful for a long moment, then shook his head slowly. "I wish I could. Thing is, you can't imagine how crazy this town gets for Halloween. The crowds are huge. I only remember Brad and…and Mary because we got talking."

"Well, thanks," Jeremy told him. "If you happen to remember anything, though…" He handed Daniel his card. "Just give me a call on my cell."

"Will do. And if you have time, come back and take a real look at the museum. We've got a section on the pagan practices that are the basis for today's wiccans' practice and another exhibit on what the Puritans thought witches were back then.…"

"Thanks," Jeremy told him, and turned to leave.

But Brad stayed put and said to Daniel, "It was that fortune-teller, the one you sent us to."

Daniel looked confused. "What was? What are you—"

"You recommended that guy?" Jeremy interrupted, wondering why Brad hadn't thought to mention that earlier. "How well do you know him? Is he a friend of yours? Do you know where we could find him?"

"No, sorry. I just went to him for a reading and was impressed, so I recommended him. I wish I could help you, but…"

When they left, Brad actually seemed determined, rather than disheartened. "That guy is out there somewhere. And when we find him, we'll find Mary. I know it."

Jeremy was silent.

"We'll find her alive. I know I must sound crazy, but I know she's alive."

"We're working from that belief, Brad," Jeremy assured him. "Where to next?"

"That shop right there," he said, pointing. "The owners are named Adam and Eve Llewellyn, if you can believe it. Mary liked them a lot. *I* even liked them, even though I thought they'd be pretty loopy. They're witches," he said with a dry laugh.

"I met them last night," Jeremy said. "But I'd like to see their place, and I wouldn't mind talking to them again, either."

Ginny opened the door at the MacElroy house, let out a little cry of joy when she saw Rowenna and gave her a big hug.

Ginny was the perfect great-aunt. Sixty-year-old widower Dr. Nick MacElroy was a pediatrician. His kids were grown, but Ginny remained with him, looking after the grandchildren when they came. Rowenna had gone to school with his two sons, who had also gone into medicine but practiced in Boston. They came out often enough with their wives and kids, and Ginny was always thrilled to see them.

Rowenna had loved Ginny when she'd been growing up. Ginny always had hot cocoa and oatmeal cookies for whoever stopped in. She had the look of Mrs. Claus, with a bun of snow-white hair, spectacles that slipped down her nose all the time, cheery, bright blue eyes, and she barely stood five feet.

"Thanks so much for looking after the place."

"It's my pleasure, dear," Ginny said. "Now, what will you have? Coffee, tea or cocoa? And I have blueberry scones, pumpkin muffins or—if you're ready for lunch—acorn squash and sliced turkey breast."

Rowenna laughed. "It isn't Thanksgiving yet, Ginny."

"I have ham, too, if you'd prefer."

"Oh, Ginny, thank you so much. But I have to go into town to meet a friend for lunch."

"A friend?" Ginny's eyes brightened. "Would that be a *male* friend?"

"Yes, Ginny, that would be a male friend. His name is Jeremy Flynn. He's renting a place in town, but I wanted to let you know about him so you won't worry if you see a strange man around my place.…"

"Is he cute?"

"More like…rugged," she said with a smile.

Ginny smiled back. "Well it's about time. I keep telling Joe that he can't hang on to you the way he does or you'll never feel as if you can date anyone else."

"Joe is a good friend, Ginny, and he's never stopped me from doing anything." She looked at her watch. "Anyway, I need to get going." She hesitated, then asked curiously, "Ginny, why did you leave the place dark last night?"

"What are you talking about? I left a light on. Nick even went over with me the other day to change the front hall lightbulbs. I know the light was on when I left," Ginny said, troubled.

Ginny was closer to eighty than seventy, Rowenna thought. Usually, her mind was as sharp as a tack. But maybe…

Rowenna knew that she forgot plenty of things herself.

"Thanks, Ginny," she said. "Don't worry about it. I'll see you later."

"I can't wait to meet your young man."

Rowenna was already heading back out to her car. "He's not *my* young man, Ginny. He's just a friend."

"Then I can't wait to meet your friend," Ginny called, grinning.

A few minutes later, Rowenna found herself driving past the cornfields. Even though it was full daylight, she tried not to look at them.

She couldn't help noticing that there wasn't another car in sight, and she shivered.

She turned her radio up and stepped harder on the gas.

Suddenly her car began to sputter. She stepped harder on the gas, but the engine quit, and she rolled slowly to a halt. At least she managed to steer the car onto the shoulder first.

Swearing, she looked at the gas gauge. It was on

empty. She could have sworn that the tank had been full when she left. Then again, she'd been gone for weeks, so she could have forgotten—just as Ginny had no doubt forgotten to turn on the light. But she didn't believe it.

"I know I filled that damned gas tank," she muttered.

No problem. She had AAA. All she had to do was call, and eventually someone would make it out to her.

Swearing, she put through the call. The dispatcher promised that someone would be out within the hour. Then she called Joe, and told him where she was and what had happened. "I'm glad I got started early," she told him.

"You need to keep a better eye on that gas tank," Joe said. "Well, thank the good Lord that it's daytime and you're not stuck out there in the dark."

"What could happen to me in a cornfield anyway?" But even as she asked the question, she felt a chill of foreboding settling over her.

"You call me when that AAA guy gets out there with your gas, you hear?"

"Will do," she promised, and hung up, then glanced at her watch. It was only ten past eleven. She didn't have to worry about calling Jeremy, since he wasn't expecting her until two.

She leaned her head back, but that only gave her an all-too-clear view of the surrounding cornfields, so she closed her eyes.

It didn't matter. She still saw nothing but rows and rows of cornstalks.

Irritated with herself, she opened her eyes, stormed out of the car and stared at the cornfield.

"You're nothing but a bunch of corn on the freakin' cob," she said aloud.

But as she stood on the shoulder and stared at the field stretching out to the horizon, the wind began to whisper.

Looking up, she saw crows.

She started when one landed on the hood of her car.

"Scat, you black rodent!" she yelled, waving her hands at the bird.

It looked at her and cawed accusingly, then flew off.

She followed its path across the sky as it went to join its fellows. A hundred of them—or it seemed like it, anyway. They were circling a spot not all that far from the road, maybe only twenty or so rows back.

She closed her eyes. "No," she whispered passionately. "I'm not going."

But then she opened her eyes again and, swearing, started to push her way through the corn.

6

"Jeremy, how nice to see you."

Eve Llewellyn gave him the same genuine smile she had offered the night before.

"And you, too, Brad," she added, giving him a warm hug. As she pulled away, she looked at both of them anxiously. "Anything new?"

"We're hoping *you* can help *us* with that," Jeremy said.

"You don't think we've already told the police everything we know?" Eve asked.

"Everything," Adam repeated.

"I just thought that maybe, with the three of you here together, you might think of something else," Jeremy suggested, looking curiously around the shop. Porcelain fairies dangled from delicate wires, and velvet cloaks were displayed on mannequins that were more realistic than many of the wax characters Jeremy had seen in the museums earlier. One rack displayed small bottles of potions, while another featured colored stones, whose labels promised they would bring power and wealth and all kinds of other things, waiting to be packed into small velvet bags. There were wind chimes, kitchen witches, books and more. Celtic music played softly in the background. Several of the displays featured carefully arranged autumn leaves, the real thing, and the candles that burned throughout the store scented the air with the unmistakable fragrance of pumpkin pie. In a nod to the upcoming holiday, Pilgrims adorned the shelves, along with other timely objets d'art.

"Well, let's see," Eve said, and looked at Brad. "The two of you—you and your wife—came in, and you were looking at the lithographs over there, right?" She nodded in the direction of several framed pictures.

"Yes," Brad said. "Mary especially liked the one of the woman sitting in the moonlight, playing the harp, because she said she has the grace of a dancer."

"Yes, we talked about it, I remember," Eve said.

"Then we started chatting about Sammhein—what you call Halloween," Adam said, unwrapping a stick of gum and sticking it in his mouth.

Eve frowned slightly, as if she were remembering the day more clearly. "We talked about how commercial things have become, and what a rip-off some of the new horror houses are. What some of those places charge for a two-minute walk-through, a couple of cheap 3-D effects and a few people in bad masks is just outrageous."

"And people line up to pay it," Adam said, shaking his head in amazement.

"We talked about how we'd been through some of them already," Brad said. "And then we talked about the museums we'd liked."

"Then we talked about the House of the Seven Gables," Eve said, "and you said you were going to do that another day, when you'd have more time. And then I read Mary's palm and saw that she was going to be a success as a dancer. The second I touched her hand, I could feel how talented she was, how full of life—"

Eve broke off abruptly, looking stricken at her choice of words. *Life.* She had said *life.*

And for all they knew, Mary was dead.

"I think we suggested that they eat at Red's," Adam said awkwardly into the silence.

"Did you also suggest that they go anywhere else for a reading?" Jeremy asked.

Adam's forehead furrowed in thought. "I think we talked about how there were plenty of readers at the psychic fair set up over on the mall."

"And we said we were already going over there," Brad said.

"Did either of you know the guy the police can't find? Name of Damien? Didn't have a permit…"

"I saw him outside his tent one time," Eve said, then hesitated, looking troubled, before she went on. "He had a…smirk on his face. I didn't like the look of him."

"Can you describe him?" Jeremy asked.

"Tall," Eve said. "Thin. And kind of exotic-looking, not just because he was wearing a turban, of all things. And I think he was wearing eye makeup, and maybe some kind of bronzer, too."

"What I wish I understood was how he created the effects in that crystal ball of his," Brad said. "He really freaked Mary out. We saw different things, which was weird. I saw the first Thanksgiving, and it seemed so real that I swear I could smell the turkey. And…then it got ugly, with people pulling out knives, like they were ready to kill someone. To tell you the truth, I thought it was scary, and I don't scare easily. Jeremy, you know that."

"Yes, I know," Jeremy assured him.

"There was something really creepy about this guy, I'm telling you," Brad insisted.

"Maybe that's why he's so hard to locate, because he's avoiding the police," Jeremy said, and looked back at the Llewellyns. "What time did you two leave the store? Do you stay open late on Halloween, till midnight or anything?"

"Of course not," Eve said.

"Why not?" Jeremy asked. "I mean, wouldn't you get tons of business?"

"We're not entirely about money," Eve said, indignant.

"I wasn't suggesting that you were," Jeremy said. "Everyone has to make a living."

"We closed a little early that day, actually, because we were joining the rest of the wiccan community for the march to Gallows Hill. It's a Sammhein tradition. I think we closed at about four, right, Adam?" she asked, turning toward her husband.

Jeremy thought there was some message in the way she was looking at Adam. Wouldn't she have known when they closed without asking him?

Unless she'd been somewhere else at the time…?

As he looked at the two of them, he wondered if theirs was a marriage made in heaven, or if the two wiccans, just like everyone else, had encountered a few bumps in their relationship.

"We closed at four, yes," Adam said.

"And then?" Jeremy asked politely.

"And then?" Eve repeated. "Then we went to meet up with the others. Like I said, it was Sammhein. A big night for us."

"A lot of people wearing cloaks, I imagine," Jeremy said.

"Of course," Eve agreed. "Oh!" she exclaimed. "You think that whoever kidnapped Mary—whether it was that fortune-teller or someone else—just put on a cloak and blended in with everyone else."

"And maybe he could have hidden Mary under a cloak and forced her along with him," Brad said.

Jeremy was startled just then when his phone rang. He excused himself to answer it and was surprised to discover that Detective Joe Brentwood was on the other end.

"I hear you're retracing Mary Johnstone's steps on the day she disappeared," Joe said.

"You have to start somewhere," Jeremy said. "How do you know what I'm doing, anyway?"

Not that it was any great secret. Nor did it surprise him that either Joe had been asking about him or the locals had told Joe about the fact that he was asking questions.

"Little birds, all over the city, just like you'd figure," Joe said.

"So you're keeping tabs on me?"

Joe laughed. "No, I'm not dogging you. People around here just trust me, and they're not sure about you yet. Anyway, call me an old worrywart if you want to, but Rowenna was going to meet me for a cup of coffee, but she ran out of gas on her way in to town."

"She ran out of gas?" Jeremy said, incredulous. Rowenna didn't seem like the kind of woman to let her tank run down to fumes.

Jeremy felt as if a slew of icebergs were cascading down his spine.

And Joe thought *he* was being a worrywart?

"You didn't go after her?"

"Can't—I'm on duty. That's why I'm calling you. She's got AAA, but I'd feel better if you'd head out after her." Brentwood's tone was gruff. Joe could tell it cost the man to ask him for help, especially where Rowenna was concerned. "I'd have sent out a car, but she'd just be mad at me. In fact, I'd appreciate it if you don't mention the fact that I called you. She doesn't like folks thinking she can't handle herself, you know?"

"Yeah, thanks. Consider me on my way," Jeremy said.

He shut his phone, ending the call, and returned to the others. "I've got to go," he said briefly. "Brad?"

"Hey, buddy, I'm with you," Brad told him.

"Is something wrong?" Eve asked anxiously.

Adam, at her side, watched him speculatively.

"No, no, nothing. We'll see you again soon. Thanks for your help. Brad, you can just wait for me here if you want."

"Hell, no. I feel like all I do is wait," Brad said.

He wasn't sure why he didn't want to take Brad with him. He wasn't sure why Joe had been so concerned, or why he was feeling the grip of anxiety himself.

There wasn't any time to argue with Brad, though. They would probably just ride out there and end up keeping Rowenna company while she waited for the service guy to get there with the gas. Of course, he could have stopped to fill a gas can himself.

Except that he couldn't get to his car fast enough.

* * *

Rowenna felt her feet sink into the dirt as she left the pavement and headed into the cornfield.

She stopped.

She could see the scarecrows in the distance, rising above the rows of ripening corn. The stalks rose high, but the scarecrows rose higher.

The crows were circling, eerie silhouettes against the autumn sky, their cawing like a forewarning.

She didn't want to move forward, but she also felt that she had no choice, that she couldn't be ridiculous and let irrational fear control her. She felt compelled, as if beckoned by the crows themselves, which scared her. But in the far back of her mind, a kernel of reason was telling her irritably that if she didn't make herself get over the absurdity of the nightmare—no doubt some messed-up, Freudian reaction to the scarecrow contests of her youth—she would spend the rest of her life being afraid. She needed to march right in and dispel all the nonsense haunting her mind.

Because the mind played tricks.

She paused just inside the first row, breathing in the redolence of the earth. This was real. She felt the ground beneath her feet, felt the nip in the air, saw the sky, autumn's hint of blue fighting against the growing sweep of thunderous gray, a warning of the winter to come.

The cornstalks grew high, in their neat rows, seeming to stretch out forever and ever.

And then, like sentinels, rising in a line above the tall stalks that bent and waved in the cool breeze, the scarecrows.

Mist swept across her vision, and suddenly what was real was lost in the dream.

She felt as if she were drifting through the corn, borne on the breeze as the mist settled over the cornfield, strangely dark against the clear light of the autumn day. She found herself looking down from above, and she fought the vision, terrified to let it win.

This wasn't a dream, this was *real*. She wasn't floating above the cornfield, she was walking into it. Her car was just behind her, steps away. Any minute, someone from AAA would show up to fill her gas tank, and then she would resume driving into town to see Joe, and then she would meet Jeremy and his friend Brad for lunch.

She had to walk into the cornfield and kill the fear.

No, she had to walk into the cornfield because the crows were calling her, because one of the scarecrows was close, and if she didn't go and look it in the face…

The day suddenly grew darker as a cloud passed over the sun, and she shivered.

Idiot, she chided herself.

On the other hand…

She despised it in movies when the stupid heroine— who always seemed to be young and gorgeous and barely dressed—walked alone into what appeared to be certain danger.

She stopped and smiled. When the AAA guy arrived, *then* she would check out what was going on in the cornfield.

Not while she was alone.

She turned back to her car. A crow was sitting on the hood again.

It stared at her and cawed, then flapped its wings furiously as it arose, soared into the sky and landed atop a scarecrow that was just visible over the cornstalks where its fellows were still circling and shrieking.

She stood by her car, refusing to be controlled by either a dream or the haunting presence of the crows. She looked toward the end of the road, where she could see the end of the fields, and the beginning of brush and trees and homes. Anything other than the corn-fields seemed very far away, but it was good to know that the fields *did* end, that people lived out there, that there were homes and trees and no scarecrows.

Golds, oranges, deep crimsons and softer yellows all dazzled from the distant trees. That was her home in autumn, the best of the seasons, the most beautiful, and she wasn't going to let anything ruin that for her. She closed her eyes and thought of the nearby shore-line, of the way the granite rose above the windswept sea.

The road remained empty. Not a single car passed.

She hugged her arms across her chest. She could hear the wind shifting, and, just standing there, she could feel an edge to the weather. Soon enough, winter would come. But for now, she basked in the ethereal beauty of autumn. To take her mind off her disturbing visions, she forced herself to think of the warmth of a harvest bonfire. Of people laughing and hot cider. Pumpkin pie. Turkey, dressing, cranberry sauce, whipped potatoes, green bean casserole…

Where the hell was the AAA man?

When her phone rang, she was so startled that she actually dropped it. She picked it up quickly, answering a little breathlessly.

It was Jeremy.

"Hey," she said.

"Hey, yourself. Are you all right?"

"Yeah, I'm fine."

"Where are you?"

She winced. She didn't really feel like telling him that she had run out of gas. That she hadn't even checked the gauge when she started out—not that she could have done anything other than call AAA even if she'd noticed the needle hovering on E.

"On the road," she said. That was true, at least as far as it went.

He was silent for a moment. As if he knew. Maybe he *did* know. She would bet anything that Joe had said something to him.

"I ran out of gas," she said flatly.

It wouldn't be good to be caught in a lie, she reasoned.

"We're on our way, and we're almost there. Just stay where you are, huh? Maybe you should lock yourself in your car."

"Jeremy, there isn't another soul around as far as the eye can see," she told him dryly. "Certainly not the AAA guy," she added with a laugh.

"Still…"

One of the crows suddenly came closer, almost dive-bombing her.

"What the hell was that?" Jeremy asked.

"Crow," she said, and she couldn't stop a shiver.

"I saw this. I saw…*this!*" Brad exclaimed, turning in the passenger seat to face Jeremy.

Jeremy was startled by his friend's outburst. Every time it seemed as if Brad had started to pull himself together, he would go off on some crazy tangent as if he'd really lost his mind.

"In the crystal ball," Brad said, and Jeremy could tell by his friend's clenched fists and tense posture that he wasn't feigning his distress.

"You saw cornfields in a crystal ball?" Jeremy asked.

Brad, staring out the window, nodded.

"Cornfields…and scarecrows. Only in the crystal ball, it was like I was flying, coming closer and closer to the scarecrows…. And then one scarecrow…it was a corpse."

"Brad, what you saw in a crystal ball was just a fortune-teller's trick," Jeremy said evenly, hoping to calm his friend down before they met up with Rowenna. All he needed was for every formerly rational person around him to begin supporting each other on a quest for a bogeyman. "Brad, the guy was playing you. And I'm not saying he's a good guy," he hurried on when Brad started to object, "but you can't get this upset about seeing a cornfield."

"Look over there," Brad said, pointing.

It *was* strange, Jeremy had to admit, following Brad's indication.

He'd never seen so many crows circling all together.

He faced forward again, and down the road he could see a car. He didn't know what Rowenna drove, but he had to assume that was her silver SUV on the shoulder.

He pressed harder on the gas pedal. He could just make out Rowenna and…

And the crows. One of them, and then another, flying around her, swooping low over her head and…

What the hell was going on?

Crows didn't attack like that!

But these crows *were* attacking her, diving straight at her.

She should have gotten in the car, dammit, but for whatever reason, she hadn't.

And they were circling her too closely now, getting between her and the car, so she couldn't get the door open. It was as if they were driving her, trying to force her off the road and into the field.

And then, when he had nearly reached her, she turned, ducking her head to protect her face, arms flailing in panic, and ran into the cornfield.

This was insanity. She knew it, but she couldn't stop. As soon as she moved, running from the crows, she knew that she had made a mistake. Wasn't instinct supposed to help you survive, not send you racing away from the safety of your car and into the unknown?

Mentally reviling herself for being an idiot wasn't going to help, she thought as she dashed wildly through the rows, the rustling stalks closing in around her as if reaching for her, then dived down low, her arms over her head in an effort to protect herself.

But even as she lay on the ground, tasting dirt, she realized that the crows were gone.

Slowly, she raised her head just high enough to see the ground near her.

She was afraid. She knew the crows…were still there.

Somewhere.

But their shrieking was gone, along with the beating of their wings, which had sounded as loud as thunder when they'd been attacking her. The whole world was silent now. Then seconds passed, and she could hear the natural sounds of the day again, the light whisper of the breeze, the cornstalks rustling as they smoothly bent and swayed.

She slowly moved, easing up onto her knees.

She commanded herself to look up, but she couldn't bring herself to obey.

Then she heard the crows again, but they were distant now, and they sounded normal, as they circled far overhead. Their cawing was the random, undirected sound she had heard dozens of times before, not that terrifying screeching they'd made as they swooped and dived at her.

She shifted and turned to look up. She could see them behind her now, far away, their black wings shimmering in the rays of sunlight filtering through the clouds.

She realized then that she was just a few feet away from the scarecrow the crows had been circling, but something in her refused to look at it. She told herself not to be ridiculous, not to be a coward, to simply look up and dispel the irrational fear coursing through her veins.

But she couldn't do it.

All she could do was remember Eric Rolfe's horrible creations, the scarecrow monsters he had created for the annual scarecrow competition back when she was young, before he had fulfilled his dream and moved on to Hollywood to create real monsters for the movies.

But Eric Rolfe's artistic endeavors weren't what was scaring her now.

The dream she had endured—time and again—was what held her in the deadly grip of fear.

She couldn't look. Not when she was so afraid the horror was going to be right there in reality.

It was just a scarecrow in a field, she told herself. Not a monster, not a rotting corpse nailed to crossed boards, just a scarecrow.

She inhaled, exhaled. Told herself she was being irrational again.

Then told herself she wasn't, because the crows' attack had been anything but rational and normal.

In the end, it didn't matter what she told herself, whether she believed she was being rational or not. She simply couldn't force herself to look up. Instead she stared at the earth and found a prayer forming on her lips.

No, no, no. Please, God, don't let it be real. Please don't let it be real....

Fear and dread began to creep through her, like cold rivers flowing in her blood. She tried to still the frantic beating of her heart by telling herself that Eric Rolfe and all his cohorts were grown up now. The competition had fallen by the wayside, and there were no longer any kids trying to terrify their friends by creating straw-stuffed monsters looming above the corn.

Whatever was in the field with her now was just a scarecrow, nothing more.

Just a scarecrow.

She had to look up.

She'd seen a car just before she'd run into the field. Jeremy was coming. She had to get up and go meet him or else he was going to think she'd truly lost her mind, but she was paralyzed. In her mind, she could already see the scarecrow.

She would look up, and it would lift its head.

Its empty eye sockets would stare at her malevolently. Its head would be a skull, with rotting, blackened flesh hanging in strips from its bony cheeks, and while she watched, one of the crows would land on it and peck at what had once been living flesh.

What was left of the mouth would be opened in a

final, silent scream. Some silly coat would be thrown over a bloated body, bones breaking through long tears in the fabric.

And then she would hear laughter, because the demon, who had left the body in the cornfield for her to discover, would somehow see her, and he would laugh at her terror. And then the corpse would begin to weep, and its tears would be blood, as its putrid fingers of bone and maggoty flesh would twitch and reach out for her....

"Rowenna!"

Jeremy, she thought in sudden relief.

She inhaled raggedly and almost laughed aloud at her own foolishness.

She lifted her head then.

And saw the scarecrow.

The mouth was open in a silent rictus of terror. The eyes were sunken pits that seemed to stare at the world in anguish. Jagged bones stuck out from flesh pecked bloody by the crows and through rents in the old coat that had been thrown over the body before it had been staked out in the field. Black hair, beneath a ridiculous straw hat, moved in the breeze, except where it had been matted to what remained of the face by dried blood.

She stared at the vision in such stunned horror that her own mouth opened and nothing came out. Her blood congealed, and she feared she would be sick.

"Rowenna!"

Jeremy's voice again.

And then another voice cried out, but not her name this time, just an endless sobbing cry of "Oh, God! Oh, God! Oh, God!"

She managed to turn in time to see Brad Johnstone fall to his knees, screaming at the sight of the savaged corpse.

7

Jeremy was paralyzed.

Rowenna was staring up at the dead woman, white as a sheet, a silent scream branded on her features.

And there was Brad, collapsed on the ground, screaming.

Not to mention the horror of the corpse staked out in the field like a scarecrow.

He pulled out his phone, hit 911 and asked not just for emergency vehicles, but that Joe Brentwood be informed about the situation. He strode forward, caught hold of Rowenna's shoulders and spun her to look at him.

"You all right?" he asked huskily.

"I will be," she said, and offered him a pale smile, so he turned and raced over to Brad.

He knelt down and took his old partner by the shoulders.

"Brad. Brad, listen to me."

"She wouldn't be here if it weren't for me. Oh, God, how she must have suffered," Brad said, tears streaming down his face.

"It isn't Mary," Jeremy said.

"What?" Brad whispered.

"It isn't Mary," Jeremy repeated.

Standing now beside the two, Rowenna breathed a sigh of relief. Until just now, he realized, she hadn't known Brad Johnstone, and she had never met Mary. But they were friends of his, and judging from the sympathetic look in her eyes when she turned to him, that mattered to her. She was clearly as horrified as he was by what they had seen, but he couldn't help feeling grateful that at least the horror wasn't compounded by the victim being someone he knew, and apparently she felt the same.

Brad wasn't looking at the corpse. He was staring at the ground, clearly afraid to look back at the mockery of a scarecrow.

"Not Mary," he said firmly, as if speaking to himself. "How do you know?"

"The hair, Brad," Jeremy said, looking down at his friend. He'd seen enough of that corpse himself, and he knew he would have to look at it again—even more closely—before this was over. For the moment, he was just trying to breathe, hoping the image of the dead woman wouldn't become permanently imprinted on his mind. "This woman had black hair. This isn't Mary."

Brad turned his eyes toward the corpse for a fleeting moment, his whole body convulsing in a shudder. "It's—it's not a wig?"

"No." Jeremy inhaled deeply to steady himself. "And she's too short… Brad, I swear to you, it isn't Mary."

At least the woman was beyond suffering now, Jeremy thought. He didn't know when she had died— a medical examiner would have to deal with that question—but he could only pray that she had been strangled, as seemed likely from the dark mottling of the flesh around her neck, before suffering the slash across her open mouth that was like a surprised and bloody grimace.

He heard the sound of sirens and something in him unwound at the thought that he was no longer going to be left to deal with the horror alone. There was something surreal about standing there in the cornfield, feeling the warmth of the sunshine struggling through the clouds and the soft breeze that was still enough to force the cornstalks to bend slightly, their rustling like the whispering of some ancient tongue.

"Excuse me," Brad muttered suddenly. Then, leaning on Rowenna for support, he made it to his feet and about ten yards away before he was ill.

It was a horrible thing to see his friend so broken, Jeremy thought.

Rowenna had regained control of herself, he noticed, though she was very carefully avoiding looking at the scarecrow. She was standing next to Brad, gently touching his shoulder, just enough for him to know she was there in case he needed her.

A moment later, three cars arrived, driving right into the edge of field before they jerked to a halt. The emergency operator had obviously gotten through to Joe, because he was the first to get out of a car; Jeremy could just see him through the green stalks. A uniformed officer was right behind him as he strode through the cornstalks, shoving them out of the way until he was standing in front of the staked body and staring up at it, horror and disbelief written across his face.

"Get the scene cordoned off—now," Joe said, and the officer, white-faced, hurried to carry out the order, calling out to the others as they exited their cars. Seconds later, while Joe was still staring tight-lipped at the body, a fourth car arrived. The man who got out was obviously the medical examiner, judging by the equipment he carried. A crime-scene unit made its appearance in his wake.

"Jesus, Mary and Joseph!" the M.E. exclaimed, crossing himself as he stared up at the body.

Joe shook his head, turning away at last. "No fuck-ups," he said curtly. "No mistakes, no evidence missed or lost or compromised, do you understand?"

No one answered him, but it was clear from their expressions that his message had gotten through loud and clear. One of the crime-scene officers began to snap pictures. Someone else stumbled away and, like Brad, was sick.

Joe made his way over to Jeremy just as Rowenna returned. Brad was sitting on the ground farther down the row, pale and shaken. Joe gave Brad a cursory look, then arched a brow to Jeremy in question.

"It isn't Mary," Jeremy said quietly.

"How the hell did you find her?" Joe asked.

Rowenna took a deep, steadying breath and answered. "I found her. My car ran out of gas, like I told you." Her tone was flat and dull. She shook her head, as if she were still trying to comprehend the chain of events herself. "I…I was attacked by crows."

Joe frowned fiercely. "What were you doing out of the car?" Before she could respond, he went on. "And what do you mean, crows attacked you?"

"I swear to you, the crows attacked me," Rowenna

said. "It was like they were…I don't know, like they were *driving* me out here."

"So you ran into the field?" Joe asked sternly.

Rowenna lifted her hands in confusion. "I just… I tried to get away from them, that's all."

"So then you found…her," Joe said very quietly.

Rowenna nodded and shoved her hands into the pockets of the light jacket she was wearing. She was still frighteningly pale, Jeremy thought. And she still wouldn't look at the corpse, not that he could blame her for that.

The clouds shifted as the wind picked up, and for a moment the sun shone brightly and the day felt almost hot.

The smell of death, which had been strangely missing before, was suddenly pungent.

Another cop ran off and, seconds later, could be heard retching. Joe let out a sigh and turned to the medical examiner. "Harold? Any preliminary thoughts?"

"Looks like strangulation," the M.E. replied. He was a man who looked just right for his job. Medium height, medium build, steady blue eyes and neatly combed silver hair.

He was as white as the rest of them.

"I could have told you that," Joe said.

So could I, Jeremy thought, but there was no point in alienating anyone by saying so.

"Fine, then you can have my job," Harold replied angrily. "I can't tell you much more until you get her down…and I've had a chance to do an autopsy."

"I want this whole damn field searched," Joe said. "Step-by-step. Jenkins, get on the radio. I want every

farmer in the county out checking on his scarecrows."
He frowned slightly. "Who owns this parcel?" he
asked.

"The MacElroys," Rowenna said quietly. "I think
the property is actually Ginny's."

"Nick MacElroy's old auntie owns these fields?"
Joe said, surprised.

"I think the income from the fields is hers, yes. She
owns the land. Nick owns the house and some fields
to the north of his house," Rowenna explained.

"Well," Joe said quietly, as if he wasn't really
speaking to anyone but himself, "I would say that lets
out the owner being the killer." He glanced over at
Jeremy and Rowenna, and then his gaze shifted to take
in Brad, who was rejoining them, though he still
looked shaky. "Go on in to the station. I'm going to
need statements from each of you. Go now, and start
writing the minute you get there. I want every detail
just as you remember it."

As if anyone could ever forget the way the corpse
looked, staked above the corn and dressed up like a
scarecrow, Jeremy thought.

As Rowenna started for the road, Jeremy gently
caught her arm. "Are you all right?" he asked. He
flushed slightly as she stared at him, a silent question
in her eyes. Could any of them actually be all right after
what they had just seen?

She nodded mechanically and glanced toward Brad.
"A lot better than he is."

Jeremy nodded. He toyed with the idea that maybe
he should stay behind to help and let her drive his car
back to town, but he'd seen the corpse, and he'd seen
the field, so Joe was going to need his statement in the

end anyway. Besides, Joe was obviously good at his job; if there was something to be found in the field, Joe would see that it was discovered. And he would no doubt resent it if Jeremy tried to hang around. He would get more information if he went about it carefully, he realized, than if he forced himself in where he was neither needed nor wanted. Besides, he hoped to attend the autopsy, which meant he needed to be on Joe's good side.

"Get out of here," Joe said now. He didn't bark the words like a command, and he didn't sound irritated, but his meaning was clear: they needed to do themselves the favor of being somewhere else.

Together, they walked through the crushed stalks, disturbed by the passage of so many people, to the road. Crime-scene tape was already stretched in a huge ring around the area that surrounded the corpse, and they had to duck under it when they reached the shoulder.

When she stepped onto the pavement, Rowenna suddenly let out a dry laugh.

Jeremy stared at her questioningly. Had she finally lost it? After what she'd just been through, it would certainly be understandable if she had.

"What?" he asked.

"I'm out of gas," she said, still laughing, clearly on the edge of hysteria.

He'd forgotten that little detail, too, he realized. "Give me your car key," Jeremy said. "I'll ask Joe to have one of his men drop it at your place once it's gassed up."

She nodded. Brad, still looking pale and barely there, got into the backseat of Jeremy's rental without a word. Rowenna took the passenger seat. Jeremy was back two minutes later and made sure she was belted in before he revved the engine and pulled a U-turn, facing the car back to town.

"Look," she said, pointing down the road.

The AAA truck was there to help her at last. She shook her head. "I'm sure Joe or one of the cops will explain," she said.

Jeremy just nodded and kept driving.

He thought that he could drive all day and all night, but it wouldn't matter. There was no driving away from what they had just seen.

News of the ghastly discovery seemed to travel faster than the breeze. By that evening, it was all that anyone was talking about locally, and it even made the national news.

The act of giving statements at the police station—which should have been fairly simple, since Rowenna had almost literally stumbled upon the body, and the others had found it only in the course of looking for her—took the majority of the afternoon. While he was still at the station, both of Jeremy's brothers called, offering advice and whatever assistance he needed, and both of them asking with concern if he was sure that the corpse wasn't Mary Johnstone.

He was certain the dead woman wasn't Mary, but at the moment the police had no idea who she *was*. He hoped, since there was now a national database that listed missing persons, that she would not remain a Jane Doe for long. Whoever she was, someone must have loved her and someone must be missing her, and they deserved to know what had happened to her, as awful as it was.

At five o'clock, they left the station. They hadn't eaten. None of them had been hungry.

It was actually Brad who said that his stomach was growling. But despite his hunger, he wanted a drink first.

Jeremy understood. Rowenna didn't say anything—she had been quiet and thoughtful all afternoon—but she seemed content to go along wherever he led.

They went to a restaurant near the water's edge, where their view was one of pleasure craft gently rocking at the dock and a peak of the House of the Seven Gables rising just over the tree line.

Brad swallowed down two whiskeys, neat, before they ordered. Rowenna joined him for the first, and Jeremy found that the beer he'd ordered was gone in a matter of seconds, as well.

Now, far away from the cornfield, with a few hours between them and the awful discovery, the world was just beginning to seem normal once again.

Jeremy had seen a lot. Hell, he'd once thought that nothing would ever dislodge the image of drowned children as the most awful thing he'd ever seen, but this had done it.

Or at least now there were two images to fill the horror chambers of his mind.

Rowenna set a hand gently on Brad's arm when the waitress brought his third whiskey in less than ten minutes. "Let's thank God it wasn't Mary," she said softly.

He drank, and his own hand trembled as he set his glass down. "The thing is…" he said, his voice husky with emotion. "The thing is…there's a psychotic killer out there. And now Mary's out there, too."

"You can't let yourself think that way, Brad," Rowenna said, and glanced at Jeremy.

He wondered how he had ever managed to keep his distance from her. The empathy in her amber eyes when she looked at Brad was remarkable.

But the way she was looking at *him*…

She looked as if she wanted to say something but was holding back, as if certain that he wouldn't approve.

He tilted his head at an angle, questioning her silently.

She looked back at Brad. "I have…I have a feeling that Mary is alive," she told him.

Brad tried to smile, but no one could have called it a complete success. "Yeah? Well, I hope you're right. I thought so, too, but now…" He shook his head as if he didn't know what to think anymore.

It was clear from her expression that she was still struggling with what and how much to say. "I know it sounds ridiculous, but you can actually ask Joe Brentwood about it. I get…feelings about things sometimes. And I feel that Mary is alive."

Jeremy couldn't believe what he was hearing. She really *did* believe in all that stupid paranormal crap. He almost said something, but he stopped himself in time.

Brad managed a real smile that time, and he lifted his glass to her. "From your lips to God's ears," he said, reaching over to squeeze her hand. He sat up straighter and offered her his hand. "You know, we were never formally introduced. I'm Brad Johnstone."

"Rowenna Cavanaugh," she returned, shaking his hand.

"And you're from…?" he asked.

"Right here in Salem. I'm a native," she said.

Brad actually managed a slight but genuine laugh as he told her that she didn't have an accent. She responded in turn that he didn't sound like a Southerner. Brad told her then that he was a Jacksonville native, and that she should never believe people who said that Florida was only a state of transients and newcomers, because his family had been in the area since the early 1800s.

It was good to hear Brad carry on a normal conversation, Jeremy thought, but at the same time, he couldn't help feeling oddly anxious, as if he were waiting for a bomb to drop.

Except that a bomb *had* dropped, in the form of a corpse in a cornfield.

He leaned back in his chair, sipping his second beer. Soup came—they'd all ordered the New England clam chowder the area was famous for—and was followed by fish.

Without discussing it, they had all decided on fish. White flaky meat that didn't resemble anything that had ever been a mammal.

They had almost finished their meal—with Brad and Rowenna carrying on most of the conversation, discussing anything and everything except local history, Halloween, Mary or the body in the cornfield—when Jeremy looked up to see Joe Brentwood standing in the doorway.

He looked old, Jeremy thought, as if he'd aged ten years in the course of one day. Old, tired and worn.

Jeremy straightened, wishing he could keep Joe from seeing them, and Rowenna and Brad from seeing Joe.

But that was impossible.

Even as the thought flashed through his mind, Joe turned toward them. He caught Jeremy looking at him, and he offered a weak smile and walked over to their table.

"Mind if I join you?" he asked.

There was nothing he should want more than a meal with the detective on Mary's case, Jeremy thought, but logic didn't matter, because in fact there was nothing he wanted less, right at the moment.

"Joe," Rowenna said welcomingly. "Of course we don't mind." She started to rise, but Joe stopped her with a hand on her shoulder.

"Sit, sit, thanks," he said, and pulled out the fourth chair and sat down himself. He ran his fingers through his white hair. "Long day. Really long, really bad day."

"Have you come up with anything you can tell us? Anything at all?" Jeremy asked him.

"Besides the press breathing down my neck? And me praying that the CS Unit doesn't give away details that may foul up the investigation? No." He glanced quickly at Rowenna, who was studying him with concern. "Ro?" he said softly. "How about you?"

She shrugged.

What the hell did this guy want from her? Jeremy wondered.

"Any ideas at all?" Joe asked her, then frowned as he glanced at Jeremy. "She's come up with some real leads for us in the past," he said flatly.

She thinks she's a psychic! Jeremy wanted to shout. A *psychic*. And he was a believer in good old-fashioned investigations, the kind that took time and turned up real evidence. Then he forced himself to stop and think about his reaction, and he was puzzled suddenly by his own attitude. If intuition could solve crimes and save lives, it would be great. He started examining his own feelings, thinking about the way he almost resented the easy flow of words between Rowenna and Joe, and the way his hackles had gone up so quickly on Joe's arrival. He would be really disappointed in himself if the reason was something as petty as professional jealousy.

But it wasn't, and he knew that now.

His mind flashed back to the unease he'd felt when Joe had called him about Rowenna and her empty gas tank earlier that day. Was that the kind of intuition she was talking about? No, his had made sense. He hadn't known then that there was a killer on the loose, but he *had* known that Mary was missing. It made sense to worry about another young, attractive woman who was alone and in a vulnerable position. On the other hand, he hadn't batted an eye when Brad had said he felt sure Mary was still alive, that he would sense it if she were dead. But Mary was Brad's wife. It made a certain kind of sense to think they might have some kind of deep and inexplicable connection. But Rowenna didn't know Mary, so making the leap to believing *her* intuition was something else again.

He glanced at Brad. Joe Brentwood had told his officers to make sure that every farmer in the vicinity checked his scarecrows.

Because there could be more dead women.

Because one woman was definitely missing.

Mary.

He could only hope that Brad hadn't thought of the same thing.

But Rowenna obviously had, because she looked at him then, as if reading his thoughts. Talk about intuition…

"I believe that Mary is still alive," she said softly, fervently.

"She has to be," Brad said passionately. "We need to be doing something. Going through the cornfields with a fine-tooth comb. Looking for that man—looking for Damien."

"Son, we have every law enforcement officer in the area looking for both your wife and that guy Damien, or whatever his real name turns out to be. There's nothing you can do right now."

"There has to be," Brad said. He stood up suddenly.

"Brad," Rowenna said worriedly.

"I'm just going for a walk. I'm going to walk these streets until he shows up. Because he *is* going to show up."

Jeremy stood up, too. "Brad, if you find him…"

Brad let out a long sigh. "I'm not an idiot. I'm not going to beat him up or anything. I'm a cop, remember?"

"Not here, you're not," Jeremy reminded him.

"But I know how to hold someone until he can be taken in for questioning by someone who *is* a cop here. Look, I'm not going to go nuts on the guy, I swear it. I'm just going to find my wife," Brad said.

"We'll walk with you," Rowenna said, standing.

"I'll get the check," Jeremy said.

"All of you, take care," Joe said warningly, and looked at Rowenna. She nodded slightly, and Jeremy knew some kind of a communication had just passed between the two of them. He felt his irritation rising again, and he knew he had to let it go.

If the two of them thought they had some sort of shared-intuition thing going, he wasn't going to change it.

And he wasn't going to allow himself to go off like a madman, either.

Not when he needed to stay in Joe Brentwood's good graces.

He paid the check, and found Brad and Rowenna out by the dock, looking out at the night and at the boats listing gently in the water. It was a peaceful scene.

They started walking, passing the House of the Seven Gables, quiet now by night, only a few lights on. They moved on past closed shops, then reached the pedestrian mall and veered off to walk down toward the cemetery, locked behind its gates now for the night.

The wall around it wasn't high, though. A determined three-year-old could scramble over it.

They looked in, and the graves were silent and eerie by night, the moonlight falling over them, shadows sweeping like living things around the centuries-old markers.

Jeremy paused, even as Rowenna and Brad moved on, their arms linked, their heads bent toward one another in conversation.

Jeremy knew that what puzzled him was the proximity of the cemetery to so many businesses where, on Halloween, even at the end of the day, there must have been hundreds—if not thousands—of people around at any given moment.

Even as dusk had fallen.

Especially as dusk had fallen and Halloween night had arrived.

How had someone spirited Mary out of the cemetery? How was it that no one had seen her being taken? Had she left willingly?

What was he missing?

"Jeremy?"

Rowenna was looking back at him, and even in the dark, he could see the question in her eyes.

"I'm coming," he said, and caught up with them. Together, they walked the rest of the way around the cemetery and back to the street, where he noted again that the cemetery sat on a rise above the traffic, both vehicular and pedestrian.

Back at the Flynn plantation, they had discovered that the graves of the family burial ground sat above a maze of dank tunnels that led to the river. Waterlogged at times, they were navigable tunnels for all that. Here, the cemetery lay higher above the water, not below sea level, as the graves at the plantation did.

Was there a similar secret passage below the earth here, its entrance hidden beneath a grave marker?

But nothing had been disturbed in the graveyard. The place had been thoroughly searched, and there had been no sign of digging, no indication that the ground had been disturbed in any way.

There were several aboveground tombs and burial vaults here. Maybe one of them opened and offered a gateway to some realm beneath the earth. Tomorrow, he would talk to Brentwood, and no matter what it took, he would find a way to legally tear apart the cemetery, and never mind that it was on the National Register of Historic Places.

Tomorrow.

How many tomorrows did they have before Mary

was discovered dead, a macabre scarecrow in a field, half-consumed by crows, a smile slashed in blood across her face?

Rowenna was looking back at him again, and he realized that he was standing still, thinking. He smiled. "I'm coming," he said again.

Now, however, Brad stopped. He was staring over the wall, and then he turned to Jeremy. "He took her. Somehow, he took her."

"Who took her, Brad?" Jeremy asked, afraid of the answer. Brad had a look in his eyes that said he was slipping away again.

"The devil," Brad said firmly.

"Brad, the devil doesn't slip into cemeteries and kidnap living women."

"That devil of a man. Damien. He's the one who took her," Brad insisted.

"Brad, we're looking for him. But even if we find him, he may not be guilty of anything other than over-acting and telling fortunes without a permit," Jeremy said patiently.

But Brad shook his head, deadly serious. "He's the devil in human form, Jeremy, I'm telling you. You don't understand. I saw it in his crystal ball."

"Brad," Jeremy said, "the man, whoever he is, knows some good magic tricks, that's all. He showed you a picture of a turkey dinner, and your imagination did the rest."

Brad shook his head in emphatic disagreement.

It disturbed Jeremy to see the way Rowenna was looking at Brad, a worried frown furrowing her brow.

"The picture in the crystal ball changed," she said softly.

"Rowenna," he said warningly, and stared at her, adding silently, *Please, for the love of God, don't encourage him. Don't get sucked into his delusion, don't encourage him to think the devil has come to earth and stolen his wife.*

"The picture changed. I saw cornfields..Rows and rows of corn, and...he was threatening me. I *know* that the man was threatening me. I saw the cornfields, and I saw something else."

The street seemed to fall dead silent then. It was as if even the breeze had hushed itself to better hear Brad's words.

"What did you see?" Jeremy asked flatly at last.

"Evil. I saw pure evil," Brad said.

Suddenly the air was split by an eerie, keening cry, as if a wolf had let out a loud and plaintive howl.

Except there were no wolves around here. Not anymore. Not for more than a hundred years.

It was a husky, Jeremy told himself. Someone in the area had a dog, and that dog was baying to the moon that even now was rising higher in the night sky.

"You can't see evil, Brad, it's a concept," Jeremy said.

"No. I *saw* evil," Brad insisted. "The man was evil, and I saw evil in the shadows, in the darkness, in the corn. It's a deadly harvest of evil, that's what it is," Brad said.

Again, the dog howled.

"Time to get you back to your room, Brad," Jeremy told him.

"I have to keep looking. I have to find Mary," Brad said.

"It's all right," Rowenna told him. She took his face

between her hands and stared into his eyes. "It's all right, Brad, really. We all know about the danger in the cornfields now. And everyone is looking for Mary. She's going to be all right."

"How can you know?" Brad demanded, anguished.

"Because I've seen the cornfields in my dreams. I've seen the scarecrows. And Mary isn't one of them," she said very softly.

She turned away from Brad, lowering her head, but Jeremy saw the movement of her lips.

And he imagined that he heard her one whispered word escape them.

"Yet."

8

It bothered Rowenna more than she wanted to admit that Brad Johnstone had seen the cornfields in the crystal ball, the crystal ball owned by the man no one knew and no one could find.

"Does that sound good to you?" Jeremy asked.

"Sorry, what?" Rowenna asked, brought back to the present by the sound of his voice.

Brad had just gone in, and he had sworn that he would lock up and stay inside until the morning came. Now she and Jeremy were alone on the sidewalk, surrounded by the quiet darkness.

"I said we can just stay at my place here in town."

"Oh. I…I can't. I need to go home."

"Why?" Jeremy asked, almost combatively.

She stared at him, her brows arching slightly. He was in a hardheaded mood, that was for sure. He seemed ridiculously tall, all of a sudden, even fierce, and she wasn't sure why. Nothing about him had changed. He was just looking at her, dressed in the same jacket and jeans he'd been wearing all day. But his tone was hard, and she suddenly found herself remembering that he'd been a cop, so arguing with him wasn't going to be easy.

She could just tell him to go to hell.

Sure she could—if she were eager to end a relationship she'd been aching to have....

"Jeremy, I don't even have a toothbrush or anything."

"We can find a convenience store, or an all-night pharmacy, if that's your big objection."

"I just got home," she told him.

"And your home is way out in the country, and it's late. And more important, I think we've both had enough of cornfields for the day."

She needed to argue a little harder.

She didn't have the heart.

Actually, once she got past her own stubbornness, she realized she was kind of glad he'd suggested they stay where they were. She was feeling seriously unnerved, and she really *didn't* need to see any more cornfields tonight—or, frankly, ever. She'd been dreaming about those fields. Dreaming about the scarecrows, dreaming that they were the dead.

And now one of them was.

What really terrified her, though, was the looming fear that another body would be staked out for the crows before this was all over.

"I should go home," she offered wearily.

"Yeah, well, not tonight," he told her curtly.

"I still need a toothbrush. And I've never heard of a guy who traveled with an extra one," she told him, managing a weak smile.

He smiled back. "Come on. Let's go find you what you need."

At least he wanted her with him, she thought.

Maybe there was hope for them yet.

And what a thing to be thinking, when she had found a corpse earlier today and Mary was still missing.

And when Brad had seen cornfields in a crystal ball, cornfields like the one where the corpse had been so gruesomely posed.

Cornfields like the ones she had seen in her dreams.

She didn't say anything as they headed for the car.

It would do no good to tell him about her dreams. He'd made it plenty clear that he didn't believe that dreams—or anything else, for that matter—could foretell the future.

They got into his rental car, and within five minutes, they came to a gas station/convenience store combo. Rowenna headed in to pick up a few essentials, while he put gas in the car. As she stood in line to pay, the heavyset woman in front of her was speaking in hushed tones to the elderly man behind the register, obviously talking about the corpse Rowenna had found.

"They haven't identified her, but she's not that woman who's just been in the papers. It's ghastly, just ghastly. But…" She lowered her voice even further, and Rowenna strained to hear. "But I've heard it's happened here before."

"When?" the old man asked. "I've been around these parts a long time, and I don't recall hearing any such thing."

"Well, it's happened before, I can tell you that." The woman let out a sniff. "It's all those uppity wiccans," she declared.

Despite the fact that she wasn't a wiccan, Rowenna found herself indignant.

"Wiccans don't practice ritualistic murder," she said before she could stop herself.

The woman turned toward her, seeming to gain girth like a puffer fish. "Are *you* one of *them?*" she demanded.

Rowenna was tired, and the events of the day were wearing on her. "No," she said, and added, "No, I'm a Satanist. We worship the devil, but we usually just sacrifice goats, or occasionally a small dog or a cat. Trying to honor the master but stay within the law. You know how it is."

The woman's jaw dropped.

Rowenna felt someone at her back then. Jeremy. He threw down a bill on the counter that would more than cover her toothbrush and deodorant, and drew her toward the door with him, apologizing as he went. "She's off her meds, ma'am. I'm so sorry. Please excuse us."

Outside, he spun her around to face him. "What the hell is the matter with you?" he demanded, eyes the color of a hurricane at full blast.

"She was just so ignorant and she's going to cause a panic or start a lynch mob or something!" Rowenna said. Oh, God, she'd been an idiot. Why was she even trying to defend herself?

"Get in the car. Before a lynch mob comes for you," he commanded.

She lowered her head, bit her lip and did as she'd been told.

She looked straight ahead as they drove, but she could feel the condemning glances he shot her way as he navigated the streets back to his rental house.

He pulled into his driveway at last, and as she got out of the car, she was uncomfortably aware of the absolute stillness of the night.

It even seemed as if she could actually *feel* the darkness, too.

She still felt him eyeing her off and on as they headed toward the back door.

"I can go home, you know," she said softly, as he turned the key in the lock. "I can just take a cab."

He stood on the porch and looked back at her. "Great. You do something stupid, I get angry—so that's it. You want to go home."

"I just meant that if you're *that* angry, maybe I *should* go home," she told him.

"No, you should accept that you have to be careful. You can't go spouting off like that to people. Why don't you just admit that you were wrong and promise that you won't go crazy like that again?" he said, an edge still in his voice. "That's a lot better than running away, don't you think?"

Run away? From him? Was that what she was trying to do? She had finally gotten what she wanted. She'd spent years waiting for someone she could care about again, and now…

Now he was here, but the dreams and the nightmares and the fear were holding her back, threatening to ruin everything.

She stared at him. "All right, it was stupid. But she just made me so mad! It's attitudes like hers that probably caused the deaths of all those supposed witches centuries ago, and listening to her, it just made me think that maybe we haven't come that far and…"

Her voice trailed away.

"We should probably go in," he suggested. "Instead of putting on a show for the neighbors."

She was relieved to see that his anger was fading at

last, and that just the hint of an amused smile was playing over his lips.

"Good idea," she said, and followed him up the steps.

A light was burning softly in the dining room, casting a gentle glow out through the old pantry-turned-back-porch where they entered. She looked into his eyes, his expression a mix of the quizzical and frustrated, like a warm stream of silver and storm, and she couldn't help herself. She just smiled and kissed him. She dropped the bag holding her new toothbrush and let her handbag slide to the floor, and she slid tightly into his arms. She closed her eyes. It had been a horrendous day. She didn't want to think about the horrible end that unknown woman had come to. The world's evil could touch anyone at any time, but she couldn't let herself think about that, couldn't let herself fall prey to the visions playing at the corners of her mind.

She fought to hold on to the wonder of this moment, to the delicious feel of his body, warm and vital and close to hers, and the sweet, expert teasing of his kiss, hot and wet and evocative of the intimate passion they had so recently shared. They broke apart and stared at each other. A smile played over his lips again, and the single dimple in his cheek deepened. She pressed herself against him, glad just to be held there for a moment, to feel his hand, large and strong, cradling her head. Against his chest, through his shirt and jacket, she could hear the beat of his heart, and when he lifted her chin, she was glad for the feel of his lips again, the wicked and tantalizing dance of his tongue.

And then his hands left her face and began dealing

with their clothing. Their jackets were discarded first, and of the rest of their clothes followed as they headed toward the stairs that led to the bedrooms, then somehow wound up on the sofa instead.

There were things she was coming to know so well about him, she thought now, as passion drove them together toward the heights. Things she loved, like the way he could be awkward and sensual and incredibly sexy all at once. Or the scent of him, subtle and unique, the sound of his laugh, and the way he would smile, until that smile began to fade as he looked at her and passion took over. She couldn't resist the deep storm color of his eyes, which could burn like cold steel. She loved the way he held her, the way he moved, the way he surged into her, as if the very survival of the world depended on their climax. She loved the way he held her, if only for a few moments, as if she were the most precious being in the world, once their ardor had been slaked. He was holding her that way now, and then he laughed as he looked around the room and surveyed the mess they'd left behind them as they'd raced for the comfort of the couch.

He went to turn off the lights while she collected their clothing, and then they made their way upstairs and back together again. Later, as they lay entwined and silent as sleep began its descent, she found herself blinking rapidly, trying to stay awake.

She was afraid of sleep. Afraid of dreaming.

She had to sleep sometime, of course. She knew that. Even so, she fought against it for hours, until, inevitably, sleep won.

When she awoke, it wasn't because of a nightmare.

Something in the room itself had disturbed her, and she didn't know what.

The little colonial house, with its Victorian gingerbread add-ons, was extremely charming. She hadn't fully inspected it yet, but the bed was pleasant, not too hard, not too soft, and the heavy comforter was wonderfully cozy. The old mahogany furniture had been stained to a warm and welcoming shade of light brown. So what was bothering her?

She was certain that Jeremy had locked the door behind them. He was an ex-cop. He would be careful that way.

But she felt as if someone else was there with them.

She stared at the ceiling, afraid to look elsewhere, and reached out, then realized that she was alone in the bed.

Where was Jeremy?

She heard him then. He was saying something, but she wasn't sure what.

She struggled to a sitting position as her eyes adjusted to the darkness.

He was standing at the foot of the bed, his hand outstretched, as if it were resting on someone's shoulder—but there was no one there. He spoke again, soft, reassuring words. "It will be all right. I won't leave you. You're going to be all right."

She stared at him, afraid to move. There was no one in the room with them; Jeremy was talking to the air.

And yet...

Goose bumps were crawling over her flesh. She was icy cold.

No. The *air* was icy cold. Freezing.

It had to be her imagination, she told herself. It was fall, and no doubt the temperature outside had dropped and the house's heating hadn't kicked in yet, but there was no way on earth it could be freezing cold in here.

She gripped the covers, wondering if she should speak to him, startle him out of whatever scene he was playing out in his sleep.

At last she found the courage to speak.

"Jeremy?"

He didn't seem to hear her. But then, she'd barely managed to draw a real breath, much less create any sound.

He smiled, then laughed softly, staring down at his imaginary friend. "It's okay, pal, I'm here. I told you I wouldn't leave you, that I'd see you through till the end."

"Jeremy!"

She'd said his name far more loudly than she had intended, maybe because she was so spooked by the chill that was cutting bone-deep.

His hand fell, and he turned to face her, then blinked and smiled.

"You all right?" he asked her.

"I'm fine," she said quickly. "But you…you were…"

He got back in the bed, lowering himself suggestively over her. "I was just—"

He broke off, frowning.

"Jeremy, you were—"

"I woke you up, didn't I? I'm sorry. I guess I must have gotten up for some water. I can never get used to the heating systems up here. I'm always thirsty," he said.

She realized that he had no idea that he had been standing at the foot of the bed, talking to someone who wasn't there.

"Damn, you're cold," he told her suddenly, levering

his weight off her and pulling her against him. "Some northerner," he told her.

"I'm…fine. Really." She curled in against him, grateful for his warmth and knowing she wasn't fine. She was still freezing. It was long minutes until the chill began to fade, and all the while he held her, cradling her tightly.

"Do you dream?" she asked him at last.

His hands, which had been caressing her back, went still. "Everyone dreams," he said.

"True. Do you ever remember your dreams?"

"Sure, sometimes. Everyone does." He moved away from her, rising and grabbing his robe from a nearby chair. "I'm going for that water now. Do you want some?"

"Sure," she said.

She heard his footsteps on the stairs and looked around the empty room.

She didn't want to be alone there—maybe because she couldn't quite convince herself that it *was* empty.

Leaping up, she found his discarded shirt, slipped it on and raced down the stairs after him.

She noticed a weak gray light trying to seep past the edges of the front-hall drapes and realized it was early morning. Very early morning.

But it was morning nonetheless, and she was grateful.

He was worried about Rowenna, Jeremy thought, as he looked across the kitchen table to see her drinking coffee and looking back at him—and apparently he wasn't the only one.

He'd been surprised when Joe Brentwood had called him—he'd thought he would have to jump through hoops to get hold of Brentwood and convince him that he needed to be fully included in the investigation. Instead, Brentwood had called him early, only a few minutes after Rowenna had joined him downstairs and they'd decided to go ahead and make coffee.

"Harold is starting the autopsy first thing," Joe had begun without preamble. "Let me give you the address. Be here by seven sharp." Then he'd told Jeremy to make sure Rowenna stayed safe and hung up.

Jeremy liked having Rowenna with him, despite the circumstances, but given her experience finding the body, he didn't think she needed to be there for the actual autopsy. It had nothing to do with her gender, because in his experience, he'd found that women M.E.s were as calm, thorough and efficient as men, not to mention that he'd seen six-foot, two-hundred-pound male cops turn green and pass out at the first scalpel cut. It was just that he'd been to a score of autopsies in the course of his career, and he was willing to bet cash money that her life hadn't included a single one.

He put his phone down and turned to her. "I've got to rush. That was Joe, asking if I wanted to attend the autopsy."

"Really?" she asked, and smiled. "I hadn't gotten the impression he liked you all that much."

"Thanks for the vote of confidence."

"Hey, I didn't say *I* didn't like you. He's just being careful, I guess. He's a good cop."

"I'll take your word for it."

"He cares. He's always cared. He knows people, and he likes them—once he gets to know them. He also believes in justice. You know, along with truth and the American way and all that."

"I'll consider myself forewarned. Listen, wait here till I get back, okay? I don't want you going home by yourself, just in case."

"Sure, no problem. I like wearing the same clothes two days in a row."

He stood and looked down into her eyes. They were such an extraordinary color. Like gold, against the dark tone of her sleek hair. Her features were beautiful, as well, her nose straight and small but not too small, her mouth well-formed and generous, cheekbones high, brows delicate and arched. He cupped her chin, relishing the softness of her skin against his palm.

"We can always drive out there later and pick up some of your things. Don't you think it makes sense to stay here in town? Close to Brad—and your friend Joe. Makes it easier for you and him to do…whatever voodoo you two do," he said, trying to make light of it.

She flushed and tried to turn away, but his hold was firm.

"Everything I do when I help the police is based on logic, you know."

"Sure it is," he said skeptically.

"I'm serious. I put myself in the place of the victim. I find out everything I can about them, and then I try to imagine what they were thinking, what they were feeling. I'm not a cop. I only make suggestions based on what I feel when I'm in that person's shoes. It's just that sometimes my suggestions have been good ones."

"While I'm gone, why don't you go out and buy something new to wear? Since you're so worried about it and all. Although your jeans looked fine to me."

She grimaced. "Jeremy, I was lying in the dirt in those jeans."

"Okay, good point. Run down the street and buy something else, then."

"They sell really nice wiccan robes down the street," she teased.

"I'm sure you'd look lovely in one," he said, refusing to rise to the bait. "I'm going upstairs to shower. I'll see you before I head out, but please, promise you'll stay in town and wait for me. Don't go out to your place without me."

"It's all right. I'll be around. I want to go to the library and maybe the museum, anyway. Just give me a call when you're back."

She was ready and waiting to take her shower as soon as he finished his, and he was downstairs, getting ready to leave the spare set of keys on the counter, along with a note, when she came down, dressed and ready to head out.

"I'm starving," she told him. "I'm going to go get some breakfast."

He handed her the keys, and she thanked him.

"Do you want me to drop you somewhere?" he asked.

She laughed. "Are you kidding? It's only a few blocks to walk, and it's nice out."

"It's cold."

She laughed. "You think *this* is cold? You ain't seen nothin' yet, mister."

Even in jeans, boots, a sweater and a denim jacket, she still somehow managed to be a picture of elegance and grace, he thought, as he pulled out of the driveway.

Jeremy wasn't sure why, but he was always surprised by the normalcy of the people who worked at the morgue. The receptionist, perky and midtwenties, seemed equally comfortable greeting the living and walking in and out of a room where human bodies lay in various stages of exposure and decomposition.

She took him back and introduced him to "Harold," aka Dr. Albright, one of the eight medical examiners working in the office. Harold and his assistant had already begun work on the unknown woman's body, and Joe Brentwood stood rigidly nearby, watching.

It was a long process. The deceased had been X-rayed when she arrived, her clothing taken away to be analyzed, and blood samples were already being processed. Jeremy learned all that by listening to Dr. Albright speaking into the microphone that was hanging down above the body, so he could describe the process as he worked. He identified the body as that of a young woman between the age of seventeen and thirty-three, standing approximately five foot three and weighing one hundred and twenty pounds. Her neck had been broken, probably postmortem, perhaps even by the weight of her skull as it fell forward due to the staging of the corpse in the fields. Death appeared to be the result of strangulation; heavy bruising was clearly visible around the neck and throat. Trace evidence taken from the body thus far included organic matter, such as dirt and vegetation, insect matter and other undetermined substances.

The stench of decomposition was strong, even in the cold autopsy room. Joe gestured toward a stainless-steel table along one wall, silently suggesting that Jeremy take a mask.

Jeremy was happy to do so.

He found it almost impossible not to distance himself a bit—to stand, like Joe, a few feet back, arms crossed over his chest, and try not to imagine that the rotting flesh and protruding bone on the table had once lived, breathed, laughed.

More photographs were being taken, but Jeremy was certain they were not for identification purposes.

Her face was too badly disfigured for that.

Not, he soon discovered, by the murderer. The damage done to the flesh of her face—other than the red slash across her mouth—had been caused by the birds of prey and insects who had fed upon her while she had reigned atop the stake in the field.

She had had sex shortly before death, and the bruising over her genitalia strongly indicated that it had been rape. Dr. Albright estimated the time of death at about a week prior to the discovery of the body. She did not appear to have been in a state of malnutrition or dehydration prior to death.

The M.E.'s voice became a drone in Jeremy's head.

The doctor made the Y incision so he could begin examining the internal organs, and the corpse became even less recognizable as human.

Heart a normal weight, two hundred and seventy grams; brain, normal, thirteen hundred grams; lungs, also normal, the left, three hundred and seventy grams, the right, four hundred.

Kidneys, both normal, left, one hundred and thirty grams…

Pancreas, spleen, liver…

Tissue samples were taken for later analysis. The assistant removed larvae found in the flesh, and Jeremy knew they would be important in establishing the exact time of death.

He became aware of a soft humming, just below the sound of the water that ran continually to keep the autopsy table clear, and he turned and noticed a computer running nearby. The screen held the image of a sightless skull covered in rotting flesh—the skull belonging to the woman on the table. Alongside it, an automated program ran a series of graphs, and as he watched, the computer began to rebuild her face, even as she lay dead ten feet away. Robbed of life, she was yet given it back.

By the time the doctor stepped aside and his assistant began stitching up the body, a human being was appearing on the screen. Statistics and math were putting her back together, just as the surgical thread was.

She had been pretty.

Young, and pretty.

But not as pretty as Mary.

Or as flat-out beautiful as Rowenna.

But the dead woman was certainly attractive enough to have drawn attention. He was surprised by how relieved he felt to know that he hadn't been mistaken, that death hadn't worked so cruelly on the body that he had been wrong to swear that it wasn't Mary. This woman was indeed shorter. Dark haired, curvy, probably quick to laugh and flirt. To live.

He hadn't felt queasy during the cutting, or even while listening to the description of her wounded flesh, which could be even worse.

But seeing her face, seeing what she had been in life…

"It's amazing, isn't it?" Joe said grimly.

Jeremy was grateful that he hadn't jumped when the policeman's voice startled him out of his thoughts.

"This will be in the papers and on the news by tonight, correct?" Jeremy asked him.

Joe nodded grimly. "I hope you're aware that we're holding back a great deal."

"I would never discuss a case with the press."

"We've held back any mention of the slashed face. I'd asked my men not to mention that the body had been found fixed up like a scarecrow, but that got out somehow anyway."

Jeremy stared at him evenly. "Not through me."

Joe shrugged. "I didn't say you had anything to do with it. Too many emergency personnel on site. Someone was going to squeal. But I'm hoping we can keep it quiet about what he did to the mouth. That's got to be symbolic of something, don't you agree?"

"I would imagine, yes."

"Come on, let's get out of here," Joe said. "Harold—"

"Yeah, yeah, yeah, I'll call you faster than I can think if I get anything," the M.E. promised.

He nodded to Jeremy, who inclined his head in return. "Thanks for letting me sit in."

Harold Albright, his eyes huge behind the magnifying glasses he was wearing, said, "Glad to have you here. You ask me, it's good to have an outsider with the right credentials in as a witness."

Joe actually set a friendly hand on Jeremy's shoulder as they headed out, saying goodbye to Miss Cheerful on the way.

Outside in the parking lot, Joe Brentwood inhaled a deep breath and shook his head. "I'll never get used to the smell of death."

"No man ever should," Jeremy told him.

Joe studied him, then nodded. "Harold won't wear a mask. Says he can smell cyanide and other stuff. He doesn't mind what he does—he just minds when he can't get an answer. We're all going to die, he says. We just deserve to die as human beings. Well, most of us do, anyway." He paused and scratched his chin, then asked, "So, you have any ideas?"

"You know this place better than I do."

"And you know your friend Brad better than I do," Joe countered.

"You can't really believe that Brad did anything to Mary," Jeremy said.

Joe smiled grimly. "That's the difference between us. I *can* believe it. I'm not the guy's friend."

Jeremy shook his head. "He's convinced that the fortune-teller they went to that afternoon, that Damien guy nobody can find, is guilty. It's as good a theory as any other at this point. Brad says he saw cornfields in the guy's crystal ball. He says he felt threatened, like the guy was trying to tell him that he was all-powerful, that he could kill people, and that it all had something to do with the cornfields."

Joe studied him again. "What do you think?"

"I think the guy could be guilty. I think he needs to be found, at the very least."

"Do you think he really showed Brad the cornfields in a crystal ball?"

Jeremy studied Brentwood, wondering if the man was trying to trick him in some way.

"I'm sure there are all kinds of tricks someone could play to make someone else think they're seeing something specific in a crystal ball, sure."

Brentwood looked away and shook his head. "John-stone must be scared to death we're going to find his wife in the same...position."

"Rowenna told him she's convinced that Mary is all right. He seems to believe her."

"And you don't?" Joe asked.

Jeremy lifted his hands. "How can she know?" he asked.

Joe shrugged. "I don't know. But the thing about Rowenna is, somehow or other she generally *does* know. Anyway, tell your buddy to stick around. Not to leave town, anything like that. Not that he probably needs to be told. He's certainly determined not to go anywhere until he finds his wife."

"He loves her."

Brentwood looked skeptical. "That's not what the parents think." He shook his head. "I'm going to have to call them when I get back to the office before they show up on my doorstep again. Having the parents around seldom helps."

"I can call if you want. I know them," Jeremy offered.

Joe looked up at the sky. It was pewter, the rays of the sun streaking through the occasional breaks in the clouds. "Thanks, but I'd better handle it. They seem to think your friend is a no-good cheating bastard."

"They'd had some problems."

"So I've heard."

"They'd solved them. That's why they were here, taking a vacation to put things back together."

"There's one sure way to fix a problem marriage—kill your partner," Joe said.

Jeremy felt himself springing to Brad's defense, but

he forced himself to speak calmly and rationally. "A husband out to rid himself of his wife doesn't usually go out and find another woman to butcher first."

"Why not? Make it look like a serial killing," Joe suggested.

"The M.E. said she's been dead about a week," Jeremy pointed out.

"I figure she died a couple of days before Mary Johnstone disappeared," Joe said.

"And Brad wasn't even in the area before that day," Jeremy argued.

"I can see where the timing gives him the better side of doubt," Joe agreed.

"You're looking for someone local, someone who knows the roads and the fields, even the people, around here. You have no idea who your Jane Doe might be, but I'm willing to bet she wasn't local, and Mary would have been a stranger, too. You have an incredibly clever, organized killer on your hands."

"A psycho," Joe muttered.

"A sociopath," Jeremy corrected him. "A smart one. Granted, the cornfield was contaminated as a crime scene because of the way the body was discovered, but this guy knew what he was doing. He took that body out there at a time when the cornstalks were high and he knew it was unlikely anyone was going to find her until she had begun to decompose and would be a lot harder to identify."

"You think I'm looking for psychopathic farmer?" Joe asked, clearly only half-serious.

"Maybe."

As they talked, Jeremy glanced across the street at the village green, across the busy street from where they stood.

An older couple, hand in hand, came walking along, smiling at one another in a way that tugged at his heart. Hell, they might have just met in a bar last night, for all he knew. But the way they looked at one another, he would have bet his soul that they'd been together for years, through good times and bad. They'd probably raised children together, and now had grandkids who turned their lives upside down whenever they came for a visit, but they were clearly happy on their own, as well, taking the time during their golden years to enjoy the waning sun of autumn and the colors of the turning leaves.

He envied them. The peace with which they moved. The smiles they gave one another. The pleasure they took in enjoying the day, and in the fact that their lives had no doubt been good and well spent.

Cars rushed by as the light at the corner changed, and when he looked again, the couple was gone.

Someone else was standing there.

A boy.

A boy of about ten, with flyaway dark hair and grave eyes.

Billy.

He stared at Jeremy solemnly and lifted a hand, as if in friendship, even comfort.

A car rushed by.

Jeremy blinked.

The boy was gone.

9

As a local, Rowenna knew plenty of places to go for breakfast, even if the main tourist attractions didn't open until nine or ten.

She opted to go to Red's for breakfast, and while she was there, Adam and Eve came in. She smiled when she saw them. Lots of people expected wiccans to go out every day wearing long black cloaks—which, admittedly, they sometimes did—but it wasn't as if there was a dress code. Today Eve was wearing a lot of silver—silver bangles on her wrists, silver cornucopias on her ears, her good pentagram and several delicate strands of silver around her neck. She wore a long wool skirt in a rich green, and a soft sweater to match.

Adam was clad in ordinary jeans and a flannel shirt.

Rowenna started to call out to them, then hesitated.

The two of them seemed to be embroiled in an argument.

She watched as Adam managed to clamp his lips tightly shut when the hostess seated them, and then, when he picked up his menu, she thought it might be safe to go over to say hi. But just then Eve leaned toward her husband and said something in a low, but—

judging from her expression—clearly heated voice. He responded with quiet vehemence, his body language betraying his anger.

Rowenna sat back and picked up the magazine she had grabbed on the way in, a local publication about events in the greater Salem area. Not that it mattered; she was only pretending to read, pretending she couldn't see two of her good friends engaged in a heated argument. They were trying to appear civil— since Salem was actually a pretty small town in a lot of ways, and no one liked being the topic of gossip— but she knew them well enough to know they were upset with each other about something.

When her waitress arrived she ordered coffee, juice and an omelet. As she drank her coffee she found herself caught up in an article on Hammond Castle, in nearby Gloucester, and the man who had built it, John Hays Hammond, Jr. Local legend said the castle was haunted by the spirits of the corpses Hammond—just like the fictional Dr. Frankenstein—had supposedly experimented on. He'd been an inventor, second only to Thomas Edison in the number of patents he held, and was known as "the father of remote control." Whether or not he had actually experimented on corpses was an unanswered question, at least according to the author of the article.

"Good morning."

Rowenna had grown so interested in the article that she was startled to look up and see Eve standing by her table, smiling pleasantly, as if nothing in the world was wrong.

"Good morning, yourself."

"When did you get here?" Eve asked her.

"Ten minutes ago, maybe. I'm not really sure. I was reading."

"Didn't you see us come in?"

Rowenna didn't lie…exactly. She just said, "I was really into this article."

"Well, how about joining us? Grab your coffee, alert your waitress and come on over."

"Sure, I'd love to join you," Rowenna said, not that she really had any choice.

She tried to hide her discomfort at having witnessed their argument as she followed her friend over to the other table.

"Hi, Ro," Adam said, rising.

"Adam," she said, accepting his kiss on her cheek as the waitress came over with their food.

"What are you reading?" he asked, noticing the magazine tucked under her arm.

"An article on Hammond Castle. Did you know it was haunted?" she asked.

"Of course it's haunted," Eve said.

"He experimented with human corpses, you know," Adam added.

"Forget that," Eve said grimly. "We have our own local corpse to worry about now."

"She's not *our* corpse," Adam said irritably.

Eve stared at Rowenna. "I can't believe you found her," she said in a horrified tone.

Great. News had traveled. Rowenna wondered if that was all anyone would think about when they looked at her now: there goes that woman who found the body in the cornfield.

"How did you know I found her?" she asked.

"Don't you watch television?" Eve responded.

"Or read the papers?" Adam queried.

"Or a little thing called the Internet?" Eve told her.

"Oh," Rowenna said simply.

"It must have been horrible," Eve said.

"It was," Rowenna agreed.

Adam leaned closer to her and asked softly, "Did he really stick her up on a stake in a cornfield and leave her there?"

Rowenna looked at her omelet and pushed the plate away, her appetite gone.

"Yes," she said flatly.

"Do you think it was some kind of ritual killing?" Adam asked.

Rowenna shook her head. "It looked like some sick psycho viciously killed a woman," she said. "Listen, guys, it wasn't a great experience, so if you don't mind…"

"Sorry," Adam said quickly.

"I just hope that maniac doesn't have Mary Johnstone," Eve said darkly, staring straight at Rowenna.

Had there been an edge to her friend's voice? Rowenna wondered. Or was she just imagining things because she was still upset from yesterday?

Adam's hands were on the table, knotted and tense. "Let's hope," he agreed quietly. But he was upset. There was a pulse beating hard at his throat.

"Is anything wrong?" Rowenna asked.

"Wrong?" Adam repeated blankly then asked, "Where's your friend?"

"Jeremy?" Rowenna returned.

"Did you bring another friend home?" Eve asked lightly.

"He's…out. He's here trying to help Brad. They used to be partners," Rowenna said.

"Brad is still a diver with the Jax police," Adam said. "We talked a bit," he told Rowenna. "I liked him."

"And his wife," Eve said, her tone slightly acidic.

"I hope they find her. She was beautiful, and really sweet. You could tell she was a dancer with every step she took," Adam said, ignoring what seemed to be a surprising jealousy that his wife was barely concealing.

"*Is* a dancer," Rowenna said.

"Is," Adam said, correcting himself. "Of course."

"Do you really think there's any hope she's alive?" Eve asked, and her concern sounded genuine.

Eve might be jealous of the woman, Rowenna thought, but she would never wish her harm.

"I believe with my whole heart that she is," Rowenna said.

"Intuition?" Adam asked.

Rowenna shrugged.

"Your intuitions are good," Eve said.

"So what are you up to in town today? You certainly came in early, whatever it is you're doing."

Rowenna didn't give them a reason for being so early. She didn't care if people knew that she was sleeping with Jeremy Flynn—she just didn't feel the need to broadcast the news. "I want to do some reading. Anyway, I think I'll go wander around a bit till the library opens," she said, standing. "I'll see you all later. I want to stop by the shop and pick up something to wear."

"You didn't eat your breakfast," Adam pointed out.

No, she hadn't, but she didn't feel any need to make them feel bad by explaining why.

"I just wasn't hungry, I guess. Not to worry—one thing you can always find around here is a place to eat," she said, then waved and left them, stopping by the counter on her way out to pay her breakfast check and her friends' check, as well.

Out on the street, the sun was rising higher, and the air was cool and clean. It was a beautiful day.

She headed to the Peabody Essex Museum, which she knew would be open, and spent some time there going through history. The reading room offered insights into the past, but she grew restless when she didn't find what she was looking for—even though she wasn't certain just what that was. When she left, she stopped for a cup of coffee from a local beanery, then meandered along. Her mind wandered back to the article she'd read about Hammond Castle, and from there she started thinking about the haunted history of the area.

Like the legend of the Harvest Man.

Was there any truth behind it?

She wasn't sure she wanted to know.

She decided to make her next stop the Eastern Massachusetts Museum of History, a small private museum known locally simply as the History Museum.

She hurried along the pedestrian mall and turned onto the side street where the museum was located. As soon as she rounded the corner, she saw the big sign that read History! Just History, and Nothing More!

Strangely enough, the museum was actually owned by out-of-state businessmen, but her friend Daniel was the manager, and he had put together a staff of full- and part-timers who all knew and loved the area, and its history and legends.

She was disappointed to find that Daniel wasn't in, but June Eagle, a junior at Salem College, was there, sitting behind the desk and reading a magazine.

"Hey, Rowenna, I heard you were home," June said, dropping her celebrity tell-all and getting to her feet. She walked around the counter to give Rowenna a quick hug. Her eyes were sparkling. "I heard you're going to be harvest queen this year."

"The rewards of being born in the area," Rowenna said, hugging her back.

"I think it's more than that. I think you really are our local queen," June teased. "So what brings you here?" she asked, and then her smile faded. "Oh. It's the body in the cornfield, isn't it? I'm so sorry—they say you found it. I can't believe something like that could happen around here. I mean, closer to Boston, maybe, but here…?"

"There aren't any cornfields closer to Boston," Rowenna pointed out.

"I have to admit, I'm frightened." June shuddered visibly. "So…what can I help you with?"

"I want to look up some of the old legends—specifically the Harvest Man," Rowenna told her.

"Okay. Hang on and I'll get you the key for the library," June said.

Rowenna felt special. Only a privileged few were given the key to the library.

June reached into the desk drawer and found the key, then handed it to Rowenna. "Call me if you need anything," June said. "Mornings are pretty quiet this time of year. People seem to like coming later in the afternoon. Anyway, I should be studying for my ancient-literature class, but I'm not in the mood. I'll just be out here delving into the latest exploits of Britney and Brangelina."

"Go for it," Rowenna told her, and headed back toward the library.

Like so many of the small local museúms, the different sections were separated by half walls and heavy drapes. The library was in the back, so Rowenna took her time, enjoying the exhibits as she passed.

The first room was dedicated to the Puritans and showed them gaining a tiny foothold in their new land. One tableau showed them building a town, with the local natives hiding in them. The area was known as Naumkeag to the natives. And although the first Thanksgiving might have been a time of friendship for the settlers in Plymouth, by the time the settlements around Salem were founded, the Puritans were beginning to realize that there were many different tribes, and some of them were warlike. Many of the settlers saw the natives as pagans, the devil's own brethren. And more than anything, they feared the devil's work.

She moved on to the display about the witchcraft trials, which covered the situation not just in the New World but in Europe and the rest of the Christian world at the time. Practicing witchcraft was illegal, but the problem was that a person didn't need to do anything in order to be accused. Fear, delusion, even jealousy, was all the motive necessary. It was difficult to understand how entire societies could fall prey to the resulting hysteria and think that it was salvation, but Salem's sad history was proof enough that it could happen.

Past the witchcraft exhibit, before she even reached the library, she found what she'd unknowingly been seeking. The aftermath.

First there were tableaus and accompanying explanations regarding the way the scandal had ended. Nothing like accusing the governor's wife to cause an uproar. And maybe the people were getting sick of the deaths of so many good people, as well. But then, as the witchcraft craze began to end, new fears arose.

And the Harvest Man was born.

She had been through the museum a dozen times before, but now she stopped at the Harvest Man display and really studied it. He was depicted as tall, wearing a flowing dark cape and a headdress of fall leaves. He was also taller and broader than the usual man, though he was human. A painting by a local artist of the early 1700s hung behind the mannequin in the display case. In the painting, the Harvest Man's cape was decorated with fall leaves to match those on his headdress. His arms were lifted to the sky as he stood in the middle of a field.

A cornfield.

The rows of cornstalks were green and lush, rich with the promise of food for the coming winter.

Around him, half-hidden by mist, women and girls cowered. They were naked but tastefully painted, ducking down and covered by their long streaming hair, arms chastely crossed over their breasts. They, too, wore headdresses of fall leaves.

Another painting, this one next to the display, also depicted the Harvest Man in his dark cape and crown of leaves, this time standing above a lone young woman, who was kneeling down as if in supplication. The Harvest Man carried a scythe, and there was something ominous about the scene. The harvest meant plenty for the people, but the painting implied that the Harvest

Man demanded blood in exchange for the bounty of the fields. It was an old belief, common all through pagan history.

Rowenna stopped to read one of the explanatory signs. Winters in the late 1720s had been harsh, and many families hadn't been able to feed all their children. Some of those starving young people had "disappeared," supporting the belief that the Harvest Man came at night and took his due.

She moved on, rubbing her arms for warmth, as if the temperature had actually dropped while she was there.

The mannequins in the next room were actually wax figures modeled on real people—real murderers, each as infamous in his own way as the Harvest Man.

The first wore a steel breastplate with a helmet circa the mid-1700s. He was Andrew Cunningham, who'd been tried and found guilty of the murder and rape of several young women in the Colonies, but he'd disappeared before his execution. Beside him was another wax figure—with eerily realistic eyes—dressed as one of Roger's Raiders, a British unit of the Revolutionary War. His name was Victor Milton, and he had also been suspected of murder—and never apprehended. Then again, he had been fighting for the British. Perhaps the hatred of the people had labeled him a murderer, just as hatred, greed and jealousy had once made people cry "Witch!"

There were two more figures in the room. The first wore a Union officer's navy dress coat. He was David Fine, and when his unit had left the area, the bodies of three young women had been discovered decaying in the woods. The last figure was dressed in a suit that was nearly contemporary. His name was Hank Brisbin, and he had gone to the gallows in the 1920s. Dying, he had announced that he would live forever, that he had already lived for hundreds of years and would never die.

The hangman's noose had silenced his words.

"You're afraid it's happening again, aren't you?"

Rowenna had been so engrossed in the figures that she gasped at the sound of the voice and jumped, her heart thundering.

"Sorry! Oh, Rowenna, I'm so sorry!"

It was only her friend Daniel.

"Dan! You can't sneak up on people like that."

He looked so distressed that she quickly laughed and said, "*I'm* sorry." She hurried over to give him a quick hug. "I'm just…edgy. I guess the entire community is edgy."

He smiled. "I swear, I didn't mean to sneak up on you."

She laughed. "I was just…thinking."

"Yeah. Scary, huh?" Daniel said, and let out a soft sigh. "They still don't know who she was, huh?"

"Not that I've heard," Rowenna told him.

He shook his head. "It's so terrible. I guess at least for now we can be thankful that she wasn't Mary Johnstone."

"You met Mary, huh?" Rowenna said.

He shook his head sadly. "Oh, yeah. I told them they should get their fortunes told—I even told them I thought Damien was good—and to make sure they saw the cemetery."

"Dan!" Rowenna said. "You can't blame yourself."

"I'm not. I don't. It's just…I keep trying to remem-

ber that day. They were both so nice, you know? They
didn't walk in and ask if we had any bones from the
witches' graves or pieces of bark from the hanging
tree, or act…fucking *ghoulish*, the way so many people
do on Halloween. Sorry."

"It's all right—I've heard the word before," she
said.

"I just feel so bad. I keep thinking there has to be
something…." His voice trailed away. "So Junie said
you're here to use the library."

"I'm just trying to find out more about the past,
about the Harvest Man."

A quizzical smile crossed his features. "The past?
You think there really was a Harvest Man and now he's
been awakened again?"

"Of course not," she said quickly. Too quickly? she
wondered. Who was she trying to convince?

"Then…?"

"I'm wondering if there's a psycho out there who
thinks he's the Harvest Man. I mean, look at your
exhibit. This guy—" she pointed to the most recent of
the suspected murderers in the gallery "—Hank
Brisbin. He died claiming that he'd live forever."

Daniel laughed. "Yeah—and he choked on his
words."

"But he *thought* he was more than human. The
world is full of nutcases." She looked away from
Brisbin as if she couldn't bear the sight of him
anymore. "Anyway, it was just an idea."

"Who knows? Maybe someone out there *is* crazy."
Daniel broke off and grimaced. "*Of course* whoever
killed that woman is crazy. But maybe he's crazy like
a fox. You know, trying to get away with murder—

maybe get rid of his wife or girlfriend by making it look like some kind of weird ritual, so he wouldn't be suspected."

"That's a stretch," Rowenna told him.

"I just don't think this was someone trying to get away with killing his wife or his girlfriend."

"Why not?"

"Mary Johnstone. She's still missing."

"Okay, but maybe—just maybe—she's missing for another reason."

"You're suggesting that she has disappeared on purpose, trying to get even with her husband for cheating on her?" she asked.

He shrugged. "It's not unheard of."

Rowenna shook her head. "Mary's the wife of a cop—she knows she'd face charges."

"For what? She's an adult. She can disappear if she wants to."

"I'm pretty sure they could find something to charge her with—make her repay the cost of the investigation or something—but that's not the point. Her purse and her phone were found in the graveyard. All her credit cards, her ATM card and her money," Rowenna said. "I never met her, but from what I understand, she loved her husband and she had a fabulous career as a dancer. Why would she run away?"

"You're probably right. I just hope they find her before... Well, I just hope they find her safe and sound."

"I do, too."

Dan grinned suddenly. "So what's going on with you and this new guy I'm hearing about?"

She blushed. She hadn't been expecting the question, especially in the middle of a far more serious conversation.

"Um, well, I worked with him in New Orleans. He's a private investigator."

"Were you on a case with him?" Daniel asked, his eyes brightening.

"No, no. I just went on a radio talk show with him. We did one of those point-counterpoint things. He was there to raise funds for a children's home, a place for orphans and abused kids, so the show was a way to draw attention to the cause. People love to listen to debates, especially when they get a little heated."

Daniel laughed. "So you argued with the guy by day and got cozy by night?"

"Something like that," she said, blushing again.

"And Joe is okay with this?" he asked.

"Joe has been after me to have a life again for a long time," she told him.

"Still, it has to hurt him some, don't you think?"

"I think that Joe is my friend, and that I'm not going to avoid him. And, I'll admit, I was actually more worried about the fact that he thinks private investigators are a pain in the ass more often than they're useful. But he and Jeremy seem to be doing all right together."

"Well, good. I'm happy for you. It's nice to know things are working out for you."

"We're not engaged or anything. We're seeing each other, that's all. I don't know where we'll go from here."

"Do any of us really know where we're going?" he asked with a philosophical shrug.

She laughed. "I do, at least right now. To the library. Want to join me?"

"Absolutely. Come on through."

They passed through several more exhibit rooms dedicated to the Revolutionary War era, the War of 1812 and the days of the whalers and the great sailing vessels. There was a room filled with pirate fact and fiction, and another focused on Laurie Cabot, who had brought not just modern-day wicca to Salem but also the tourist boom that was now so crucial to the area's economy.

At last they reached the library, where only teachers, professors and serious students were allowed. It was Daniel's favorite part of the museum, Rowenna knew. He liked to let the college students work with the exhibits—they were all more artistic than he was, he'd once told her—but the library was his domain. He was a voracious reader, and he kept a bookcase here of his personal books for whenever he had a spare moment, apart from the scholarly works, and antique books and manuscripts, the museum had bought or that had been donated by local residents.

She found herself glancing through his personal collection, thinking she might borrow something to read later, when she had finished with all her stops for the day.

She wasn't going back to Jeremy's rental house without something to keep her mind off things.

"You love books," she said aloud.

"Yeah, anything," he agreed cheerfully.

He was telling the truth. He had two shelves of classics, including Poe, Shakespeare, Dickens, Defoe and more. Contemporary fiction came next, with alphabetically arranged sections devoted to fantasy and science fiction, mysteries and thrillers, and horror. She was a little startled to see that he also had a collection of romance and erotica.

"Don't laugh," he said.

She didn't laugh, but she couldn't help but smile. "Hey, a good book is a good book."

"I read for knowledge as well as entertainment." He grinned. "I'll have you know my knowledge of so-called *women's* fiction makes me very popular with women when I go out at night. And I, unlike those macho types who look down their noses at my choice in reading material, know what women are looking for in the bedroom."

"Good for you," Rowenna said cheerfully, and then her smile faded as she remembered the corpse she had found and the fact that Mary Johnstone was still missing. "I feel guilty for having fun, you know?" she asked him.

"Yeah, I know," Daniel said, his voice husky. He shook his head in frustration. "I really wish I could help."

"Well, let's see what we can find," Rowenna said. "Dare I hope there's a section on the Harvest Man?"

"Are you kidding?" he asked. "I have a section for everything."

"You're beyond anal," she accused him.

"You bet," he told her with a grin. "To your left, behind the desk, in the glass enclosed case. I'll even trust you with one of our real treasures. It was written by a man named Ethan Forrester in 1730."

"Okay, let's go by era, then," she said as he reverently handed her the book. She took it with the same respect.

"No coffee or anything else to eat or drink while we're in here," he told her gravely.

"I wouldn't think of it," she assured him.

They read in silence for a while. Daniel finished with one book, frowned and picked up another.

Rowenna immersed herself in Ethan Forrester's *The Way of the Devil.*

Forrester had probably been considered a forward thinker for his day. Of course, he had had the advantage of hindsight. He could look back on the witchcraft hysteria as a man who had been a child at the time of the executions and had seen what happened firsthand, though through a child's eyes.

He wrote about the hardships in Salem at the time the hysteria began, the severe cold of the winter, and the complete and utter boredom the children of the time experienced. The society was rigid, with scarcely room to breathe. Girls were expected to do their chores and pray.

Forrester's book was rambling, but it made for intriguing reading. He spoke of people in a way that made them very real, noting that Giles Corey—a man who was pressed to death under heavy stones when he refused to enter a plea of guilty *or* innocent—had testified against his own wife, who had been executed. He wrote about John Proctor, who gave his servant girl, Mercy Warren, a good thrashing, which made her lose all sense of hysteria—until the other girls got hold of her and she once again cried "Witch!" against her neighbors.

Then, he wrote about the aftermath, how the shameful didn't end so much with a bang as with a whimper. Massachusetts had been a British colony at the time, and the powers that be had looked to the mother country for guidance. In those days, correspondence moved slowly, with questions and their subsequent answers having to cross the Atlantic by boat. And just because the governor's wife had been accused, he hadn't been able to stop the whole frenzy with a single word. But the executions had ended at last, though some of the convicted had continued to wither away in jail, until the trials slowly became an uncomfortable topic of conversation. Eventually, as the world moved into another century, many began to regret their mistakes.

But there had been so much to fear in those days. The cold, hostile natives—even hostile neighbors.

And it was onto this stage that the Harvest Man had made his entrance.

Perhaps he had been there all along, unnoticed at first because the collective concentration of the people had been on the persecution of the witches, those who had supposedly signed the devil's own book. Yet even in the height of the witch frenzy, a young girl had gone missing. Her friends thought she had found a way to leave the area before she could be accused. Her enemies were certain that she had run from justice.

She was never found. Perhaps she really had gone on to live elsewhere, changing her name and leaving behind no record of her existence.

But as the 1700s began, so did the periodic disappearances. And then bones—human bones—were found in a cornfield.

Rowenna, staring at the text, gasped.

"What?" Daniel said.

"In the seventeen hundreds, they found bones in a cornfield!" she exclaimed, looking over at him. "Why have I never heard this? I need to read more."

He set his own book aside and came to stand behind her. Rowenna began to read aloud.

"'She was picked bare of flesh, and she left no blood. Scratch marks on the skull indicated that beaks had pecked the eyes. Other carnivores and carrion eaters had come, and thus they had scattered those pathetic bones that were found. No man came then to justice to pay for the act of murder, nor would any man pay for the indignity for years to come. Only after the disappearance of Annie Rigby, in seventeen twenty, would there be a suspect. The people had whispered of the Harvest Man. They sometimes said that he was a black man, for it was poor Tituba's race and color that made the people think she had the mark of a witch. She was from a foreign land, and thus she innocently began the witchcraft hysteria that created the age of darkness here. Those days were over, though. Witches were not to blame. Then they claimed that it was the Devil himself in the dress of the Harvest Man. But Annie Rigby had been seen in the company of a man, and when his cottage was stormed, it was seen that though he laughed at the charge of witchcraft, he told his accusers that he did indeed worship the Most Divine, and that the Most Divine being was none other than Satan himself. At trial, Andrew Cunningham said that he was the Devil in the flesh, that the Devil cohabited within his bones, and that the Devil demanded his due. They ate, they survived, because the Devil was given his due. Thus was Andrew Cunningham—who also claimed he became Satan in the flesh—condemned, and thus should he have gone to the gallows, but for on the day of his scheduled execution, he was not to be found. Indeed, they searched the dungeon—that same dungeon beneath the sheriff's office where so many had waited their fates not three decades earlier, that pit of rankness and leaking sewage and rats that none had escaped before. Cunningham was gone, and the people were very afraid, not that he might walk among them again, but that the Devil was at large. In their rage they dragged from his house and hanged the old hag who was his housekeeper, as it was always said that the Devil needed a handmaiden.'"

Daniel peered over her shoulder to see that she had reached the end of the page. "Is that it?" he asked.

Rowenna stared at the next page. There was only one sentence to finish the chapter.

She looked up at him, and then she continued reading.

"'The Harvest Man will come again.'"

10

By noon Jeremy was back at the bar in the Hawthorne Hotel, sitting with Joe Brentwood and going over every recent missing persons report from the Northeast, a time-consuming process.

He'd been surprised that Joe was more or less willingly including him in all facets of the investigation, but when he had thanked him and asked why, Brentwood had merely shrugged and told him, "Hey, my pop always taught me, keep your friends close and your enemies closer."

"But I'm not your enemy," Jeremy had told him.

"The jury is still out on that one," Joe had replied.

Jeremy had chosen not to argue the point.

Maybe Joe had decided that even if he *was* the enemy—because of his relationship with Rowenna?— he had the skills and training to help in an investigation that had boiled down to looking for a needle in a haystack without knowing whether it was even there.

So they went over data and, when they got hungry, headed to the bar and ordered sodas and hamburgers.

The numerous federal and state agencies had finally learned to cooperate in trying to apprehend kidnappers, rapists and murderers; technology had been the key. Despite that, they found themselves engulfed in information.

They had extended their search as far south as New Jersey, as far west as Pittsburgh, and north to the Canadian border. If they couldn't find the identity of their Jane Doe within those parameters, they would have to extend their search cross-country. But Halloween wasn't like Thanksgiving or Christmas; it wasn't a holiday when people traveled to join their families or went far because they had extra vacation time. Since their Jane Doe apparently wasn't local, she had most likely come from somewhere not too far away.

They had an approximate height of five-three, weight of one-twenty. In decent physical shape. Age, seventeen to thirty-three. They had no eye color, given that she no longer had eyes, and her hair was dark brown to black.

"Here," Joe said, indicating one of his data sheets. "Lily Arnold, last seen at her parents' place October twenty-eighth, went out for a date with a new guy." He looked pleased with his discovery, but then he swore softly. "Never mind. There's an addendum. The mother called in to say that she'd heard from her—she'd quit her job and gone up to Toronto."

Computers didn't catch everything.

"How about this woman?" Jeremy asked, reading from the sheet in front of him. "Dinah Green, from Boston. She fits the physical description, and she didn't show up for work on October twenty-seventh. She'd been on vacation and had told co-workers that she was going to drive up the coast, but when she still didn't show up the following day and didn't answer her phone, her boss reported her missing. She lived alone, but her apartment was empty and didn't look disturbed when the local police went to check. They questioned her friends and neighbors, and she had told the woman next door, a Clare Faith, that she would be back for a Halloween party she was throwing. She didn't make it, and apparently Clare also called the police and reported her missing. Dinah still hasn't shown up, and she didn't pay her rent for November or any of her bills. No one has heard from her, and her cell phone hasn't been used since October nineteenth."

Joe took the data sheet from Jeremy, frowning as he studied it.

"There's not much more here," he muttered. "Where's this girl's family? She kind of went off the radar, and it looks like no one was out there hounding the police."

"Claire Faith seems to be worried. And her co-workers."

Joe shook his head. "There ought to be a parent out there somewhere. Hell, I don't get it. I mean, kids have to grow up, but you invest a lifetime in them—don't people keep up with their kids, at least? Then again, maybe she just left home and forgot about them, so they tried to forget about her. If you distance yourself, I guess you don't hurt as much when something does go wrong."

Jeremy held awkwardly silent for a moment, then said, "I'm sorry about your son, Joe."

Joe nodded and looked away for a long moment. "Hell, I'm sorry for your folks. Three boys—all in law enforcement, one way or another. They must worry."

"My folks are dead." Apparently Joe had only checked out his current circumstances. "Maybe Dinah Green's are, too."

For a minute, Joe stared back at him. Then a rueful smile curved his lips. "Well, I'm sorry for you boys, then."

"We managed. They were great when we had them. We have the memories."

"Memories. Yeah, my memories are all good," Joe said, smiling in reminiscence. Then he frowned suddenly. "Why the hell did you up and resign the way that you did? According to my sources—and yes, even we local-yokel types have them—you found guys who had decayed in a six-seater Cessna, a woman dropped into a canal chained to a block of cement and a couple who crashed and died twenty feet down in a souped-up dragster. You even saved some lives, so what made you throw in the towel?"

"The kids," Jeremy said.

"The kids?" Joe echoed.

"A van full of foster kids."

"Because they were dead?"

"Because one of them wasn't. And because I was about two minutes too late to save him," Jeremy said flatly.

Because he's alive in my dreams.

Not that he was about to admit *that*.

But Joe was still looking at him curiously, studying him. Jeremy wasn't sure why he wanted the man to think well of him; he didn't have to prove himself to anyone.

But Joe's good opinion mattered to him.

Because Joe mattered to Rowenna?

He didn't want to think about that.

"You learn in this business that you can't save everyone—and you can't blame yourself for that," Joe said at last.

"I don't blame myself. I put the blame where it belongs, on the idiot foster father who went drinking, then drove into that canal, but it doesn't help. I didn't blame myself. I was just ready to leave. Anyway, I like what I'm doing now. Working with my brothers… We make a good team. And I like the flexibility. Brad needs me, and I can be here. It all works."

Joe nodded slowly, still staring at him. Jeremy had no idea what he was seeing, but the older man's gaze was too penetrating for comfort.

Besides, they were getting off subject, and he was certain that Joe Brentwood was as eager to solve what was going on as he was, so he tapped the paper Joe was holding and asked, "What does the credit card trail show?"

Joe looked down and skimmed quickly. "She checked into a hotel in Saugus, just down the road, on October eighteenth. Checked out Halloween morning… No, wait. She was due to leave on the thirty-first, so the charge just went through as an express checkout. Nothing left in the room, so no reason for the hotel staff to suspect a problem. She made a withdrawal at an ATM there for a few hundred on October twentieth. That looks like the last credit or debit card usage."

"What about her car?" Jeremy asked, and Joe slid the paper over to him.

Jeremy's eyes skipped over the page while Joe stared at him. He found what he was looking for and turned back to Joe. "It was found abandoned off of I-95 north, just south of the Maine line. It was towed on November first, but the authorities don't know how long it might have been there. It was reported the day

before by a state highway patrolman who had seen it
there at least two days before."

"I think we may have something here," Joe said. He
pulled out his cell phone and put through a call. He
gave Dinah Green's name to one of the deputy sheriffs,
and crisply informed him that he wanted any addi-
tional available information requested from Boston
and any dental records patched through to Doc Harold
immediately. He wanted current pictures, and he
wanted his men canvassing the area bars and shops
asking if anyone had seen her, and if so, when and with
whom. Then he snapped his phone shut. "Anything
else? Any*one* else?" he asked Jeremy. "I have a feeling
you've found our Jane Doe, but just in case she doesn't
pan out…"

They spent another twenty minutes flipping
through the rest of the missing persons reports, and
in the end, Jeremy pulled out three of them. "These
fit the description but not much else. There's a girl
from Princeton who apparently had a huge fight with
her boyfriend, but according to the police in New
Jersey, she made a withdrawal in person from a
branch of her bank in New Hampshire. And here's a
woman from New York City, but she took off with her
boyfriend—the mother called it in. She told police
she hates the boyfriend, he's Italian and probably
Mafia, and he kidnapped her daughter to an island in
the Caribbean."

"You're kidding me. He's Italian, so he has to be
Mafia?" Joe said in disgust.

"The mother hates him. She has to find something,"
he said calmly, then returned to the files. "Here's one
more that's worth looking into—Charlene Nottaway,

left New York City for a cabin in Maine, but she hasn't shown up there yet. She left the city the last week of October and hasn't used a credit card since." He looked up at Joe. "She's thirty-eight. A little older than the M.E. seems to think our cornfield corpse could be."

"Yeah, well, I think your first girl is the one, but I'll pull more information on this one, as well," Joe told him grimly.

He frowned suddenly, staring at Jeremy suspiciously. "Where's Rowenna?"

"She was going to do some research," he said.

"In town?" Joe asked sharply.

"Yes."

"She didn't drive in alone, did she?" Joe demanded.

Jeremy shook his head. "No." He hesitated for a moment. Rowenna wasn't Joe Brentwood's daughter. She was over twenty-one. Her life was her own. So why did he feel like a college kid who had kept a girl out too late? "She stayed with me here in town. I'm renting a house over on Essex Street."

"I see." Joe stared at him and let out a long sigh. "The thing is, I want her to have a life. I just didn't want her having a life with a cop or another serviceman," Joe said. "And I don't imagine your profession's a whole lot safer."

Jeremy looked down at the remains of his hamburger. Well done. He usually liked his meat rare.

Not after an autopsy. He was a carnivore, and he had no interest in going vegetarian. But there was something about seeing the remains of a human being that just wasn't conducive to enjoying rare meat.

He looked back up at Joe. "There are no guarantees in life," he said.

"No. There are no guarantees. But there *are* statistics. And statistics aren't good for servicemen, cops—anyone who messes with perps. Why don't you just play your guitar?"

Jeremy laughed. "I'm not good enough to make the big bucks."

"I hear otherwise."

"That in the file you're putting together on me?"

Joe just grinned.

"I like to play, don't get me wrong. But I like investigating, working with my brothers, more. There's a real satisfaction in it. It's important to me. And, I might add, I don't see you putting in for early retirement."

Joe was quiet for a minute. "Well, I kind of feel like I'm on borrowed time anyway, if that makes any sense. Wife and son, both gone. I have friends. I'm not the suicidal type. But my work *is* my life now."

"It's not really a life if you don't find some kind of meaning in it," Jeremy pointed out.

Joe shook his head and changed the subject. "She worries me."

He didn't have to say who he was talking about. Jeremy knew he was referring to Rowenna.

"She worries you—but you go looking for her to help you out with potentially dangerous situations," Jeremy reminded him.

"She's going to get into things with or without me," Joe said. "The thing is, I know I would take a bullet for her. The question is, would *you?*"

He was serious. Deadly serious.

Jeremy smiled. "It's part of the training, you know. Not just because I care about her, but you know the drill. Protect and serve. Protect. Be the front line. That means you take the bullet."

Joe nodded, then rose impatiently. "Just… You have to be careful with her. Really careful."

"Because she…rushes in?" Jeremy asked.

"Because you never know quite what she's seen," Joe said. He picked up the check the waitress had left when she brought over their food. "You got my dinner last night. I can do lunch. I'll call you when I've got something." He picked up the files and headed out. Jeremy watched him go, then found himself reaching for his phone.

To his irritation, he found that Joe's words had made him anxious.

But Rowenna answered on the second ring.

"Jeremy?"

"Yeah, it's me. Where are you?"

"Having lunch with my friend Dan from the History Museum. I was there this morning, and I found out all kinds of stuff."

"Yeah?"

"Jeremy, men have been arrested through the *centuries* for claiming to be the Harvest Man."

"Well, I don't know who the Harvest Man is, but I do know that twenty people were executed for being witches and none of them really were," he said. "I don't see how the past has anything to do with a corpse in the field now."

"The Harvest Man is a local legend—I'll tell you about him later. But I think our guy is crazy, and that he thinks he's the Harvest Man reborn or something," she said.

"Well, our guy is definitely crazy in one way or

another, and given the way that body was rigged up, I'm willing to bet he knows the area and its legends backward and forward."

"You really have to go through the research," Rowenna said. "Honestly, I'm sure I'm onto something."

"Even if that's the case," Jeremy told her, "he's still flesh and blood, very dangerous—and out there some- where." He found himself rising as he talked. "Where are you, exactly? I'm on my way over."

She gave him the address of the little sushi place off the main drag where she and Daniel were. It was close enough that he decided to walk. He cut through the pe- destrian mall, envisioning where Damien had set up his tent. Assuming he'd been the one to abduct Mary, how had he pulled it off? Somehow he would have had to close up and store his tent, then spirit Mary out of the cemetery. Of course, according to Brad the area had been deserted, so that meant no one around to see what was going on.

As he passed the shops, he noticed Rowenna's friends Adam and Eve Llewellyn changing the display in the front window of their store. They seemed to be arguing as they arranged brilliant purple fabric to provide the backdrop for whatever merchandise they planned to feature.

Eve looked up, as if instinctively, and saw him. The scowl she'd been wearing disappeared as if it had never existed. She smiled broadly and waved, and elbowed Adam in the arm so that he could wave and smile, too. It was interesting, Jeremy thought. Adam hadn't seen him, so he'd been arguing away, the tension in his features betraying his anger. But just like Eve, he slipped an instant grin onto his face and waved as if he were as happy as a clam.

With no alternative, Jeremy smiled and waved back.

Eve escaped from the window and reached the door before he could stop at a wave and keep going.

"Where's Rowenna?" she asked.

"Having lunch with Dan," he told her.

"Lunch? Where?" Eve asked.

"Some sushi place off the main drag."

"Asaki," Eve said knowingly. "Wait for me? I'm starving, so I'm just going to tell Adam to hold the fort."

Before he could answer, she had hurried back into the shop.

Through the window, he could see Adam frown, then argue.

Eve ignored him and hurried back outside, wrapped in a long black cape and smiling broadly, as if she hadn't a care in the world.

Smiling far too broadly, it seemed to him.

"Let's go, shall we?"

She linked an arm through his. "Do you like sushi?" she asked brightly.

"Sure. I like just about anything. I've already eaten, though. I'm just catching up with Rowenna," he said. "She was over at the museum researching something called the Harvest Man."

Eve laughed, and it seemed as forced to him as her smile had been. "Well, I'm sure she'll be glad to see you. Dan's a nice guy, but he can be a little dull. I'm sure they've had their noses stuck deep into some old book all morning. How they think that looking into the past can help solve a modern murder…" Her voice trailed off, and she paused, shuddering. "Do they know who the woman is yet, or where she came from?"

"They're looking into it now," Jeremy told her. But I've got a pretty good idea, he added silently.

Eve shuddered again and tightened her grip on his arm tightly as they kept walking at a brisk pace. "It's so horrible," she said. "I mean, you read about things, but they happen other places. Or they're awful, but make some kind of…sense. A wife kills her abusive husband, a drug dealer shoots a rival drug dealer. This…this just gives me chills."

"Hopefully they'll catch the killer quickly," Jeremy said.

"They know it was a man?" Eve asked.

"She was sexually assaulted, which certainly suggests a man," he said. They had all been working off the assumption that the killer was a man, but there had been no seminal fluid to collect. A condom would have seen to that, but it was possible that she had been sexually assaulted with a foreign object, though there had been no unusual injury to support that theory. Definitely an organized killer, but every killer eventually made a mistake.

This killer would, too.

Except that Jeremy had the sinking feeling that if they didn't catch him in time, this killer's next victim could be Mary.

"How is your friend holding up?" Eve asked, as if following his line of thought.

"I haven't seen him today. I'll check in with him soon," Jeremy told her.

A moment later they opened the door to the restaurant. Rowenna and Daniel were at a booth in the back, deep in conversation. She looked beautiful, Jeremy thought. And when she saw him, she looked up with a smile so genuine that he couldn't help smiling back. He wondered how she had managed to slip into his life, his heart, so easily. Arguing with someone was one thing, attraction was another and sex—even great sex—was still another. She was all three of those things and more. Maybe he'd kept away from her so long because he'd known she was going to have this ability to rock his world with merely a smile.

Daniel turned and looked up, and gestured invitingly. They made a strange duo, Jeremy thought. Dan looked like a stereotypical professor, with his slightly ruffled hair and glasses. He was even wearing a tweed jacket with leather elbow patches.

In contrast, Rowenna was an image of vibrance. Her coloring was electric; even sitting still, she seemed to exude energy and life.

Eve added to the diversity of the picture. Rushing up in her flowing cape and dangling pentagram earrings, she was the personification of a Salem "witch."

"Hope you don't mind me barging in on lunch," Eve said now. "I saw Jeremy passing by and accosted him. When I heard where he was going, I forced him to bring me," she said, sitting and, without compunction, diving right in and snatching a piece of California roll from Rowenna's plate.

"I'm always happy to see you," Rowenna said.

Daniel, looking up at Jeremy, rolled his eyes. Jeremy had the feeling that they were friends because they were both friends with Rowenna, not because they really had much in common. Daniel's love of history and books seemed pretty obviously at odds with Eve's free-spirited approach to life.

He found himself suddenly anxious for Rowenna's

safety, even though he could see that she was safe, and no doubt would stay that way so long as she stuck with her friends. In fact, there was no reason to assume that she was at any more risk than any other young woman walking the streets of Salem.

That was what a smile could do, he thought. Twist a man's psyche so he found himself afraid for a woman just because she was a woman. No, if he were honest with himself, he had to admit that it was more. It was because she was edging into being part of his world, part of life as he knew it. What an idiot he was. He'd somehow managed to avoid her in New Orleans despite seeing her on a daily basis, but now…

Just then Daniel stood to shake his hand, interrupting his thoughts. "We did some interesting reading this morning," he said.

"I got a hint of it on the phone," Jeremy said, sliding next to Dan in the booth, since Eve had taken the spot next to Rowenna and was busily sharing her sushi.

"Remind me that I need a to-go order," she said. "I told Adam I'd bring something back for him."

"What about you?" Daniel asked Jeremy politely. "You hungry?"

Jeremy laughed. "I wasn't. I just ate, but those rolls look good." He figured they were going to have to dispense with the meal before they did any real talking. And though he knew that no legendary killer had come back from the dead to murder women, he thought it was definitely possible that someone was playing a modern game of death based on the past.

When their waiter approached, Eve ordered quickly. "Edamame, please, a salad with ginger dressing, a dragon roll and a miso soup. And just double the whole

order and pack the second one to go, will you?
Thanks."

Having ordered, Eve looked very happy. The simple
things in life, Jeremy thought.

The rolls really did look good, and seafood didn't
seem quite as…*dead* as his hamburger had.

Jeremy opted for two rolls, one tuna and one
salmon.

"The decorating is coming along great for Thanksgiving," Eve said as the waiter promptly arrived with
two more water glasses, another teapot and little cups.
"And then we'll do it up for Christmas."

"Christmas?" Daniel teased. "But you're a wiccan."

"And we have our own holidays, but I—unlike some
people I know—respect all kinds of beliefs. We carry
items to appeal to wiccans, Christians, those who recognize Mohammed, Buddha, Confucius—we even
have customers who celebrate Kwanzaa. Oh," she
added, nodding sagely toward Jeremy, "we also have
a few things for anyone who's into voodoo."

Jeremy realized that she didn't know that he wasn't
originally from New Orleans, nor that not everyone in
the city practiced voodoo.

"Yeah?" Daniel asked, his lips quirked in amusement. "Is that what those hideous masks on the wall
are all about?"

Eve made a face. "I don't like them at all," she
admitted.

"But you sell them," Daniel said.

"What masks?" Rowenna asked.

"We just put them out this morning," Eve said. "I
have so much beautiful stuff—and Adam decided we
had to buy those masks. They're by a local artist. Well,

a guy who grew up here and made it big doing special effects in the movies, and then decided to come back home. His name is Eric Rolfe."

"Eric? I remember Eric," Rowenna said, and looked across the table at Jeremy. "He was a few years ahead of me in school. He wanted to do special effects, even when he was a kid. He always made the creepiest scarecrows." A troubled look crossed her face. "In fact…his scarecrows were almost as scary as a real corpse."

Jeremy knew he needed to look up this Eric Rolfe immediately.

"So he just moved back here recently?" Jeremy asked.

"Yeah, a couple of weeks ago, but don't go getting ideas about him being a homicidal maniac," Eve said, waving a dismissive hand in the air. "He's the sweetest little thing you'll ever meet," she said in a mock Southern accent.

"Sweetest little thing?" Jeremy repeated.

Rowenna laughed. "He's actually about six-three, and he was built husky, even back in high school. But he *is* a really nice guy, the kind who wouldn't hurt a fly. I heard that a few years ago, one of the high schools managed a senior trip out to California when he was working on some monster movie. He gave all the kids a tour of his shop, got them on the set—he was really generous to them. I'm kind of anxious to see him. I didn't know he was back."

"What's the story with his masks?" Jeremy asked Eve.

"Eric was always interested in what makes people tick," she said. "He thought it was fascinating psychologically, the way the Puritans believed in witches and actually thought people could sign the Devil's book and all that. So now he's made a series of masks depicting what the Puritans thought the Devil might look like. And let me tell you, they're creepy as hell. Adam insisted we carry them."

Was that what they'd been fighting about? Jeremy wondered.

She sighed. "At least I managed to hide them in the back of the store. Oh, on a brighter note… Ro, do you remember Angie Peterson? She's doing beautiful jewelry designs in silver—she got her degree in New York—and she's come home now, too."

When the two women started discussing Angie's life and art, Daniel turned to Jeremy and said, "We found a reference to a body being left in a cornfield almost three hundred years ago."

"Rowenna said something about centuries ago," Jeremy told him.

"I think it could be important, don't you?" Daniel asked, and gave him a rundown on the Harvest Man and the related history they'd uncovered.

"Could be. It certainly looks as if the killer is local and knows this Harvest Man legend," Jeremy agreed. "Then again," he added, "whoever did this obviously knows the local fields and when the roads were likely to be empty so he could go out and put up his 'scarecrow.'"

"Local?" Eve looked positively ashen. "I know just about everyone who lives around here," she said. "And I don't know any homicidal maniacs, thank you very much."

Rowenna looked at her friend, clearly worried by her pallor.

"Sorry," Eve said, looking around the table. "It's just—it's just very upsetting."

"Of course it is," Rowenna said soberly.

There was silence at the table.

At that moment the waiter arrived with the miso soup and salad.

Eve bent over her soup immediately, as if it were the most important thing in the world.

"Are you afraid?" Daniel asked her quietly.

She paused with her spoon midway to her mouth and looked up. "Me? Why should I be afraid?"

She obviously was, though.

"You should both be afraid," Jeremy said bluntly. Daniel stared at him, surprised, so he went on to explain. "I don't mean hiding-under-a-table afraid. I mean aware and careful. One woman is dead. Another is missing. I hope there's not a panic, but you should be extra vigilant, yes."

Rowenna was staring at him with a frown puckering her brow.

"Rowenna, where is your car now?" Jeremy asked.

"At the police station," she said, her gaze absent. She was concerned for Eve, he could see.

"What are your plans for the afternoon?" Jeremy asked her.

"I was going to go back to the museum with Dan and do some more reading," she said.

"Good, stay there until I come for you, all right?" Jeremy asked.

"Hey, you said you'd stop by the shop," Eve said, hurt.

"Fine, I'll stop by the shop, and then I'll go back to the museum," Rowenna said. "Why? Where are you going?" she asked Jeremy.

"I have a few errands to run, and I want to check on Brad," he told her.

The sushi arrived, but Eve, who had been starving earlier, seemed to be having a problem swallowing.

Conversation petered out.

Daniel tried to get it moving again. "Hey, I just remembered, we're sitting in the company of a queen."

"Oh, yeah, that's right," Eve said, smiling. "Rowenna is this year's harvest queen."

"Just what does it mean, being the harvest queen?" Jeremy asked.

"We have a parade on Thanksgiving day," Daniel explained. "It's kind of a silly thing. A lot of the local businesses create floats. It's kind of cool—art majors from the local colleges get involved. They get extra credit, and sometimes they even wind up on TV. We usually end up with about twenty floats. It's not like the Macy's parade or anything, but it's fun. It starts out—"

He broke off abruptly, staring at the women across the table.

"It starts out in the cornfields," Rowenna said with forced brightness. "The queen rides on a big fixed-up hay wagon drawn by four horses. The route is only a few miles long. The harvest starts right after. Or it used to. Now, sometimes, it's already started. It's just for fun these days, though I guess it had more significance years ago."

"It's part of a pagan ritual," Eve said.

"There's nothing pagan about it," Daniel protested.

"Yes, there is," Eve insisted. "It's a way of giving thanks for the harvest. According to pagan belief, the harvest queen was like the goddess, Mother Earth, the one who shares her bounty with those around her."

"Well whatever it used to be, all it is now is a good time," Rowenna said, stepping in to end the argument. "Local farmers—and just people who have houses along the route—set up fruit stands, they serve hot apple cider, and there's a dinner-dance at one of the colleges that night. You'll enjoy it," she assured Jeremy.

He smiled, but he wasn't as sure as he was pretending to be. Anything with the word *harvest* connected to it was suspect in his book these days, as if the very word carried an aura of evil.

"So there's no harvest king?" he asked.

"The harvest king is chosen at the dinner," Eve told him. "Think of Rowenna as Queen Elizabeth the First, choosing her king from among her courtiers. And the dinner will be really nice, I promise. I'm on the decorating committee."

"Am I invited?" he asked Rowenna.

"Of course. Anyone can come." She smiled then, as if to let him know he would have been invited anyway.

Jeremy looked at his watch and stood. "I'll catch up with you at the museum, then," he told Rowenna. "I need to get going."

She nodded. "Sounds good."

As he headed to the front, he saw the waiter bringing Eve her to-go order. He wondered what she and Adam had been fighting about. Married couples squabbled, he told himself. That was life. Still, there seemed to be something off about the way they'd tried to cover for their fight. Maybe there marriage was in real trouble and they just didn't want anyone to know.

He found the hostess and paid the bill, then hurried out.

He was sure Joe would call him as soon as he had any information to share, but meanwhile, he had a few stops he needed to make, and he was anxious to get moving.

He wanted to stop by the MacElroy farmhouse at some point, for one thing.

The farmhouse by the cornfield.

The MacElroys were Rowenna's next-door neighbors—even if "next door" meant something different out in the country than it did in town—and they owned the cornfield where the body had been found. The police had undoubtedly already contacted them and asked every imaginable question.

But he wanted to get a few answers himself.

However, he now had a new plan. He wanted to find Eric Rolfe.

He had only gone a few steps down the sidewalk when he heard his name called. He turned around and saw that Rowenna had come running out of the restaurant after him.

She stepped up to him awkwardly, a hesitant smile on her face.

"What is it?" he asked her. "Is something wrong?"

He had grabbed her by the shoulders, he realized, and eased his hold.

She shook her head, her smile deepening, her eyes dazzling.

"No, I was just worried about you," she said.

"Me? Why?"

"I…I just wanted to make sure you were okay. Last night…last night you seemed to be a little restless," she said. "And then this morning, you went to that poor woman's autopsy."

"It wasn't my first autopsy," he said.

"I'm sure that…it still must have been horrible."

"It *was* horrible. Murder is always horrible. And that's why this guy has to be stopped." He winced. "And why Mary has to be found."

"You think she was taken by the same person," Rowenna said, and it wasn't a question.

"I don't want to think it, but…yeah. And he has to be found. And stopped."

His grip on her tightened again. He didn't know why, but he felt as if he were in the vise grip of fear himself.

"Please, be careful out there. Stay with friends at all times, and don't go wandering off in the dark," he said. "Promise me."

"I promise," she assured him, touching his cheek. "You, too," she told him softly. "You be careful, too."

He grinned. "I'm always careful. And I carry a gun."

"I guess that's good," she said doubtfully, then added, "Since I'm sure you know how to use it."

"People shouldn't have one unless they know how to use it," he assured her.

"I carry pepper spray, and I'm not afraid to use it," she said.

"The point is, don't get into a position where you'll need it," he said.

"I don't intend to, I promise."

"Go on. Get back inside with your friends. I'll find you at the museum later."

She nodded and turned. He watched her until she was back in the restaurant, then glanced at his watch and realized he needed to hurry. Darkness came quickly to New England in the fall, and he wanted to accomplish a few things before it began to descend—and before it was time for the museum to close.

If he couldn't make it this afternoon, he would forgo the farmhouse until tomorrow.

But he was going to find Eric Rolfe.

The man who had recently returned to the area.

The man who had once created the creepiest scarecrows.

And who was now creating images of the Devil himself.

11

Rowenna stood by the doorway, watching Jeremy as he walked away.

He really didn't remember last night, when he'd been standing at the bottom of the bed, naked and sound asleep, talking to someone who wasn't there.

But at least he was going to come get her at the museum, so there would be no reason to go back to that house by herself.

She wondered why she was so afraid of something that seemed so simple. If she was afraid of anything, it should be the fact that there was a killer on the streets, a killer who did terrible things to his victims. And she *was* afraid, of course, but she was going to be intelligent and stay in the company of friends.

And then there were the dreams. She was afraid of her own dreams.

She really didn't need to fixate on Jeremy's, too.

But her own dreams were something that she needed to pursue. Because that was where she had first seen the corpse in the cornfield. And if she could figure out how to access what she saw in her subconscious…

"Ready?"

She turned. The others had joined her at the door.

"Did you say an extra goodbye to your *special* friend?" Eve teased.

"What is this? Are we back in high school?" Rowenna demanded. "Let's not forget that he's here because a friend of his is missing."

"I don't want to think about it," Eve told her. "I want to enjoy the fall, and I want to be a little bit happy. We can't take every death to heart or we'll go crazy. Do I sound terrible?"

Daniel stared at her, arching a brow. "How about we go show Rowenna those nasty masks in your store? There's a cheerful thought for you."

Eve shot him an icy look, then lifted her chin and hurried away, carrying her to-go box of sushi.

The other two grinned and followed.

Eve had been busy, or rather, Eve and Adam had been busy, Rowenna thought. The front window was enticing, draped in a majestic purple, with a dazzling display of silver jewelry and seasonal decorations. Colorful leaves were strewn seemingly at random against the purple backdrop, and Thanksgiving and harvest-themed items were arranged in eye-catching ways.

As they entered, bells chimed softly from above the door. Adam looked up and acknowledged them, then went back to showing a customer what was clearly one of Eric's ghoulish masks.

"Ugh," Eve whispered. "Come on back and see the rest."

As they passed the counter, Eve set Adam's lunch beside him, then led the way to the back of the store.

And there they were.

Carved wood, for the most part, they had been enhanced with various materials. From one, glass eyes gazed out with a malevolence that was truly frightening. Another had horns fashioned from discarded deer antlers. Another sported what seemed to be genuine goat horns. Some were painted, but it was the plain wood masks that seemed the most eerie to Rowenna. They were like dark figures that the imagination could see in the natural knots of a tree.

"Fantastic, aren't they?"

She spun around. Adam was behind them, and he seemed pleased with himself as well as with the masks.

Eve grimaced.

"Hey, this *is* a business, and we just made a very nice profit on the one I just sold," Adam said, defending himself. When Eve didn't say anything in response, he turned to Daniel. "What do you think?" he asked.

"I think they're remarkable."

"Rowenna?" Adam asked.

"They're…well, they *are* art," she said, her tone tepid.

"Hey, Rowenna," Eve said, "come to the back room with me. I just got in some gorgeous silk blouses I want to show you."

Rowenna glanced at Adam, who rolled his eyes. She offered a weak smile, and followed Eve.

Rowenna oohed and aahed appropriately over the blouses and decided to buy a couple, but that clearly wasn't why Eve had pulled her aside.

"Ro, I'm really scared," she said.

"You just need to be careful," Rowenna told her.

Eve shook her head. "Not that. It's Adam!"

"Adam?"

"He's gone on this horrible kick. Some guy was in here about a month ago, going on and on about how he couldn't figure out why any man would want to be a wiccan when women are in charge of everything and turn the men into lapdogs. It was stupid—the guy didn't know anything about wiccan beliefs and practices. But it was after that when Adam started demanding that we broaden our horizons. Which is fine with me—really. But then he started studying up on Satanism. As if we're not always trying to fight against misconceptions that wicca and Satanism are the same thing.... I just hate what he's doing. It's like he has to prove he's a man suddenly. And he's always slipping out of the shop now—that's why I decided to go to lunch without him today. Rowenna, can he be having a midlife crisis when he isn't even thirty yet?"

Rowenna fought the temptation to laugh, her friend was so serious.

"I'm sure he'll get over it, Eve. Honestly," she offered.

"He worries me," Eve said.

"Why? Is there something else?" Rowenna asked.

For a moment she thought that Eve was going to tell her that there *was* something more, but her friend just looked unhappy and shook her head.

"Come on, you two have been together for years. This will work itself out," Rowenna said.

"I guess. I mean, I'm not ready to call a lawyer or anything, but…" Her words trailed off, and she suddenly hugged Rowenna. "Thank you. Thank you for being back, for never being judgmental, for being my friend."

"Of course I'm your friend."

"Hey, Ro!" Daniel called. "You ready to head back to the museum?"

"I'm coming," she said, then grinned at Eve. "You ready to face the world again?"

Eve nodded, then swept out ahead of Rowenna. "How's lunch?" she asked Adam, who was behind the counter, his meal spread out before him.

"Wonderful, thank you," he said.

Rowenna's phone rang, and as she slipped it from her handbag, she noted the number. It was Joe Brentwood's private line.

"Hey, Joe," she said.

"Hey. What are you up to?" he asked her.

"I'm at the Llewellyns' store," she told him. "I was about to head over to the History Museum. Dan and I have been doing some interesting reading."

"Great. I'll see you there in a bit."

"Okay," she said, and was about to hang up when he spoke again.

"We've gotten a positive ID on the woman in the cornfield," he told her.

"Oh?"

"Dinah Green, from Boston." He was silent again for a second. "I've told Jeremy. We'll have pictures to show around soon. We need to try to find people who saw her in the area."

"Of course."

"I'll see you in a bit."

She closed her phone to see that Adam, Eve and Daniel were all staring at her. "They've identified the woman from the cornfield," she said.

They all waited.

"Please tell me she wasn't anyone we know," Eve said.

Rowenna shook her head. "I don't think so. Her name was Dinah Green. She was from Boston."

She could hear Eve exhale loudly in relief.

"I've never heard the name," she said.

"I'm sure the police will be around with a picture to find out if she was in the shop," Rowenna said. She reflected for a second, then grimaced. "Wait. I *know* the police—and probably Jeremy, too—will be around with a picture."

"I know he's really gotten involved in this because Brad's his friend," Eve said. "But it's still possible that the murder and Mary Johnstone's disappearance aren't related, right?"

"It's possible. I certainly *hope* they're not," Rowenna said.

"I have to get back," Daniel said, checking his watch. "I'm worried I might have left the reading room door unlocked."

He sounded so serious that Rowenna turned away to hide her grin. She just didn't think there were too many people who plotted each morning to get into his reading room, but she was ready to move on. "All right. Just give me two seconds. I just want to quickly buy something to change into. I've got to get out of these filthy jeans." Eve wound up supplying her with an entire new outfit. Rowenna wasn't certain that the skull bra-and-panty set would have been her personal choice, but they were comfortable and well made, and beggars couldn't be choosers. She picked up another set of undergarments—this set decorated with cherubs—just in case she didn't get home again that night.

Finally she and Daniel headed back to the museum to see to the safety of his books.

At least he didn't mind when she slipped in a bookmark wherever she found a section of text that she thought the police and Jeremy should read.

She was reading about the third notorious murderer from the tableau when Joe arrived. He chatted with Daniel for a minute, but it was evident that he didn't have time to spare, so when he asked Rowenna to take a stroll out with him, she cast a quick excuse-me look Dan's way and headed out with Joe.

"Turn up anything interesting in all those old books?" Joe asked.

"There may be something there," she said, and quickly explained what they'd found.

"What do you think about Brad Johnstone claiming he saw cornfields in the crystal ball? Is he making too much of this Damien person?"

She stopped walking. People were strolling by, looking into windows, enjoying the day. She looked Joe squarely in the eyes, took a deep breath and spoke.

"I've been having dreams about the cornfields. They started right before Halloween. I kept seeing them as they were when I was young, maybe twenty years ago. Remember when the town used to run competitions for best scarecrow? Eric Rolfe always created the scariest one. In my dream, I'm approaching one of his scarecrows, but I know it isn't going to be a scarecrow, that it's going to be real. And when I get there, it's a rotting body, just like…just like the one I found."

He looked back at her solemnly.

"You didn't happen to dream about what the killer looked like, did you?" he asked. His tone was dry, but there was an odd hopefulness in it, too.

"Come on, Joe, if I had any idea, I would have told you right away."

"Yeah, I know," he said wearily.

"I don't know why, but I feel as if reading about the past is very important. I mean, beyond the obvious—that someone is playing off things that have happened before."

"We have to go back to that field," he said.

"We?" she asked warily.

"The crime-scene people have gone through it with a fine-tooth comb. Harold and the lab staff have found everything the body and the clothing can tell us. We've got nothing but some crow feathers, and I can hardly lock up a crow." Joe sounded disgusted. "I have a suspect of a sort, some guy named Damien. Of course, no one can put him near the cemetery, no one saw him come into town and no one saw him leave, not to mention that no one knows who the hell he really is or where to find him. At least we know who the victim is now. I've got fliers circulating now, so with any luck we'll know soon if she spent any time in town. I can only pray that someone can give us a lead, because right now, I have an invisible man and a bunch of birds. And Mary Johnstone's husband, of course, but assuming that his wife and Dinah Green were victims of the same perp, Brad is starting to look very much like a man in the clear." He paused for a moment. "I need to call the parents and tell them that their son-in-law is most probably just as innocent as they are. Meanwhile, I know it won't be easy, but I'd really appreciate it if you'd come back out to that cornfield with me."

"What do you think I can find that all your techs missed?" she asked. She knew she sounded skeptical, but she couldn't help it. She didn't want to go back to that cornfield. Not ever.

"I don't know what you'll find with your own strange brand of logic," he said. "But I sure as hell hope you'll find something."

"When?" she asked, feeling a sense of fatality settle over her.

"Now," he told her gravely.

Jeremy was glad that he had made a point of getting and staying on good terms with Joe Brentwood, because Brentwood's acceptance seemed to give him access to any information he needed.

On the way to his car, he pulled out his phone, hoping to get Brentwood on his cell, but the man didn't pick up. A call to the station put him through to Detective Ivy Sinclair, who supplied him with an address for Eric Rolfe. He thanked her for her help and headed out of town on the road that eventually led to the MacElroy house, Rowenna's house, and then, a bit farther down and to the left, the Rolfe property.

Apparently Eric Rolfe was not a man who needed to bask in his success.

The old farmhouse needed paint, and the front yard was filled with a melange of materials—wood, metal scraps, twine, stone and marble—all stacked untidily on the ground or on a series of mismatched broken-down chairs. There were paint cans in the yard, as well, along with a pile of fabric, and plastic bins filled with various bits and pieces of what seemed to be debris.

Rolfe was seated in a chair, sanding a length of wood. He looked up curiously when he saw Jeremy's rental pull into the drive, and gave a pleasant nod when Jeremy got out of the car.

"Hello," Rolfe said simply. He was a tall man, as Rowenna had said, but he'd lost weight as he matured and would no longer be considered husky, though his arms, bare below the pushed-up sleeves of an old gray sweater, were well defined with muscle. He had long, light blond hair, but his full beard and mustache had streaks of red. He smiled again beneath all the hair and said, "Hiya. Something I can do you for?"

Jeremy strode forward and introduced himself.

"Up from the Big Easy, huh?" Rolfe said politely.

"Recently, yes," Jeremy said. "I didn't realize it was common knowledge."

Rolfe grinned broadly. "I know all about you. Salem's a pretty small world when you get right down to it." He waved a hand toward town. "Nice to meet you. To what do I owe the honor of your driving way out here?"

"Dinah Green," Jeremy said bluntly.

The other man frowned slightly, and appeared to be thinking. Then he shook his head. "No, can't say I know who she is. Am I supposed to?"

"She's the woman whose body was found in the cornfield."

Rolfe smiled slowly. "I see. And I make devil masks and live near the cornfield, so…"

"And you just returned to town after a long time living away," Jeremy added evenly.

"No alibi. I'm living alone," Rolfe said agreeably.

"Those are some pretty weird masks you make," Jeremy told him, changing the subject.

Rolfe nodded. "Yeah, I was a weird kid, too. I always loved the movies. Did you ever see *An American Werewolf in London?* That was it for me.

They created a new Academy Award for special effects that year, it was so damned good."

"I did see it," Jeremy said. "I liked it."

"Want to come in? Have a beer or something?" Rolfe asked.

"Sure."

"I didn't kill that woman, you know," Rolfe told him. "I'm all artist—a lover, not a fighter. But I guess I can understand why you have to eliminate me as a suspect."

He got off his broken chair, and headed toward the rickety porch and unpainted house.

"Guess you're wondering how I could have done so well in Hollywood and own such a ramshackle place," Rolfe said after telling Jeremy to watch out for a broken step.

"I was finding it interesting," Jeremy admitted.

He was even more interested by how surprisingly different the house was inside. It was neat and clean, with a typical parlor to one side of the entry, and a long hallway that branched off to the right and led to the rest of the rooms. The parlor had new leather furnishings, modern end tables and an overall appearance of being well kept. Far more livable than the exterior had led him to expect.

"I picked up some new stuff when I came back," Eric explained. "I hadn't been home in maybe five years. My father died, and my mother moved to Florida. I have a sister in Las Vegas. No pressing need to come back, except that it's home, you know? I always loved the fall. Anyway, when you don't come around in five years, things kind of go to hell, especially in New England. The weather takes its toll." He moved on through the house. Jeremy noted that he was lean, but fit. His hands were powerful, calloused from the work he did. Papers strewn on the dining room table were evidence of his expertise in design and electronics, but it seemed evident that he was a hands-on man, that he enjoyed bringing his visions to life— sometimes literally.

"Light or full-bodied?" he asked Jeremy.

"Whichever," Jeremy said.

Rolfe took two cans of beer from the refrigerator. He handed one to Jeremy, then popped the top on his own. "So you're here with Ro, huh?" He grinned.

"I met Rowenna in New Orleans, and I happened to be coming up here right when she was coming home," Jeremy said.

Rolfe studied Jeremy. "Well, it's good to see her with someone, and from what I've been hearing, you're a stand-up kind of guy. Half the guys in high school had a thing for her, but she was in love with Jon Brentwood from the get-go. It was hard to hate him for it, though a lot of us tried. Strange thing, him becoming a soldier. He was always the kid who broke up everyone else's fights. The kind who never felt he had to prove anything to anyone. He got teased to death in school, his dad being a cop and all. When we were smoking in the boys' room, or sneaking off to try pot, we'd all rag him, saying he was likely to turn us in to his dad." He took a long swig of beer and shook his head. "He never ratted on anyone, though. Of all the guys who shouldn't have left this world too soon, Jon Brentwood was at the top of the list."

"His father must have taken it hard," Jeremy said. "And Rowenna."

"Yeah. Yeah. I wasn't here—didn't make it back for the funeral. But it must have been tough. Joe kind of adopted Rowenna after Jon's death. Her folks were gone, his only child was gone, she would have been his daughter-in-law anyway. I guess it was natural." He made no effort to hide the fact that he was staring at Jeremy, studying him. "So what does Joe think of you?"

"We seem to be getting along."

"Good. I'm glad to hear Ro's moving on finally. You can't dig up the dead, and that's a fact. Strange, though, coming back here. This place is still the same in so many ways. Pretty different from…"

"From…?"

Eric Rolfe laughed. "Hollywood. Coming home to Salem…it's like taking a giant step back into the past. You just get swept right up into all the old stuff, the same routine, the same 'witches are silly' or 'don't show witches on broomsticks, it's such a stereotype.' Personally, I'll take the witches, past or present, over those Puritan Fathers any day. Man, those guys were messed up." He shrugged and gave a dry grin. "But they left some great stuff for an artist to work from."

"Like your masks? Where did you get the pictures you modeled them on?" Jeremy asked.

"The Internet. I've got a bunch of them printed off, if you'd like to have them, if you think it will help you in any way."

"Sure. Thanks." Jeremy wondered if the guy really was innocent or just ingenuously pretending he had nothing to hide.

Rolfe went to the bookcase in the living room, behind the leather recliner that faced the state-of-the-art television. He dug around in a folder, then handed the whole thing to Jeremy. "Take it. I'm done with the masks. I'm working on a Christmas monster for a film that's supposed to start shooting in Vancouver in January."

"So you're not staying in town?"

"It's home. I guess I'll always come back. Strange thing about New Englanders—we leave, we come back. I think it's the draw of the autumn colors," he said.

"When did you get back to town?" Jeremy asked him.

Eric Rolfe thought about that a moment. "I drove cross-country. All by my lonesome, with my audio-books and CDs. Stopped here and there… I think I got in on the seventeenth." He smiled slowly. "Just in time to commit murder, right?"

"The timing fits," Jeremy agreed equably.

Eric shook his head. "I'm clearly your man, then. I must've done it."

"Did you spend Halloween in town?"

"Yes, I did. And please, for the love of God, don't ask me if I saw anything strange," Rolfe said, rolling his eyes. "It was Halloween in Salem. It would have been a miracle if I *didn't* see something strange."

"I was about to ask you if you happened to meet a fortune-teller called Damien."

He had.

Jeremy was sure of it.

Something had briefly flickered in the other man's eyes.

Eric Rolfe hadn't just seen the man. Jeremy had somehow hit a nerve.

"Yeah, I saw him."

"Had you seen him before?"

"No…." Rolfe answered slowly. "No…I don't think so."

"Okay, that's a leading answer," Jeremy told him.

"Well, the guy was out shilling for customers when I walked by. I was on my way to see Eve and Adam, and I was just kind of looking around, watching the kids in their costumes, catching the displays—looking down my nose, if you must know, at some of the cheesy effects some of those people use—when I almost bumped into the guy."

"And then?"

"Then I backed up and said excuse me or something like that. But the guy was staring at me as if…"

Rolfe stopped talking. He appeared to be deep in thought, as if he were trying to remember exactly what had happened. He stared at Jeremy suddenly. "He looked at me as if he knew me. For just a split second it was as if he thought *I* might know *him*. You know, I wouldn't even have remembered that—except that you just asked me. He laughed and said he could tell me the future. He said—"

Rolfe broke off abruptly.

"What?" Jeremy prompted.

"He said he could show me the mysteries of the cornfields. The *cornfields*."

He stared at Jeremy as if puzzled himself.

"And then?"

"Then I said something about having an appointment and kept moving, because to tell you the truth, he kind of creeped me out."

"What did he do? Anything—"

"He just laughed and said I was going to be sorry," Rolfe said. He looked pensive for a moment, then shrugged—almost as if he were shaking off uncomfortable memories. "Who knows? Could have been coincidence. Or maybe he did know me and knew I used to make scarecrows. What do you think? Do you think he knew me?"

"Probably," Jeremy said. Eric Rolfe was either telling the truth or he'd learned a hell of a lot about acting out in Hollywood.

"Do you think that guy is the killer?" Rolfe asked suddenly.

"I don't know what to think. No one can find him."

Rolfe shook his head thoughtfully, his features scrunched into a frown. "I swear, I didn't recognize him, but then again…he had on a turban. And makeup. Facial hair—fake facial hair, I can assure you of that. It's like trying to recognize Santa Claus, you know?"

Jeremy pulled a card from his pocket. "If you come up with anything concrete…"

"Yeah, yeah, call you."

Jeremy laughed. "If you come up with solid facts, call the cops. But if anything occurs to you that you're not a hundred percent sure about, then yes, call me."

"A pleasure. How's Ro, by the way?"

"Good."

"Good?" Rolfe echoed doubtfully.

"Beautiful," Jeremy said.

Rolfe's grin deepened. "Give her my regards. I can't wait to see her."

"I'm sure you'll see her soon. And you know, I really am here to help out a friend."

"Brad Johnstone," Eric said.

"You've met him?" Jeremy asked.

Rolfe shook his head. "No, I haven't met him. But I read the papers, and it's all the talk around town. Or it was." He sighed. "The way of the world. A corpse beats a missing woman." Eric paused. "I did see him on Halloween, though. Him and his wife."

"Where?"

"They were holding hands, walking into the cemetery."

"You saw them go in, but you never saw Mary come out?"

"I was walking down the street, not hanging around spying on them," Rolfe said, sounding tired and impatient. "You couldn't miss them, because they were beautiful. I admit it. I was thinking they would have made the perfect opening for a horror movie. The beautiful couple, dusk coming, the ancient tombstones. I saw them go in. I walked on by."

"No one saw anything," Jeremy muttered, disgusted.

"Hell, it was Halloween. Pretty much anything could have happened and no one would have thought a thing about it," Rolfe said.

He stood and walked out of the kitchen, and Jeremy had no choice but to follow him back toward the front door.

But on the way, Eric paused in the living room and stared at his bookcase.

"You know, I've done some macabre makeup in my day. I've made a gorgeous woman look like a crone and the heartthrob of the month look like a three-thousand-year-old mummy. I've made people look like trees, goats, dogs, bears, you name it. And yet…"

"And yet?"

Eric Rolfe turned and stared at Jeremy. "And yet, no matter what you do—even with contact lenses—there's still something about the eyes. I can always recognize anyone in makeup, because of the eyes." He hesitated for a second. "And that's what's bugging the shit out of me now. It was his eyes. That Damien guy. He stared at me…and I felt like I knew him and didn't like what I knew. There was something in the way he looked at me."

"What about his voice?" Jeremy asked.

Eric seemed startled by the question.

"I don't know."

"Well, what did he sound like?"

Rolfe thought about it. "He didn't have a heavy accent, but…he sounded a bit English, maybe. He definitely didn't have a Boston accent. He was kind of formal, proper. I don't know. I'm a visual guy. Sorry."

"But voices are telling, too. If you heard him again, would you know him?"

"Maybe. Maybe not."

"Well, do me a favor. Keep thinking about it," Jeremy told him.

"Sure. Does that mean I'm off the hook?" Rolfe asked. He spoke with dry amusement; clearly he already knew the answer.

"Not yet," Jeremy assured him.

They kept walking then, and Jeremy headed out. He was almost to the car when Rolfe called to him and he turned back.

"If I could see him, maybe. I'm telling you, even with the contact lenses…there was something about his eyes. Something I *knew.* And I really do think—I'm actually afraid—*he* knew *me.*"

12

It was daylight, and still relatively early. The darkness wouldn't come for another hour, at least.

Besides, Rowenna thought, she wasn't alone. She was with Joe.

And the corpse was gone. The corn, just days away from harvest, rose high into the sky, even after being trampled by so many people, Mother Nature protecting her own. The earth might not be eternal, but she would go on for millions of years, even if man didn't. Life sprang from her, organisms tinier than the eye could see and as huge as elephants and whales—and as egotistical as man.

But all her creations returned to her, became part of her, in the end.

And she accepted them all back, just as she had accepted the blood that had dripped from Dinah Green.

Rowenna felt the strength of the ground itself, and the whispering, growing corn.

Maybe even the corn could sense that its time was coming.

She tried to shake the feeling of dread and finality that had seized her there in the vast field. She tried to tell herself that the rich scent of nature was sweet, and that the breeze was like a caress.

It didn't matter. Nothing could change her mind.

She didn't want to be there.

Joe was standing a short distance away from her. "Well?" he said softly.

She shook her head. "I'm not sure what you think I can do. The crime-scene unit has already been through here. What do you expect me to find that they didn't?"

"What do you *feel?*" he asked her.

"Joe, I've told you, all I do is put myself in the victim's place and try to think logically."

"Okay, think logically."

"Do you think she was killed here?"

He nodded.

"Where was she found? Exactly?" Rowenna asked.

He pointed next to her. She felt like an idiot. Nature was taking back her own, but there was a numbered marker right by where she was standing, and if she'd looked down, she would have seen the stake thrust deeply into the ground.

He walked over to her and handed her a color photocopy of Dinah Green's driver's license.

The woman had been pretty. Hair: dark brown, almost black. Eyes: brown. Height: five-three. She'd managed a shy smile for the photographer at the driver's license bureau. She looked like a woman who had a lot of living to do, and was eager to get out and do it.

The breeze began to blow harder, or so it seemed. Rowenna looked up as it whipped her hair. The sun looked strange, with an opaque haze haloing it. And it was dropping. All too soon, darkness would come.

Rowenna closed her eyes and lost herself in that place where the intuitions came.

She thought she could hear someone pleading. A feminine voice, fraught with terror and, amazingly, hope... The human heart lived on hope, even against all odds.

Rowenna winced as, somewhere far away, as if in the memory of another time in this very place, she heard a scream.

And then laughter. A man's cruel laughter.

There was a struggle, and then the woman's voice again.

"I'll be good, I swear."

And a man talking. A deep voice, with a note of implacability in it.

"It's too late."

And then a struggle. Moaning.

Another scream. This one of choking agony.

And then...

Then she understood everything—what he did, where he did it, even, to a degree, *why*. And she was terrified.

Suddenly Rowenna found herself fighting for breath, her hands clutching her throat as if to fend off an attacker. She fell to her knees in the cornfield, knowing his hands were around the woman's throat, feeling them around *her* throat, his strength...brutal and impossible to combat.

She heard a snap as a tiny bone at the back of the throat broke....

"Ro!"

Joe was at her side, shaking her, dragging her back to her feet.

She blinked rapidly.

That eerie haze no longer obscured the sun, whose rays shone down gently on her.

"Ro, are you all right?"

Joe was anxious, she thought, but at the same time, he didn't appear to be the least bit sorry for what he had just put her through.

"Yeah, I'm fine," she said. And she was. The sun was warm. The breeze was gentle. Life was normal.

"What did you see?"

"I don't *see* things," she whispered, and she didn't know if she was protesting to him, or to herself. Because this time what she'd felt had gone way beyond imagining the victim's final moments and had taken her straight into the twisted mind of a killer.

"What did you feel?" Joe pursued.

"Okay, looking at it logically, this is my theory. He kidnaps his victim. He has someplace where he takes her, a place where he can keep her a prisoner without being afraid of being caught or seen. I doubt this place is in the city, unless he had a soundproof room built. And I have a feeling of darkness. As if he uses darkness itself as one of his tactics for terrorizing his victim. He keeps her alive, he makes her his plaything, except…"

"Except?" Joe's hands were on her shoulders, and he was staring at her intently.

She looked up at him. His hold was so strong that she almost protested, because in another second he would probably cause bruises. He was a strong guy and still spent a lot of time in the gym, and she was feeling the results. But he was so intent, and he seemed so desperate, that she held her tongue.

"Except that she has to play his way. She has to be

afraid, but…she has to understand that he's all-powerful. She has to worship him. And if she goes against him, if she tries to escape, then she has to pay the price."

His fingers tightened again, twitched.

"Ro, can you see him? Think, Rowenna. Concentrate. Can you see his face?"

There *was* an image in her mind. Something…

"Ro?"

She shook her head. "No, I can't see his face. You know what I *am* seeing? One of those ugly devil masks Adam and Eve are selling." She winced as his hold tightened painfully. "Joe, let go. You're hurting me."

The sudden blaring of a horn startled them both. Joe released her, a look of apology on his face, and stepped back. They heard a car door slam, and seconds later Jeremy came striding through the corn, heedless of the stalks, crashing through them as he raced toward them.

His face was tight with anxiety as he came to a dead stop five feet away and stared at her. She saw that his hands were knotted into fists as his sides.

"Jeremy," she said. "Hi."

"What the hell are you doing out here?" he demanded.

"She's with me," Joe said.

"You're supposed to be at the museum," Jeremy told her accusingly, completely ignoring the older man. "I couldn't believe it when Dan said you'd come out here."

"I said she's with me," Joe repeated.

"It's not safe for you to be running around out here in the cornfields," Jeremy challenged, staring her straight in the eyes.

"You said you'd be at the museum," he went on. "That you'd be there, in town, waiting for me."

"Jeremy, I'm with Joe," she said placatingly, wondering where all this anger was coming from.

He turned from her to Joe, as if noticing him for the first time, his eyes thunderous. "Why would you bring her out here?" he demanded.

"Hey, simmer down. This is my home, my stomping ground. *I'm* the law here, and Ro's here to help me. I've known her practically all her life—you two have just become friends. Or *whatever*," he added with a glower. "So don't go all ballistic on me, son. If anyone doesn't belong here, it's you."

Jeremy didn't back down. He stood his ground, arms crossed over his chest. "Night is almost here. You may be a big strong cop, maybe a crack shot, but once it's dark out here… Joe, the killer is a clever man, maybe even an illusionist. Cop or not, it isn't safe for Rowenna to be out here."

"It's daylight," Joe pointed out.

"It's three-thirty, and night comes fast."

"Excuse me, both of you," Rowenna snapped, striding past Joe to confront Jeremy. "I was going back to the museum. I would have met you there, just as planned. Joe and I have been doing this kind of thing for a long time. And, by the way, he *is* a crack shot."

"Crack shot—or crack*pot?*" Jeremy said heatedly, looking past her to Joe. "You can't use her this way— it's dangerous. You'll get the killer thinking she really *can* see things, and then he'll target her, make her his next victim."

"But I can help!" Rowenna insisted. She looked at the two of them, staring at one another, nostrils practically flaring. She had a sudden image of the two of them stomping the ground and rushing each other like a couple of angry bulls.

"Both of you, stop. Jeremy, the killer isn't going to think anything, because he doesn't even know I exist— Joe and I came out here alone. I know you're just worried about me, and I'm grateful. I'm also legally sane, over twenty-one and more than capable of taking care of myself." She marched past him, trembling— but whether with anger or fear, she honestly didn't know—and headed for the road.

She could hear the two men pushing their way through the whispering stalks in her wake.

Jeremy spoke first. "Wait! I'll take you back to town."

"Hey, she came out here with me," Joe said firmly.

She spun around. "Screw you both! You're acting like a couple of five-year-olds. I'm hitchhiking."

Even as she said it, she knew perfectly well that she had no intention of hitchhiking.

She had far too strong an instinct for self-preservation.

"No, no, wait. Ride back with Joe, and I'll follow," Jeremy said, catching up to her.

"No. It's okay. Go with Flynn and *I'll* follow," Joe said.

"Look, it doesn't matter," Jeremy said. "Maybe I was overreacting, but come on, Joe. You'd overreact, too, if you knew that Rowenna and I were at the scene of such butchery…. Especially after this morning."

"Yeah, I guess," Joe muttered. "Hey, was that an apology?"

"I'm apologizing for being a jerk. I still don't think she should be out here," Jeremy said.

Joe ignored that, turned to Rowenna and asked, "You two are going back to the museum, right?"

"Yes," she said.

But when she looked to Jeremy for confirmation, he looked hesitant.

"Sorry, *I'm* going back to the museum," Rowenna said to Joe.

"I'll meet you there before five," Jeremy told her. "Joe, you'll see to it that she gets there safely, right?"

"You bet," Joe promised him.

Jeremy walked over to her and paused, meeting her eyes briefly before taking her hand and kissing her cheek. Then he nodded to Joe and headed for his car.

Rowenna watched him go, puzzled, suddenly feeling as if the entire focus of the last few minutes had been argument for the sake of argument, like some kind of bizarre male bonding ritual, and she'd just been the excuse.

Joe joined her on the shoulder of the road, then walked with her over to his car.

"That was weird," she said as she settled herself in the passenger seat.

"Not really," he told her, glancing in his rearview mirror as he pulled out on the road.

"Yes, it was," she assured him. "First he was going crazy worrying about me, and then it was like he forgot all about me."

He just grinned and glanced at her. "He was in a panic when you weren't where you said you'd be. Now he knows you're safe, and he had something else on his agenda."

"Am I hearing this right? You're standing up for him?" she said, eyes widening in surprise.

He shrugged. "The kid's okay," he said.

She laughed. "He isn't a kid."

"Hell, if you're *me*," Joe said, "he's a kid. And so are you. Leave it at that, huh?"

She fell silent and stared out the side window, watching the rows and rows of corn sweep by them. After a while she glanced over at him. "I take it you think you know where he's going?"

Joe's lips twitched. "Logically?" he asked her.

"Logically."

"He's stopping by the MacElroy place. He'll want to meet Ginny and Doc MacElroy himself."

Rowenna leaned back, thinking of the ridiculousness of little Ginny MacElroy dragging anyone weighing more than ten pounds through a cornfield.

But then there was Doc MacElroy. She had gone to school with his kids, and MacElroy himself would have fit in in Beverly Hills. He was lean and tanned, with a full head of thick, silver-white hair. His eyes were blue like the sky, and he'd always been a handsome man.

Dr. MacElroy a murderer? No, never. She remembered how he'd made her laugh about teddy bears or Barbie dolls to take her mind off the sting whenever he had to give her a shot. She remembered him at her parents' funerals, telling her that he was right there next door if she ever needed him. She could picture him holding up one of his granddaughters, making her giggle with delight as he spun her around the room.

No. No way was he a killer.

Joe glanced at her. "MacElroy was out of town on Halloween."

"Oh," she said.

"Medical convention in Orlando," he elucidated.

She smiled, relieved to have her faith confirmed.

"You know, I'm sure he's been out to see Eric Rolfe," Joe said. "He called the station, asking for the address. Now…there's a strange fellow."

Rowenna frowned, turning to stare at Joe. "He's not strange, he's artistic."

"You don't think our murderer was 'artistic'?"

She shook her head. Yes, she could see why Joe would find it easier to see Eric Rolfe as a sadistic murderer than the kindly Dr. MacElroy. But they both seemed like equally unlikely suspects to her.

"I admit I haven't seen Eric since high school," she said, "but he was a nice guy."

"He was *weird.* Just because he found a place to go where weird is in, that doesn't change the fact that he was one weird kid who built some really twisted scarecrows, then grew up into a pretty weird adult," Joe said firmly.

"Joe Brentwood, that's exactly the kind of attitude that forced Eric to run out west. Well, that and the obvious fact that that's where he could use his talents to make good money," she said.

He looked at her. "We both know it was a local who did this," he said. "When you were doing your thing today, you knew it. He targets out-of-towners. He keeps prisoners. He knows where to put up his displays. He knows the area."

She felt a sinking sensation. Joe was obviously thinking that he needed to keep an eye on Eric Rolfe, which was just ridiculous. Eric was just…Eric.

Then again…

How well did she really know him? She hadn't seen him in years. In fact, just how well did anyone ever know anyone else?

She looked at Joe. She thought she knew him. Thought she knew him well. And yet he had surprised her just a little while ago by actually defending Jeremy Flynn.

They had reached the edge of town, and Rowenna felt a strange sense of relief to see that even though it was still relatively early, the streetlights had come on. The homes they passed were beautiful—but looking a little indecisive. Pilgrim lawn ornaments were out in abundance, along with wagons heaped with pumpkins whose bright orange complemented the brilliance of the autumn leaves. But some people already had their Christmas lights up, as well. One house already sported a giant Santa and sleigh on the roof.

"Can't we just get through the one holiday before starting on the next one?" Joe complained. "I mean, seriously. Could we just celebrate Thanksgiving without getting confused with Christmas? It's a good old American holiday that deserves its due."

"As American as apple pie?" Rowenna suggested with a smile.

"Yeah. Apple pie," Joe agreed, as he pulled up to the curb in front of the museum. "Take care, you hear? I don't want Jeremy coming after me with a mad-on." He grinned, and then his expression turned serious. "And thank you."

"You're welcome, Joe. See you later."

As she got out of the car and walked the few steps to the museum, Rowenna noticed that the night was coming on fast, almost as if the darkness were racing down from the sky.

She hurried up to the door.

There was a poster on the notice board outside, a

poster with two photos, and it hadn't been there when she'd left. She was certain that the same poster was up all over town. The notice below the pictures, which were identified as Dinah Green and Mary Johnstone, read: PLEASE HELP. If you have seen either of these women, please contact the Salem Police Department at 555-TIPS. Dinah Green went missing on approximately October 20th. Mary Johnstone has been missing since Halloween night. If you saw either of these women, particularly in the company of anyone suspicious, please step forward and help.

Rowenna found herself staring at Dinah Green's photo. As she did, she once again felt as if the breeze suddenly started to whirl around her, catching her in its vortex. She could hear whispers in her ear.

The woman, crying and desperate.

The man, cold as ice, ruthless, merciless. Unstoppable.

She blinked, as a strange sense of cold surrounded her and her peripheral vision began to cloud. The darkness crowded around her, and the air grew redolent with the scent of growing things, as if she were still standing in the cornfield.

Taking a step back, she found her equilibrium again.

Poor Dinah. She was gone, and she had died in an agony of fear.

And Mary was still out there somewhere, in the possession of that same calculating killer. Rowenna was convinced that she was still alive, though she had no logical way to explain her certitude.

The killer played with his victims. They were toys to him. He was a god, and they were to worship him. He was kind. The harvest king. And they were to bow down and offer themselves willingly, lovingly, to the king of abundance.

She focused on the picture of Mary Johnstone. She was a gorgeous woman, with laughter in her eyes. The photographer had caught something gentle and sweet in her features, in her full and generous smile. She had been hurt, Rowenna knew, but she had forgiven, because she loved her husband.

The swirling sensation came again, along with that foggy darkness. She was there, but she wasn't. She heard voices again, and she knew that she was hearing Mary Johnstone, feeling what Mary had felt, but when she'd been happy, not as she was now. She was laughing and sliding her hand into Brad's, a sign of the trust she was willing to give.

She was Mary, or she was in Mary's head, and she was walking along the street and then going into the museum.

"There you are."

She was startled back to the present. Dan was standing in front of her.

"I was going to give you up for lost and call it quits for the day," he said.

"Is it five?" Rowenna asked. It couldn't be. She was sure that it hadn't even been four-thirty when Joe dropped her off.

Had she been standing here staring at pictures for over half an hour?

"It's five," Daniel confirmed.

Her cell phone rang. She gave him an apologetic smile and answered it quickly, recognizing Jeremy's number.

"I'm sorry. I'm running late. I'm close to town, though."

"That's okay."

"You *are* at the museum, right?" he asked with a hint of skepticism.

"Yes."

"I arranged for us to meet Brad for drinks at six, at the Hawthorne Hotel."

"Okay, I'll be there."

"Are you alone?"

"I'm with Dan."

"Okay, good."

"Did you come up with anything else?" she asked Daniel once she'd hung up.

He grinned. "Well, I don't know if the cops will think so. They're pretty interested in the here and now. But I think you were right and someone is replaying the past, even though the cops aren't interested in all the details."

"I'm interested."

"You are, aren't you?" he said, and his expression grew sad as he looked at the pictures on the poster. "I saw her, you know, at the Hawthorne bar. I called the police and told them what I could."

Rowenna sucked in a breath.

"Did you see who she was with?"

To her surprise, he nodded. "I described him to the police, and I bet I'm not the only one who'll be able to give a description. It was busy there that night, so someone else is bound to remember them."

"Was the guy…local?" Rowenna asked.

"I've never seen him before, but that doesn't mean he's not from the area."

"What did he look like? Did you ever see him again? Maybe the day Mary Johnstone disappeared?" she asked anxiously.

"I wish I could say that I had, but no. He was tall, good-looking. Built, like he worked out a lot. I got the feeling that he was blue collar. I don't know— mechanic, construction worker, something like that. He had that…bad-boy kind of edge, I guess."

"Blond, dark, white, black, Hispanic, Asian… What?" she asked.

"Blond, white," Daniel said. "Hopefully they'll put a sketch out, someone will recognize him and they'll get him. Quickly, I hope. While Mary's still alive."

She nodded at him and smiled slowly. "I'm glad you think she's still alive, too. Brad believes it, of course, but he almost has to, to keep from going crazy. But I think most people think that she's dead. Especially now that Dinah Green…" She couldn't bring herself to go on. The mental image was bad enough without putting it into words.

He touched her face. "I think *you* think she's alive because you want to," he said softly.

"That's not true. I really believe it."

"You're a good kid," he told her. "But will you be a good queen?" he teased, making an effort to lighten the mood.

She shrugged. "It's hard to think about celebrating anything right now."

"Yeah, but…that's what the world does. It goes on. The seasons will always come and go. Until we blow up the planet, of course," he added dismally. "Well, long day, and longer day tomorrow. I'll see you then, I assume?"

"Yeah, but wait! I want to hear what you found out."

He waved a hand dismissively. "Nothing huge. I'll fill you in tomorrow, okay?"

"Sure, thanks."

His brow furrowed. "Hey, are you all right alone? Should I take you somewhere?"

"No, no, I'm just going up the street."

"Well, be careful."

"I'll stick to the main roads, and I'm only going a few blocks. I'll be fine."

He waved goodbye and started off down the street. She watched him go and hesitated, thinking she should have asked him to walk with her and considering calling him back. But she really was going only a few blocks along sidewalks filled with people, and she couldn't go letting Jeremy and Joe make her afraid of the town she'd lived in all her life.

When she turned the corner, she saw that Adam and Eve hadn't closed up. In fact, there were still several customers in the store.

She noticed that Eve had taken a corner of her display window to put up the police department's request for assistance.

She forced herself not to look at the pictures; she still couldn't understand how she had lost so much time in front of the museum, staring at them. She hadn't been trying to figure out where they had been or what had happened, but somehow her mind had slipped into those channels anyway.

Maybe she *should* try to figure out where Mary was, since she was still alive.

For how long?

A sense of urgency tugged at her. If only she had some magic window or a real crystal ball, or if she could even go into a trance to discover the truth. But she couldn't do that. Despite the way she had felt earlier, the things she had seen, all she had was logic.

All she could do was let herself feel and *become.*

But it was frightening, painful. And she couldn't do it now, not here, and not alone.

She was all set to move on when Eve saw her, waved and hurried outside, offering Rowenna a worried smile.

"What are you doing out here on your own? You're not going to drive home alone, and stay in that big old house all by yourself, are you?"

"I'm staying in town with Jeremy," Rowenna said. "I'm on my way to meet him now."

"Smooth move," Eve said teasingly.

"Eve!"

"Oh, don't get huffy. I know you wouldn't sleep with someone just because you didn't want to go home. Especially not him. I mean, I'd sleep with him without any extra incentive. Wait, that didn't come out right."

"Like you'd ever cheat on Adam."

"I'm married, not dead," Eve said indignantly. "I can look, at least." But she glanced back into the store and frowned.

Rowenna had a feeling that there was a lot more than an argument over what merchandise they carried in their shop creating a rift between Adam and Eve.

"Oh, God," Eve said suddenly, appalled.

"What?"

"I just said *I'm not dead.* And that poor woman… Oh, God, Ro—we met her when she came in the store. She was just here having a good old time, and now…she's dead."

"Dan told me he'd seen her, too."

"She was nice, just like Mary…. She came in and

bought some jewelry." Eve hesitated for a moment, looking unhappy, then shook her head. "She said she lived in Boston and hadn't been up this way in ages. She came here to see the leaves and then…then she died here."

Eve looked stricken, ready to cry.

Rowenna gave her a hug. There was nothing to say.

Eve drew away. "Hey, hurry up. Go meet your guy."

"Are you all right?"

"Of course," Eve said.

"All right, then, go back in, close up," Rowenna told her.

Eve still looked anxious.

"Eve, is something else wrong?" Rowenna asked, worried. She didn't want to get to the bar late and send Jeremy into a panic, but she didn't want to leave her friend standing there, looking so lost.

"Nothing."

"Eve?"

Eve laughed. "Nothing. Really." She looked away, as if trying to hide her feelings. "Nothing you can fix, anyway. So go meet Jeremy, and don't stop along the way to talk to strangers."

"Yes, ma'am. I'll see you tomorrow, okay?"

Eve took a deep, steadying breath, then nodded and ducked back into the store. Rowenna waved and walked on along the pedestrian mall.

The other shops had closed. It seemed impossible, but in a matter of minutes, the streets had cleared.

The chilly autumn breeze suddenly blew. A scattering of leaves whirled up from the pavement, then settled again at her feet. She quickened her pace.

A strange buzzing sound reached her ears, and she

glanced up. A streetlamp was flickering, and as she watched, it buzzed again, burned brightly for a moment, then went out.

A perfectly natural occurrence, she told herself.

There was still plenty of light.

But where there was light, there was also shadow.

Moving quickly now, she looked at the bricks beneath her feet and nearly jumped at the sight of a shadow on the ground.

Of course there was! Her own.

She listened to her own footsteps and wondered if she was hearing a slight echo to each one, as if someone were following and trying to match his footsteps to hers.

The breeze stirred again, and the leaves were swept into a minor cyclone, dancing wildly through the air before falling at her feet with a dry rustle that sounded just like an insinuating whisper.

The shadow was growing, as if she were getting taller, larger. Broader. As if a mountain was looming behind her, massive and dark.

No, it wasn't a mountain, it had a shape.

Like a man, a man in a cape, rising from the bowels of the earth.

Her imagination was taking charge, and even though she knew she was being ridiculous, she quickened her pace even more.

The echo of her footsteps seemed to come a beat too late.

Like a pulse, a heartbeat out of sync.

Fear suddenly swept through her. Somehow whatever was creating the shadow was no longer behind her, but had moved in front of her.

She turned and ran, fleeing the mall along the

nearest side street, knowing she was being forced away from the business district and toward the less populated side of town.

No longer did her pursuer make a pretense of stealth. She *was* being followed.

Every shop, every restaurant she passed was closed and dark.

The footsteps following her now were loud and fast and all too real. She knew they had to belong to a human being, yet it felt as if she were being followed by something more than human, something that whispered of evil.

Where was everyone?

This was leaf season, for God's sake.

A pair of Pilgrim salt-and-pepper shakers smiled benignly from a shop window as she passed. A historic building, closed to the public, was next. The witch memorial was across the street.

And the cemetery.

Bizarrely, the gate was standing open, but why question fate?

It was insane, given what had happened there, but she knew the cemetery so well that she could streak across it, hoping her pursuer would get confused in the dark, maybe even trip on one of the old headstones, while she raced out the other side.

With nowhere else to go and her stalker coming closer, she raced through the gate and past the old tombs and broken stones to the other side, where she came to an abrupt halt.

The evil was no longer behind her.

It was in front of her.

She stood dead still, the pitiful stones marking the

little children's graves to her right, broken stones to her left, an aboveground tomb before her.

And she was aware that someone, something, had somehow herded her to this spot, then managed to circle past her again to block her path and keep her here.

Words whispered through her mind.

"Come closer, closer, bow down before me, come…"

It was in her head. It beckoned. It made her think of a hill, where power and vengeance, life and death, were all to be found.

"Honor me. Worship me…."

The darkness was growing, taking on form and mass, like something living.

There was a tomb just beyond the graves of the little children, and in that thick darkness, the age-old etching began to gleam red—red, the color of blood….

Bloody ink, spelling out the name of the deceased.

Rowenna Eileen Donahue.

13

Brad was waiting at the bar when Jeremy arrived.

He was running his fingers up and down the glass of beer he was drinking, evidently fascinated with the frost that had formed on the outside, but at least he appeared calm and in control.

"Anything?" he asked hopefully, as Jeremy slid onto the stool next to him.

"Not really, but I've had some interesting conversations," Jeremy told him. "How are you doing?"

Brad nodded gravely. Jeremy could tell that he was sober; it looked as if the beer was his first. "I got a copy of the police flier—you know, with the pictures of Dinah Green and Mary." His voice went husky at the end. "I couldn't just sit around all day, so I drove north, stopped in every town I could find and showed the flier to people. Everyone was sympathetic, but no one had seen either one of them."

Jeremy already knew that neither woman had ever gotten north of the area; he knew the trail for both had ended right here. But Brad was right; he'd needed to be doing something, and it was always a mistake when investigating to count on what you "knew" without eliminating every possibility.

"So what about your conversations?" Brad asked.

The bartender came over with a beer for Jeremy. It was the same guy who'd been on duty before, Hugh. Thirty-something, balding, stocky and pleasant. "Hi, good to see you again," he said.

Jeremy nodded, and thanked the man for his beer.

"So you know she was in here, right?" Brad said, before Jeremy could answer his earlier question. "Dinah Green? Seems like half the town saw her in here with some guy. Big tough-guy type."

The bartender hadn't gone far, and now he moved back over to them, looking at Jeremy, and leaned on the bar, speaking in a confidential tone. "I served her. I served Dinah Green. Did Brad tell you?" he asked. "She drank Cosmos, and the guy was a whiskey, neat."

"So you must have been able to describe him for the cops."

"Yeah. They sent a sketch artist right over, but they're not going to need all that—I had something better to give the cops," he said, clearly pleased with himself.

"The guy's credit card receipt?" Jeremy asked.

Hugh looked deflated, and Jeremy felt immediately sorry for having spoken.

"Yeah. How'd you… Oh, yeah. It's what you do," Hugh said.

"The thing is," Brad said, "and I don't know whether it's a good sign or a bad one, but if this guy—"

"His name is Tim Richardson," Hugh volunteered. "Address in Little Italy, in Boston."

"I wonder if they knew one another back in Boston," Jeremy said.

"The thing is, no one saw Tim Richardson here on Halloween," Brad said, then went on hopefully. "So maybe…maybe Mary is safe somewhere." A tormented look came over his face. "But then, where is she? And why? Mary wouldn't disappear on purpose. I know it. But after finding Dinah's corpse, the cops think all we have to do is find Dinah Green's killer and then we'll find Mary. But if the two cases aren't connected, we're wasting time when we could be looking for Mary while she's still alive. And she *is* still alive. She *has* to be."

"Brad," Jeremy said, setting a hand on his friend's shoulder, "just because Dinah Green was with this guy at the bar, we don't know that he killed her."

"It was the last time she was seen," Brad said stubbornly.

"And he *was* with her," Hugh added.

Jeremy studied Hugh. "Did they leave together?" he asked.

Hugh frowned and flushed. "I don't know," he admitted.

"They were both at the bar, right?" Jeremy asked.

"Yeah, but it got busy real fast that night. I ended up running a few of the tables, too. The guy had paid his tab, and they were still talking when…I served a veal Oscar. Yeah, over there, table two. I could see that the girls were rushed off their feet out on the floor, and one of the kitchen guys brings the food out to the end of the bar when it's busy, so I helped out. So no, I didn't actually see them leave."

"Maybe someone else did," Jeremy said. "Did the police take the receipts from that night?"

"Hey, we're talking weeks ago now—the receipts are all turned in," Hugh said.

"So how did you get the info for the police?" Jeremy asked.

"The computer."

"Can you print me out a list of the receipts for that night? Not now, I know you're working, but later? I can pick it up in the morning."

"Sure." Hugh seemed pleased to be asked. Then he looked past Jeremy and Brad to the door, and a smile lit his face. "Hey, Eric. Good to see you."

Jeremy turned and saw Eric Rolfe coming into the bar. He was alone, and though he was only wearing jeans, a T-shirt and a denim jacket, he looked like a man who had showered and shaved in preparation for a night out. Except for a single autumn leaf sticking out of the top of his left boot.

Brad seemed not to have heard Hugh's greeting, nor to have noticed Eric's arrival.

He was staring morosely at his beer.

"The morning," he said bleakly. "Everything is always something we're going to get to in the morning." He looked at Jeremy. "We're getting nowhere. How many more mornings will Mary have?"

Jeremy's thoughts turned back to the man Hugh had seen with Dinah, even though he didn't know if she'd left with him or not.

Boston wasn't far away. The man could be their killer. Just because Hugh hadn't seen him on Halloween, that didn't mean he hadn't been in town.

Whoever had killed Dinah Green was still on the streets.

Mary was still missing.

And Rowenna hadn't arrived yet.

Jeremy stood abruptly and said goodbye to Brad,

nodding to Eric as he passed and looking once again at the leaf protruding from his boot.

Shower, shave and take a walk in the woods? He didn't think so.

He wanted to grab the man as he walked by, shake him and demand to know where he was keeping Mary Johnstone. Somehow, he refrained. Until he had more to go on than a hinky feeling and a stray leaf, he was going to have to hang back. Meanwhile, he was worried about Rowenna, anxious to get to the street and take the shortest route from the bar to the museum.

"No." It was only a whisper of protest. She was too shocked to manage anything more.

That was her name.

On a tombstone.

And there was a shadow in the cemetery, taunting her, calling to her.

No. It was all in her mind.

It was nothing but the power of suggestion, nothing real, only her fears given substance by her own traitorous mind.

It was as if the skills she used when she put herself in a victim's place, feeling what had happened, using logic and intuition to let her imagination run free, had suddenly all turned inward and created a monster from all the fears that had been haunting her. Perception was truth and reality, so now she had to change her perception and defeat this shadow monster.

She'd been in this cemetery a hundred times. Her name wasn't on any tombstone. And she wasn't going to be anyone's victim, not even the Devil himself if he had risen from hell just to find her.

"No," she said loudly and firmly, staring into the dark graveyard.

It was empty. No one was there, not even a shadow.

She stared back at the stone where she had so clearly seen her name in blood.

There was nothing there.

The moon came out from behind a cloud, dispelling the darkness that had seemed so tangible only moments before. In the silver light she could see autumn leaves lying on the ground, and when she examined the stone, the writing that was the only memorial to some stranger's death was too eroded by the passage of time to say anything, much less her name. The breeze blew lightly, and when she looked around, there was no one else in the cemetery, real or imagined.

Then, suddenly, she heard her name called in a real, solid and worried voice.

"Rowenna?"

She spun around.

"Hey, Rowenna, are you all right?"

Adam Llewellyn was standing by the gate—closed now, she noticed, but she wasn't going to dwell on the strangeness of that—as if he were afraid to venture into the graveyard by night. He was staring at her as if she had lost her mind.

Had she?

As she stared at him, a couple, hand in hand, came walking down the street, talking about the restaurant they were heading to.

A car passed along the nearby street, its headlights cutting reassuringly through the darkness.

It was just a night like every other night.

A man was passing the wax museum, walking a yapping Pekingese. Big guy, small dog.

"Ro?" Adam asked again.

She squared her shoulders and strode quickly in his direction, and made it easily to the low wall.

"Adam, hi. Were you following me?" she asked, studying him. He was just Adam, the same Adam she had known for years.

Had he just helped save her from her own mind— or from someone or something else? Or was he somehow involved in whatever had just happened to her? She dismissed the idea out of hand. Nothing could be more ridiculous.

"I was trying to catch up with you," he told her, still looking confused.

"Did you see anyone else?" she asked him, and though she tried to sound calm, even blasé, she knew there was an edge of hysteria in her voice.

He seemed troubled by her question, and he gave it some thought. "Um, Libby Marston was closing up her shop, but the streets were pretty quiet." He shrugged. "I'm sorry if I scared you, though," he said. "Ro, especially after everything that's happened, why would you climb over the wall to get into the cemetery at night?"

"I didn't climb the wall. I went through the gate. It was open."

He lowered his head, but she saw his brow arch skeptically before he did so. He didn't believe that the gate had been left open. They didn't like graveyard ghouls around here—people who thought it was cool to hang around with the dead at night.

This was just Adam, she told herself. Her good friend's husband, her own friend.

And now, with him standing there, the two of them chatting, cars passing in the background, pedestrians going by, the whole night felt surreal.

And yet, like the books at the museum, something to think about.

"Never mind," she said. "I just thought I saw…someone."

"In the graveyard? At night?"

"Why were you following me? Do you need something from me?" she asked. "Because you scared me."

"I didn't mean to scare you. I'm sorry."

He shook his head. "Ro, if you think you're being chased, running into a dark cemetery is not a good idea. Especially not when Mary Johnstone disappeared from that same cemetery."

She opened her mouth to speak, then closed it again. How could she possibly explain that she knew it had been a stupid thing to do, but she had been *chased* here, given nowhere else to go?

She would never be able to explain it. She didn't understand it herself.

"Whatever. Hey, I need to go meet Jeremy. Walk with me?" She hated the tremor in her voice as she asked, but she couldn't help it. She was spooked.

"Sure," he told her.

"Wait—where's Eve?"

"At the store, unpacking a box of Thanksgiving stuff. Interested in a gravy ladle shaped like a Pilgrim?" When she shook her head and laughed, he added, "How about an Indian?"

"Just don't let her leave there alone, okay?" Rowenna said, suddenly sober.

"Don't worry. I won't. Now come on, I'll walk with you," he said.

She was glad of his company. "So why were you following me?" she inquired as they headed toward the hotel.

"I'm worried about Eve," he admitted.

"What?" she asked, shocked. Eve was worried about Adam, and now *he* was worried about *her?* "Why?"

"I don't know what's up with her lately. Just because I think Eric Rolfe's masks are incredible and thought we should carry books about Alistair Crowley and Satanism, she thinks I've become something evil. I don't understand her. Eve and I always shared our thoughts, talked about everything that interested us. And now…it's as if she's turned into a little old lady with a mind-set straight from the sixteen hundreds." Adam frowned as he spoke, looking truly mystified. "She keeps on saying how worried she is about me."

"Have you given her anything to worry about?"

"No," Adam said firmly. "But all we do now is argue. And sometimes she looks at me as if I'm not a person anymore. The other night, when I touched her, she flinched. I don't know. I love my wife, I really do. I've loved her since we were kids."

Rowenna grinned. "And I care about both of you, you know that. But it sounds as if maybe you two should see a marriage counselor."

"Yeah, maybe," he said. "But if she comes to you about me, please, let her know how much I love her."

"Of course," she promised.

Adam had stopped walking. They were at the corner and the hotel was just across the street.

"I'll watch you go in, then go back for Eve," he said.

"Thanks," she told him. "It's—it's okay. There's a doorman outside. I'll be fine. You go on."

"I'm watching till you're inside," he told her. "So don't waste time arguing with me."

The light changed, and a car stopped right in front of her, with another car stopping behind it. Suddenly there seemed to be people everywhere.

Some were even gathered around one of the hotel's front windows, reading the same missing persons poster that was up all over town.

The murmur of life was all around her.

She felt embarrassed. The fear that had sent her racing through the dark earlier seemed foolish, the curse of having too much imagination.

She squared her shoulders, smoothed back her hair and crossed the street. Just as she reached for the door to the bar, Jeremy came bursting out, a frown deeply etched between his brows. It eased the second he saw her.

He gripped her shoulders and pulled her close for a moment. She smelled the rich leather of his jacket, sensed the vibrant tension in his body, and she felt a bit like melting. It was too good. Too good to be true…

No, it was horrible. He was only here because his friend had disappeared and another woman was dead.

Still, for the moment, he was tall, handsome, solid and, most of all, real, so she smiled, determined *never* to tell him that she'd thought she was being chased by an evil shadow and had run into the cemetery to avoid it. He wouldn't understand. He *couldn't* understand. Real was real to him. The imagination was…suspect.

Yet he sleepwalked and talked to people who were only there in his dreams.

"Sorry, I got worried when you didn't show up," he told her.

She smiled, and kept that smile plastered to her face.

She knew she should tell him the truth, even if he thought she was ridiculous. And anyway, maybe he wouldn't. Maybe he would want to comb the streets, looking for whoever might have been terrorizing her.

It was too late, though. If anyone really had been chasing her—if it hadn't just been the combination of darkness, the blown streetlamp and her nightmares preying on her mind—he was long gone by now.

Maybe sitting in some bar already, swilling down a beer.

"Sorry," she told him. "Adam and Eve were just closing up, and she came out to chat. I knew you'd be worried. I should have extricated myself a bit faster."

He held the door, and she stepped inside ahead of him. She recognized Eric Rolfe—thinner now, but still clearly the same guy she had known in high school—immediately and hurried over to say hi. He recognized her, too, and rose and gave her a big bear hug. Then he stepped back, and she saw him looking over her shoulder.

At Jeremy.

"Your friend thinks I'm a murderer. He doesn't like my masks," he whispered.

Rowenna glanced back at Jeremy. To all outward appearances, he looked casual, just a guy out for a drink with friends, but she already knew him too well to be fooled. She could almost see the tension radiating from him and filling the air. He really didn't trust Eric, she realized.

She wanted to tell him that she'd known Eric since she was a kid.

Then again, she had grown up here. She'd known a lot of the locals since she'd been a kid.

And their killer was a local, she thought, then shivered.

Jeremy's phone rang. He waved at her to excuse himself and stepped through a side door into the hotel lobby.

Eric followed Jeremy's progress, then looked down into Rowenna's eyes. "Great timing on my part, huh? No sooner do I come back into town, bringing my masks with me, than a woman gets murdered and staked out in a cornfield right near my house. But come on. You know me. How can anyone see me as a killer?"

"Eric, I'm pretty sure they're talking to a lot of people," she said. "And Jeremy's a good guy. Really."

He rolled his eyes, then grinned at her. "He's good-looking, I'll give you that."

She laughed.

"You two an item?"

"Yes." She could feel herself blushing. Talk about ridiculous…

"Good. He looks like the protective type. Not a bad thing, what with everything going on around here. I bet he's good with a gun," he said speculatively.

"He is, and he also plays the guitar," Rowenna said.

Eric laughed. "Sorry, I just find that a little hard to picture. He's a pretty scary guy, if you want to know the truth." He dropped his voice. "Not like me. I needed my scarecrows back in high school because most of the guys thought I was a fag. I had to scare them somehow."

"So how are you doing *now?*" she asked him with a smile. "I haven't seen you in ages. Hollywood treating you well?"

He laughed. "It is, actually. I'm on an A-list for effects guys. I get paid really well to be my creepy self." He grinned. "Not to make light of that fifty bucks I won for best scarecrow or anything. How about you? I've seen your name on the bestseller list. We've both made it. Cool, huh?"

She smiled. "Well, there's high school, and then there's real life."

"Ain't that the truth?" he said, and winked. "Have a seat. I want to check out your boyfriend's artistic side."

"Oh, Eric, I don't think—"

"Sit."

He pulled out a chair, so she sat and watched him as he walked over to the band that was just setting up to play, motioning to the keyboard player.

She looked for Jeremy, but he hadn't reappeared. Brad was at the bar, talking to Hugh.

She got up and walked over to the bar. "Brad, how are you doing?" she asked him.

"I'm okay," he said, but he didn't sound okay.

"Hey, Hugh," she said, smiling.

"Hey, Ro," Hugh replied, then headed off to serve another customer.

Brad leaned over and whispered something to her, but she couldn't make out what he said.

"What?"

"Is he a witch?"

"Hugh?"

"Yeah."

"No."

"You know what?"

"What?"

"There's something really freaky going on around here. I mean it. And I'm not just saying that because I'm drunk. Because I'm not. Drunk, I mean. The thing is…"

"The thing is what?" she asked.

Brad looked grave. "Jeremy doesn't believe me. I know he doesn't."

"What are you talking about, Brad?" she asked. "What doesn't Jeremy believe?"

"Satan," he said seriously.

"What?"

"The Devil. The Devil is here. I'm telling you, the Puritans weren't crazy. The Devil is alive, and he's here." He looked around the room, then back at her. "He could be right here, drinking with us, right now," he said gravely.

"…last name's Richardson," Joe was saying over the phone. "There was no problem. He hadn't disappeared, wasn't in hiding. The Boston police picked him up coming off his shift—he's a construction worker. He's claiming he's innocent, of course, that they don't know what they're talking about, that it's not illegal to flirt and buy a girl a drink."

Jeremy was glad he had moved out of the bar, into the hotel lobby. In the bar, he couldn't hear.

And he didn't want to be heard.

"Has he gotten a lawyer? They can't hold him very long, not unless they have something to charge him with."

"They can keep him in the lockup overnight. They told him he could get a lawyer, of course, but it seems he thinks if he exercises his constitutional right and gets a lawyer, he'll look guilty," Joe explained. "So…bright and early?"

Jeremy was surprised that Joe seemed to have taken him on as a de facto partner, but he wasn't about to look a gift horse in the mouth. Maybe it was just Joe's way of watching him.

"Yeah, thanks," Jeremy said. "But back up. This guy admits to spending the day in Salem with Dinah Green?"

"Yup. He recognized her picture right away. But he denied knowing anything about what might have happened to her."

"He could be telling the truth."

"Most murderers deny their guilt," Joe said. "Hell, he was with the woman most of the day. We have his charge slip from the bar."

"Yes, but—"

"He can't prove where he was on Halloween. Boston is a short hop away. His shift ends at three-thirty. He could easily have gotten up here in time to grab Mary," Joe said.

That was true enough. Jeremy just didn't think it gelled. Why? he asked himself. There was no reason, nothing but his gut feeling that the murderer was somebody local.

No, there was evidence of a sort: the cornfields. No one but a local would know the fields well enough to have pulled off that scarecrow scene. It was logic, plain and simple.

If only it *were* Tim Richardson. Then they could— maybe—find Mary alive. They could end the fear, and he could stop looking at every person he met on the street—at Rowenna's friends—and wondering which one of them was a monster.

"Bright and early," Joe said again.

"See you then. Thanks."

He hung up, not certain why he wasn't more interested in a trip to Boston to question a possible murderer.

He knew the answer.

He didn't want to leave here.

Why not?

He knew that answer, too.

Because Rowenna could be in danger.

He hesitated, about to call Joe back and tell him to go without him, but before he could dial, his phone rang again. He looked at the number and smiled.

"Hey, bro."

"Zach, good to hear from you," Jeremy said.

"Yeah? Hope so. Aidan and I were just talking. We've been watching the news—about the corpse found in the field."

"There's a real maniac on the loose," Jeremy said.

"Sure looks like it. No sign of Mary, huh?"

"Not yet. I feel—I *think* the killer is local, and I think we're getting closer to narrowing down our list of suspects."

"We?"

"The lead detective on the case, Joe Brentwood. He's let me in every step of the way. That's been a real blessing." He hesitated and shrugged, though his brother couldn't see it, or the grudging smile that tugged at his lips. "He even listens to me."

"Great," Zach said. "Listen, I can come up, if you'd like."

"Hell, yes!" Jeremy said. With Zach there, he wouldn't constantly worry about leaving Rowenna on her own. He could go with Joe in the morning, knowing Rowenna would be with friends, or even Brad. Undoubtedly Zach could book a flight that would get him in by tomorrow night.

"You can catch me up when I get there," Zach said.

"I'll be asking you to do some bodyguard duty, if you don't mind."

He heard his brother's soft chuckle. "So long as I'll be guarding a beautiful woman with black hair and amber eyes, that won't be a problem," Zach assured him.

Jeremy grinned. "Great. Get here as soon as you can."

He hung up and leaned against the wall. There was no one he trusted like his brother. He could accompany Joe tomorrow morning with a clear conscience. And after all, they would only be gone a few hours.

He looked up, still smiling…

…and froze.

A boy was standing against the opposite wall, near the check-in desk.

He was about ten, with brown eyes, and tousled brown hair, wearing jeans and a T-shirt.

"Billy," Jeremy breathed.

The boy stared at him solemnly, a hesitant smile flickering across his lips.

A heavyset man passed in front of Jeremy, who moved to the side, trying to reach the boy. Then a luggage cart blocked him, a bellman and young couple alongside it.

When they had passed, the boy was no longer there.

Jeremy strode to the front door and then out to the street. He looked in every direction. There were plenty of people out, taking advantage of the mild autumn night.

But there was no sign of a boy.

Swearing softly, he headed down the street and around the corner.

A sightseeing carriage, drawn by a single horse, the driver a pretty woman with reddish-blond hair, rumbled by. He could see a hearse leaving the mortuary down the street, and a group of uniformed high-school-band members were heading back from the green, two chaperones in the lead, two more in the rear.

Life still went on, obviously, but under supervision. No one was feeling lax regarding security these days.

He walked around the back of the hotel, through the parking lot, and looked down the street with its tree-lined median. It was dark, and, except for a few people walking dogs, there was no activity going on.

And there was no boy.

He turned and walked back into the lobby, looking thoughtfully toward the elevators.

He told himself that he had simply seen a boy who looked like Billy, and who had gone up to his room. Squaring his shoulders, he reminded himself that there was nothing he could do for Billy, but there was a good chance Mary was still alive, which meant there were things he *could* do for *her.* He also reminded himself that Brad and Rowenna were waiting for him in the bar.

He strode back in, shrugging his shoulders as if, in doing so, he could shake off the memory of the boy he had failed.

14

Rowenna was glad to see Jeremy walk back into the bar. She was trying to be supportive, but she was having a hard time putting any more credence in Brad's theory about the Devil than Jeremy had. She'd tried to get him to order some food, thinking dinner might take his mind off his dire thoughts, but he'd announced that he wasn't hungry.

He was Jeremy's friend, and Jeremy could no doubt deal with him better than she could. She didn't want to admit it, but...

He'd been creeping her the hell out.

"Who was that?" she asked Jeremy as soon as he arrived, glad to have him back by her side. It occurred to her almost immediately that his phone call might have been private, that she was barely a part of his life, and he might just tell her it was none of her business.

But he answered right away, looking thoughtful and a little distracted. "That was Joe," he told her. "First."

She inclined her head, waiting.

Brad, too, had perked up to listen.

"They've found the guy who was with Dinah Green here at the bar. The Boston cops picked him up."

"Oh, my God, has he said anything?" Brad demanded. "Does he have Mary?"

"He claims he wasn't here on Halloween, that he spent the night with a hooker in Boston. They're holding him, and I'm driving down with Joe to talk to him."

"When?" Brad asked anxiously.

"First thing in the morning."

"I'm going, too," Brad said.

"No, you're not. You're too emotionally invested to be in on this, Brad," Jeremy told him, his tone compassionate but firm. "I'm lucky Joe is letting me go along, and you know I'll ask all the right things." Then he hesitated. "Besides, I'm sure he didn't do it," he said after a moment. "But we have to clear him so we can get down to figuring out what *did* happen."

Rowenna frowned, looking at him. "How do you know he didn't do it?" she asked. "How can you be so sure?" She would like nothing better than to find out that some Boston guy was the killer, because she hated the thought that someone she might know, might even think she knew well, could be the psychopath they were seeking.

"Our killer has too much local knowledge, for one thing. And for another… Gut feeling, and I've been around too long to ignore that," he told her. He glanced toward the band, and at Eric Rolfe, who was talking to the keyboard player. "We need to be looking for a local, someone who knows who owns what land, who manages it and knows what's going on with it. Ginny MacElroy may own that land, but she doesn't go walking around her fields making sure her corn is growing well. She leaves that to the real farmers, and I doubt they inspect it daily, either, as if their lives depend on every stalk out there."

"The cornfields," Brad said, turning to look at them solemnly. "I'm going to walk through every damn one of those cornfields if I have to."

"Brad, everyone who has anything to do with those fields has been alerted. They've been searching the fields for days," Jeremy told him. "And they haven't found...anything."

Another body. That was what he'd been about to say, Rowenna thought. Mary's body.

"I'm losing my mind," Brad said. "I can't stand it. Not knowing where she is, how she is, believing she's alive—and knowing that every moment nothing is done brings her closer to death."

Rowenna's heart went out to him.

"That's always the hardest part," Jeremy said. "You know that. The waiting. Think of the hours that we've sat around together, scuba gear on, scuba gear off, waiting. Dive here, dive there. And then the next day, try farther over there. Or for the guys working the streets, it's watch that house, a pedophile lives there. Watch him. And then you go crazy with the boredom of sitting and sitting, and drinking coffee, and trying to stay awake. And then you get your chance. We're doing everything right, Brad. We stick to the plan, we eliminate everything we can, we follow every clue—and we'll find her."

Brad stared at Jeremy and nodded, as if trying to believe.

Just then Eric walked up behind Jeremy and laid a hand on his shoulder. Jeremy turned to look at him, and Brad followed suit. Eric didn't seem to notice the way Brad's eyes narrowed at the sight of him.

"I hear he makes devil masks," Brad whispered to Rowenna.

"Yes, he makes masks. Relax, Brad," Rowenna whispered back.

"Mr. Flynn," Eric said, "I've heard that you're an amazing guitarist. The band over there wants you to sit in."

There was a dead, flat look in Jeremy's eyes for a moment. He turned to stare at her—as if it were *her* fault, she thought. Then something in his expression changed, and she was coming to know him so well, she realized, that she actually knew what he was thinking: that it wouldn't hurt to get tight with the locals.

Even the locals on his list of suspects—or perhaps *especially* the locals on his list of suspects.

Then he got up and walked over to the band, talked with them for a minute and picked up an extra guitar.

He really could play, Rowenna thought, remembering the times when she had seen him sit in with one of the bands on Bourbon Street in New Orleans.

She had wondered if he would touch a woman with the same knowledge and tenderness as he gave to a guitar.

And now she knew.

"Shit," Eric said. "He *can* play."

"Of course he can play," Brad said indignantly, then looked at Eric and laughed. "You were hoping he'd make a fool out of himself."

"No!" Eric protested. "Well, okay…yeah, I was."

He wandered off, closer to the stage. Rowenna felt Brad staring at her.

"When are we going to find her? Will we find her *soon?*" he asked intently.

She felt a flow of crimson come to her cheeks. "Brad, I'm not sure what you think I can tell you."

"I think you know things," he said. "You told me not to give up hope. You keep saying she's alive."

"And I do believe she's alive."

"But we have to find her quickly."

"Yes," she agreed.

He grabbed her hand. "If there's anything, anything at all, that you can do, please, I'm begging you, do it."

"I will, Brad. You know I will."

His sense of urgency filled her, and she felt dread settle heavy in her heart. Time was of the essence. And the thing was, she had a feeling that there *was* something she could do. She just didn't want to do it.

The answer lay in the cemetery. She was sure of it.

Just as the thought came to her, she noticed Adam and Eve entering the restaurant, and for once they weren't arguing.

Daniel came in by himself behind them, said something to them, and then the three of them sat down at a table together. She was surprised, given that they weren't great friends, despite having known each other a long time. Daniel had a tendency to air his feeling about "failed Catholics" embracing pagan beliefs as a way to make money.

He looked up and saw her at the bar, waved, then looked around. He seemed surprised to see Jeremy playing with the band, and he drew Adam and Eve's attention to the musicians.

Eve grinned, then looked over at Rowenna and gave her a thumbs-up sign. A moment later, Daniel spotted Eric and walked over to where the other man was sitting. They chatted for a minute; then Daniel pointed out the table where he was sitting with Adam and Eve. Eric shrugged, and accompanied him back over to join their group.

More people began to file in, some going straight to the bar for a drink, others filling the tables and perusing the dinner menu.

When Rowenna saw Ginny and Dr. MacElroy enter, she nearly fell off her bar stool. It was almost as if people were flocking in just to be together and try to forget the horror that had touched their once-safe little town. She hadn't seen Dr. MacElroy in a while, so she excused herself to Brad, and walked over to the table Doc and Ginny had just taken.

"Rowenna, so nice to see you." Ginny's face brightened at the sight of her.

"Rowenna, hello." Dr. MacElroy had just taken his seat, but he rose, smiling. His given name was Nick, but he had been her pediatrician when she was a child and she could never bring herself to refer to him as anything other than Doc or Dr. MacElroy, especially to his face.

He welcomed her with a grandfatherly hug, then he held her away for a moment, studying her as if she were still a child and might have grown since he'd last seen her. "You look as lovely as always. Ginny says you're doing well."

"Very well, thank you."

Doc MacElroy was slim and dignified. His hair was thinning and white, his eyes a powder blue, like Ginny's. He held out a chair for her, and she perched on the edge, explaining that she could only stay for a second, because she was with friends.

"Nasty business, this. Very nasty business," Dr. MacElroy said sadly, shaking his head. "You sure you're all right? Ginny said you found that poor woman's body."

"I'm okay. Really."

"Your young man came by," Ginny explained to her, a sparkle in her eyes. "He'd been out to meet Eric, so he dropped by to see me, too. He knew *I* hadn't been out there running around in the corn, but he hoped maybe I had heard something, seen a car, anything unusual. But I'm afraid I'm a homebody and never notice much of anything outside the house."

"She watches game shows with the TV on full blast," Dr. MacElroy said fondly. "Of course she never notices anything."

"But I *do* own that land. Father left it to me," Ginny fretted.

"Ginny, please, you can't let that worry you," Rowenna told her.

"She's been upset ever since, well, you know. So I thought a nice dinner out would be a good idea," Dr. MacElroy said, looking around the room. "I'm seeing half of my patients in here tonight—all grown up now, of course. Time does fly," he added softly.

"And to think I've lived to see a time like this," Ginny said. "It makes you wonder what this world is coming to."

"Ginny, bad things can happen anywhere," Rowenna said. After all, she thought ironically, the witch trials certainly counted as bad things.

"At least the harvest festival is coming up to take people's minds off things," Ginny said. "I'm helping out with the costumes this year, and I've made a beautiful dress for you." She frowned. "You'll have to come by soon. The festival starts in a few days."

"Of course. Day after tomorrow, will that be all right?" Rowenna wanted to get back to her research tomorrow.

Ginny nodded. "So long as I have time for alterations, anything suits my schedule."

Dr. MacElroy nodded toward the band. "Is that your young fellow playing the guitar, Rowenna?"

She smiled. It seemed so strange to hear Jeremy referred to as hers.

"That's Jeremy Flynn, yes," Rowenna said. "Well, I've left Brad alone at the bar long enough. I'd better get back."

"Of course. Good to see you home," Dr. MacElroy said.

"And it's good to see you out, Ginny," Rowenna said.

"We were out not so long ago. Halloween night, and it was lovely." She frowned suddenly. "That was the night that poor woman disappeared. Your friend must be in agony, wondering if they're going to find her in a cornfield, too. Oh!"

She broke off, staring in horror. Rowenna turned to see what Ginny was looking at, but the only thing she could see was a column.

"Ginny, what is it?" Dr. MacElroy asked in concern, clearly as puzzled as Rowenna was.

Ginny stared from one of them to the other. "Lights. I saw lights."

Rowenna and Dr. MacElroy exchanged worried glances.

"Oh, stop it, you two! I haven't gone daft. I just thought of it suddenly, being here, talking about that woman. I haven't heard anything, but the other night, I woke up and looked out toward the northwest, and I swear, there were wiggly-waggly lights out there, like a UFO."

"Ginny, there's nothing out there but brushland," Dr. MacElroy said.

Ginny turned to Rowenna. "You make sure you tell that man of yours what I said. He told me it was important to tell him anything—anything at all—that came to mind."

"Of course I will, Ginny. Thank you," Rowenna said.

She left them at last, and paused on her way back to the bar to say hello to Adam, Eve and Daniel. Eve kissed her cheek and said, "He's really good," as she tilted her head in Jeremy's direction.

"A regular rock star," Adam said, smiling, then asked, "How did Ginny seem to you?"

"Fine, why?"

Adam shook his head. "I don't know, I think she's starting to slip. I'm kind of worried about her. She called me at midnight about a week ago, asking about a costume, and thought it was early evening."

"Ginny will be fine. I'm helping her with the details," Eve told him, her voice cool. They might be trying to appear as if everything was copacetic in public, Rowenna thought, but Eve still wasn't happy.

And everything seemed to come back to the Harvest Festival.

Rowenna glanced at the bar. "Excuse me, will you? Brad seems to be slipping into his beer. I'm going to go back and keep him company."

"Of course," Eve said sympathetically.

When Rowenna returned to her stool, Brad was so deep in his thoughts that he didn't even notice her at first.

"Here you go, Ro," Hugh said, setting a cold beer in front of her. "On the house," he added.

She smiled her thanks and touched Brad's shoulder.

He jumped, then looked at her with anguished eyes. "Sorry. The waiting is getting to me. The not knowing."

She nodded. "But you're a cop. You know how investigations work, and that's got to help."

He straightened and nodded back. "Don't worry. I won't fall apart." He turned on his stool, and watched Jeremy and the others playing. "I wish I played guitar," he said, pointing at Jeremy with his beer bottle. "He works things out in his head when he plays, did you know that?"

"I wish I could play an instrument, too," she told him.

"You're great the way you are, Rowenna. You don't need to be more."

"Thank you."

He pointed to the table where Eric, Daniel, Adam and Eve were sitting. "But," he said, his words slurring just the tiniest bit, "you sure as hell have some really weird friends. I mean, they're nice enough, but…they're kind of scary-weird." He turned back to the bar. "Except for Hugh, here. Hugh's normal. He likes a good beer and a football game, and he doesn't worship trees. Right, Hugh?"

Hugh looked apologetically at Rowenna. "Um, right, Brad." He moved away, looking uncomfortable.

"Let's just listen to Jeremy," she suggested.

"One of them could be the Devil," Brad whispered.

"Brad, seriously, they're all just people," she assured him.

"I'm sorry," he told her.

He didn't say anything else, and she couldn't help but wonder, glancing over at the table where her friends were sitting, just what he'd been apologizing for.

Was he sorry that he had insulted her friends?

Sorry that her friends were weird?

Or sorry because one of her friends was the Devil?

She silently thanked God when Jeremy, to the sound of applause from the audience and thanks from the band, returned to them after the next number. When he reached the bar, he told her that he was famished and they needed to order dinner.

Brad needed to eat, she thought. He'd been drinking too fast and too long without anything to eat.

"I'm not hungry," Brad protested

"I am," Jeremy said. "So we're going to have dinner."

They moved to a table, and Jeremy watched people while they ate. He waved to Ginny, and asked Rowenna to introduce him to Dr. MacElroy, which she did when the two of them stopped by their table as they were leaving. Ginny spoke encouragingly to Brad, while Dr. MacElroy seemed to study Jeremy just as Jeremy studied him.

"Did you tell him?" Ginny asked Rowenna anxiously. "Did you tell him what I saw?"

Jeremy looked at Rowenna, his expression inquiring.

"No, not yet," Rowenna admitted.

"Lights," Ginny told Jeremy gravely.

"Lights?"

"In the night—just like a UFO," Ginny said. "To the northwest of our house—and Rowenna's, too. I forgot all about them until tonight."

Dr. MacElroy looked uncomfortable, as if embarrassed for Ginny.

But Jeremy thanked her solemnly and asked, "When did you see them?"

"Well, I'm not sure. Let me think…. Oh, dear. I'm so sorry. I think I've noticed them a few times. I just don't know how I could have forgotten."

"Don't worry about it," Jeremy said reassuringly. "And thank you very much. If you see them again, will you let me know?"

"Of course," Ginny promised gravely. "Of course."

"Good night, then," Dr. MacElroy said, and he and Ginny exited.

"UFOs?" Brad said wearily as they walked away. "Give me a break."

"Lights to the northwest. What's out there, Rowenna?" Jeremy asked.

"Nothing. Just brush. It's not even good farmland," she told him. "And, Jeremy…" She hesitated to say anything, but it really did sound as if maybe Ginny was losing it a bit.

"What?" he asked.

"I hate to say it, but I think maybe Ginny's getting a little senile, so you…you might not want to put too much stock in what she says."

Jeremy didn't say anything. He just looked thoughtful as he started eating again.

Eventually they finished their meals, walked Brad back to his B and B and then went on toward the house Jeremy had rented.

"What a strange night," Rowenna said. "I don't think I've ever seen that many locals all there at once.…"

"Interesting," Jeremy agreed.

He looked pensive, though, and he sounded distracted.

"What are you thinking?" she asked after a long silence.

"Just that…I think interviewing this guy tomorrow is going to be a waste of time."

"But he was the last person seen with her."

"If his alibi checked out, he'd be walking and I wouldn't even be going," Jeremy said. "Even so, they don't have any hard evidence, and they can't hold him past tomorrow, so this is the one chance we have to talk to the guy. And who knows? I don't think he killed her, but maybe he'll remember something that points in the right direction. The thing is…"

"What?"

"I know our killer's local, and I can't help feeling that there's something I should be seeing, but I'm just not seeing it."

"You grilled Eric today, I hear."

"I'm not a detective," he said, his tone dry as he gazed her way. "I don't 'grill' anyone."

She hesitated, then said, "It's possible that the man you're going to talk to has just studied the area. I mean, Boston is only thirty miles away. If traffic's not bad—"

He laughed. "When is the traffic near any large city *ever* not bad?"

"Four in the morning?" she joked. "Seriously, maybe it *is* this guy."

He mulled that over, then shook his head. "Brad is convinced it's Damien. The guy with the crystal ball. The problem is, no one has been able to find him. He never applied for a permit, so there's no paper trail. He came to town, he disappeared. Do you know what that means?"

"No, what?"

"That Damien isn't really named Damien. I'd guarantee it. I was thinking about it the whole time I was playing, going over everything we know, everything we don't know and all our dead ends. First, the guy is incredibly smart. He knows the area, knows when things will be so busy that he can put on an entire charade, complete with tent, and no one will notice. Then, he knows enough to cover his tracks. Dinah Green was sexually assaulted, but they couldn't find DNA, they couldn't get a scraping from beneath her nails, they couldn't find a single fiber that told them anything. Then Mary disappears from the only deserted place in town on a massively busy day. He didn't go underground with her—there are no secret passages to the street from the graveyard. That means he knows just how crazy Halloween is going to be, so once he gets her out of there, who's going to notice some guy in costume with a woman over his shoulder or tucked against him like she's drunk or whatever he did. The thing is…" He paused, took a deep breath and finished the thought. "I'm afraid that if we don't solve this quickly, Mary will run out of time."

They had reached the house. He looked at her and said, "You didn't get home today, did you?"

"No—but I'll have to at some point. I bought these clothes at Adam and Eve's, and I got some extra underwear, so I'm covered for tomorrow, but after that, I'll have to go home."

He nodded. "Do you want to drive into Boston with Joe and me tomorrow?" he asked.

She shook her head. "I know you think I'm looking for something that can't possibly exist, but I want to keep researching. There are books at the History Museum I haven't even opened yet."

"I wish I could send Brad with you," he said.

"You can," she said. She did like the guy, and sober, he was fine.

"I can try. Brad is a doer, not a reader, I'm afraid."

"Just tell him to come get me for breakfast, because you're worried about me, and that he has to walk me to the museum and keep an eye on me. That will make him feel like he's doing something," Rowenna suggested.

"I like that," Jeremy said. "I should be back around lunchtime, anyway. And Zach will get here at some point tomorrow, too."

"Zach?" she said. "Here?"

He nodded. "I guess I got sidetracked. After I talked to Joe, Zach called. He's going to catch a flight up here tomorrow. Once he gets here…well, then I won't have to worry about you so much."

"You don't have to worry about me now," she said. "I don't really need protecting during the day in my own stomping grounds."

"Look, being careful is…just not being stupid."

"I am *not* stupid."

"I didn't say— Look, forget it, okay? I think I'm just on edge. Zach will be here, and you like Zach," he said.

She thought she heard a touch of bitterness in his voice.

"Of course I like your brother. He's a nice guy," she said coolly, wondering about the bitterness in his tone. Had he thought she didn't like him?

He pushed the door open. She preceded him in.

As soon as they were inside, he spun her around and into his arms. At first she felt as if everything within her constricted. She was angry, and she couldn't help it. She wanted to tell him that she liked his brother, but she had fantasized about *him*. It wasn't her fault he had been so distant with her until that last night in New Orleans.

"Hey," he said huskily when she pulled back and stared up at him. "Hey."

It wasn't an apology, but his eyes held the words that he couldn't quite seem to manage to say.

She melted.

He closed the door, and it was as if they tacitly agreed that they were closing the door on the outside world of fear and sadness that had sucked them into its vortex all day. Her handbag hit the floor, along with his keys, and then their jackets. She forgot that she had ever been angry, forgot whatever had come between them. The natural intimacy they shared came sweeping back with a vengeance.

He picked her up and started to carry her up the stairs.

He bumped into the wall.

She cracked her head and laughed.

He apologized, and she only laughed harder.

They made it to the second floor, to the bedroom. And then, in the combination of hot, wet kisses and clothes flying every which way, he came upon the skimpy skull underwear she had bought and decided it was sexy. He kissed her through the silk that barely covered her, and the feel of his mouth on her in such intimate ways through the fabric was incredibly sensual. She wanted desperately to return the erotic favor, and she explored his skin with her hands, her fingers stroking, and with her tongue. Then he spanned her waist with his hands, lifting her above him, holding her so that she met his eyes, and he groaned, a deep, husky sound that was nearly as arousing as his touch. He brought her down on the length of his erection with an earth-shattering slowness that drove her wild, and they tangled in the bedclothes. At first she was on top, but then he rolled her beneath him and thrust with a rhythm that made the room fade away. There was nothing left but his body, his breathing, his whispers, and the pressure of him inside her, until she shrieked with the violence of her climax and lay beneath him, heart shuddering as he came seconds later, then cradled her in his arms and slid to her side.

They lay there then in a silence that was precious to her, it was so natural. Then, as their damp bodies began to cool, they teased and laughed, trying to straighten out the covers, which had been left in absolute disarray, finally managing to snuggle together beneath them.

It had been a long day, a very long day, and there was no encore.

She didn't remember trying to fall asleep, she simply *was* asleep, and at first it was deep and pleasant.

And then she was back in the cemetery, listening to a guide she couldn't see talk about the witchcraft trials. He was talking about the way the convicted had been executed on Gallows Hill, explaining that none of them were buried here, in a cemetery for those who had died in God's good graces.

But any cemetery harbored the dead.

And even if it was hallowed ground, the Devil could still sneak in.

And it was there.

The whisper, the shadow, the malice that had come through time to find her.

It was dark, for darkness was the Devil's realm. And she knew it would claw its way free from the earth with skeletal fingers that dripped blood, but those fingers would not be the yellow-white of natural bone but dark, black and red, the colors of blood and death.

The others were still listening to the guide as he told them about the upcoming Harvest Festival, promised that there would be vendors out on the streets selling apples and cider and soup, dolls made from the corn husks and ceramics to dress a Thanksgiving table.

She still couldn't see the guide, but she had to make people understand that they needed to get out. That he had led them there because he drew power from the dead and would use that power against them.

And then she saw him, the guide, the evil, the source of the danger. She couldn't quite make out his face yet, but he was there, a dark figure of menace and malignancy. And…

She knew him.

She knew him, even though he was in costume. A turban around his head, a false mustache and goatee. Makeup accented his eyes, and…she knew he was wearing contact lenses to hide the color, but still, if she just looked closer, she would know….

She stepped forward and was greeted by the sound of laughter, his laughter, swelling in the air and drowning out everything else in the world.

He wanted her to come closer.

He had herded her toward the cemetery before....

And now he was in her dreams, beckoning to her.

She had to stop herself. As much as she wanted to know who he was, she had to stop herself.

She heard a chanting now, rising above the laughter.

"Don't fear the Reaper

Just the Harvest Man.

When he steals a soul

It's a keeper, so

Don't fear the Reaper,

Fear the Harvest Man,

For when he steals a woman's soul

She'll go to hell or deeper...."

The other people were moving away, and he was coming toward her. The others didn't know, she realized. They still thought this was all a performance, part of the festivities.

"Get out!" she cried. "Please, just go!"

He stopped then, angry at her for interfering. He shape-shifted right in front of her. First he was a man, and then he was a demon with horns, the classic image of the Devil: bloodred, his tongue as forked as his long thrashing tail...

Then he was a man again, the stereotypical swami in his turban and long cape flowing as if in the breeze, though the air around her was still, so still.

"You see me," he said. "You can see me."

She didn't know if the words were an invitation or a realization.

"Look," he commanded, pointing.

And there, in front of her, was the tomb.

The tomb that bore her name.

Dread filled her, but she dragged her eyes away

from it to face him again. "You are in my mind. You are only in my mind. You are not real. None of this is real."

He laughed, a high-pitched sound that assaulted her like a weapon.

"You're wrong. I *am* real. And I am here."

The cemetery disappeared in a sudden fog, and then she was no longer there at all. She was in a field.

Rows and rows of cornstalks stretched out before her.

And there were scarecrows. She knew she had to reach the one closest to her, had to see it, and yet it was the last thing she wanted to do.

"Go to it," he whispered in her ear.

Because he, too, was there, in all his dark evil.

But she couldn't go, couldn't look. Because she knew that if she went, if she lifted her eyes to see, she would see herself. She would see that she had been staked out in the cornfield, a sacrifice to his ego and insanity.

"The queen of scarecrows, the queen of blood," he mocked.

"No!"

She had to fight it. She had to fight *him*. He was real, and yet he was not. To best him, she had to fight him in her mind as well as in the real world.

"No!" she said again.

His laughter deepened, and against her will, she found herself moving closer and closer to the scarecrow, knowing that in moments she would see…

Herself.

Blinded by the pecking crows.

Dripping blood…

Feeding the harvest gods.

15

"Rowenna!"

At first Jeremy had been disturbed but not alarmed. She had nightmares that tormented her? He understood. He had his own.

When she was just tossing and turning, he didn't wake her up.

But then her breathing grew shallow. Beneath their delicate lids and long black lashes, her eyes were rolling and in a frenzy.

"Rowenna?" He shook her gently, but when she didn't respond and he drew her into his arms, she was like a rag doll.

"Rowenna?" He laid her back down, straddled her and shook her shoulders firmly.

She gasped, her eyes flying open, and stared at him in raw panic.

"Rowenna, it's me. You were having a nightmare."

She blinked, nodded, then closed her eyes for a long moment. Her rapid breathing began to subside.

"Are you all right?" he asked her.

She tried to smile, but it was a weak effort at best. "I'm fine. That was one hell of a nightmare."

"What was it about?" he asked, lying down by her side again and taking her into his arms.

She was silent for a moment, and he was certain she was carefully crafting her answer.

"All this," she said softly.

"'All this' meaning…? The body in the cornfield? Mary's disappearance?" he asked.

She nodded.

He held her closer.

"You know, you have some terrible dreams, too," she told him.

He shifted slightly. "Yeah, I know. We all have nightmares. Every kid's afraid of the monster in the closet at one time or another."

"Your dreams aren't about a monster in a closet, though, are they?" she asked him.

"I've seen a lot of bad things," he said, shrugging.

She drew away from him, propped herself up on an elbow and stared at him. "I'll show you mine if you show me yours," she teased.

He smiled, and realized that exploring the scary realms within their souls was, for the two of them, more intimate than lying together, sweaty and naked, in bed.

"You haven't really told me yours," he reminded her.

"You just told me—"

"What every woman in the area is probably having nightmares about right now," he said flatly.

"I beg to differ," she told him solemnly. "Every woman in the area did not find that corpse staked out like a scarecrow in the cornfield."

"No," he agreed. "But you're not telling me everything. You were having nightmares before you found that body, weren't you?"

She inhaled, her eyes on his, honest and wide in the shadows of the night. "I dream of the cornfields, the way I used to see them when I was young. I dream of them stretching forever. I see the scarecrows Eric Rolfe used to make—they were terrifying, and so real. I promise you, one day he's going to win the Oscar for special effects—"

"If he's not doing life," Jeremy interrupted her, his tone deadly serious.

She gave him a scathing glance.

"Sorry. Please, go on," he urged her.

"There's not much more. The scarecrows suddenly become real women. Dead. Some of them look at me. And I hear someone talking. He thinks he's the Devil—but he's real."

She spoke the words almost lightly, as if the dreams had no power over her. But he knew she was telling him the truth—and that the dreams terrified her far more than she was willing to admit.

"You know, you're just falling prey to the power of suggestion," he said gently.

"Your turn," she said, ignoring his words.

He arched a brow. "I think there's more."

She shook her head, smiling. "I've given you pretty much the whole of it. That's everything I can remember," she said. "Except sometimes I see the cemetery in my dreams, too."

"Because Mary was last seen in the cemetery, that's why," Jeremy told her.

"Probably." He could hear the edge of doubt in her tone, even though she was trying to hide it.

He frowned suddenly, feeling a little spasm of unease. "You need to stay out of the cemetery."

"Don't worry about me and the cemetery. I've known it since I was a kid. I could probably draw you a map of it with my eyes closed. Now. Your turn," she persisted.

He crooked an elbow behind his head and stared up at the ceiling. "I had awful nightmares after my folks died. I got past those because of Aidan. He kept telling me I had to be strong for Zach. He was the one pulling to keep us all together, so we shaped up fast. The only movies that ever really scared me were the *Nightmare on Elm Street* series, I guess because they made me realize how helpless we are when we're asleep."

"Those movies scared me, too," she assured him. "I think they scared everybody. What I *wasn't* frightened by were all the movies about idiot teenagers who went off exploring the same place where dozens of other idiot teenagers had already been killed. I was never going to be stupid enough to do that." She got a strange look in her eyes then, and she quickly looked down and traced her fingers in a line down his chest, creating a stirring in his groin.

Was she trying to distract him? he wondered. Or herself?

Neither, apparently.

She was being persistent.

"You had a nightmare last night," she said.

"I did?"

"And you were talking to someone in the middle of it."

"Who?"

"I don't know. But I think you do."

He was annoyed to feel color suffusing his cheeks. At least they were in the dark, so she wouldn't see.

He felt strange, though, as he opened his mouth and admitted, "Billy."

"Billy?" she repeated softly, questioningly.

"Well, you know my story already. Billy was the boy who was alive when I reached him. I got him to land, up on the embankment, and gave him CPR. He was alive. His heart was beating, and he had a pulse. I talked to him. I rode with him in the ambulance. I could swear that he looked at me, that he thanked me, that he knew me…and then, at the hospital, he was declared DOA."

"I'm so sorry," she said.

"Being a forensic diver…you see horrible things. You wonder how one human being could ever perpetrate such cruelty on another human being. But there was something about those kids… They never had a chance. They went from one abusive home to another." He was silent for a moment, feeling the empathy in her eyes. "Hell, according to the psychologists, after what they'd been through, they probably would have grown up to be monsters themselves."

"You don't believe that."

"I believe it can happen. I also believe that we're all responsible for ourselves. That whatever went on when we were young, once we're adults, we have to get over it and become the people we want to be."

She rested her head on his chest. "And what about others?" she asked. "Can we make them into what we want them to be? *Should* we want to change them, or can we grow to accept that people are different?"

He frowned and shifted, looking down at her, her

face averted, the wealth of her silky black hair fanning over him in a way he was afraid he was getting much too used to. Her tone had been wistful and deep, and he knew what she was talking about. She was talking about the two of them, because she was no fool, and she knew that when they had first met, he'd thought she was either a sham or on the mentally unbalanced side.

He touched her hair. "I think we're crazy if we don't learn to see the world from every angle," he told her, surprised at the tremor in his own voice.

And even more surprised that he meant it.

He lay there then, his hand on her hair, her cheek against his flesh. He closed his eyes, knowing he wouldn't sleep again but hoping she would. And that her sleep would be free of dreams.

No matter what, though, dreams or no dreams, he would be there.

Was this love? Could a man fall from "avoid this woman at all costs" into sexual attraction-fascination-obsession and from there into love?

How the hell could either of them really know, when this had all grown so intense at the rate of a speeding bullet?

He lay there for a while, resting, thinking. He didn't sleep. She did. Deeply and apparently dreamlessly.

He tossed everything he knew around and around in his head. He would talk to Joe on the way to Boston, even though Joe was, like Rowenna, in denial.

Joe didn't want to believe that someone local, someone he knew, maybe knew well, maybe even had known all his life, could be a psychotic killer.

But someone was.

Jeremy didn't think he could sleep, didn't think he did.

But there, in the misty shadows, he saw Billy. Billy, alive and well, a typical kid in jeans and a T-shirt, hair a little tousled. He was grinning, and Jeremy got the feeling he liked Rowenna, approved of her. He wanted to deny that Billy was there, told himself he was just seeing Billy in his mind, imagining him. That if he tried to touch Billy, get up and walk over to him, he would disappear.

He closed his eyes and remembered the feeling of the kid's hand in his. It was almost as if he could feel it again, as if it were real. As if Billy had lived.

But Billy hadn't lived.

Billy had died.

He opened his eyes.

And Billy was gone. Misty daylight was creeping in through the drapes. He shifted Rowenna carefully to his side and rose.

As Rowenna began to awake, she stretched a hand across the bed, seeking Jeremy's warmth.

She touched…nothing.

She jerked up in a panic, remembering all too clearly she didn't want to be in the house alone. Jeremy's strange behavior had spooked her. She leaped up, then tiptoed to the door and looked out into the hallway, listening. The house was quiet.

"Jeremy?"

No answer.

Had he already left for Boston? Without waking her up to say goodbye?

She swore out loud and moved back into the bedroom, took a deep breath, remembered that her purse with her change of underwear in it was downstairs and swore again. She ran into the bathroom and fumbled with the faucets in a rush to shower as quickly as possible, then get dressed…and leave.

But as she stepped beneath the spray, a strange sense of calm suddenly descended over her.

Soap in hand, she smiled to herself.

Billy. Jeremy had been talking to Billy in his dream. At least, if Jeremy was seeing a ghost, it was a good ghost. The ghost of a little boy he had tried to save, someone to whom he had shown the best of human nature.

She reminded herself that she didn't believe ghosts existed, not really. And they didn't haunt this house.

But if they *did* exist, in more than mind, in more than memory, then Billy would definitely be a good ghost.

She had raced back upstairs, wrapped in a towel, after running down to collect her purse, when she heard a knocking at the door. She struggled into her clothes and hurried back downstairs, looking through the peephole before opening the door.

It was Brad.

Jeremy had obviously taken her suggestion last night and asked Brad to spend his morning playing bodyguard for her.

"Hi," she said, as she opened the door to him. "Thanks for agreeing to hang around with me this morning."

"No problem," he said solemnly. "And…I'm sorry. I was a little drunk last night. I didn't mean to be so…to scare you."

"You didn't scare me," she lied. Besides, in morning's light, all kinds of creepy things seemed to fade away.

"Are you up for breakfast?" he asked.

"Absolutely," she assured him.

They went to Red's, where, once again, the missing persons poster was on display in the window. And inside, the snatches of conversation she overheard made it clear that Dinah Green was very much the topic of the day.

Maybe she shouldn't have come here with Brad after all.

But then, people knew who he was by now. Those he hadn't met had seen him around town or on the news pleading for help, or seen his face in the newspaper.

Several turned away to whisper when he walked by.

They sat at a booth and ordered omelets. Trying to talk about anything other than what was uppermost in his mind, Rowenna asked him about working with Jeremy.

"He was the best partner ever," Brad told her. "I miss him. Don't misunderstand me, there's nothing wrong with the guy I partner with now. He's good—you have to be to make the squad. It's not like diving in the Caribbean, where the water's clear. The river can be pure murk. But there was just…something about the way Jeremy worked. He never saw it, but it was like he had a sixth sense, you know? He could home in on things."

"You were with him when the kids were found?"

"It was a bad day, bringing up those little corpses. Hope is a hard thing. It's great when it pays off. But when you hope for something and it doesn't come through, then hope becomes vicious."

Hope. He was hoping and praying that his wife was alive.

They finished eating and had second cups of coffee, then he walked her down to the History Museum. "Aren't you coming in?" she asked him.

He'd paused outside to look at one of the window displays, one that was new since yesterday.

A mannequin dressed as the Harvest Man.

"No. Jeremy was pushing for me to hang out, but you'll be okay with your friends, right?" When she nodded, he went on. "I think I'll walk in a different direction today. Or maybe I'll go back to the cemetery. I won't go off the deep end," he promised. "When should I come back for you?"

"Say noon? We grab some lunch, or find out what Jeremy is up to and go from there."

"Sounds good. You have my cell number, right?"

"I do. You just gave it to me at breakfast, remember? And you have mine."

He smiled, waved to her and started off down the street, his hands shoved into the pockets of his suede jacket.

Rowenna headed on into the museum. An older couple was paying for admission, and two young women were already starting through. June Eagle was at the desk.

"Hey," she said cheerfully to Rowenna after she had sent the couple on their way.

"Hey. If you don't mind, may I have the key to the reading room?" Rowenna asked her.

June shook her head, grinning. "No need. Dan is already in there. He wanted to get an early start."

"Thanks, June."

June nodded and turned her attention back to the latest issue of *People*.

Rowenna quickly bypassed the people who were visiting the exhibits and kept going toward the section on the Harvest Man. Though she knew that they were only mannequins, she found herself pausing at the display dedicated to the four real-life murderers who had come after the legend.

They were just mannequins, but there was…something about all four of them….

They had been designed and manufactured by the same company, of course, but it was more than that. They were positioned differently, and dressed in the appropriate period clothing, so what was it…?

The faces, she thought.

They were all lean and narrow. It was as if they had been specifically designed to wear a look of cold, calculating ruthlessness.

She felt a chill just looking at them, and she hurried on, anxious to reach the reading room and another living, breathing human being.

Daniel was sitting back, fingers laced behind his head, books open in front of him. Anyone else, she thought, would have had his feet up on the desk.

"So what have you found?" she asked, after a quick hello.

He shoved one of the books toward her. "Read about our boy Hank Brisbin."

She sat down across from him and looked at the page he had indicated, then leafed back. The book had been written in 1959, she saw, by Sam Jackman, professor of law, Harvard University.

"Impressive," she said.

Daniel leaned forward. "Back then, it wasn't as hard as it is now to convince a jury to see beyond a reasonable shadow of a doubt. There was no physical evidence connecting the man to the murders that occurred. They found the girls' bodies rotted down to nothing but bone, picked clean by crows, and lying in the fields near scarecrows. Brisbin lived out that way in a farmhouse that has since been demolished. The night he was hanged, the townspeople burned it to the ground."

Rowenna glanced over the text. Jackman said that it had been difficult to piece the story together, because so many of the references to it in the records had been excised. Apparently Brisbin had been arrested because he'd been seen with the last of the three girls to die and because he had "behaved suspiciously." He was indicted, and the case went to a jury. He was condemned, with a comment by the jury foreman that the verdict had been unanimous.

Still, if there had been any lingering question in anyone's mind as to his innocence, it had been eliminated by his gallows speech.

Rowenna looked up at Daniel when she finished reading.

"Okay," he said, and pushed two more books toward her. "Now check this guy out. Victor Milton. Once again, you've got bodies found in a cornfield. And look at this reference to the old records. 'She was found by the stake where should have stood a scarecrow.'" He sat back again. "I think these guys were imitating the Harvest Man, and our guy is imitating *them*."

"Dan, this can't just be coincidence—the police need to know this," Rowenna said.

"I've told Joe. He agrees that we have someone on

our hands who's imitating the past, bringing the legend to life. Whether it's because he really thinks he's the reincarnation of these men, the tool of the Devil and the Harvest Man reborn, or whether he's just some clever psycho trying to hide his real motivations behind a historical mask, he doesn't know yet. Anyway, I've marked what I found for you."

"Thanks."

He stood up. "I'm going to spell June so she can take a coffee break. If you need me, I'll be at the desk."

"Thanks."

She started reading. It turned out that Hank Brisbin's wife had also disappeared mysteriously. There was a photograph of him in one of the books. He had the narrow-faced, evil-eyed countenance of all four mannequins. Maybe the mannequins had been designed from this picture.

She picked up another of the books. Victor Milton's presumed victims had also been found in the local cornfields. He had never been apprehended or brought to trial, but the locals had been convinced of his guilt.

She yawned and stretched, about to reach for the next book, when her cell phone rang.

It was Eve.

"Hey, you," Rowenna said.

"What are you doing?" Eve asked her.

"I'm at the museum. Reading."

"Can you come over here? Right now?"

Rowenna glanced at her watch. It was only ten-thirty.

"Are you at the store?"

"Yes, and I need you to hurry. He's gone now, but he'll be back."

"Who's gone? Did you see someone you recognized?"

"No! Adam. I'm talking about Adam. Please, Rowenna, please!"

"All right, I'll be right over." Brad wouldn't be back to pick her up for another hour and a half. And Jeremy wouldn't be back from Boston at least till then, either.

"Hurry. *Please.*"

As soon as she hung up, Rowenna carefully closed the book she had been reading, rose and headed out.

She averted her eyes from the mannequins as she passed, ridiculously afraid that if she looked at them, they might come to life.

She stopped at the desk on her way out and told Daniel that she would be back in a bit, warning him that he had the key, so she hadn't been able to lock the door and some unauthorized tourist might wander into the sanctum sanctorum.

He grinned and assured her that he would take care of the door.

Outside, the day seemed colder than when she'd arrived. The sky was an iron-gray, and not even the brilliance of the fall leaves could combat its oppressive effect.

Maybe the tourists felt the same way she did, because the streets were nowhere near as crowded as they usually were this time of year. Everyone was probably inside, drinking coffee and hot chocolate, fortifying themselves to face the cold on the streets.

The minute she entered the shop, Eve grabbed her arm, locked the door and hung a sign that read Back in Five Minutes—Promise!

"What on earth is the matter?" Rowenna asked, genuinely worried by her friend's behavior.

"You have to see this," Eve said urgently and dragged her into the back of the store. There were two small curtained-off rooms near the door to the store-room, separated from the rest of the store by deep cobalt velvet drapes embroidered in gold thread with the sun, the moon and the planets. One was the room Eve used when she did readings, and the other was Adam's.

Eve led her to Adam's.

A tapestry covered a small table holding a crystal ball and a deck of medieval tarot cards. The only decoration in the dark-painted room was a Colonial candle holder with a scented candle, standing on a small desk along the back wall.

Rowenna looked at Eve. "Okay…I'm supposed to see…what?"

"I'll show you."

Eve walked around the table, opened the top drawer of the desk and produced a book.

"Is it on Alistair Crowley? Satanism?" Rowenna asked, still baffled as to why her friend was so upset.

"No. It's a spell book," Eve said.

Rowenna lowered her head to smile. She would never mock Eve or her beliefs, but she simply couldn't bring herself to believe that mixing a few herbs together and reciting some words could create a love spell or any other kind of spell.

"Eve, you have tons of spell books in—"

"Open it to the marked page," Eve told her.

Rowenna did, but could barely read what was written. The light in the room was too dim, and it didn't help that the printing was archaic. Finally, as her eyes adjusted to the low light, she began to make it out.

"'Seven,'" Rowenna read aloud. "'The number is seven. And when the seventh is taken in the prescribed manner, the man becomes the god. Be it known that the god is male, and that woman is subservient to man, and so shall it be. But he who would be the god must perform the prescribed sacrifice, and the number is to be seven. The harvest must be fed, and nourishment must be returned to the earth.'" Rowenna looked up at Eve.

"Keep reading," Eve said.

"'The god must first be a man, and act in the carnal way of man,'" Rowenna went on.

"She was raped, right?" Eve demanded.

"What?"

"Dinah Green. She was sexually assaulted," Eve said.

"Yes, but—"

"I've been lying. I've been lying to protect Adam. Because I believe in him. I love him." She paused, and the look of desolation that came over her face nearly broke Rowenna's heart. "I *did* love him. I *did* believe in him. But, Rowenna, he won't give up these awful books. He says he needs them. Oh, Ro! He left here on Halloween, and he was gone a long time—right around the time Mary Johnstone disappeared. He was in and out all day—but he was out then. And then... before...that other woman. Dinah Green. When she was in the store, he was flirting with her. She came on to him first—I guess she thought I was just someone who worked here—but he was definitely flirting back. And when she left the store, he left a few minutes later. Oh, God, Ro! I think I might be married to a murderer!"

Joe had to talk the talk, Jeremy thought. The guy was a cop, and he had to do some things by the book.

And as they drove into Boston, Joe ran through the cop playbook.

This man was the first real lead they'd had on the case, and his alibi for Halloween was so full of holes, rabbits could have leaped through them. But as Jeremy listened, he got the feeling that Joe didn't believe his own words, no matter how logical they sounded. They were following clues the way all cops followed clues, but Jeremy didn't think Joe expected those clues to lead anywhere any more than he himself did.

Finally Jeremy turned and asked, "Joe, do you honestly think this man is our killer?"

Joe frowned, glancing over at him. "He was the last person seen with the victim."

"Dinah Green was seen all over the city—she met a lot of people. Any one of them could have arranged to meet her later. I just think our killer has to be someone closer."

Closer. That was better than saying flatly that the killer had to be a local, someone Joe might know and like. At the same time, he knew it didn't matter how he phrased it. Misplaced tact wasn't going to help them find a killer, and anyway, Joe was no fool. He knew what Jeremy was really saying.

"There's still a possibility this man did it. Scenario—they get into a lovers' spat. Or he's picked her up, planning to sleep with her, only she doesn't come through and he gets mad. He rapes her and kills her. What then? He has a body, and he has to get rid of it."

"So a guy who just happens to get into an unplanned argument with a woman and kills her just happens to have gloves on, so his prints aren't found anywhere, like on the stake he's miraculously found hanging around beside the road to tie her up on?" Jeremy said.

"I should have left you back in town with the moping husband," Joe muttered.

"No, sorry. I know it's important that we talk to this guy, even if all we do is eliminate him from our pool of suspects."

The Boston cops were happy to help and led them straight through to an interrogation room where Tim Richardson was waiting.

He was fit enough, with just the beginning of an armchair quarterback's paunch. He was rough-hewn, with the kind of weathered, once-classic features that appealed to women.

When they entered the room, he made no attempt at false bravado. He ran his fingers through his hair and told them right off, "I didn't do it. I swear, I didn't. I couldn't believe it when the cops came to get me, when they brought me in for questioning. I met that woman in a shop, we went to a bar, we had some drinks. I asked her to come home with me—to Boston—and she said she had other plans. I didn't sleep with her, I didn't manhandle her, nothing. I came right home," he told them.

"Is there anyone who can vouch for that?" Joe asked him.

"My cat," Richardson said wearily. "I fed the poor sucker when I got in."

"All right, tell us about the bar," Joe said.

Richardson frowned, confused. "It served alcohol." He really didn't intend to be a wise guy, Jeremy realized. Richardson honestly didn't understand the question.

No way was this the guy who had planned and carried out such an elaborate murder.

"Tell us about that night at the bar," Joe clarified. "Who did you talk to? What did you see? Did Dinah seem to know anyone else there?"

Richardson brightened. "Yeah, she did. She said hello to a bunch of people. Some students—she told me they were students, anyway—and some people she said she met earlier in the day. In the stores, at the museum, you know?"

"Do you remember anything in particular about that night?" Jeremy asked.

Richardson thought about it, shrugged and slumped in his chair. "It was just people at a bar, drinking, talking, laughing, eating…nothing special."

Richardson groaned and dropped his head in his hands.

Joe began to ask questions again. "Did Dinah tell you anything about her plans?"

"Yes, she wanted to keep going north. She had vacation time, and she intended to use it." He looked up then. "We went into a couple of haunted houses that afternoon. It wasn't Halloween yet, but they get all excited up there for the whole month of October. I met her in that area where no cars can go—"

"The pedestrian mall?" Joe suggested.

"Yeah, yeah. At a joke shop. That's when I met Dinah. She was looking at the books."

"So you just started talking?" Joe asked.

"Yeah, yeah. Figured out we were both from Boston. Both up to see the leaves. So we decided to go for coffee. I thought she was cute, and she said she thought I was rugged. And cool," he reflected mournfully.

Jeremy thought it was the appropriate time to bring out Mary Johnstone's picture. He watched Richardson's face as he thrust the photo in front of him.

If anything, the man looked perplexed. He frowned, looking up at the two of them. "That isn't her," he said. If he'd recognized Mary in any way, he hadn't betrayed it with so much as a blink.

"No, that's the woman we're looking for right now," Joe said.

"I've never seen her 'cept on the news," Richardson claimed vehemently.

"She disappeared on Halloween," Jeremy said.

Richardson groaned. "I was with a hooker on Halloween."

"And her name was?"

Richardson stared at them, shaking his head.

"Sugar," he said at last.

"Did Sugar have a last name?" Joe asked him.

Richardson groaned again. "Plum."

"Being a smart-ass isn't going to help you," Joe informed him.

Richardson laughed dryly. "I'm not being a smart-ass. That's the name she gave me when she got in the car. Sugar Plum. She even asked me to go in and buy her a bottle of plum brandy. While we were waiting for the guy to run my card, she said she was just like the sugarplum fairy, she'd be in my dreams forever."

"Any reason you picked up a working girl on Halloween?" Joe asked.

"Yeah. I was horny," Richardson said.

The man was wearing down, Jeremy thought. He'd been through all this with the Boston police. It was amazing he hadn't demanded a lawyer yet.

"Wait a minute," Jeremy said. "Did you just say you used your credit card in a liquor store?"

"Yeah."

"Did you tell anyone this before?" Jeremy asked.

"No."

"Why not?" Joe demanded.

"Because I just remembered it now," Richardson said irritably.

How dumb was this guy? Jeremy wondered. He didn't seem to realize he'd finally given himself an alibi that would hold water.

Joe rose and banged on the door for the guard. "I'll get them right on it," he said.

The cell door closed in Joe's wake. Richardson looked at Joe. "Good cop, bad cop?" he asked.

"I'm not a cop at all. I'm just a private investigator trying to help my friend. He's married to the woman in the picture. I would really appreciate any help you can give me."

Richardson sat there, chewing his lip. "I wish I could give you something. Believe me—I wish I could get myself out of this place. I never met your friend's wife. I did meet Dinah. We went to some haunted houses, a couple of shops, and we stopped by a museum, but we left when she saw I was bored with all that history stuff. Then we had dinner at the bar. Did I think I was going to get laid? Yes. Did I kill her when it didn't work out? Hell no. That's why they make working girls, you know?"

"What happened when you left?" Jeremy asked him.

"After dinner, she said she wanted to talk to someone she'd met during the day. I said I could wait and walk her to her car. She said not to bother, that it was just over by the cemetery, a couple of blocks away, and she could get there by herself."

The cemetery, Jeremy thought. Everything kept going back to the cemetery.

He needed to get a list of everyone who had been in that bar the night Dinah Green had last been seen. He was certain now that someone in that room—maybe the person she had spoken to, maybe someone else—had followed as she walked to her car.

And then...

Jeremy handed him his business card. "If you think of anything else, anything at all, call me."

"Sure. If they let me," Richardson said.

Jeremy glanced around...just in case. "Ask for an attorney," he said.

Richardson frowned. "They said I could have one. But I'm not guilty."

"Innocent men need attorneys, too," Jeremy assured him.

Just then Joe returned to the cell. Jeremy looked at him. "Your Halloween story checks out." Joe turned to Jeremy. "The guy at the liquor store actually remembers little miss Sugar Plum. Imagine that."

Jeremy shrugged. He extended a hand to Richardson, who stared at it for a few seconds, then accepted it. "If I could help you, I would. You know that, right?"

"You never know what might come to mind," Jeremy said.

As he and Joe left and headed for Joe's car, Joe was scowling.

"The man is innocent," Jeremy said quietly. "They'll have to let him go in the end."

"Yeah, I know," Joe said. "That poor sucker is too damn dumb to have done it," he added in disgust. "Wasted time."

"No," Jeremy disagreed. "He said that she stayed in the bar after he had left because she wanted to talk to someone she'd met that day."

"So? That may not even be true."

"I think it is."

"We're still looking for a needle in a haystack."

"I think the haystack just got smaller. I asked Hugh to pull his receipts for the day, and I'll pick them up later. We can start looking at every local who was in that bar that night."

Joe eyed him dolefully. "We can start looking, and we may still be wrong."

"And we may be right," Jeremy said. "Richardson said she told him she was parked by the cemetery."

"I told you—there are no tunnels in that cemetery. No tombs doubling as a secret hideaway."

"That's not the point," Jeremy said. "The cemetery figures into this somehow. This guy has decided that he likes the whole Harvest Man idea. Being worshipped. He's taking these women and entertaining himself with them. Making them adore him, beg for their lives, maybe. And then, when he tires of them, or they try to escape, or maybe because it's Wednesday or it rains, he decides it's time to kill them and find another. And I'm telling you, Joe, whoever he is, he was at that bar that night."

"Maybe," Joe said.

"We narrow it down. We find someone who was there, and who has land, so no one will hear what goes on. Or a soundproof room. Somewhere where he kept

Dinah Green before he killed her. Somewhere where he's got Mary Johnstone right now."

"Let's just hope he paid with a credit card," Joe muttered.

"Let's just hope he doesn't get tired of Mary," Jeremy replied.

"Amen," Joe said solemnly.

16

Rowenna had no idea what to say to Eve.

She couldn't believe her friend was accusing her own husband of being a murderous monster.

And looking into Eve's tormented eyes, she knew that Eve didn't want to believe it, either, but things had built up inside her until she was ready to self-combust, and she'd desperately needed to speak with someone. Someone she trusted.

"Well?" Eve whispered.

"Well, the fact that he wasn't in the store doesn't make him a murderer. And even if he flirted with her...well, we all flirt sometimes. It's a way of feeling...appreciated, I guess," Rowenna said.

"What should I do?" Eve asked quietly.

"Have you confronted him with any of this?" Rowenna asked.

"I've argued with him about the books. And we had a big fight after he followed Dinah Green out of the store.... It didn't help when we saw her again later. At the bar," Eve said.

Rowenna sucked in a breath, watching her friend closely as she asked, "Did he leave you at all that night?"

Eve frowned. "Yes. He got up from the table and went to the bar to get our drinks. Then, when he didn't come back, I went to ask Hugh what the hell was going on that it took so long to get a drink, but I couldn't find *him,* either. I was angry, so I said screw the check and left."

"And then—did Adam come home?"

"Of course he came home. Do you think he'd leave a house he feels he paid for?" Eve asked bitterly.

"Eve, I meant *when* did he come home?"

"I don't know!" Eve exclaimed miserably. "I'd had a few drinks, and I was so angry—I shouldn't have, but I took a sleeping pill. And I was out like a light."

"What happened in the morning? Was he there when you woke up?"

"Yes. He was there. I got up, ignored him and went into the store without him."

"Did he come into the store later?"

"Yes. He got there a few minutes after me."

Rowenna studied Eve, at a loss for reassuring words. *Adam?*

Could her friend be right? Was her husband a killer?

"What should I do?" Eve begged. "What should I do?"

If Adam *was* the killer, Rowenna thought, was Eve safe with him? No, what was she thinking? It couldn't be Adam. It *couldn't.*

Why not?

Because it just had to be someone else.

But should Eve be staying with him if there was any possibility, any possibility at all?

"Oh, Eve…"

"I know. If I'm wrong, I've destroyed my marriage.

But if I'm right, I might wind up dead in a cornfield," Eve said miserably.

"I have to tell Jeremy," Rowenna said.

"You can't!" Eve gasped. "You can't. He'll make them bring Adam in for questioning, and then Adam will hate me. He'll kill me!" She realized what she had just said and started to laugh, but it was a sad and bitter laugh.

"Eve, I can tell Jeremy to talk to Adam himself and to be careful. He isn't Joe, Eve. He's not a cop anymore. But…you have to be careful. I mean, honestly? I don't believe it. I'm sure Adam can be a pain—he's a man, for God's sake," she said, trying to lighten the tension. "But I have to say something to Jeremy about this."

Eve shook her head vehemently. "Couldn't you…couldn't you do your thing?"

"What are you talking about?"

"Your thing—where you commune with the earth, or your mind, or whatever it is you do for Joe when you let the spirits talk to you."

Rowenna groaned inwardly. "Eve, I'm not a psychic. I'm not sure I even believe in psychics." Though given what she'd been through recently, she was getting closer to believing all the time.

"You keep saying that!" Eve snapped. "But you're lying to yourself. I don't care what you call it, but you…know things. And if you let yourself, you could see what happened that night. And you could find Mary, too," she added stubbornly.

"Eve, if there was any possible way for me to find Mary Johnstone, don't you think I would have done it by now?" Rowenna demanded, exasperated.

"Adam said he found you in the cemetery last night," Eve said accusingly.

"Yeah, well, I thought I was being followed."

"And you thought the cemetery would be a good place to hide?" Eve asked, nakedly skeptical.

"It was…a series of circumstances," Rowenna told her. "And stupid."

"But it's daylight now," Eve told her.

"So?"

"Please, let's go there. It's day, people are out. You can try to figure out what happened. You can pretend it's Halloween and see what happens."

"Nothing will happen," Rowenna said tensely, lowering her head and shivering.

She had to admit, she'd been thinking that she needed to go there. Not by night, not when she thought that she was being chased and no one else was around. In daylight. And with or without Joe, who still wanted to get her out there, too.

Even if this was a day cursed with a gloomy pewter sky.

"Please. Before we say anything to Jeremy about Adam. You said you'd do anything possible to find Mary Johnstone."

Rowenna let out a sigh. "All right."

"Thank you," Eve breathed in genuine relief. "Let's go now."

As Eve spoke, Rowenna's phone rang. She answered it by rote.

"Hey, where are you?" Brad asked. "I actually came back to the museum early, thought I'd poke around, and Dan told me you'd headed over to Eve's."

Rowenna hesitated, thinking it might not be a bad thing if he went with them.

"Who is it?" Eve whispered.

"Brad," Rowenna mouthed in return. "Should I…?"

"Bring him? Yes. Tell him to meet us outside Red's."

"Brad, meet me outside Red's. I mean, meet us. Eve's with me."

"Okay. Why?"

"Just come," Rowenna told him.

"*Now*," Eve begged.

"Now," Rowenna said.

"All right, I'm on my way," Brad told her, and hung up.

"Let's *go!*" Eve insisted.

Determined, Eve headed back out to the front of the store. She paused, collecting one of the little bags of herbal spells near the door. "It's for long life," she told Rowenna.

"Let's hope," Rowenna muttered.

Just as they reached the door, Adam entered. He was frowning. "Why is the Closed sign on the door?" he asked irritatedly. Then he noticed Rowenna and smiled.

Great, Rowenna thought. He thinks I'm telling his wife she's lucky to be married to such a great guy who loves her so much, and really I'm planning to go to the cemetery to try to figure out if he's a murderer or not.

"Ro and I were going to hop out for coffee, and I didn't know when you'd be getting back," Eve lied easily.

"Oh." Adam seemed to accept that happily enough. "Well, have fun. Bring me back a cup."

"Sure," Eve said curtly, and swept past him.

Adam stared at Rowenna in confusion. Her smile felt too wide and plastered on, as if she'd just had a triple dose of collagen injected.

As she slipped by Adam, she brushed against him, and thought, Adam? A killer?

He couldn't be.

But she couldn't forget what Brad had said about her friends at the bar the night before.

"They're kind of scary-weird."

And then, *"One of them could be the Devil."*

Thank God, Rowenna thought, when she saw that there were lots of people thronging the mall. And she was even more relieved, when they took the turn for the cemetery, to see that there were still plenty of people in the area.

The tourist tram went by, and she could hear the conductor cheerfully passing on information to the riders.

Outside Red's, they waited for a few minutes for Brad to arrive. "Why didn't you just have me meet you at the shop?" he asked.

"She doesn't want Adam to know what we're doing," Rowenna explained.

"Oh?" Brad said, frowning. "What *are* we doing?"

"Going to the cemetery," Eve replied, then apparently realized how painful that might be for him and hurried to add, "Ro's going to do her magic trance thing to try to figure out what happened to Mary."

A series of emotions flashed through his eyes. He hated the cemetery, but at the same time, he was eager to revisit it if doing so could provide any shred of hope. Rowenna could tell that he was even worried about *her.* He probably thought she and Eve were heading over the edge. Crazy. Of course, he hadn't sounded so sane himself recently, ranting about visions in crystal balls and the Devil out drinking alongside the locals.

"All right, let's go," he agreed. "I'm willing to try anything," he added under his breath.

The cemetery looked bleak. The trees there were almost leafless, as if they had shed their brilliant beauty overnight.

Rowenna realized that she really didn't want to go in.

"Come on," Eve urged her. "You promised. And Mary might still be alive," Eve said.

"She *is* alive," Brad said. "You said so," he insisted to Rowenna.

"We'll go back to Halloween," Eve said. "Brad can talk you through it."

As they walked in, Rowenna, forcing herself every step of the way, found herself remembering the night before and where the shadow had stood. Staring unwillingly at the tomb where her name had been written in dark, dripping blood. She felt almost as if she were entering her nightmare again, and she was terrified.

"Okay, concentrate," Eve said. "It's Halloween. Crowds are everywhere."

"There are vendors set up out there in the street," Brad said, taking over. "But it's getting near dusk. I'm in the cemetery. Alone with Mary. She had a book about what the symbols on the tombstones meant and she was telling me about them, but I was getting tired, so I walked over there—to that aboveground tomb." He pointed to show her the one he meant. "And then I lay down on it and closed my eyes."

Rowenna half closed her own eyes, letting her lashes shield her vision from the present reality. She imagined the crowds, the laughter, the little kids running here and there. Costumes. Everyone in costume…

And Mary. Exploring, and then…

Rowenna felt the breeze and had the overwhelming sense that, if she were to open her eyes wide, she would be standing on a hill. Mary had stood above a grave, and somehow Rowenna knew that Mary had seen her own name on it. Etched cleanly, as if the letters had just been chipped into the stone that morning.

Then *he* had come, powerful and somehow unseen, and he had kept Mary from crying out, even though she had been terrified. He had taken her from just feet away from where she herself had stood last night, paralyzed in terror. And Mary had known him, had recognized him, from earlier that day, but he was a master not just of effects but of hypnotism, and he had kept her mesmerized so she never cried out. Then he had silenced her with a drug-drenched rag. And with the entire city around them in costume, he had spirited her away. She had been in a cemetery, and then she was on a hill.

Looking down on the cornfields.

"Ro!" Eve gripped her arm, shaking her.

Rowenna opened her eyes. Eve and Brad were both staring at her anxiously.

Rowenna looked at Brad. "Her book—did you find her book? The one you were just talking about?"

"No. Only her purse and cell phone were on the grave. That one." He pointed. "You can just read the initials on the stone. Her initials," he added emphatically.

"Ro, what did you see? It was like you were somewhere else," Eve told her.

"I just imagined it, imagined the way it must have been," Rowenna said. She looked at Brad. "I'm sure you're right. That fortune-teller, Damien, is the one who took her." She kept her eyes on Brad. She didn't want to add, And he's one of us, someone who knows how everything here works, people's habits and schedules, and how to slip through a crowd in costume, dragging a drugged woman, and make it all look like some sort of macabre show, so no one would even notice with everything else that was going on.

Brad stared at her, nodding. They all jumped when his cell phone went off. "Jeremy," he said apologetically when he looked at the number.

A tour guide, dressed as a Pilgrim, was leading a group through the cemetery. Suddenly it was a normal place again, sad, but not evil.

"Let's get out of here, huh?" Eve suggested.

"Absolutely," Rowenna agreed. "Don't tell Jeremy where we are," she whispered to Brad.

He glanced at her curiously, but he nodded. "Yeah, she's right here. We're having coffee. We'll see you in a bit…. No? Okay, well… Sure. Where do you want to meet?"

Eve caught Rowenna's arm, dragging her toward the gate. Brad followed.

Rowenna wanted to tell Eve that after what she'd just experienced, she had to say something to Jeremy about Eve's suspicions of Adam, so Jeremy could get to the bottom of things, one way or another, but she didn't want to say anything in front of Brad, just in case he took the information and went off half-cocked. Anyway, she still couldn't believe Adam was guilty. But if there was even the slightest chance…

Then Eve wasn't safe with her husband.

She was going to have to find a way to say something soon, but her thoughts as to how and when were interrupted when Brad closed his phone and turned to face her curiously.

"Where are we supposed to meet him?" she asked quickly, to stop him from asking why she hadn't wanted Jeremy to know where they were.

"Down by the water in half an hour," Brad said. And then, clearly not willing to be deterred, he asked, "Why can't we tell him we were in the cemetery?"

"I just don't think it's a good idea," Rowenna said, then hesitated. "You know Jeremy. He was your partner. He wouldn't think much of me trying to…relive Mary's experience."

Brad nodded, and she knew he wouldn't tell Jeremy, even if he was his close friend. He wasn't willing to put a damper on any efforts to locate Mary, no matter how crazy they might look to other people. No matter how crazy they might look to *her,* Rowenna forced herself to admit.

"Good—there's a café right there, across the street. We can make sure that we're not complete liars and get some coffee," Eve said.

"Don't forget to bring some back to Adam," Rowenna reminded her.

"We'll walk you back on our way to meet Jeremy."

Eve nodded, tight-lipped, and looked imploringly at Rowenna.

Don't say anything to Jeremy, she pleaded silently.

Rowenna tried to convey her own answer silently, too. *I have to.* But she promised herself that she would make him be subtle when he went to talk to Adam.

They strode to the café, ordered their drinks, sat for a few minutes, then walked Eve back to the shop.

"She's nice," Brad said, after Eve had hugged Rowenna goodbye and gone inside.

"Yes, she is."

"For a demon worshipper."

"She's not a demon worshipper," Rowenna said impatiently. "Anything but. She's a wiccan."

But her husband might be a Satanist.

"Let's get down to the waterfront," she suggested, hugging herself to keep from shivering.

The restaurant Jeremy had chosen was busy, and lots of the diners were clearly tourists. Apparently a body in a cornfield couldn't stop people from enjoying the fall colors. Most of the tourists appeared to be either young and childless, or retired and enjoying their golden years, which made sense, Rowenna thought, since schools were in session.

She and Brad were shown to a table and ordered more coffee while they waited for Jeremy and Joe. Brad suggested an appetizer, too, and they decided on an order of calamari.

"You really do have a unique talent," Brad told her as soon as the waiter had gone.

"No, I don't. Not really," Rowenna said, pretending to study the menu.

"You can find her for me. You can see things."

"Brad, I'm not—" She broke off. There was too much hope in his eyes. "Brad, I would do anything in my power to help you, but I don't have any magical power." *I don't,* she insisted to herself. "I just think and feel things out. That's all I do. All I *can* do."

"But you should have seen yourself in the cemetery. For a minute…you *looked* like Mary."

"I've seen her picture, I've heard you all talk about her. I can envision her. *You* can envision her, too. That's why I looked like her."

He wasn't convinced. "I think there's more we can do. Like get a hypnotist or a medium, someone who could really guide you through…whatever it is you do."

Rowenna looked up. Jeremy and Joe were threading their way through tables toward them.

"Brad," she said. "Please don't—"

He shushed her with a wave. "Not a word," he promised.

Jeremy paused by her chair, and for a split second, he seemed awkward. Then he brushed a kiss on the top of her head and took the seat next to her. Joe slid into the chair opposite him.

Jeremy had a folder, and he set it on the table, his fingers drumming. He was obviously anxious to get to it.

"Have you two ordered yet?" Joe asked.

"Just some calamari," she said. "We were waiting for you."

"Thanks," Joe said, and picked up the menu, then looked at Rowenna over the top of it. "Have you taken care of your costume yet?" he asked her.

She stared at him and blinked. Admittedly, life did go on. But he and Jeremy had just been talking to a murder suspect, and even though he didn't know it, she was still feeling the effects of the experience at the cemetery and worrying that one of her friends was married to a murderer. "Costume?"

"Yes, costume. The thing you're supposed to wear when they drive you through town on a horse-drawn float," Joe said.

"Oh, right. Ginny's making it for me," Rowenna told him.

"What happened in Boston?" Brad asked tensely, his impatience with the current conversation obvious.

"He isn't our man," Jeremy said.

"The guy wasn't the sharpest tool in the shed," Joe said wearily. "Quite frankly, he wouldn't have been capable of pulling off anything as complex as Mary's abduction, and I doubt he had anything to do with Dinah Green's death, either."

Brad looked at the other two men. "I know I'm playing devil's advocate here—" He stopped and flushed at his own choice of words. "Look, you know I think it was that Damien guy, but even so…sometimes perps act dumb on purpose."

"Not this guy," Joe said confidently. "Trust me, he's a fair amount of brawn and not a hell of a lot of brain."

"And he had an alibi for Halloween," Jeremy added.

"Airtight?" Brad asked.

"Sugar-Plum tight," Joe muttered.

Rowenna looked at Jeremy, who explained, "He used a credit card to buy liquor for a hooker named Sugar Plum, and the timing clears him in Mary's disappearance. The Boston cops checked it all out."

"So it was a waste of time," Brad said. "And Mary is still out there somewhere."

"It's never a waste of time to eliminate a suspect," Joe said.

Rowenna was eager to finish the meal and get a chance to talk to Jeremy alone, so she could tell him about Adam. "Let's order, shall we?"

The calamari arrived, and they put in their entrée orders.

When the waiter had gone, Jeremy leaned toward Brad and said, "Richardson *was* with Dinah Green at the bar, and then he says he left. He claims he offered to walk her to her car—which was parked by the cemetery—but she said she wanted to stay and talk to someone she had met earlier in the day."

Brad shook his head. "So…?"

"So Hugh went into the computer and pulled up all his receipts for that night so we can get at least a partial idea of who was there," Jeremy went on.

"It was Damien," Brad said stubbornly.

"Could be," Joe agreed. "But whoever the hell he really is—because I can pretty much guarantee you his real name isn't Damien—he disappeared into thin air…or back into his own skin, his own life. We have to track him down."

Brad looked glum. "He might not even have been the one who paid the bill. Or maybe he paid cash. If Dinah Green and Mary were even abducted by the same man."

"It's something to start with, at least," Jeremy said. "Brad, one way or another, we'll track down everyone in the bar that night, I promise you. And Zach is coming up to help."

"Great. He can look for a needle in a haystack, too," Brad said.

Joe cleared his throat. "Quit bitching and be glad you have friends with resources the cops can't afford— like extra manpower. Every qualified person working this case is something you should be grateful for."

Rowenna quickly lowered her head, hiding a smile, surprised that Joe had so quickly leaped to Jeremy's defense.

When she looked up again, Brad's face was flushed.

"You don't understand," he said. "You don't know what it's like to love someone and be desperately afraid that they're going to turn up dead."

"Yes, I do," Joe said harshly, staring at Brad, who had the grace to look abashed.

Rowenna wondered if he knew that Jonathan Brentwood had been killed in the service or if he had just gathered from Joe's speech that there was a story to be told.

"What time is Zach coming?" she asked Jeremy, trying to move past the awkward moment.

"Not till late this afternoon. It was the earliest flight he could get."

"So what's your plan now?" she asked him.

"Are you thinking of doing some more research this afternoon?" he asked her.

"Yes," she said slowly. An idea had occurred to her; it had been forming since she had been at Eve's shop, looking at Adam's book, and she was interested in following up her theory. But she still needed to talk to Jeremy—alone—before dusk came and Adam and Eve closed up for the night.

"I'm assigning two officers to follow up on the list Jeremy got from Hugh. They'll find out exactly who was in the bar that night, and who talked to Dinah before she left," Joe said.

"I'm going to take a drive," Jeremy said.

"A drive?" she asked, surprised.

He shrugged. "I want to go see if there's anything out where Ginny saw those lights," he explained.

"She's...getting old. Slipping a bit," Joe warned Jeremy.

"I know. Rowenna told me. But I still want to see what's out there." He turned to Rowenna. "I'll come get you at the museum before dusk. I promise."

"I want to go out there with you," Brad said.

"Sure," Jeremy said. "Two sets of eyes, you know how that goes." He frowned. "But, Rowenna, wait for me there this time, all right?"

"I will," she promised.

When they were leaving, she slipped an arm through his. "I need to talk to you," she whispered.

"What's up?" he asked. She hesitated. Brad was hovering just a few feet away.

"Can it wait till tonight?" he asked.

"Can you come get me by four-thirty?"

"All right."

She nodded.

Joe bade them goodbye and headed for his office, and Brad and Jeremy walked Rowenna to the museum. June wasn't at the desk this time, but Rowenna knew the coed who was—Lily Valentine—and Lily handed her the key and sent her back to the reading room, explaining that Daniel had popped out for lunch but would no doubt come join her when he got back.

Rowenna was actually glad to be alone. She started reading about the four killers who all seemed to have followed the pattern set by the Harvest Man, jotting down notes as she went, paying special attention to the number of victims each killer had claimed. Three in one case, four in another, then three again.

Hank Brisbin, the most recent link in the murderous chain, had also been the most prolific. Five corpses had been laid at his door, all of them found in the cornfields, one down to nothing but bones strewn by a bare stake.

He'd given a newspaper interview shortly before his execution, and he'd told the reporter, "Seven must come and seven must go, and thus wilt thou Satan forever know."

Seven.

Was it possible, she wondered, that in each case the killer, the incarnation of the Harvest Man, had been trying to make seven sacrifices but had been stopped before he succeeded?

She leaped up, hurrying toward another bookshelf. She glanced past the volumes on paganism and wicca until her eyes lit on a book with the ridiculously long title of *When Worlds Collide: Satanism and the Practice of the Ancients, Runes, Gods, Goddesses, Devils and Demons*.

She took it back to the table with her and started reading.

The number seven was often associated with magic, the book said. It was considered a lucky number by some, but according to some of the primitive peoples who had inhabited Europe before the advent of Christianity, it was also the number of sacrifices that needed to be made in order to gain the approval of the harvest gods. Seven goats were still slaughtered at each fall's harvest festival in certain remote villages on the continent. The seventh son of a seventh son was still widely supposed by many to be a magician, a god or a man possessed of godlike powers.

She turned the page to see a sketch, rude, poorly crafted, hundreds of years old, of a red devil seated upon a high throne, horned and stroking his goatlike beard. His feet were cloven hooves, and his tail—with an arrow-shaped spike at the end—protruded from beneath him.

His other arm was stretched out, his fingers sporting ridiculously long talons and curling around the throat of a woman wearing a crown of leaves and a golden cloak with vines growing from it. The devil's head was cast back; he was strangling her with one hand alone.

In front of him, upon a black altar, in sheer white gowns, their eyes and mouths opened in their final terror, six young women lay slaughtered, blood pooling around them. The caption beneath the picture read, He must come to know them, and to love them. And so shall he be fed to new life by the blood of the seven he has cherished and taken. Seven, and he will reign over all, for all time, the God of Fornication.

She pushed the book away, feeling ill. This was the New World. This was the here and now. But it didn't matter.

They might not have found them yet, but there were more bodies out there.

And more to come.

The Harvest Man believed that he had to sacrifice seven women to the earth, to nature, to ensure the harvest and his own eternal power.

And he needed to complete his bloody work before Thanksgiving Day.

17

The road that led northwest of the MacElroy house was in bad shape, forcing Jeremy to drive slowly. Not that he had planned to speed, since he and Brad needed to look carefully at everything they passed, looking for anything suspicious.

All he knew for sure was that if the killer was seizing women and keeping them somewhere, it had to be a quiet somewhere. And if Ginny MacElroy was seeing lights where there shouldn't be lights…

They had passed miles of cornfields before finally reaching the empty scrubland where the ground was too thin and rocky to support corn or any other crop. He had noted that the barren lands began when they made a turn less than half a mile past Eric Rolfe's house, which indeed seemed like the beginning of the end of the world. There was one small cornfield, and then, for miles and miles, nothing but bracken-filled land, with occasional outcroppings of granite.

He stopped the car when the road ahead narrowed and turned to rutted dirt, and sat for a long minute staring out at the desolation surrounding them.

"What are you doing?" Brad asked.

Jeremy left the car, walking to the edge of the

broken pavement, where the high grass, thorns and brush began. He shaded his eyes with his hand and stared toward the fields and the houses to the southeast. The dirt road meandered on, disappearing in the distance. He started walking, his eyes scanning from side to side.

"I'll walk back the way we came and see if I can find anything we missed," Brad said.

Jeremy nodded and kept going.

A needle in a haystack, Jeremy thought. Hell, that sounded easy, compared to what he was trying to find.

It was so overgrown and wild here that any sign of a body, a shack, an old cellar, would be almost impossible to find. But he moved doggedly forward anyway, searching the brush nearest the road for any sign that it had been trampled or otherwise disturbed. At first he couldn't find so much as a bent leaf or a cracked twig. He felt the hard-packed dirt of the road beneath his feet, and despite the coming winter, the sun beating down on him was hot, burning. It was already beginning its descent, but here, away from tall trees and taller buildings, its rays were still strong.

"Hey!" Brad called out to him excitedly, his voice barely carrying from the distance.

"What?" he shouted back.

"Come here!"

He turned and ran back to Brad, who didn't say a word, only pointed.

Brad had found a place along the road where a wild cherry bush had been all but flattened, though clearly the damage had happened some time ago. The bush was struggling to straighten itself, but it still grew at a slant— like a palm caught in a hurricane and bending to its will.

Any footprints in the area were long gone, erased by rain and wind, so Jeremy didn't worry about obliterating evidence as he followed the trail marked by damaged brush, as if someone had dragged a wagon or a wheelbarrow through at some point.

The trail kept leading them back.

Back to the edge of the last cornfield.

The door to the library opened. Rowenna looked up, expecting Daniel.

She was stunned to see Adam standing there.

"Adam!" she said, surprise quickly succeeded by alarm. "Is something wrong? Is Eve all right?"

For a moment he didn't speak or move. He just stared at the table, at the books, his eyes empty, as if he had blacked out while standing.

"Adam?"

She felt her skin crawling, because there was something so odd about his eyes—and the situation didn't help. She was alone with him in the back of a museum, with a wax murderers' row just beyond the door.

And Adam—her friend whom she had once thought she knew so well—was reading books on Satanism and spells to let the Devil into his own flesh, so he could become immortal through the blood sacrifice of women.

Atmosphere and Adam were kicking in. Goose bumps began to form on her flesh.

She longed to jump up and run, but he was blocking the door.

"Adam?" she said quietly, reassuringly. "Let's go outside. I've been in here too long—I need a break."

Should she scream? Maybe someone would hear

and come help her. Was there anything here she could use as a weapon?

Books. All she had were books. She almost laughed as she supposed she could do her best to beat him over the head with a priceless volume on Satanic ritual. At least there would be a certain poetic justice in that, she thought.

He seemed to snap back to the present. His eyes cleared and focused on her. "I came for you," he said.

"What?" she breathed.

He shook his head. "I mean I came to see you. I...I haven't been completely honest with you."

"You don't always have to be completely honest with people," she said uneasily.

He didn't seem to hear her. "I told you I love Eve, and I do. But something's wrong, really wrong. She's afraid of me." He moved farther into the room. She shrank back, and he paused, frowning. "You're afraid of me, too," he said bitterly, then pulled out a chair opposite her at the table and sank into it, looking worn and dejected.

He wasn't going to hurt her, Rowenna realized.

Not there and not now, anyway.

"Adam, go on. Talk to me," she said.

"Blackouts."

"What?"

He shook his head, then looked at her, his eyes bleak. "Rowenna, I'm having blackouts. I'll find myself standing somewhere, and I won't have any idea how I got there. And then Eve gets mad at me for taking off. Ro, I'm afraid."

You're afraid? she thought.

Could a man kidnap, rape, torture and then murder

a woman in the midst of a blackout? Or was this just a clever act?

"Adam, if you're having blackouts, you need to see a doctor," she said.

He looked at her and shuddered. "I don't like doctors," he told her.

"Adam, no one likes going to the doctor, but if you're sick, you don't have a choice."

"What if…what if I've done something horrible in the middle of a blackout?" he asked, his eyes and voice filled with torment. He reached into his jacket pocket for gum, started to open the pack, then looked at it in confusion, as if he'd completely forgotten what he was doing.

"Let's just deal with the blackouts," Rowenna said. "You have to get help. I think you should go to an emergency room right away, before you get hurt or…or something." She just couldn't bring herself to upset him any more than he already was by saying *or hurt anyone else*. She looked at him with more confidence than she felt and said, "Come on. We'll go tell Eve together."

Adam was still for a minute. "She'll leave me," he whispered. "If something is really wrong, she'll leave me."

"She loves you, Adam. She always has, since we were kids. She won't leave you." Unless you're a killer, a little voice inside her brain pointed out.

He was very still for a long moment, his expression thoughtful, and then he rose slowly.

"I'm going to tell her myself. I *need* to tell her myself. Now. I'll put the Closed sign on the door and tell her. And we'll make arrangements. Then we'll call you," he said gravely.

"It will be okay," Rowenna said, mentally crossing her fingers in the hope that she was right.

He breathed a thank-you and left.

With trembling fingers, she reached for her cell phone. She had to call Jeremy. Or maybe she should call Joe; he was the real cop. No, she would call Jeremy, and have *him* call Joe, assuming there was a need to call Joe at all. Because if there really was something wrong with Adam, that could explain everything that was worrying Eve and prove that he wasn't a killer after all.

She snapped her phone closed when the door opened. This time, it *was* Daniel. Luckily, he didn't notice her panic, because he was staring back over his shoulder as he came in. "That was nice. I haven't seen Adam in here in, well, forever."

She stood. "That's great, but listen, I've got to run.... I'll be back later. See you."

She fled past him, anxious to get Jeremy on the phone and tell him everything that was going on.

Alone.

"Oh, God," Brad breathed, then buckled over, shaking.

The remains were just inside the first ragged row of corn, the one so far to the rear that the farmer would be unlikely to inspect it often. It was almost like a buffer row, the one in which he would expect some loss. It was also clearly a row the searchers hadn't yet reached.

There was very little left of the body. The elements, rodents and crows had seen to that.

It had been there some time. At least a month,

maybe two, Jeremy thought. He wasn't an M.E., but he'd seen enough bodies. This much decomposition didn't happen in a matter of weeks. The face was mostly gone, the white of the skull gleaming in the sun. The flesh of the body had been so consumed that the clothing was only a dirty, matted tangle, and the bones of the arms and legs lay at strange angles, disarticulated by the attentions of the carrion eaters.

Brad was on his knees by then, sobbing.

Jeremy set a hand on his shoulder. "It's not Mary, Brad. It's not Mary," he repeated.

Reason would take over, Jeremy knew. Brad had seen the ravages of time and the elements on the human body at least as often as he had. As soon as he got over the shock of their discovery, he would realize that these sad remnants couldn't be his wife.

Brad gasped, drawing a long, cleansing breath, then stared at Jeremy.

"But she's gone. Mary is gone. And now we've found two…"

"We don't know that Mary was taken by this man," Jeremy said, but even as he spoke, he knew the words were patronizing. Brad wasn't stupid. The truth was becoming more and more obvious. "Mary is strong, and smart. If he has her, she's found a way to stay alive," he said.

"But for how much longer?" Brad whispered. "This woman, oh, God, this poor woman! Someone thought she was just missing. They've been hoping all this time. And here she is."

"Maybe he made mistakes this time, Brad. Maybe the crime-scene unit can find something. And now that it's a serial case, the FBI will come in on it. We're

going to find Mary, Brad. Let's back up and not contaminate the scene any more than we already have."

He took Brad by the arm and dragged him away. He
didn't think they could contaminate the scene much
more than nature had already managed to do, but he
wanted to get Brad away from there, and any excuse
would do.

He called Joe Brentwood and tensely informed him
of what he had found. Joe told him to stay put, he
would get cars out there immediately. Then he said
something else, but Jeremy didn't hear it, because his
phone went suddenly dead.

"What the hell?" Jeremy muttered.

He looked at his phone. Searching for Service was
streaking across the screen. He swore.

"What?" Brad said.

Jeremy showed him. "At least I got through first,"
he said.

Brad pulled out his phone, but it was showing the
same message.

"What'll we do while we wait?" he asked.

"Keep looking," Jeremy said.

"For what?"

"I'm not even sure."

"Well," Brad pointed out, "we already know that
Ginny was right. There *were* lights out here. Someone
was dumping a body," he added bitterly.

"Yeah, but there's more," Jeremy said.

"More what?"

"I don't know, but it's nagging at my mind, and we
have to figure it out. Let's keep searching."

Brad nodded, his constant struggle evident in his
face. He was trying to be strong, but it was impossible

for him *not* to be afraid that they would find Mary's body out there in the corn.

The sun was slipping farther down in the sky, the air shifting from warmth to the chill of late afternoon. Jeremy raised the collar of his jacket and, hands in his pockets, walked along the rows, his eyes searching the ground.

"Holy shit!" Brad called.

Jeremy swore and turned, then raced back toward Brad.

Brad had gone a fair distance from the first corpse. He had moved to an area that was bordered by a thicket of trees, an area where the neat rows were out of kilter. The corn there had grown from seeds that had fallen off the back of a seeder, and it was tangled in with brush and trees.

Brad was staring between two trees at a tall stake standing with a straw hat caught on it.

The body it had once held was so badly decomposed that it had fallen from the wood, the bleached bones lying below it on the earth.

This time Brad knew that the bones couldn't be Mary's without Jeremy telling him.

But there was horror in his eyes nonetheless.

"We've hit the jackpot," he said bleakly. He was trembling.

Jeremy suspected Brad was as afraid as he was to keep searching. They had found two bodies now.

How the hell many more could there be?

Rowenna couldn't reach Jeremy. He must be on the phone or out of range, she thought, because her call went straight to voice mail, which made her decision easy. She had to call Joe. But he didn't answer his cell phone, and when she reached the station, she was told that he had gone out on an emergency call. She hesitated, but she didn't *know* that Adam was a killer, so she could hardly say so in a message. She asked the officer to please let Joe know that she had called as soon as possible.

At a loss, she wandered around the corner, wondering how Eve and Adam would react if they caught her peeking through the door at them. She certainly didn't want to make the situation any worse.

If Adam was a killer who had blackouts, should he be alone with his wife?

She walked to the shop, but the Closed sign was nowhere in evidence, so she took a deep breath, opened the door and walked in.

Eve was behind the counter, straightening out a jewelry display. She looked up when Rowenna came in. "Hey," she said, then hesitated, studying Rowenna. "You look as if someone stole your Thanksgiving turkey."

"Where's Adam?" Rowenna asked.

"He ran out about fifteen minutes ago. Said he had an errand to run. He should be right back. Why?" Her tone rose at the end; Rowenna could tell that she was worried.

"Oh, I saw him, that's all. I thought he'd be back here by now."

"Rowenna, what's going on?"

"He's…he wanted to talk to you himself."

Eve frowned, looking angry. "Wait a minute, there's something going on and my husband told you first?"

"He's afraid. And he loves you."

"He's afraid of what? And *love* is just a word," Eve said, growing visibly tense. "Rowenna, what the hell is going on?"

Rowenna looked outside. There was still no sign of Adam. "He came and told me that he's been having blackouts. He's afraid there's something seriously wrong with him, but he's scared to go to a doctor and scared to tell you. He's afraid he'll lose you."

"Blackouts?" Eve said, her tone skeptical. "He isn't having a 'blackout' when he flirts," she said, sounding hurt.

Rowenna felt uncomfortable. She wished she hadn't come, hadn't spoken.

She wished to hell that Adam had done what he'd said he would do and told Eve himself right away.

"I'm going to go look for him. And once I find him you two need to talk. Not argue—talk," Rowenna said.

She hurried out before Eve could say anything else. Suppose Adam was having neural issues? The pressure of coming to her might have brought on…something. Or maybe he had chickened out and gone to get a drink to shore up his courage before talking to Eve.

She hesitated when she got to the cross street that led to the cemetery. She felt as if she was being drawn there, but she told herself that the feeling was absolutely ridiculous.

Then she thought that maybe Adam had wandered that way.

She turned the corner, and as she did, she had the acute feeling of being watched. She stopped and turned around. A couple of schoolkids, out for the afternoon, were dancing around outside the joke shop behind her, laughing. The elderly wiccan who owned Lamp, Bell and Candle walked by in a long black cape and smiled at Rowenna. "Blessed be, Ro."

"Blessed be," Rowenna echoed, forcing a return smile.

There were people out now. The streets were not inconveniently empty. But she still had the sensation of being watched.

She looked up the block toward the cemetery.

She could have sworn she saw a large shadow rising at the back, but the people walking through didn't seem to notice anything strange.

At least, most of them didn't seem to notice.

Rowenna saw an attractive young blond woman somberly studying the grave markers where several children of the same family, who had all died very young, had been buried. Then the woman looked up suddenly, as if disturbed.

The shadow seemed to be lumbering toward her.

Rowenna could have sworn that she heard the old children's song in her head.

Don't fear the Reaper,

Fear the Harvest Man...

She hurried into the cemetery and up to the woman. "Hello," she said.

The woman didn't seem to hear her, even though she was standing right in front of her.

"Excuse me," Rowenna said, trying again. She reached for her arm and touched her gently. "Miss?"

Startled, the blonde turned and stared at Rowenna. "Oh, I'm sorry. Were you speaking to me? How odd.... I just had... Oh, never mind. What can I do for you?"

"This may sound silly, but it's getting close to dusk and—" She broke off. A lie would have to do. She couldn't very well tell the woman that a shadow was after her.

"I saw a man in a dark cape and hat watching you, and it just made me uneasy. If you're alone, I think you might want to go somewhere with lots of people, or…even go back to your hotel for the night."

The woman smiled. "Don't worry. I'm with my husband. He just went to buy a new camera battery before I meet him for dinner."

Rowenna's heart sank. She was certain that the woman *had* been about to be a victim.

Of what? A shadow? In broad daylight, with people all around?

But the woman had clearly been under a spell of some sort, which she had only shaken off when Rowenna forcefully caught her attention. She wondered what the woman had been seeing.

A vision of a hill and cornfields?

Rowenna was sure the blonde was going to politely tell her goodbye, but she didn't.

"I'm supposed to meet him at the Clam Shack at the waterfront. Can you tell me the best way to get there?"

"I'll walk you over," Rowenna told her.

"Thank you. I appreciate it. I'm not real sure of the streets here."

"It's easy. I'll show you."

"I hate for you to go out of your way."

"Not a problem," Rowenna assured her.

On the way, they introduced themselves and Rowenna discovered that Sue was from New York. When they reached the restaurant, Sue's husband was outside, enjoying the view of the docks. They asked Rowenna to join them, but she demurred, waved goodbye and hurried back. Adam should have shown up by now. And if he hadn't, Eve was going to be having a fit.

She hurried back to Eve's, avoiding the cemetery, but that uneasy sensation of being watched returned. And she knew that those unseen eyes were definitely hostile. She kept moving quickly, and she made sure to keep where there were crowds.

At the shop, she pushed the door open. "Adam? Eve?" Nobody answered. She kept calling their names as she peered into their little reading rooms behind the drapes, and then back in the storeroom. Neither of them was anywhere to be seen.

They never left without locking the door. Never.

A wave of unease swept through her. She was alone in the store. And she was certain someone out there had been watching her.

Following her.

She started for the door, planning to go straight to the police station, and on the way, she was going to get back on the phone and get hold of Joe—no matter what.

But as she neared the front of the shop, a shadow loomed outside and the door began to open.

Police were called in from all the surrounding cities. Joe was furious; warnings and instructions had been sent out to all the farmers, and in his opinion, the bodies should have been discovered already. Precious time was elapsing, precious time for Mary Johnstone—if she weren't among the dead already.

As Jeremy had expected, the crime-scene crew weren't hopeful of finding much, but they were grateful that he and Brad hadn't trampled the scene once they'd found it.

Harold came out. There were so many mitigating circumstances that he was reluctant even to hazard a guess at either woman's date of death, but when pressed, he estimated that the first woman had probably been dead six to eight weeks, and the other one, possibly three months.

A cry went up while Joe and Jeremy were talking with Harold.

A third set of bones had been found.

Harold groaned, and they all winced.

Spotlights went on, because the light was starting to fade, and the third set was scattered.

The police kept searching, and in the end, parts of a fourth victim were found. She was going to be hard to identify, because her skull was missing....

"Who owns this field?" Jeremy asked.

"I don't know," Joe said. "We'll have to check the county records. I know Ginny's land stretches pretty far, and the Rolfes owned land out this way once, too, but I'm pretty sure Eric's mother sold everything but the house when she moved to Florida."

One of his men cleared his throat. "Sir, this is MacElroy land now. They picked it up, since it bordered Ginny's land."

"Makes sense," Joe muttered, shaking his head. "Ginny hires people to work it, and folks who are hired aren't as thorough as folks who own."

Dr. MacElroy deserved some scrutiny, Jeremy thought. Could the kindly pediatrician be a killer?

He'd heard of stranger things.

Jeremy looked up to the sky. The last of the day's

light was going. He turned to look out across the nearby stretch of bracken. The last rays of sunlight must be playing, because he saw the boy again. Standing there, just looking at him, looking like a real live boy, with his tousled hair and T-shirt, his hands jammed into the pockets of his jeans.

Jeremy shook his head, as if to clear his vision, and told himself that the obvious explanation was almost always the right one. No doubt there really *was* a boy out there. There were houses around here. Somewhere. Farmhouses. And farmers had sons.

But then the boy moved, pointing toward the sky, as if to draw Jeremy's attention to the fading light. Then he pointed again, toward Jeremy's car.

He was a good distance away, but Jeremy could swear that the boy mouthed a word.

"Hurry."

And then he vanished.

It was almost dark.

Rowenna. He had to get Rowenna.

He knocked Brad in the shoulder. "Let's go."

Joe looked at him. "You're not hanging around?"

"I've got to pick up Rowenna," he explained.

"Something else may turn up here," Joe said. "I'll call you later if we find anything. You get going."

His stride long as he hurried, heedless of the rough ground, Jeremy tripped over something as he passed close to where they had found the first body. When he looked down as he caught his balance, he noticed something sticking out from under the rock that had nearly brought him facedown in the field. He pulled a tissue from his pocket and carefully picked it up.

He frowned. It looked like a business card, but it,

like the body, was the worse for the elements. It would probably have dissolved already if it had been paper, but it had been laminated.

In the fading light, he could just make out the curlicue writing, the pentagram in the upper left and the fairy on the right.

It read Magick Mercantile, Adam and Eve Llewellyn, Proprietors, followed by the store's address and phone number.

Anyone could have dropped a card, he reasoned. But there was something stuck to the back of the card.

It looked like gum. Old, dried-up gum.

And Adam Llewellyn was always chewing gum.

It would have to be tested, to see if his guess as to its identity was correct.

But even though he didn't know for sure, Jeremy's blood chilled in his veins.

"Joe!" he shouted.

"Hi, there, Ro. You working for the Llewellyns now?"

She felt frozen where she stood. She'd been just about to reach for the doorknob when the door had opened, and she'd jumped back to avoid being hit by it. But now she couldn't move.

It was Eric Rolfe. He had looked like a menacing giant seen through the glass of the door, but up close he was merely a fairly tall man in a big Windbreaker.

"Ro? You look upset. Is everything all right?" he asked.

"I…I can't find Adam or Eve," she said.

Eric frowned and looked at his watch. "I had an appointment to meet Eve here. She was going to give me a reading. I can't believe she would just stand me up."

"I can't believe she would, either," Rowenna said, and started behind the counter.

"What are you doing?" Eric asked.

"Something's wrong. I'm going to call 911," she said.

"Ro, wait. I don't think you should do that," Eric said.

"Eric, a woman is dead, another one is missing…and now Eve!" She couldn't bring herself to say that Eve thought her husband might be a killer and point out that her husband wasn't there, either.

Eric shook his head. "Rowenna, what if you get the police all stirred up and then it turns out they just ran out for coffee? Or a quickie? You could cause all kinds of trouble for them. When did you last see Eve?" he asked.

"About twenty minutes ago," she said.

He arched a brow. "Twenty minutes?" he said.

"Yes, she was here. Twenty minutes ago."

"You're going to try and tell the cops that a woman is missing because you haven't seen her in *twenty minutes?*"

Eric was coming closer to the counter, and she suddenly found that whether she had known him all her life or not, she was nervous.

He had made those horrible scarecrows when she was a kid, and now he made movie monsters and devil masks. Why couldn't Eric be the killer?

He hadn't fit in as a kid, so he had created creepy scarecrows to win prizes and look cool.

She stared at him, praying that her fear didn't show in her face.

First Adam, now Eric. They couldn't both be killers. Could they?

"She didn't lock the door, Eric. She always locks the door."

"Which probably means she's right nearby, maybe getting coffee or something."

"We need the police." She reached for the phone and nearly screamed when his hand settled over hers.

"Ro, I'm telling you, do *not* call the police."

In the car, Jeremy tried calling Rowenna. Her phone rang once before his cut out and the "Searching for service" message filled the screen. He swore in aggravation.

"Mary is going to be okay," Brad said, as if trying to reassure himself. "Joe has men out looking for Adam. They'll pick him up right away, and they'll get him to tell them where Mary is."

Brad was like a ball of electricity, Jeremy thought.

"We don't *know* that it was Adam," he pointed out. "Anyone could have picked up that card at the shop." He had been discreet in telling Joe about the possible gum, hoping not to give Brad reason to go flying off the handle, but it looked like it had been wasted effort.

"That card means he was out there," Brad said flatly. "I wish you hadn't shown that card to Joe. I wish I could have gotten to him first. I could have made him tell me where Mary is."

"We're going to find her," Jeremy promised, wishing he felt as certain as he managed to sound. Undoubtedly they *would* find her. But in what condition?

Dead or alive?

Why had the dead boy in his dreams begun to haunt his waking moments? Why had he pointed to the sky, and then to the car?

And why had he told him to hurry?

It was that last question that worried him most of all, because he'd promised to pick up Rowenna—and what if he was too late?

"He's a wacko, that's what he is. A homicidal wacko," Brad said. "I bet that bastard left his own shop, ran to that tent, put on a costume and waited for us to show up. He's a hypnotist or something. And he buys all that weird shit for his shop. Maybe their incense is drugged. I should have seen it. Oh, God, this is all my fault."

"It's not your fault," Jeremy said, but he was distracted, replying by rote.

There was a tractor in front of him. He gritted his teeth, praying for patience. He beeped, hoping it would move to the side of the road, but it just lumbered on.

Hell, he couldn't see around the guy, but there was never anybody on this road. He floored the gas pedal, and they veered around it.

Luckily the truck coming from the opposite direction was still a good distance away. Jeremy just managed to pass and swerve back into his own lane.

"Fuck!" Brad said, staring at him.

"Sorry."

"Hell, no, they should put you in control more often," Brad said.

Jeremy reached for his phone, which finally had service, and hit Redial. Rowenna didn't pick up. His sense of panic increased.

"Gun it," Brad told him.

He did.

"Rowenna," Eric said. He was staring at her, and suddenly, his tone turned pleading. "Don't go causing trouble for them. They're a nice couple. I know they've been having a few problems, but they'll work things out. If you get the police involved, it will just make everything harder for them."

He lifted his hand from hers.

She stared at him. "Eric, I think something is really wrong."

"But…the police?"

There was a killer out there. And even though he had taken his hand off hers and was looking so sincere…

She still didn't feel secure.

"All right, you stay here. I'll go look and see if I can find them somewhere nearby," she said.

To her relief, he agreed. "Okay, and if they don't show up in an hour…well, I don't know. We'll worry about that if we have to."

She headed for the door, trying not to run. She realized that she had left her purse somewhere in the store, but she wasn't going back for it. She was going to get out to the street—where there were people.

But once again, as she neared the door, it burst open.

And this time, three uniformed police officers poured in.

"Officer O'Reilly?" Rowenna gasped, recognizing the first man through the door.

"Rowenna, are you all right?" he asked.

"Yes. What's going on?" she demanded.

"Where's Adam Llewellyn?"

"We don't know," she told him. "Why?"

"He's wanted for questioning in the murders of Dinah Green and four unknown women, and the disappearance of Mary Johnstone," O'Reilly said.

18

They were nearly at the museum. Jeremy could read the banners out front that advertised the upcoming Harvest Festival, promising music, munchies and mayhem.

Jeremy jerked his car to a stop in front of the museum and leaped. Brad followed, but Jeremy didn't even notice as headed straight for the door.

His heart sank. It was locked.

He looked at his watch. It was five-thirty. An hour after he'd promised to meet Rowenna.

He kicked the door in frustration.

He pulled out his phone again, afraid that it was futile, but he hit Redial anyway.

This time, to his amazement, she answered.

"Jeremy?" She said his name in a strangely tremulous voice.

"Rowenna, where are you? Why didn't you answer before?"

A second's silence made him think he had lost service again. His heart plummeted.

Then she spoke, and her voice was stronger. Defensive, maybe.

Or just indignant.

"I tried calling you," she informed him. Anger. It was anger. But that was okay; she was all right.

"Where are you?"

"Looking at you," she informed him dryly.

He turned, and there she was, coming down the street. She wasn't alone, either. To his vast relief, he saw that Zach was at her side.

He closed and pocketed his phone as Rowenna ran the last few feet to him, and then he took her in his arms. He saw the amusement in Zach's eyes, but he didn't care. He just offered his brother a shrug and went back to hugging Rowenna. When she finally eased away from him, he greeted his brother with a hug just as heartfelt as the one he'd given Rowenna, though substantially less intimate.

Brad stepped up then, and he and Zach exchanged hellos, shaking hands.

"This is one active place," Zach said.

"What are you talking about?" Jeremy asked, looking from his brother to Rowenna.

"I came walking down the street just when Rowenna was coming out of a place the police were raiding," Zachary explained. "They told us you'd found four more bodies."

Jeremy nodded grimly.

"Did they get Adam Llewellyn?" Brad asked anxiously.

"Not that we know about, not yet," Zach said.

"Joe will let us know," Jeremy told him.

"Eve is missing, too," Rowenna said worriedly. She shook her head. "It's all my fault," she said miserably.

"Your fault?" Jeremy said.

"Maybe we shouldn't be having this discussion out

in the street," Zach suggested. "My bags are still in my rental car. I wouldn't mind a chance to wash my face, sit down and get the rundown on everything. And I think that Rowenna has a few things to tell you." He looked over his shoulder, then looked back at Rowenna. "Where did your other friend go? I thought he was right behind us."

"When the police let us go and you arrived, he said he was going to go get a drink," she answered.

"What other friend?" Jeremy asked sharply.

"Eric. He was at the shop, too."

"Wait a minute. You were at the shop? And Adam and Eve weren't?" Jeremy demanded. He knew he sounded overbearing, but he didn't care.

"I could hardly wait at a museum that had closed," she replied sharply.

"Let's get to that house of yours," Zach suggested.

"Go on," Brad said. "I'll see you later."

"Wait," Jeremy told him. "Where are you going?"

"I'm going to look for Adam Llewellyn. I have to find Mary, and he knows where she is."

"Brad, no. If you lay a hand on him, you'll go to jail and possibly ruin the cops' case, as well," Jeremy said. "You have to let the local police find him. Dammit, Brad, you're coming with us."

Brad stared at him, his eyes narrowing. "If Rowenna were missing, you'd be out looking for Adam, and don't lie to me and say you wouldn't."

Jeremy stared at his friend, then turned to his brother, a question in his eyes.

"Rowenna, will you take me to the house?" Zach asked. "They can come along in a while."

She offered them all an icy smile, then met

Jeremy's eyes. "I'm not going anywhere until I tell you what I know."

"Okay, go on," Jeremy said.

They all listened as she told them about everything Adam had confided about his blackouts, the book he was reading, and everything Eve had told her. Jeremy knew he was frowning when she told him about going to the shop, seeing Eve and then going back to find it empty.

"So even his wife thinks he's a killer?" Brad said when she was done.

"That doesn't mean she's right!" Rowenna insisted. "But..." Her voice trailed off, and her brow was furrowed in a frown. Her eyes were a deep amber as she turned to Jeremy. "You say that...you found four more corpses? You're sure it was four?"

"Yes, four. Why?"

"So with Dinah Green, that's five."

"Yes, why? There may be more somewhere, God knows."

"He needs seven," Rowenna said.

"Seven?"

She reminded them of what she had read in Adam's book, then explained that she had gone back to the museum and found the reference to the fact that the Harvest Man needed to sacrifice seven women to take on the powers of the Devil.

"Mary," Brad said weakly. "My God, we have to find her."

With nothing to do but wait for word from the police, they took Zach's things to Jeremy's house, then went to have dinner, though none of them managed to eat much of anything as they brought Zach—and each other—up to speed on everything they knew to date.

At ten, when they were all sitting over drinks with no idea what to do next, Rowenna suddenly said, "The cemetery."

"What?" Jeremy asked.

"He's gone to the cemetery."

"It's closed at night," he pointed out.

She gave him an incredulous stare. "Jeremy, a Pekingese could get into that place!"

He sighed. He didn't want her anywhere near the cemetery. Mary had disappeared from the cemetery.

But he was there, and Brad and Zach were there. "All right, we'll try the cemetery."

As they approached it a few minutes later, Jeremy was stunned to see a figure seated cross-legged on top of a tomb just inside the wall.

"Son of a bitch!" Brad roared from behind him.

"Brad!" Jeremy tore after Brad, leaping the wall right behind him. He managed to grab Brad two seconds after he had all but crushed Adam to the ground and taken a swing at his jaw.

"You son of a bitch!" Brad roared. "Where is she? Where's my wife?"

Jeremy had Brad, but Brad was strong and powerful and running on adrenaline. Jeremy struggled to hold him, while Zach tried to get Adam up and protect him.

Adam didn't seem to give a damn. There were tears streaming down his cheeks. "I don't know. Oh God, I don't know. I wish I did. I'd help you. I swear I'd help you!"

Jeremy, on the ground and still trying to control

Brad, was dimly aware that Rowenna was on the phone. In seconds, he heard the screech of sirens. Adam didn't run; he just stood there, looking bleak and broken. Jeremy rolled on Brad, finally pinning him.

Then the police filed into the cemetery and Adam was taken away.

Only then did Jeremy dare get up. Brad just lay there, panting as Jeremy stumbled to his feet. Zachary watched both of them warily.

Another police car, lights blazing, drove up. Joe Brentwood jumped out, and as soon as he was introduced to Zach and apprised of what had just happened, he pointed a stern finger at Brad. "I know what you're going through, son. But we don't have a lick of proof against that man. If he took your wife, we'll find out and then we'll find her. Tonight, you get off the streets. If any of my men see you out, you'll be under arrest, and I'll find a way to keep you under lock and key until this is over. You understand me?"

Brad seemed to visibly deflate.

"Get in the car," Joe said, his voice gentler now. "I'll get you back to your B and B." He started leading Brad away.

"Joe," Rowenna said, stopping him. "You haven't found Eve yet?"

"No," he said quietly. "I'm sorry. And get the hell out of the cemetery, will you? This place is starting to give *me* the creeps."

Despite the lateness of the hour, they drove out to Rowenna's house, so she could pick up some clean clothes, and then went back to Jeremy's place. Driving past the MacElroys' place, Rowenna commented that she needed to stop by soon so Ginny could do the final fitting on her costume.

Someone had to stop the Harvest Festival, Jeremy thought. Surely the town fathers, with five corpses on their hands now, would call a halt.

"I'm going to shower, if you two don't mind amusing yourselves," he said once they got back.

He turned the water up as hot as he could stand, hoping to wash away the memories of the corpses along with the dirt. He was amazed he didn't dwell on the dead women, on Adam Llewellyn, or on the boy he had seen, but he was just too tired, as he let the hot water pour over him.

When he got downstairs, Rowenna and Zach were sitting at the kitchen table drinking beer. He helped himself to one and sat down next to her.

A sudden noise in the house made them all jump. Then Jeremy laughed. There was a fax machine on a Victorian desk in the parlor. He rose and went over to it. Picking up the paper, he saw that it was a list compiled from the credit card receipts Hugh had given them from the night that Dinah Green had last been seen. There were phone numbers next to the names of the locals, who were listed first, and addresses and phone numbers next to those from out of town.

He explained the sheet to Zach.

"So what does that mean?" Zach asked. "That we just got the fax, I mean. You think Joe doesn't believe Adam is guilty?"

Jeremy hesitated. "I don't know. I didn't mention this to anyone else. Brad was already crazy enough." He glanced at Rowenna. "Anyone could have dropped that card. But it looked as if there was gum stuck to it.

And Adam…Adam always has a stick of gum in his mouth. On the other hand, the land where the bodies were found belongs to the MacElroys, so Joe will be questioning them again. Ginny doesn't have the strength to hurt anyone, but…Dr. MacElroy—"

"He was my pediatrician!" Rowenna snapped.

"And Adam is your friend," Jeremy reminded her. He turned to his brother. "To answer your question as best I can, Joe's a good cop, and so far he hasn't got proof that Adam is guilty, so he'll follow every lead until he's sure."

Zach looked at Rowenna. His tone was gentle. "What do *you* think?" he asked her.

She shook her head, looking anguished. "I don't know. But…Eve is missing now, too, and…the killer needs seven sacrifices. They've only found five dead women, but with Mary and Eve…"

Zach put his hand on hers. "We'll find them. Both of them."

"The fourth killer," Jeremy said, mulling over everything she'd told them earlier about the four killers. "You said they burned his house to the ground. Rowenna, where was that house?"

She looked at him. "I don't know. It didn't say."

"What was his name again?"

"Brisbin. Hank Brisbin."

"I'll get on it in the morning," Zach said.

"No, if you don't mind, I'd like you two to stop by the MacElroy place tomorrow. Just chat with Ginny. See if she can remember anything else. She's the one who told us about the lights, and that's why I was out there to begin with," Jeremy said.

"I can tell her I'm there to get my fitting," Rowenna said flatly.

"That's good, it's a good reason for you to be there," Jeremy said. His brother would see things through fresh eyes. That might help.

"Oh!" she said suddenly.

"What?"

"There was a book."

Both brothers stared at her.

"Brad…told me that the day Mary disappeared, she had a book. A guide to the symbols on old tombstones. They found her purse and her cell phone, but they didn't find the book. It may not mean anything, but I just thought of it."

"If we find the book…" Zach mused.

Rowenna sighed. "They sell that book from Boston to Maine, and God knows where else." She rose. "If you two will excuse me, I'm going to shower and go to bed," she said.

Jeremy nodded. She had sounded stiff, and he watched her go with a frown. He knew she was upset that one old friend seemed to have gone crazy, another was missing—and he was still suspicious of everyone in her hometown, but even so…

"So this is a breakdown of who was at the bar the night Dinah Green disappeared?" Zach asked, after Rowenna had gone upstairs. "Because some of these people saw her and might have information about who she left with?"

"Yeah. We cleared the guy who was drinking with her of anything to do with Mary's disappearance," Jeremy explained. "And I'll lay you any odds you want that he didn't kill Dinah or any of the other women." He gave his brother all his reasons for being certain the killer was local.

Zach agreed and started reading the list of names, starting with the locals. There were a lot of names Jeremy didn't recognize, but plenty he did, including Adam Llewellyn, Ginny MacElroy, Eric Rolfe and Daniel Mie.

"Hey!" Zach said, catching his attention. "Joe Brentwood was in there that night."

"Yeah?"

Zachary squinted at the fax. "He paid for three beers at midnight. There's a note that two other cops were there with him, an Officer O'Reilly and an Officer Macnamara. Celia Preston—there's a note here, says she's seventy-one, lives alone and runs a wiccan shop. If it turns out Llewellyn didn't do it, then you've got a hell of a long list of possibles, including three cops." Zachary shrugged. "But I have to say, Llewellyn didn't look too sane to me."

Jeremy took the sheet. "Ginny MacElroy was on the list. That means Nick MacElroy was there, too. Ginny owns the land where we found the first corpse, and either she or the doctor owns the land where we found the remains today."

"What about Brad?" Zach asked. "What do you want him doing tomorrow?"

Jeremy was thoughtful. "We make him act like a cop. He can call all the out-of-towners on that list, see what he can get from them. We've got to keep him busy or he'll wind up getting himself arrested for harassing the police about Adam."

"Sounds like a plan. And he may learn something," Zach said.

Jeremy stood, realizing that he was exhausted. "Make yourself at home. It's bed for me."

"Yeah. I'm going to go online, see what I can find out about Brisbin's house," Zach told him. "There's got to be a record somewhere of where it was."

"Go for it, little brother."

Jeremy left Zach downstairs and went upstairs to find Rowenna already asleep.

She curled into his arms when he got in bed, and that night, he just held her. And when he fell asleep, he slept like a log.

And so did Rowenna.

She had always liked Zach, Rowenna reflected as they drove out toward the MacElroy house. He looked a lot like Jeremy, though where Jeremy had storm-gray eyes, Zach's were more like a Caribbean lagoon, and he had more red in his hair than either of his brothers.

Like Jeremy, Zach liked to escape into music. As a sideline while he'd worked forensics for the Miami PD, he'd invested in several recording studios, so he could produce some of the local acts he found in coffeehouses and bars. He'd decided to quit the force and join his older siblings in their investigation agency when he had been called into a crack house where a father had gotten angry that his baby was crying and decided to put him in the microwave. He had always been friendly and easy to talk to, a complete contrast to Jeremy's original standoffish attitude.

Now she found herself telling him things she hadn't mentioned to Jeremy, because she'd been too afraid of him treating her dreams—and anything else that hinted at the paranormal—with disdain.

Zach listened gravely and without judgment when

she told him how she had started dreaming about the cornfields—and the corpses. She even confided about being in the cemetery and her certainty that whoever was guilty had some knowledge of hypnotism or mind control.

"That may be true," Zach pointed out, "but how could he have controlled your mind when you were in New Orleans?"

"I don't know. Maybe he couldn't have. I don't understand any of it," she told him.

They drove in silence for a few minutes, and then she asked if he would mind going by her house first, because she wanted to check something on her bookshelf. He agreed, got her permission to use her computer to go online and followed her directions to her place.

She felt cold and sick with worry about Eve. But she wasn't sure what she could do; the police were looking for her everywhere. And Jeremy was at the station, talking to Adam, who kept repeating that he didn't know where she was. A psychiatrist had even been brought in, so she couldn't do anything that wasn't already being done.

Except go to the cemetery. Because she was convinced that the answer somehow lay in the cemetery.

When she walked into her house, she remembered how surprised she had been that the light had been out when she had first returned. Ginny was normally so careful, but apparently she was starting to slip. Then again, she reminded herself dryly, Dr. MacElroy was still on the suspect list.

She went over to her bookcase and started going through it. She owned a book on funerary art, and she wanted to grab it and ask Brad if it was the same book Mary had been reading.

It wasn't there.

She frowned. She wasn't compulsive, but she loved books, and she was careful with them. It should have been there. She went through the whole shelf, looked through the titles again, and still didn't see it. It was gone. On the heels of that realization, she felt deeply uncomfortable. She couldn't imagine that Ginny would have borrowed it.

Which meant that someone else had been in her house.

She hadn't thought about the book in a long time, she reminded herself. Maybe her memory was faulty. Maybe she had loaned the book to someone.

But she knew she hadn't...

She went to find Zach, who looked up at her excitedly. He pointed at the computer screen. "Take a look at this," he told her. "It's a complete record of Brisbin's speech on the gallows. He claimed that he was Damien, the Devil's servant, and said he would return in the flesh to wreak vengeance on the heirs of his killers when he completed the seven and ruled the world."

"Damien," Rowenna breathed. "Like the fortune-teller."

"I know," Zach said.

"Adam was reading some pretty creepy stuff, so he could have found this and decided to take the name Damien," she said and hesitated. "Eve did say that he left the shop for a while that day."

"But apparently Damien's setup was pretty elaborate," Zach said. "It would have taken time to pull it together, more time than a guy running a store with his wife would have."

"True," she agreed.

"Let's get over to the MacElroys'," Zach said. "I'll call Jeremy and see if anyone's been able to track down the current ownership of Brisbin's land. Something's missing in the online records, so someone's got to go through the actual paperwork. We should know by tonight."

"Tonight." Rowenna sighed. "And tomorrow the Harvest Festival starts."

"Isn't this kind of early?"

"It runs till Thanksgiving. Not that I'm feeling very thankful this year."

Jeremy and Joe sat talking over coffee in a café near the hospital where Adam was undergoing tests while they waited for word on his condition, and for the business card and the substance on it to be analyzed for prints and DNA. Joe sounded disgusted as he told Jeremy, "The organizers and the mayor and everyone involved with the Harvest Festival had a meeting last night, but they say we've got someone in custody and they've already paid for the kiddie rides, ponies, union electricians, yada yada yada, so they're not going to pull the plug. But we'll have every officer we can muster on duty, and all the neighboring departments have offered to send men, too. But if Adam's not our guy and the killer's the master of disguise he seems to be, I don't see how we're going to spot him.

"We're getting FBI help soon," Joe added glumly. "They'll be sending someone out from the Boston field office as soon as they can spare a man." Joe looked at him quizzically all of a sudden. "What were you doing way out there yesterday, anyway?"

"Lights."

"Lights?"

"Ginny MacElroy told me she'd seen lights—like UFOs—out there."

"Out of the mouths of…well, not exactly babes, huh?" He laughed self-deprecatingly. "I probably would have thought she was just going a little senile and seeing things. I sure as hell wouldn't have raced out there to investigate," he admitted.

The man looked tired, Jeremy thought. No wonder. He hadn't stopped since all this had begun.

"Joe, the fax you sent me last night, the one of everyone who was in the bar the night Dinah Green disappeared—your name and two of your men's names were on it."

"Yeah, but none of us ever noticed her."

"But you sent me your name."

"I sent you *every* name. Hell, so *I'm* a suspect now?"

Jeremy lowered his head, trying to hide his grin. "Well, you *are* a local."

"Touché. You'd have disappointed me if you hadn't been honest."

The two of them sat in gloomy silence for a few minutes, and then Jeremy asked, "So none of your men has seen any sign of Eve Llewellyn?"

"No," Joe said. "Adam swears he never saw her, doesn't know where she is. Says he went to see Rowenna at the History Museum, then started back to the store. He doesn't remember anything else until he found himself sitting in the cemetery. That's his story.

He's like a mass of jelly. Terrified that he's the killer, but he keeps swearing that he would never in a million years hurt his wife, that he doesn't believe he'd hurt anyone. But like I said, the fact that we have him in custody has the festival committee convinced that it's safe to go on."

"You don't think its Adam, do you?" Jeremy asked him.

"Hell if I think I know anything at this point. This used to be a nice town that had gotten past its sad history and made a nice living off a bunch of modern-day wiccans who draw the tourists.... A serial killer who thinks he's the Devil…" He shook his head in what looked to Jeremy suspiciously like defeat. "That's way beyond anything we've ever had to deal with here."

Just then his phone buzzed. When he finished the call, he turned to Jeremy and said, "Come on. The shrink had a neurologist checking Adam out. Let's go see what they found."

"Is he insane?" Joe asked the psychiatrist the minute they got into the room where she and the neurologist were waiting to meet with them.

"Not in the least," the woman, Dr. Detweiler, said. "He's been tormenting himself because he didn't know what was going on, but he's not suffering delusions of any kind and he doesn't show the signs of being a classic split personality, to use the layman's term. In talking to him, I felt that the man was dealing with a physical problem, so I called Dr. Lauder," she went on, nodding toward her colleague.

"We still have tests to run," Dr. Lauder said. "And the results on the tests I've done so far aren't all in yet, but I believe he is suffering from a rare form of epilepsy. He doesn't go into physical spasms, as in the classic form of the disease, but parts of the brain shut down, leading to so-called blackouts. There isn't a cure, but there *is* medication. You can talk to him now, if you'd like."

Adam was under guard in the hospital. He was in restraints, and he looked like hell.

But he was clear-eyed, and he spoke rationally when he saw them.

"Any sign of my wife?" he asked miserably, as soon as they entered.

"No, I'm sorry," Joe told him.

"I would never hurt her," Adam whispered. "I love her. That's why I was so afraid."

"Adam, we found a business card from your store out where we found four more bodies," Jeremy told him.

"I couldn't have done it. I couldn't have blacked out that long. Could I?" The look in his eyes was horrified, pleading. "Oh, God, if I did do it, I want to be executed."

"Massachusetts doesn't have the death penalty," Joe pointed out dryly.

"A card from the store?" Adam said then. "But…anyone could have one of those cards."

"Adam, there was what looks to be gum on it," Joe told him.

Adam frowned. "No. No, I'm being set up. By someone who figured out I was having problems. I swear, I couldn't have done this. I must be being set up." His arms went rigid with tension as he struggled against the restraints. "I didn't do it," he said pleadingly to Jeremy. "You have to believe me. And you have to get out there and find out who *did* do it. I've been reading up on the past myself, reading about Satanists. He's going to kill seven. And he has my wife!"

Ginny greeted them at the door. "Oh, my God! I heard about Adam, and it's so terrible. I never would have thought… But now that they have him, I hope they find poor Eve and she's all right. But at least he's in custody, so now we don't have to be so worried. Come on in, dear. Oh—you're not Jeremy," she said, studying Zach as he came in behind Rowenna.

"Zachary Flynn, Miss MacElroy," Zach said politely. "Jeremy's brother."

"Nice to meet you," she said, looking him up and down. "Well, you just go on into the kitchen over there while I get Rowenna decked out. I made biscuits, and there's coffee on the stove. Unless you prefer tea?"

"Coffee is fine by me," Zach said, and started in the direction of the kitchen.

"You. Upstairs," Ginny said.

As Rowenna obediently followed orders, she noticed that Zach hadn't gone to the kitchen after all. He was silently returning to the foyer—and crossing through to Dr. MacElroy's study.

Upstairs, Ginny chattered on about everything and nothing. The festival was so much work, but it was good for tourism. It was terrible, just terrible, all those women dying right under their noses. Thank God Jeremy was such a nice young man. He listened to her and checked out the lights.

Rowenna found herself hoping it wasn't going to be

too cold for the duration of the festival. The harvest cape itself—rich brown velvet with fall leaves cut from satin sewn on it—was warm. But beneath it, over brown tights and a bodysuit, the queen's gown was pure gauze, scattered here and there with more satin leaves. At least there were brown fur-lined boots to go with it, and long, fur-trimmed brown gloves, as well.

When Rowenna was fully dressed, Ginny stepped back. "Oh," she said, clapping her hands together in delight. "You're perfect. Absolutely perfect. Let's show Mr. Flynn, shall we?"

Had Zach had time to finish searching through the doctor's desk? Rowenna wondered.

"I think we should keep the outfit a surprise," Rowenna said.

"If you say so," Ginny said with a sigh. "If only I could look like that. I did, once, of course. I was quite beautiful in my youth."

"You're still beautiful," Rowenna assured her.

She took her time getting dressed again.

When they got downstairs, Zach was waiting for them at the foot of the stairs. "Ginny, your back lock has been jimmied," he told her. "Did you know?"

"What?"

He waved for them to follow him through to the kitchen and over to the back door. There were marks on the door and the frame, and the lock was broken.

"Oh, my God!" Ginny gasped. "Someone broke in here."

"I've called in the police—and a locksmith," Zach told her. "With your permission, I'll walk through the rest of the house and just make sure things look secure."

Ginny nodded fervently. "Do you think someone is hiding in here now?" she asked, clutching Rowenna's arm.

"Zach will make sure you're safe," Rowenna assured Ginny. "But I'm sure whoever did this is long gone."

She couldn't believe Zach had broken the lock just to get a chance to inspect the house. That was going a little overboard, Rowenna thought.

But she didn't give him away.

She let Ginny cling to her, and by the time Zach finished his inspection, a policeman was at the door. Zach explained the situation, and they left Ginny in the hands of the officer. On their way out, they saw the locksmith's truck arriving.

"That was quite a ruse," she told him. "What happens when they find your fingerprints all over that lock?"

He looked at her in surprise, his brows drawn together very much the way Jeremy's often were. "That wasn't a ruse, and they won't find my fingerprints. Her house really was broken into."

"What?"

"It probably happened last night, and I think it was because someone was planting this. I found it on the doctor's desk."

He tossed something on her lap. It was a book about New England funerary art, the same book she owned and hadn't been able to find. She looked at him in shock. Was this in fact her copy? If so, why would someone take it from her house and leave it on Doc MacElroy's desk?

Or was the book Mary Johnstone's? Had Doc MacElroy really had it in his own possession, or was someone out there trying to frame both Adam *and* the doctor?

19

Leaving Joe and the hospital behind, Jeremy was just about to call Zach when his phone rang.

He didn't know the number, but he recognized the area code. Southern California.

"Eric Rolfe?" he asked as he flipped the phone open.

"Yeah," Eric said in surprise. "Uh, yeah… Listen," he said bluntly, "can you meet me? Now. Right away? It's urgent."

"Where are you?"

"Meet me at the shop—Adam and Eve's shop."

"The cops locked it up last night."

"No, you have to come to the back. Through the alley by the movie theater."

Since he was personally convinced that Adam was innocent, and since Eric Rolfe was high on his list of suspects, Jeremy decided meeting the man made sense. But he intended to be careful. Very careful.

He followed Eric's directions. He had never realized just how many crevices and hidey-holes there were in the area. When he reached the back of what he was certain had to be the right shop, there was no one there. But then the back door opened.

Eric Rolfe popped his head out. "Come in," he said in a whisper. "Quick."

His gun was holstered beneath his jacket, so, alert and ready for anything, Jeremy went in.

They were in a storeroom. Boxes were everywhere, along with an old Victorian sofa and a tiny refrigerator. Suddenly someone started to emerge from a curtained dressing room, and Jeremy nearly reached for his gun, then stopped in shock.

It was Eve.

"Eve, what the hell are you doing here?" Jeremy asked her softy. "The cops are looking for you everywhere."

"I know. And I'm sorry. But...this is all my fault. I have to clear my husband. Somehow."

He looked at her, waiting for her to explain.

"I told Rowenna that I thought that he might be... Oh, God, how horrible of me. And then she told you, and you told the cops, and..." She trailed off on a wail.

"No, Eve. We found your store card—with what look likes gum on it—by the remains of another dead woman," Jeremy told her. "What suddenly changed your mind about Adam—and why are you hiding?"

"Before Adam went to see Rowenna, we'd had another fight. He told me that even though he'd been reading up on Satanism and thought we should carry books about it, he didn't know where that spell book had come from—he'd never seen it before. And I didn't believe him at first, but then when Rowenna came and said Adam should be there, and she left...and he still didn't come back, and I was worried, so I went out to look for him myself, only I guess I was so upset I forgot to lock the door...and then I came back, but there were cops everywhere, so I got scared and hid. And then this morning I was going to keep looking for him, but I saw in the paper that they found him. But he's not guilty. Jeremy, you have to prove that he's not guilty. And you have to keep looking for that woman, for your friend's wife."

"I read the spell book, too," Eric said, clearing his throat. "Eve called me this morning. Sorry. I told her she should call you. You have to read it yourself, though. It's all about sacrificing seven women and becoming Satan. And there are spells for illusion and hypnotism, so you can put the woman under your power." Eric handed him the book.

"There's a secret page," he said. "At the back."

Jeremy found the page. It showed an artist's rendering of the devil, with six dead woman staked up in front of him. They were decked in leaves, and their necks were broken. Behind the devil stood a woman who appeared to be his handmaiden. Half her face was old and decrepit; half seemed to be regaining youth and beauty as the devil came into his power.

Another woman stood before the devil, wearing a crown and a cloak of leaves, and looking toward heaven, as if for salvation.

But the devil was reaching for her.

"I'm not sure what it means," Eric said, "Except that once again there are seven victims."

The seventh victim was beautiful. There was something especially innocent and pure about her as she looked skyward.

She was decked in leaves and wearing a crown.

She was the harvest queen.

Terrified, Jeremy reached for his phone.

* * *

Zach's phone was ringing. He glanced at it.

"Jeremy?" Rowenna asked.

"No, our older brother, Aidan," Zach said. "I'll take it out here. You go on in, I'll be right with you. I'll give Jeremy a call, too, let him know where we are, what we're up to."

She nodded and headed into the museum.

June Eagle was at the desk. "A friend of mine is right behind me. Send him on back, will you, please?" Rowenna asked as June handed her the key.

"Sure. Dan is around somewhere," June said. "If I see him, I'll tell him that you two are going to be back there. You know how he is about that reading room."

Rowenna nodded, then made her way through the exhibits toward the back of the museum.

She didn't want to look at the Harvest Man or the killers who'd come after him. Just entering the area where the tableau stood made her skin crawl now. But she had to go past them to reach the reading room.

As she hurried through, she noticed that figure of Andrew Cunningham, in his eighteenth-century garb and high hat, seemed to have moved, as if he'd turned to watch people go by. She shuddered and averted her eyes, hurrying on and reminding herself that Zach was right behind her and Dan might already be in the reading room.

The reading room door was open.

She was glad to see that books she'd been reading yesterday were still lying on the table, so it would be easy to show Zach what she had found. She wandered over to the bookshelf, looking for something similar to the spell book Adam had been reading. As she searched the titles, she gasped.

Her heartbeat quickening, she pulled out the guide to local funerary art.

Her phone started to ring, and as she fumbled in her bag to retrieve it, she heard a sound behind her, turned…and gasped.

The wax figure of Andrew Cunningham hadn't just turned, it had come to life.

It was standing right there behind her, but with a face she knew.

She opened her mouth to scream, but she was too late.

Before she had a chance to make a sound, Cunningham slammed her in the head with the butt of an eighteenth-century hunting rifle.

She fell to the floor, a stygian darkness closing in.

Rowenna hadn't answered her phone. Just as Jeremy was about to call Zach, his phone started ringing. Brad.

"Brad, what is it? And hurry. I have to reach my brother."

"You're not going to believe this, but I found a woman in Memphis who not only saw who Dinah Green was talking to in the bar, but who she was with outside it that night," Brad said.

"Who?"

"Adam and Eve Llewellyn, Eric Rolfe, Dan Mie and Dr. MacElroy."

Jeremy's heart tightened in his chest. Five people.

Adam was in custody. Eve and Eric were right there with him, staring at him anxiously.

That left two people.

"Good work, Brad. I'll call you back as soon as I can. I have to reach Zach."

He hung up without another word and was about to dial Zach, but his phone rang again. His brother had beaten him to the punch.

"Zach, where are you?"

"The History Museum. Listen, Joe just called me— your number went to voice mail. Long story, but Brisbin's scrubland belongs to Ginny MacElroy."

"Ginny?" Jeremy said, stunned. That meant Nick MacElroy had access to it, as well. And he was local. He was bound to know the history of the place.

The house had been burned to the ground.

But houses had basements.

"Zach, we've got to get out there. Where are you now?"

"Outside in front of the History Museum. Where are you?"

"Around the corner. I'll meet you there."

"I'll go in and get Rowenna," Zach said.

Eric and Eve were staring at him as he hung up. "I need to go meet my brother and Rowenna," Jeremy said. "Rowenna…she's the harvest queen. We thought he had seven—the five he'd already killed, Mary Johnstone…and you, Eve."

"Oh, my God…" Eve breathed.

"Sorry," he said quickly. "But it's Rowenna he wants for his finale. The harvest queen."

"So who owns the property?"

"Ginny MacElroy."

"Ginny? You think *Ginny* did it?" Eric looked ready to laugh at the ludicrousness of the idea.

"No. I think it's the doctor," Jeremy said.

"No, it can't be," Eric protested.

"Why not?"

"I told you, the eyes… I saw Damien. And it wasn't Dr. MacElroy. MacElroy is too old. I know it wasn't him."

Eve gasped. "It's Dan," she breathed. "Dan Mie."

"Dan Mie," Jeremy repeated, scrambling the letters in his mind to form the name Damien.

"Oh, God," he said.

"I've got to get out to the old Brisbin property. You two, stay here. Eric, call Joe and tell him Eve's okay, and that the old Brisbin property is connected to this somehow."

His phone rang again. Zach.

"Zach, what? I'm on my way."

"It's Rowenna. She's gone. I don't know how—no one used the emergency exit, and the girl at the desk swears there's only one other way in and out, but she's gone. The police are on their way, but you've got to get the hell over here now!"

The blackness began to recede, and she thought she heard people talking. She looked up and saw the late autumn sky, a soft gray-blue punctuated with clouds, and she could feel the gentle touch of the breeze.

She was lying on something soft and yet firm, redolent of growing things.

The earth.

She was lying with her hands folded corpse-fashion over her chest, and she had the sense that she was in the graveyard, on a grave. She blinked and realized it wasn't real, and yet she could feel the grass beneath her, she could smell roasting chestnuts at a stand not far away.

She felt rather than saw the shadow coming.

"You're not real," she said. Her voice was weak, and her head was pounding.

Then he was there. She knew him, even though he was wearing a turban, makeup and a magnificent cloak. He looked so different. Handsome, which was funny, she thought hysterically, because she had never thought of him as at all good-looking. "Dan," she breathed.

"Not Dan," he said with a wolfish grin. "Damien, the Harvest Man, and I'm about to rule the world. I won't just worship Satan, I will *be* him in the flesh."

She was amazed to hear herself laugh, but all the time, her mind was racing. She had to buy time, had to keep him talking, had to find a way to throw him off balance. "Damien. Dan Mie. It's an anagram. Was that what made you think you were supposed to be the Devil's heir? When you figured out that you could turn your name into his? Or was it the fact that you were always a nobody? You needed something to make you feel important, so you decided to be the Devil?"

She could tell from his expression that she had found his weak spot. She was making him angry. Good. Angry people got careless. They made mistakes.

Right. Like there was any salvation for her now. She didn't know where she was. She couldn't really be in the cemetery, because there would be people around, so somehow he had created an illusion.

So where *was* she?

She fought with her own mind, trying to dispel the fantasy he had created and let reality in.

She felt the breeze, and suddenly she wasn't lying down. She was running. She was in a cornfield, running for her life. The stalks bent as she forced her way through them. The sky overhead was steel-gray, and the very heavens seemed to rumble and roar.

Crows screamed, dive-bombing her, their calls deafening as they darted around her, chasing her.

Leading her to the stake where her life would end. *No!*

It was another illusion. She had to fight it.

She closed her eyes, ignoring everything but her sense of touch. She felt the ropes that were binding her arms. She felt the cold, and felt the dankness of the air. Felt the hard-packed earth beneath her.

She was somewhere…underground. In a grave?

Had she been buried alive?

No, that wasn't the Harvest Man's way. She opened her eyes and looked around her.

Damien was gone. She could hear him, though. He wasn't far away. He was talking to someone. She could hear a low, muted voice replying to him. A feminine voice.

Mary Johnstone?

But then she heard a low, sobbing moan, and it was very close, but outside her line of sight.

She strained to hear past it to what Dan and the woman were saying.

"You'll ruin everything," the woman said. "You have to kill the first one now—quickly—or they'll find you before you finish. You cannot be the true king of kings, Satan on earth, unless you complete the ritual perfectly."

That voice…

As Rowenna tried to shift into a more comfortable position, she realized that she was dressed in her harvest queen costume.

And she recognized the female voice.

Ginny MacElroy.

Her mind fought against such an absurd possibility, but she knew Ginny's voice too well to be mistaken, and she knew what she was wearing, knew that the nearby sobbing had to be coming from Mary Johnstone.

She began to test the ropes that were binding her. How long did she have? Minutes?

No, longer. Because Mary…

Mary had to die first.

Desperation and hopelessness nearly overcame her as she realized that the ropes binding her were too tight for her to slip free.

Then she went dead still, terrified, certain she was losing her mind.

There was a little boy standing by her feet. Just a regular little boy in jeans and a T-shirt, looking at her so sadly.

She started to say something to him, but he raised a finger to his lips to warn her to be silent.

And then he faded away.

Rowenna was nowhere to be found. Joe and the police had torn the place apart, a tearful June hovering nearby and trying to help.

Finally Jeremy had explored the library and found the shelf that was really a false door, opening into a tunnel.

He didn't know how Eve had managed to follow him, how she had gotten past Joe and the other policemen. But she was next to him.

"Go back and tell Joe I'm checking this out," he said.

Zach had already gone to pick up Brad and then head out to the old Brisbin land.

Eric had gone with him, because he knew the area and had the best chance of finding the foundation of the old house.

"I'm going with you," Eve insisted.

"No! Go back and tell Joe."

She nodded unhappily and left, and he bent low, following the tunnel. They had checked out the cemetery, Joe had told him, and there were no hidden tunnels there.

And this tunnel didn't lead to the cemetery. It led to a sewer line.

And the sewer line led to the street adjacent to the cemetery.

He clambered up the ladder to the street and stared at the cemetery.

He jumped when Eve climbed out behind him. "I told Joe," she hurried to say before he had a chance to get mad at her. "But there's something there," she breathed, staring at the old graveyard.

"Go back. Tell Joe that Dan took her out through here and is probably already back at the property. Zach is on his way, but they have to get the cops out there right away."

"All right. But remember this. Love is stronger than evil, and there is more than you know in this world...."

She left, and he started running for his car.

But then he paused.

The boy was in the cemetery. Billy. And he was beckoning him closer.

Despite his panic for Rowenna, Jeremy walked into the cemetery. He couldn't help himself. There were people around, but he didn't bother to ask them if they had seen a man trying to kidnap a woman. He walked straight to Billy.

And this time Billy didn't disappear.

The boy took his hand and mouthed the same word he had spoken from the stony ground near where the five women had been found.

Hurry.

Jeremy felt the rush of the wind. He was no longer in the cemetery. He was on a hill, corpses hanging from a nearby gallows, and the sound of mocking laughter came to his ears. Somehow he knew that the corpses swaying in the wind belonged to innocents who had died so that evil might rule.

The hill faded away, and he found himself in the cornfields, fields that seemed to stretch forever.

He started running, his feet hitting solid ground. He smashed through the stalks as he ran, until finally he burst out of the corn and into the field of bracken granite.

Billy was still there, holding his hand, and now the boy tugged until he started running again.

Because Billy knew where they were going.

Rowenna managed to find a sharp stone and run the rope holding her hands back and forth over the edge until she had cut through it. As soon as her hands were free, she untied the rope binding her ankles and rose as quietly as she could, then inched her way through the murky darkness to the wall. The place was filled with debris, littered with the dirt of centuries, and the only light came from the direction from which the voices had come earlier. On the far side of the room, she could see another woman lying, bound hand and foot as she had been bound.

Ginny's voice. Because Ginny was part of this. She still couldn't believe it. *Why?*

"Mary?" she dared to whisper.

For a moment, there was silence. Then a whimper, as if Mary had tried to keep silent but hadn't been able to control her fear.

Mary was probably afraid to speak, Rowenna thought. No doubt she had long ago realized that Ginny was not a kindly old lady there to rescue her, and now she was frightened of all new voices.

Rowenna felt her way along the wall, which was damp and covered with algae, toward Mary, moving carefully to avoid making any noise that would alert Dan and Ginny that she had gotten free.

She passed a chink in the stone of the wall, which she recognized as the foundation of an old house, and the pale glimmer of light reaching through illuminated a tray of food that was currently giving sustenance to a large rat.

Finally she reached Mary and saw that the rope around her ankles was anchored to an iron ring hanging attached to a beam overhead. She swore under her breath, then prayed that Mary wouldn't cry out.

"Mary, please don't scream," she whispered. "I'm a friend of Jeremy Flynn's. My name is Rowenna."

She heard a gasp and moved closer. Mary was pale and gaunt. Her face was dirt-streaked, the look in her eyes tortured. She was decked out like a doll—or a scarecrow. There were even tufts of straw sticking out from the cuffs of the denim pants she wore. Beneath the grime, her face was painted up to look like a harlequin.

Mary just stared at her, eyes huge and wide, as if she had no strength left at all.

Rowenna felt her nails break as she worked frantically at the knots of Mary's bonds, but they had been well-tied and pulled tighter by Mary's struggles. At last she freed Mary from the ropes.

But they still had to get out.

And she didn't even know how they had gotten in.

Plus it looked as if she would have to carry Mary, who lacked the strength to stand. And the other woman looked as if she weighed practically nothing, but she would still be a burden.

She had just heaved the unprotesting other woman over her shoulder when she heard footsteps.

Ginny and Dan were coming.

The blinding light of a storm lantern suddenly illuminated the room.

"Rowenna Cavanaugh!" Ginny said, distressed. "What are you doing? You're going to ruin your lovely costume."

"Put her down, Rowenna. She's half-dead already," Dan said patiently. "Put her down or else I'll make you."

She shook her head. "No, Dan. You can't make me."

"Of course I can. I can make you see or do whatever I want you to."

"I see and do what *I* choose to," she said with far more confidence than she felt. "I saw your crimes before you wanted me to," she told him.

He stared at her and began to frown as she stared back without flinching. He was trying to make her see something, she realized. He was trying to make her envision herself putting Mary back down on the ground. But she knew what he was up to, and she wouldn't do it.

He swore and strode toward her, and she had to put Mary down then, so she could protect herself. She struggled, using everything she had ever heard about self-defense—knee to the groin, elbow in the ribs. She threw him off finally, but then Ginny rushed her.

To her amazement, she had no difficulty at all in sending the old woman who had fed her cookies all her life flying right across the room and into the wall.

But then Dan was on her again. She fought him wildly until…

She felt the knife against her throat.

"You have a few minutes left. A few minutes of precious life. So use them wisely," he whispered, the blade cold and sharp against her flesh.

There were no cars around, but Jeremy saw tire tracks in the dirt, faint but perceptible, as Billy pulled him along.

Without Billy's help, he never would have seen the trap door, which had probably led to a storm cellar but was now covered with leaves and refuse. He pulled the door open and stared down into the darkness.

But there was a ladder; as his eyes adjusted, he could see it. He turned to Billy for guidance, but the boy was gone again. He inched down the ladder….

And heard voices.

"You might as well slit my throat now, Dan Mie, because I will never stand here quietly and let you strangle that woman. Besides, *he* won't let you."

Thank God! It was Rowenna's voice. She was alive.

"Who? Your hotshot investigator boyfriend?" Dan

mocked. "It will take him forever to get here—if he even figures it out. He should be out looking for the good Doctor MacElroy right now."

Jeremy inched closer until he could see what was going on, could see that Dan was holding a knife to Rowenna's throat.

"No, I'm not talking about Jeremy, actually. I'm talking about that little boy right there," Rowenna said.

My God, Jeremy thought. Billy *was* there—and Rowenna could see him, too.

"There's no little boy," Dan said.

He heard a woman's faint gasp. Someone else was there. Mary?

"There...*is* something...."

It was Ginny. Ginny MacElroy. She sounded weak and hurt.

"I think he's here to protect Mary and me," Rowenna was saying. "See how he's glowing? He's from a very good place, I think. And he's here to send you to burn in hell forever. Isn't that what you want? To be with Satan?"

"I will *be* Satan. I will have my seven!" Dan Mie roared.

Enough was enough, Jeremy thought, and strode forward, heedless of how much noise he made. He had his gun drawn, and he aimed it at Mie.

"Billy can't shoot you, Dan. But I can," he promised grimly.

But the knife was still at Rowenna's throat. He was a crack shot, but...

All it would take would be a twitch.

Her eyes met his. Amber gleaming gold, and strong, so strong.

"Dan, watch out for Billy," she said. "Don't you see him? He's right there beside you."

Dan twisted slightly, but Jeremy decided not to chance the shot. Instead he dove for the man, yanking him away from Rowenna, and together they tumbled to the floor.

The knife glittered in the light as Dan tried to drive it into Jeremy's chest, but Jeremy sat up, head-butting Mie.

The knife flew out of the other man's hand just as Jeremy heard a shrill cry, like the cawing of a crow, and looked up to see Ginny MacElroy rushing him.

Rowenna tackled her just as he slammed a fist into Mie's jaw, driving him back against the wall.

Suddenly gunfire split the air, freezing them all in place.

His brother had arrived at last, and Brad was right behind him.

On the floor, Ginny started sobbing and swearing at Dan. "I told you to hurry up and kill the first one, that you had to complete the ritual before they caught you. You don't deserve to be the Prince of Darkness!"

Brad let out a deep, harsh sound and ran past everyone to where Mary lay.

"Mary, Mary," he sobbed, cradling her in his arms.

"Took you long enough," Jeremy told Zach with a grin.

"I broke every speed limit known to man," Zach said. "How the hell did you get here so fast?"

"You wouldn't believe me if I told you," Jeremy said. And then he stood and helped Rowenna to her feet.

"It was Billy," she said softly, and then fell against him, shaking.

Epilogue

"I swear, I'll never understand it," Joe said, shaking his head and frowning. "Why?"

"Well," Jeremy said, helping himself to a slice of turkey, "Ginny had heard the legends all her life. She believed that if she was Satan's handmaiden, she would be restored to youth and beauty and live forever, so she was more than happy to help Mie become Satan. She was the one who planted the idea in his mind.

"It probably started years ago—when he was eating cookies and milk in her kitchen. They're both completely crazy, of course, but their delusions fed each other, and five women died." And two more almost did, he thought, looking gratefully at the woman sitting by his side.

"It's still so creepy to think that people we've known our whole lives are killers," Eve said, then smiled tentatively at her husband. He hadn't had another blackout since starting his medication, so the two of them had a lot to be thankful for this Thanksgiving.

He smiled in return. "I'm still trying to piece it all together."

"I have it figured," Rowenna said. "Dan targeted tourists, women just passing through. He met them in bars or at the museum. He picked women who wouldn't be missed for a while. Until it got close to Halloween. Then he had to speed it up, so he took a chance and grabbed Mary, even though Brad was right there to call in the cops. He knew about Adam's blackouts—he'd been watching you," she said to Adam. "So he got one of your cards and stuck some of your gum to the back, and planted it by one of the bodies. That way, if someone looked suspicious, it would be you. Ginny tried to make Doc look guilty. Poor guy. He's still in shock."

"Okay, I understand all that," Joe said. "And I get Dan could come and go from the museum at will through the tunnel, while anyone working the desk would swear he'd never left, because as far as they knew, he never had. But…Mary said she was on a hill, and then in a cornfield and then tied up in the basement—and she didn't know how she got to any of those places or even if she was really there."

"Dan studied hypnotism," Jeremy explained.

"But can anyone be that good?" Joe demanded.

"He was very good," Rowenna said quietly. "He could plant things in your mind. Mary and I even saw our names on a tombstone. But…there are some things we'll probably never really know or understand. Maybe that's what life and death are about."

She was thinking about her dreams, he knew. And about Billy. How could anyone explain those things?

He still had questions, too. Questions he could never ask, because most people would think he was insane.

Not Rowenna, though. She smiled at him, and he remembered arguing with her about the possibility of the paranormal really existing. He had been convinced that the world was whatever you could see and touch, hear and taste and smell. Earth and sky and sea. Evil was flesh and blood. Goodness was the same.

And that was true, as far as it went. Dan and Ginny were flesh and blood, certainly. But at the same time, he couldn't help believing that some evil from the past had slipped into their souls. The Devil? Maybe.

So did that make Billy an angel? He didn't know and didn't care. He was just grateful for the boy's help in saving the only woman he would ever love.

Did the paranormal exist? He couldn't prove it, not the way his cop training insisted things needed to be proven, but he sure as hell couldn't discount the possibility.

Rowenna had always known, of course.

"There's another question," Joe said. "How the hell did you get out there so fast? You were in the museum, then in the tunnel. How the hell did you beat us out there?"

"Without a car," Zach said beneath his breath, then looked at Jeremy and shrugged.

"I don't know," Jeremy said. "I honestly don't know."

"I do," Eve told them, gripping Adam's hand tightly. "It was the power of love. Evil can be strong, but love is stronger than any other power on earth."

Jeremy was pretty sure he was blushing.

"So what about it?" Joe demanded.

"Pardon?"

"She *is* practically my child," Joe said. "So I think I have a right to know."

"He wants to know your intentions, bro," Zach said, laughing.

Joe looked into Rowenna's eyes. Magic. There were so many facets to the human mind, the human heart, and she had touched him on every one of them. She was more important to him than life itself. She believed they could touch the unknown.

And she was right. They could.

If she suddenly decided to wear long green robes and chant to the sea gods, he simply wouldn't give a damn.

"My intentions —if she'll have me, of course—are to love and cherish her until death do us part…and beyond," he said softly.

He saw the amber in her eyes sparkle to a magnificent gold. Then she leaned over and kissed him.

He was pretty sure he had his answer.